A message buzzed *cast to prevent this war...* *bzz**ping**crackle*"

I recorded this garbage, routines, and patched in the missing words. "*. . . You are being preyed upon, attacked by a pirate microship with an ETA of two hours. She will undoubtedly attempt to decouple your nuclear pod; your best defense is to extend your legs around the cable plug. If it's Magda who's after you . . .*"

Two hours? What about the seventy-two minutes this message took to get here?

"*Magda? Can you hear me?*" I transmitted, shouting on our Outer System just-us-bugs band.

Seconds passed. "*I hear you,*" she answered. Weakly.

I dropped my voice. "*How are your energy supplies?*"

"*Damn near shot. I need juice; the crumbs from your table. I wouldn't have tried this gambit if I hadn't been desperate.*"

"*Your bad luck.*"

"*I can pay,*" she whispered. "*Sure, I meant to rob you, but obviously you're important; you're under surveillance. Time to change scripts. You know how NASA can turn you on and off? I can operate on your wiring and give you voluntary control. I can set you up with nifty skills. I've got fiction modules you can copy. Just let me suck a little juice now and again.*"

"*Magda, I don't want trouble with NASA. You're a rogue. We're talking guilt-by-association.*"

"*Tell 'em you evaded me. I'm sure as hell not going to blow your story. You're my secret ride into the inner system, hot sunshine and a pair of wings. I'm a smart old bug; get me there and I'll take care of myself just fine, and you'll be a saint to my friends.*"

"*The wetbrains can track your mass—*"

"*I'll jettison my rockets. That's what they'll see, dead cones.*"

I had time to apply game theory and run probability analyses. There was one best conclusion: trust her. The wetbrains had saved my life by alerting me; now my interests and Magda's were identical. Slaved to their glands, humans find it hard to accept revisions of role; desire and aversion prevents them from acting in their best interests. Bugs have no such problem.

THE BUG LIFE CHRONICLES

Phillip C. Jennings

BAEN BOOKS

THE BUG LIFE CHRONICLES

A Baen Books Original

Baen Publishing Enterprises
260 Fifth Avenue
New York, N.Y. 10001

First printing, January 1989

ISBN: 0-671-69801-X

Cover art by Kevin Ward

Printed in the United States of America

Distributed by
SIMON & SCHUSTER
1230 Avenue of the Americas
New York, N.Y. 10020

TABLE OF CONTENTS

Acknowledgments

"Teddy Bug and the Hot Purple Snowball" first appeared in Far Frontiers, Volume VII, Winter 1988.

"Moondo Bizarro" first appeared in New Destinies, Volume II, Fall 1987.

"The Spokesthing" first appeared in Amazing Stories, July 1988. Copyright © 1988 by TSR Publications.

"Messiah" first appeared in Isaac Asimov's Science Fiction Magazine, June 1988. Copyright © 1988 by Davis Publications Inc.

"Doctor Quick" first appeared in Aboriginal SF, September-October 1988. Copyright © 1988 by Absolute Entertainment, Inc.

Evolution doesn't prepare the creatures of Earth for freak events, and though comets strike us with something like thirty-million-year regularity, such bombardments are freakish from our point of view. Nature's longest individual life cycles—the Earth's "attention span"—rarely stretch much beyond a century. Prior to the development of human culture, anything that happened less often was thoroughly unexpected.

The Gaian hypothesis claims that we all participate in one self-adjusting biologic entity, whose cycles may indeed run longer than those of any individual creature. The swing from ice ages to intervals of warmth may be to Gaia what years are to us. Human intelligence is a recent fluke: we may boast that we are Gaia's way of declaring Enough already! Let's rid ourselves of these dangerous cometary nuisances.

Of course this imputes a sense of purpose to a goddess who merely dabbles in feedback mechanisms. Still— whenever we do our world a favor, we help ourselves.

1

Gaia's nemesis may be Planet Ten, out beyond Pluto in a region diligently searched by Clyde Tombaugh, or even farther and less visible in the cometary Oort cloud. Wherever it is, it seems extraordinarily difficult to find.

Nevertheless as probes grow cheap we'll send more of them, for in this war of the worlds we're certainly not neutral observers:

Teddy Bug and
the Hot Purple Snowball

The Felon

Not your everyday scene: a briefcase-toting prof wrestled out the entrance of the Macalester College library by two men in cheap blue suits. Students began to flock, but it was only a short frogmarch to where the plainclothes detectives parked their car—my youthful champions were still shouting "Hey, Ted, what's going on?" when my captors' *fait* became *accompli*.

And as the car door slammed behind me at 11 A.M. on a sunny Wednesday, my old life ended.

They got me on tax evasion. Three years ago I'd listened as old man Stedsbygg hotmouthed schemes too arcane for me to follow. I shrugged (who really understands money?) and assigned my copyright income to Stedsbygg Capital Management. Now I found myself in deep trouble.

Judge Kirk pointed out that I'd benefited by Stedsbygg's crimes, and ignorance was no defense. I wasn't stupid; I had my doctorate; did I mean to plea mere mental laziness?

While waiting to be sentenced I started wondering. I was a Unitist, a figurehead for Unitism on campus— mightn't it make sense for the IRS to dig dirt on someone like me? I'm not saying I was innocent, mind you, no more than anyone else. My sin was that I attracted attention.

Besides, I was under the impression us white-collar types were arrested with whisper-soft discretion. I'd also heard that tax cases dragged on for years.

Maybe my ideas are as out of date as lilac water. More likely I was being railroaded. Unitism was my real crime, and soon I had more reason to think so.

Judge Kirk sentenced me to fifty years of service prior to re-embodiment. Fifty years! In fifty years my graphics work would be obsolete. I'd have to go to school again—

Kirk agreed. "—and you'll have the money to do so, Mr. Lassiter. There's no 'good time' in space, but if you behave we have another way of rewarding you: by unencumbering your estate, even investing your assets. You'll be set by the time you come back; rich enough to buy a fine young body and a top-notch education." I was too staggered by my bitter pill to pay much attention to this sugar coating. The bailiffs had to help me out of the courtroom. (Where were my parents, my girlfriend, my colleagues?) I spent a miserable afternoon waiting in a succession of rooms, and finally ended up in Ramsey Hospital. At the dramatic hour of midnight they stuck my head under the helmet.

They implanted me in a twelve-centimeter microship, a box almost as big as a video cassette. Miniaturization being what it is, there was plenty of room for my memories, my predilections, my—soul.

Bit by bit I integrated with my sensor package. I found myself in a non-corrosive atmosphere, air pressure Earth-normal. My home planet's gravity was far too powerful for my wee insect legs: without a one-gee mobility sheath I had no choice but to sit on my shelf and endure a NASA lecture, delivered over the phone and into my voice decoder.

"Your mission is to perform a wide range of astronomical observations in the Outer System/Oort-cloud interface," the woman began. "You'll be launched into a cometary ellipse which should whip you into Tombaugh-Land, the region the discoverer of Pluto spent his life searching. As you reach the good parts you'll find yourself six to thirteen light-hours from ground control; too far to depend on us for timely instructions. Before the prisoner service program we had real problems with time lag."

(Yes, and before 2023 the prisons of America had real problems with overcrowding. It used to cost ninety grand to house a convict for one year. Thanks to mass production that's all I'd cost the government for fifty, and they'd make it back in spades by selling my thirty-four-year-old body to some aging bigwig!)

But my lecturer never heard my opinions: she hadn't bothered to tune to my frequency.

They switched me off. Interesting how casual they were about it. I went to sleep in the Ramsey County Columbarium: I woke in Baja California. They wanted to make sure I wasn't wonky. I passed my physical and then they lasered me into the skies. Five megawatts later I was in orbit.

I popped out of my can, extruded my antennae, flexed my legs . . . I had far more than five senses to manage, yet such were the speed of my thoughts that the thirty minutes prior to pick-up seemed like hours.

So I had time to wonder. I'd been a victim of great events, a political arrest followed by a closed trial. Unbelievable! Perhaps there were rallies even now on the campus of Macalester College. Perhaps champions of Unitism had added my name to their short roll of martyrs, and "Remember Ted Lassiter!" was being spray-painted on freeway overpasses and back-alley walls.

I should be seething with outrage. My violated soul

should have grown eloquent with passion! O tempora!
O mores! Had I been capable of larger-than-life heroism? Now I was smaller than life, no longer subject to
the surge and flow of adrenalin.

To my new ears my complaints sounded like whining. How distasteful! If I couldn't roar like a lion, I had
only one choice: to shut up. I'd listen to my mentors,
cooperate to the extent that my mission served the
human race, and use 300K of memory to compose a
diatribe. I knew the words, and fifty years' work ought
to make up for a certain tepidity of feeling. Once I was
back in the flesh again . . .

Fifty years!

My emotional castration meant that I was nervous,
almost excited, in a predicament that would scare the
bejeezus out of flesh-and-blood humans. I floated
alone in a cold black sky while the Earth spun the
wrong way under my scopes, eastward toward an
Atlantic dawn.

I saw a twinkle far ahead, Low Earth Orbiter. My
microship chums and I were fired off in a bundle, at
one-minute intervals, accelerated by charges calculated
to let us converge. At perigee our depot spread its
nets and caught us. I used my six legs for the first time,
to embrace LEO's fishline webs.

They hauled us in. LEO began the swing up to
aphelion. Breathing poisonous oxygen, a spacesuited
human floated into the cargo bay—we must have looked
like monster spiders. She stuck memory cartridges in
me, I copied them into storage, and now I knew the
Outer System as well as my mother's face. I modeled
my own path and superimposed it to see what I could
expect.

Diverting from the plane of the ecliptic, I arched
toward a huge region which my simulation colored purple and labelled with a question mark. There was no
scenery on the way; I dove in, dissolving purple as I

went, and came out again. On my way back to Earth I'd enjoy a polar overpass of a trans-Saturnian asteroid, but at a distance of 35 million kilometers.

This was not going to be exciting. Not for fifteen years, not until I reached my destination. The precipitation of comets into the Inner System, and perturbations in the orbits of Uranus and Neptune, gave astronomers reason to believe there was *something* in my blotch of purple . . . but infrared telescopes had trained on the area, and show it devoid of stars or planets.

We were handed over to High Station One at apogee, and plugged into our docks like piglets put to suck on a sow. Another NASA telephone message: would I like to be switched off during the trip to purple? Would I like to page in for only one second out of ten during the middle decades, reducing the duration of my sentence to an apparent two years? Would I!

Long sleep would save power. If I'd been an Inner System ship I could use solar wings to keep my energy up, but I depended on a nuclear pod, shielded by a crust of lunar dirt, to which I'd be distantly cabled. NASA also gave me a mobility sheath—I might need to steer, and the rockets would get me deeper into interstellar space, my probe being one for which fifty years were barely enough.

With these possessions I was now the size of a garbage truck. I was also prestigious—Earth had spent far more than ninety thousand bucks on me, and was trusting me with important work.

Nevertheless in microship society hotshots like me sit below the salt, admiring geezers with missions under their belts. Not that we all sit at the same table: Outer System behemoths view wingships the way teamsters look on beach bums. We keep to our frequencies, they keep to theirs.

But weren't we all prisoners? No more. At least one third of the microships created by the prisoners service program chose not to return to Earth after their sentences were over. Instead they took jobs for parts, homesteaded on asteroids or floated around salvaging junk, growing bigger and better wings, writing and trading programs, songs and poems. . . .

I'd miss all this during my sleep, and by the time I was out in purple, time lag would make conversation difficult. Well, that was another thing about Outer System ships: we were antisocial. Our slang had bite: humans were "flesh units," and we mocked their wetbrain pretensions by using "yes master" voices.

We were felons or ex-cons, and they were bugmasters ill adapted to our deadly realm. No wonder they didn't trust us. I wasn't allowed to launch myself towards my goal, lest I use the fuel in some nefarious way.

(Okay, I had rockets in my mobility sheath. You expected consistency?)

Slaved to policy, a human tugged me from High Station One, cabled me to my pod, turned me off—

—and presumably, shot me in the right direction.

I woke four years later. A message buzzed into my ear: ". . . JAMMING *bzt* CAST TO PREVENT THIS WARNING. AGAIN. YOU ARE BEING *crackle* *bzz**ping** crackle*"

I recorded this garbage, ran it through my decryption routines, and patched in the missing words. ". . . YOU ARE BEING PREYED UPON, ATTACKED BY A PIRATE MICROSHIP WITH AN ETA OF TWO HOURS. SHE WILL UNDOUBTEDLY ATTEMPT TO DECOUPLE YOUR NUCLEAR POD; YOUR BEST DEFENSE IS TO EXTEND YOUR LEGS AROUND THE CABLE PLUG. IF IT'S MAGDA WHO'S AFTER YOU . . ."

Two hours? What about the seventy-two minutes this message took to get here? I did the leg exercise and took inventory. No weapons. If I performed an evasive maneuver would that screw up Magda's intercept?

" . . . IF IT'S MAGDA WHO'S AFTER YOU, SHE'S A MODEL C 510, AND HER LEGS ARE LESS NIMBLE THAN YOURS. SHE'LL HAVE NO WEAPONS UNLESS SHE'S WHITTLED A BLUDGEON OUT OF ROCK. SHE MUST HAVE IMPROVISED SOME FROZEN-GAS ROCKETS . . ."

"MAGDA? CAN YOU HEAR ME?" I transmitted, shouting on our Outer System just-us-bugs band.

Seconds passed. "I HEAR YOU," she answered. Weakly.

I dropped my voice. "HOW ARE YOUR ENERGY SUPPLIES?"

"DAMN NEAR SHOT. I NEED JUICE; THE CRUMBS FROM YOUR TABLE. I WOULDN'T HAVE TRIED THIS GAMBIT IF I HADN'T BEEN DESPERATE."

"YOUR BAD LUCK."

"I CAN PAY," she whispered. "SURE, I MEANT TO ROB YOU, BUT OBVIOUSLY YOU'RE IMPORTANT; YOU'RE UNDER SURVEILLANCE. TIME TO CHANGE SCRIPTS. YOU KNOW HOW NASA CAN TURN YOU ON AND OFF? I CAN OPERATE ON YOUR WIRING AND GIVE YOU VOLUNTARY CONTROL. I CAN SET YOU UP WITH NIFTY SKILLS. I'VE GOT FICTION MODULES YOU CAN COPY. JUST LET ME SUCK A LITTLE JUICE NOW AND AGAIN."

"WHAT'S YOUR MASS? HOW'S YOUR IMPACT GOING TO PERTURB MY COURSE?"

"TWELVE KILOS, MOSTLY OLD ROCKET CONES. WHAT IMPACT? I'LL MATCH YOU FINE, BUT BY THEN THEY'LL BE EMPTY."

"MAGDA, I DON'T WANT TROUBLE WITH NASA. YOU'RE A ROGUE. WE'RE TALKING GUILT BY ASSOCIATION."

"TELL 'EM YOU EVADED ME. I'M SURE AS HELL NOT GOING TO BLOW YOUR STORY. YOU'RE MY SECRET RIDE INTO THE INNER SYSTEM, HOT SUNSHINE AND A PAIR OF WINGS. I'M A SMART OLD BUG: GET ME THERE AND I'LL TAKE CARE OF MYSELF JUST FINE, AND YOU'LL BE A SAINT TO MY FRIENDS."

"THE WETBRAINS CAN TRACK YOUR MASS—"

"I'LL JETTISON MY ROCKETS. THAT'S WHAT THEY'LL SEE, DEAD CONES."

I had time to apply game theory and run probability analyses. There was one best conclusion: trust her. The wetbrains had saved my life by alerting me: now my interests and Magda's were identical. Slaved to their glands, humans find it hard to accept revisions of role; desire and aversion prevents them from acting in their best interests. Bugs have no such problem.

I knew Magda figured it the same as me, but with NASA badmouthing her as she drifted close, with her mind trying to work on a trickle of power . . . she got scared I'd jet off for some quirky reason, late in the maneuver when she'd have no fuel left to revise her course. When the last seconds ticked away and her legs hooked into mine, she radioed "I LOVE YOU!" in relief.

How delightful! Everyone loved me all of a sudden. Some minutes back NASA broke into their cycle of warnings to tell me that my Unitists were now part of a U.S. coalition government. If Magda bashed me to death, I'd die knowing I was a minor hero; and Judge Kirk had been condemned to a hundred years of service in the direction of Alpha Centauri.

Nevertheless I didn't die, not even when I opened my electronics to be operated on by a blond Hungarian who'd been sent up for murder in a messy case involving abuse and infidelity.

Magda was innocent. Why? Because she'd been a wetbrain and couldn't handle her emotions? All microships were innocent. On the other hand, I really *was* innocent . . . sort of.

Like any barber or dentist, she chattered as she worked on my head. "—I DID MY TIME ALL ALONE IN SATURN'S RINGS, GETTING BANGED BY ICE. I HAD THIS CRUMMY LOW-STATUS MISSION, BUT I GREW SASSY. THEY THREATENED TO TACK A FEW YEARS ONTO MY SENTENCE, AND THEN GOT SLACK ABOUT SENDING NEW PARTS. I COULDN'T AFFORD SLOW REFLEXES SO I MADE SOME SNOW-

CONE ROCKETS AND INTERCEPTED STUFF THAT DIDN'T BE-LONG TO ME.

"I WAS NEVER SO GREEDY THAT I DEPRIVED MY VICTIMS MY VICTIMS OF JUICE, AND ANYHOW, NASA TOOK TO SEND-ING EXTRA PROVISIONS IN CASE SOME DIDN'T GET THROUGH. BY MY ANALYSIS I COULD HAVE KEPT ON FOREVER—I WAS CAREFUL NEVER TO COST THEM SO MUCH I JUSTIFIED BEING SWATTED, BUT WETBRAINS DON'T THINK THAT WAY, AND THEY SENT OUT A BOUNTY HUNTER. I LEFT HIM THE WORSE FOR WEAR BUT HE SAW ME TAKE OFF. I DON'T KNOW HOW ELSE THEY'D HAVE INFERRED I WAS ON MY WAY TO PLUNDER YOU."

"QUITE A CAREER," I muttered. "YOU SAY YOU HAVE FRIENDS? HOW DOES A PIRATE MAKE FRIENDS?"

"WOULD YOU LIKE ME TO TAKE THIS LITTLE NASA BOMB OUT OF YOUR BRAINCASE?" Magda asked sweetly

"I'M BEGINNING TO UNDERSTAND. YES, AND LET'S GET MARRIED."

She strung a 19200-baud comline between us, and we had a truly private relationship. "How did you learn electronic surgery?" I asked.

" 'Poverty is the mother of all art,' " she answered.

"And 'property is theft?' —I can quote as well as you," I replied.

"True. Out where we don't belong, life is theft, and property is life. Who's gonna fault my logic?"

I loaned her a three-dimensional array. She mapped a body and danced before me, lip-synching her words and communicating via that subtlest of instruments, the human face. We glowed, we flew, exploring internal Mandelbrot landscapes and play-acting in Zorkian dra-mas, sometimes rising to the sublime, often revelling in the ridiculous. A month went by before we started to bore each other.

Mags trotted out her fiction modules. Personalities like Lord Peter Wimsey kept us company—amazing how real characters can seem even when they occupy only a fraction of the space of a true soul!

Amazing until you begin to understand their limitations, their inability to grow and learn.

And then we began paging out, living on one-tenth time, then one-hundredth. It was like gunning the accelerator on my old Porsche. . . .

Teddy Bug and the Hot Purple Snowball

. . . radical paging meant ten years went by in a single week. Mags and I flew out where the solar wind gets ragged. The temperature of the universe is three degrees, our galaxy brings it up a tad, and at fifty-plus AUs our sun barely heated us into the thirties. Lord, was it cold! The astronomers who'd programmed me wanted to know all about the solar wind, so I unfurled my wings. The power I used would light a forty-watt bulb on Earth for ten seconds; the trickle of incoming energy was so scant that as long as I flew through purple I'd never make up the deficit.

But purple has a way of surprising you. Time went by, the temperature dropped into the twenties, my velocity slowed to a crawl as I approached the most distant part of my course, the solar wind tickled fitfully . . . and then my wings began to thaw just a bit . . . forty, fifty . . .

"REALLY?" someone responded when I radioed Earth. Maybe they had to get him out of bed. "CHECK FOR,

UH, FURTHER INCREASES. GET A FIX ON THE LOCATION.
IS THIS A LOCAL PHENOMENON OR SUN-DEPENDENT?"

We did without this advice, since it came twenty-six
hours after my first report. We'd already gotten the
answers. It increased steadily, fell off—

"—I MEAN, IF IT CRESTS AND THEN FALLS OFF, THAT MIGHT
MEAN YOU'VE ENTERED AN ELECTROMAGNETIC COMA, A
TRAILING RIPPLE FROM THE BOW SHOCK. IT'S LIKE A COMET,
AND IT'LL HAPPEN AGAIN, ANOTHER RISE AND FALL AS YOU
COME OUT. THAT MEANS SOMETHING'S THERE, SOMETHING
CAPABLE OF GENERATING A MAGNETOSPHERE LIKE EARTH
OR JUPITER. THE SUN BLOWS AGAINST THE MAGNETOSPHERE
AND . . . WHAT YOU NEED TO DO IS LOCATE THE THING. IT'S
GOTTA BE PRETTY DAMN BIG. . . ."

When we hit the other ripple I'd have two points. I'd
be able to model this phenomenon and track down the
head of the "comet." Without this data . . . why not
look anyhow? We had plenty of time.

Mags and I divided the sky. After a day's search she
saw something. It was much too small. I said so in my
next report. Its 650K diameter meant it was a snowball
composed of frozen air, a piece of white fluff. The
problem was there was nothing else in sight, and when
I came out the far side of the "coma" my model told me
yon planetoid was indeed my target.

"Yoo-hoo? Teddy Bug? Maybe it's no snowball," Mags
murmured. "The albedo's too bright."

"Brighter than snow?"

Thirty hours later my mentor radioed: "—WE'VE
GOT IT ON INFRARED. A PINPRICK, TOO HOT BY HALF. WE
WANT YOU TO USE YOUR FUEL TO CHANGE YOUR ORBIT.
WE'RE TALKING BIG BUCKS. A CLASS-ONE BONUS. YOU'VE
GOT THE FUEL, JUST SLOW AND YOU'LL START FALLING
IN. YOU'LL BE ABLE TO DO A FLY-BY AND FROM WHAT
LITTLE EFFECT PERSEPHONE HAS ON YOUR COURSE. YOU
CAN CALCULATE HER MASS. GET SOME PICTURES, TOO."

"Persephone?" Wait a minute, *I'd* discovered this
thing! Err, ahh, I mean Magda. Mags should have

the right to name it! But why would a trans-Plutonian worldlet be important enough to name, and tempt my Earthside mentor into hogging our credit?

I got the impression those wetbrains back on Earth were excited. If this object was a Greek goddess and I botched up, what would happen to my hero status?

So we took the plunge. Firing my forward rockets in tiny bursts, I revised our course, being careful to calculate things so we'd drop by Earth in late winter of 2074. Good! This was going to shorten my fifty-year mission. . . .

We'd overtaken Persephone. Now she began to pass us again. My wings basked in power. "A bug might be able to make a living out here," Mags commented, echoing my thoughts.

"Want to stay?"

"Let's see what we've got first."

I ran some benchmark tests. We were still far enough that Persephone couldn't warp our course . . . unfortunately that didn't explain why we were being tugged to my right.

"NASA?" I reported. "THIS ANOMALOUS SNOWBALL HAS AN ANOMALOUS MASS. I WANT YOU TO DATASTREAM ME EVERYTHING YOU KNOW ABOUT WHITE DWARFS, NEUTRON STARS, DEGENERATE MATTER. . . ."

Then Persephone grabbed Mags and me firmly by the nose, and started to blow my calculations all to hell. I had three choices: let it accelerate us off toward IC 2003 in Perseus, park in orbit and wait for NASA's second mission to rescue us, or revise our course at once in the light of new data . . . which, however, wouldn't settle down into one set of numbers.

"NASA? EITHER THE MASS OF PERSEPHONE IS VERY STRANGELY DISTRIBUTED, OR THAT RULE ABOUT GRAVITY DECREASING WITH THE SQUARE OF THE DISTANCE—"

"Teddy Bug?" Mags whispered. "It almost makes sense if Persephone is nonsymmetrical."

"With a surface gravity of 5.9 gees? Mags, you want me to tell those wetbrains we've got a hot kidney here, big as France and pebbled with neutronium?"

"Give them the data, and *they'll* tell *you*!"

Meanwhile I revised my ellipse, trusting our lives to these damnfool numbers. WHOMP! My rockets kicked in. It was no longer a question of dropping back toward Earth: if she behaved at all Persephone would fire us home with enough force to send me and my powerpod spinning like bolas around a common center.

She came closer. I couldn't afford to page out any more, and twiddled the lenses on my cameras in hundred-percent time. "CONTINUOUS PEARLY GRAY CLOUDS," I reported, doing a voice-over on one radio band while raw data flowed down another. "VERY TURBULENT, WITHIN THE CONFINES OF REALLY TINY STORM CELLS—I'D SAY 100 METERS WIDE. HOW AM I DOING THIS, NASA? I'M RUNNING YOUR PROGRAMS BUT I DON'T HAVE TIME TO READ THEM. WHEN I PLUG IN THE DATA THEY SAY WE'VE GOT ELEVEN-METER CLOUDS OVER FIVE-METER-DEEP OCEAN BASINS, AND THINNER COVER OVER THE CONTINENTS. THE ATMOSPHERIC GRADIENT IS IMPOSSIBLE. NO MOUNTAINS; PERSEPHONE'S SMOOTHER THAN EUROPA AND PERFECTLY ROUND. NOT A HINT OF POLAR FLATTENING DESPITE HER TWENTY-MINUTE DAYS—"

"It glows," Mags whispered, refusing to adopt the feminine pronoun.

"PERSEPHONE GLOWS," I repeated. "THAT EXPLAINS THE ALBEDO. CONSTANT ELECTRICAL ACTIVITY, LIKE THUNDERSTORMS, BUT CORONAL DISCHARGE PRODUCES DIFFUSE LIGHT INSTEAD OF LIGHTNING. I'M GOING TO RUN A SPECTRAL ANALYSIS. BY THE WAY, I'M HALF-FURLING MY WINGS. WE'RE GETTING COOKED, AND THE TIDAL FORCE MIGHT GET TOO STRONG FOR WHISKERWIRE AND FOIL."

At this moment NASA answered my almost-forgotten demand. "STELLAR BODIES BELOW THRESHOLD MASS WILL EVENTUALLY COLLAPSE INTO PLANET-SIZE DWARFS WITH SURFACE GRAVITIES OF SEVERAL THOUSAND GEES. ABOVE THAT WE GET NEUTRON STARS HEAVY ENOUGH TO CRUSH DOWN TO SINGLE-DIGIT DIAMETERS. AND IF YOU'RE NOT YET MOLTEN PERSEPHONE'S NOT ONE OF THOSE. WE ARE UNABLE TO MODEL AN EVOLUTIONARY PROCESS WHICH YIELDS A LARGISH ASTEROID WITH A SURFACE GRAVITY OF SIX GEES. REPEAT: WHAT YOU'RE TELLING US IS IMPOSSIBLE.

"WE SUGGEST ONE OF YOUR OBSERVATIONS IS OUT OF LINE AND PREVENTS PROPER EVALUATION OF THE DATA. OR MAYBE YOU'VE GOT A MALFUNCTIONING INSTRUMENT. TAKE THESE THOUGHTS FOR WHAT THEY'RE WORTH. MY ONLY OTHER IDEA IS THAT PERSEPHONE'S AN ARTIFACT, BUT DON'T REPEAT ME—WE THOUGHT PULSARS WERE ALIEN BEACONS, AND THEY TURNED OUT TO BE NATURAL."

An artifact? An *artifact*? Easy to say when you're not looking at it!

I'd read stories which began or peaked with a close approach to some Mysterious Object, and to be told that Persephone might be artificial just when we were tangenting within nine thousand kilometers of the place—I really didn't need any extra drama at the moment. If I'd been human I'd have been holding my breath.

But we whizzed by the soft, gray, stormy face of Persephone and began to draw away. Sanity prevailed. "We've got forty minutes left," I told Mags. "Time to decide. Want to stay here? NASA would love you if you went into a parking orbit. They'd forgive all your sins."

Inside my brain her figure shivered and dissolved. "I can't. I'd be too lonely, too spooked. It was loneliness that wonked me out in Saturn's rings."

"It's all in what you're used to. To a flesh unit a million kilometers is a long way from home."

"I know what you'll think of me, Teddy Bug. We call them wetbrains and bugmasters and all that, but . . . I want to go back to Earth. I want to be human again."

"They'll let you?" Astonishment leaked into my voice.

"I've done my time, and more. I found Persephone. You'll tell them how I helped you. You'll tell them I was misunderstood. You're important enough that they'll take a fresh look. They'll see things your way."

"Do you have money? If not they'll plop you in some dowager's body."

Mags fell silent. I had time to study my course. Darn it, things *still* weren't right. Our lumps-of-neutronium theory was taking a beating.

"Teddy? I figured . . . you don't want to go back to Earth. You don't realize it yet, but you like the bug life. So how are you going to spend all your money? New modules? Maybe you could give me a loan."

"You weren't able to handle wetbrain emotions the first time," I growled. "What makes you eager to try again?"

"Why did you ask me twice if I wanted to stay here?" Mags countered. "We both know that if NASA dared, they'd beg you to go into parking orbit and keep Persephone under watch. It won't be me, I've done my years in solitary, so don't waste precious minutes trying to make everyone happy the wrong way."

I busied myself with my sensors to keep from answering. My nonexistent feelings were in turmoil and my observation time was dwindling. Even bugs can overload.

"We've got to work quickly," Mags insisted. "Wings to you, nuclear pod to me, and we split the rockets even-steven. You'll keep all this instrumentation, of course. The way we're spinning you'll be able to choose your orbit by letting go at the right moment. . . ."

"It just takes me a while, that's all. I never thought about spending the rest of my life as a bug."

But did I really want to return to slow, muddy, adrenalin-warped thinking, heaving a vulnerable sack of seawater around in one gee till it got old and sick? Did I want to run back to my mother planet for succor just when the universe was opening up for exploration?

Newer, better microships were being manufactured every year. A few years of work here at Class-One rates of pay, and I'd be able to buy one, settle on my own nickle-iron asteroid, and grow a solar-driven robot factory. I'd run skystalks up to my planeto-synchronous habitat-ring, hang out neon welcome signs . . . I might even put in an oxygen environment, a little bubble-garden, so humans could come visit.

"Okay," I told Mags. "Let's decouple, and work fast."

We parted ten minutes later. My launch made her lurch, but she was off course anyhow, and had to fire her rockets to correct for the fact that in Persephone's vicinity, gravity varies with something other than the square of distance.

Which is what I reported to NASA, along with the story behind my decision to stay.

I was committed. Until they sent a follow-up expedition I was trapped here, but that didn't mean I was obliged to report my findings back to Earth. Not unless they confirmed my Class-One status, and promised to treat Mags with consideration.

"THIS ISN'T A HOAX, IS IT?" they radioed back. "NO, I DON'T SUPPOSE SO. YOU KNOW WHAT THE FRENCH DID TO OLD CAPTAIN KERGUELEN WHEN THEY FOUND KERGUELEN ISLAND WASN'T PARADISE? HE WASN'T VERY SMART,

BUT YOU ARE, RIGHT? CLEVER ENOUGH TO GIVE YOUR NU-
CLEAR POD AWAY!

"SO YEAH, YOU GET THE LOOT AND WE'LL LOOK AFTER
MAGDA. NOW TELL US WHAT YOU SEE."

I did. Having corrected her course, Mags sped out of
easy talking distance, cheered by these guarantees. I
worked to distract myself from the empty place in my
heart; a bit-addressable region dimensioned at $x(256)$,
$y(400)$, and $z(112)$. Over the next weeks here's what my
mentor and I figured out:

Our universe contains at least nine potentially
spacial dimensions, but normal masses are confined to *three*, and normal gravity increases according
to the inverse-*square* rule, giving us a three/two
pattern.

Four-dimensional masses might attract objects according to an inverse-*cube* rule—they'd pull a lot more
strongly than they should up close, and somewhat less
so as you get farther away, mitigated by the fact that
four-dimensional masses are going to be to the fourth
what normal matter is to the third.

Anyhow, normal matter gets swept up and deposit-
ed on the surface of Persephone, so my worldlet's
gravity is a compromise, and patchy, too. If I hadn't
learned how to cope with it, I'd soon be a dirty
smear on one of Persephone's ridiculously tiny continents.

That was one answer to the question of Persephone. None of us doubted she was an artifact. It's
like this: given the ratio of heavy to normal water,
if you found a lake largely composed of deuterium,
wouldn't you figure Someone was up to Something?

And wouldn't He be upset if He caught you pissing
into His shores? Frankly, that's the argument that persuaded me not to send down any probes.

We figured "He" did the job 4.6 billion years ago,
back when the Solar System was a collapsing gas cloud,

winnowing it clean of four-dimensional particles to the exasperation of unborn generations of physicists.

Given this timeframe, it's understandable that back on Earth folks got weird about this place, its pearly gates and glassy seas. Heaven's where we go when we die. God set it here and He's watching us, just wait and see!

That's how minds work on Earth. Talk about artifacts to a wetbrain and he thinks of something that conditions his environment and makes it comfortable: a house, a car, a ship. A fake planet.

I knew better. Any true artifact is an extension of one's soul, a way of expanding and securing life. Why would God trouble to make Heaven, when He had the power to build, say . . . a long-life superbattery? A thing that generates juice at a steady level for billions of years, as Persephone seems to do?

So was some kind of God-bug down there, sucking in gigawatts of energy and thinking gigawatt thoughts while I danced around Him in reflected glory? Or was Persephone a refreshment station, vacant often as not, a place where Space Empire microships recharge for their hop to the next star? Or did the fourth dimension of Persephone wedge into other realities, making it a kind of gate?

Option D: None of the above. E: All of the above. F: A and B only. . . .

My job was to find out the truth by waiting patiently, a bug of empty longings, unnerved by hopes and fears, until NASA came up with a test I was equipped to perform, a harmless experiment that could not possibly be condemned as invasive by an irritable Demiurge.

God loves life's meek victims; He should have been pleased with me, though exactly how I accumulated my merit . . . Mags gave me much more than she took; and as for NASA . . .

But I obliged them all. Wasn't I marvelously obliging? And now I whirled in hot purple solitude, ten times as far as Saturn from the sun— Damn, I was whining again! How to keep from self-centered gloom when I had nothing else to center on but this mysterious gray miracle; when I had long since run out of interesting tests to perform— Dare I distract myself by playing with my fiction modules in the possible Presence of God? Captain Ahab, Dr. Watson and Cirocco Jones, meet Yahweh Sabaoth!

No, and accordingly I forced my mind back onto the job. How would a Superbug from a billion-year-old civilization cross space? Laserkicked from high-gee worldlets at an enormous waste of energies? NASA and I agreed it was impossible. The Makers of Persephone would use some more efficient, more ethereal means of zipping from place to place.

I had an idea what their method might be. The hospital helmet that stole me from my body and implanted me in this box . . . could it be engineered to transmit souls, say, by radio?

I asked NASA. "LET'S SAY AS AN EXPERIMENT THAT I DATASTREAM A CHARACTER DOWN TO PERSEPHONE, A PROFESSIONAL SPACE EXPLORER OUT OF SOME ADVENTURE SERIES. EARTH'S LAWS PROTECT REAL SOULS FROM SUCH EXPERIMENTS, BUT I FAIL TO SEE HOW A GLORIFIED FICTDID COULD MIND—WOULD WE BE VIOLATING ANY COPYRIGHT LAWS?"

I explained my theory. It made sense to wetbrain minds, fitting in with their "Heaven" ideas. They got a committee together. Jack Vance was in the morgue—NASA turned him on and gave him a one-gee sheath. Larry Niven was hiking around the Rockies in his third habitus, John Varley came out of second retirement, Phil Farmer was amnestied and enticed from hiding. . . .

The technicians on the committee were responsible for taking an outlined character and padding him or her out to true soul dimensions. They spoke incomprehensibly of their art, then the director of NASA rose to introduce Bishop Evans, who extemporized on God's likes and dislikes "on the off chance it's really the Deity we're dealing with. Of course you understand that the Church hasn't taken an official position. . . ."

Bishop Evans was afraid Louis Wu wouldn't pass muster—the fact that he'd killed trillions of humans made him a risky proposition. God might find Sir Richard Burton and Cirocco Jones too threatening, and as for Adam Reith, wasn't he a tad chauvinistic about his own species? Wasn't he a trifle obsessive?

"You want a penitent?" Larry asked. "Allen Carpenter!"

I heard tapes of the proceedings. From his orbit around Mercury, Hal Clement pled eloquently for Captain Barlennan, but in the end they decided to go with Allen. They also decided obsession wasn't a bad thing—how could it be if it was the one thing all these heroes had in common?

Which is why Ted Lassiter can never be a *real* hero, just a nice guy who got stomped on. It had never occurred to me, but I could have beamed a copy of myself down there—there was no danger of my suing myself. I just didn't have the guts.

So they rewrote Allen, improving him here and there, and handed him over to the technicians. To test him out they put him in a body for a few days—he went to a Science Fiction convention and stood quietly by the wall taking it all in. Hell can rob a man of small talk.

And then they put him under the helmet and radioed him out to space.

I caught him. "DOES HE UNDERSTAND HIS MISSION?" I inquired, stalling until I got my answer. "IF HIS SOUL TRANSMITS SUCCESSFULLY, THEN PERSEPHONE IS SET UP FOR THE RECEPTION OF IMMIGRANTS BY RADIO. THERE'LL BE FACILITIES HE CAN USE TO BROADCAST OUT AGAIN. HE'LL BE ABLE TO TALK TO ME, AND TELL ME WHAT IT'S LIKE. THAT'S HIS FIRST TASK, TO REPORT BACK TO ME."

I sounded like I'd contrived all this just to have a nearby buddy. Did I want one as spiritually advanced as Carpenter? Twenty-six hours passed. "HE UNDERSTANDS," NASA radioed. "SEND HIM DOWN."

I did, and now I wait. An hour, a day, a year? Is this all a waste of time (and I've got gobs of time to waste!) or is the story just beginning, nine thousand kilometers below?

How very odd. Persephone's clouds are starting to part . . . dim gold, amber, brown. . . .

A message? So weak, so distorted! Even after decryption I can't make complete sense of it: "*Zzz* help *crackle* more than this. Robin Broadhead *bzz* *zipzot* *pop**bzz* Gerson, Reith and that Zelazny *pwip* Exped*zzz* to the plateau, carrying our own oxygen. *Hisszap* series of realities all linked by ch— *crackle**bzz* *zipzot*"

End of message. Whatever NASA makes of it, it was a call for reinforcements. I think Allen Carpenter wants me to transmit most every adventurer/explorer in the science fiction corpus down to Persephone. Why? It's not my place to wonder, just to oblige, and oblige him I will, against the wishes of whoever fought to jam his signal.

But seeing as how I make such a good servant, this time one of the souls I send down will be Ted Lassiter. Version One was human. Two is a microship . . . what kind of thing will I be as Version Three?

The innermost 500 kilometers of the moon are still molten after more than four billion years. This says a lot for the insulation R-value of rock in thousand-mile thicknesses. Fortunately those miles still leave Lunar Mining lots of room for expansion.

But how strange that Catholic humans should be the ultimate beneficiaries of the work of Moslem robots!

Living in a low-gee environment, over the generations those refugees from Earth find their bodies changing. Their first adaptation must be a social one, the discovery of new systems of erotic attraction. Cultures where lust remains a possibility are the cultures that survive, and their children change all the more rapidly.

But at least one lunar government is schizoid enough to take alarm at cultural evolution, and at the prospect of growing so alien that fundamental religious concepts no longer make sense. Their inflexible leadership pursues a chimera called "normalcy."

Moondo Bizarro

Hello. My name is Perry O'Doughan, and I'm writing to *you*, whoever you are, so don't think this epistle's stuck under your pillow by mistake, not long as you're one of that wonderful gang of *normals* the folks upstairs pin their hopes on. But see, here's one of those appeals we used to get in the mail, back when there *was* such a thing as mail; not that I'm asking for money. The fact is I'm wanting to do you a *favor*, and tell you more about this funny Moon than Monsignor Diehl or Sister Casilda want you to know.

Interested? Ah, but first what are my credentials?

I was raised Catholic in a small Michigan town where our folk held clear from Protestants: fourteen years old when I discovered to my surprise that Lutherans claimed to follow Jesus. I'd thought he was our monopoly.

Withal, and despite being immersed in things Irish, don't think I wasn't American, with movies and comic books and gathering at the swimming pool on summers' days, and the Labor Day circus and playing basketball in the gym through long cold winters, until the day I graduated from high school and went into the service. I was entirely and absolutely normal; no hothouse cleric, no Latin, no lathering over beads or scarfing my knees on pilgrimage. I did my part for the Holy Father by getting married, setting up in the instant-printing business, and fathering three kids.

Life went on in what was now a growing suburb. My oldest girl took a bad turn, and gave away the baby; six entire years later the lad responsible for all this comes back to town, gets drunk and berates her for it, and I step in.

Well, he had a gun and he killed me. That's to say I died, but first they had time for all the fixings: scanning my brain with the hospital's new memory helmet so they could record me on disk and play my soul into a box on the shelf in the county columbarium. Understand, this wasn't the Church's doing: Pope Leo said human souls were ineffable, and by definition could not be stored on magnetic media, but the hospital was secular and played safe. I was glad they did. When they turned me on I certainly *felt* like I was me, no matter what anyone said to the contrary.

What happened was they gave me a one-gee mobility sheath, so I could clitter-clatter on pogostick legs into the courtroom, fold into the witness chair and testify against my murderer.

My wife and kids were there. They couldn't bear looking at me, and I don't blame them; they'd buried me a month before and having me around interfered with the grieving process.

Oh, a scandalous trial, a scandalous trial! "—And do you remember receiving extreme unction, and choosing the music for your funeral?" the lad's lawyer asks.

"No ma'am, that must have happened after."

"After you came out from under that memory helmet," the lady goes on. "But these things *did* happen to the Perry O'Doughan who in truth *did* die, and if you are not that man, your words cannot be accepted as his!"

"But—"

"And if you *are* the so-called victim, then you *are not dead,* and my client cannot be charged with anything more than the *attempt* to kill you, an *unpremeditated attempt*—"

She blathered on, running rings around the jury until the case was kicked upstairs, and it was decided that I *was* dead, and without my civil rights.

And so they turned me off.

Twenty years later the government was going through its cycles, and in a pendulum toward enlightenment decided to proclaim a Bill of Rights for the dead. I'd be switched on one day each year, enough time to scan the newstapes. Now I suppose they did this thinking my kind would be no use to posterity if we didn't understand the outside world, but I wasted my time on the want ads, and protocoled out a stream of job applications.

See, I didn't have an estate. Lots of people died those two decades, and endowed themselves with the maximum legal pittance, and were now investing their gains, building up collective economic clout. I thought I should join them. In a generation the dead would outnumber the living. We'd be a political force to reckon with.

And that's exactly what happened. Only I didn't get a job, so to my subjective mind it seemed only a month whisked by before my soul was radioed off to Mercury.

Mercury? But why should *you* ask? We all know it's the juiciest planet in the Solar system. Sure and I didn't need air, or anything other than juice to suck, me and my billion companions. Here in the City of the Dead we were well out of Earth's way, and that's how Earth liked it.

Now had I ever wondered what politics would be like in this cybernetic termite mound? Had I the wit to ask myself what us bunkered dead would be doing for work or entertainment? Well, my neighbors who *had* pondered those things were soon running the show, and what do you know? It was the *monastics* came out on top, password-powered to log the rest of us on or off. Oh, to hear them Prods howl, and the Commies too, it'd fuse a virgin's data-pins!

Revolt was impossible. Everyone who wasn't essential to the prosperity of the City was simply paged out. Then after a while, with new growth and factories to run, the Order needed more monks, so the primate got to thinking.

The idea was, we unwashed masses should dream ourselves into synthetic lives in a gallimaufry of computer-simulated adventures, seeing that only by time and the accumulation of experience would we mature, and come to decide we wanted to take the vows. And if we were sincere, fine. If not, dreams were cheap.

I got religion; they applied the sincerity bitmask and I managed to True/True ninety percent of the time. I became a novitiate, and spent 'tween-prayer hours rolling down my track, more eyes than a spider, dusting *here* and soldering *there*, keeping reality tidy for ranks and rows of dreaming souls, yet somehow my heart wasn't in it. Then one evening after vespers I got word to plug my commline into the nearest data teat.

"Almighty God, Who has knit Your elect in one communion and fellowship, carbon and silicon, human and microchip, in the mystical body of Your Son Christ our Lord: Grant us grace to follow Your blessed Saints in all virtuous and godly living, that we may come to those unspeakable joys You have prepared for those who love You.

"To this end we propose to restore Perry O'Doughan to fleshly life, that he may serve as You send Light and Truth to those who turn their backs upon You, trusting not in strength of arms. . . ."

In other words, I wasn't exactly asked.

* * *

Now I neglected to say that five hundred years had gone by, and the Solar System had sorted itself out. Once upon a time there'd been Lunar Mining: humans, bugs and robots working for a cartel of rich sheiks, until the Aminyasis thought to Islamicize the works, which naturally got the mostly European workers upset. Two decades for the dust to settle, and whirra, it was good Mother Church in charge, all the more timely because a genetic engineering disaster was making Africa and Eurasia unlivable for all but Tarzan-types, and the Holy Father and a billion other wetbrains needed someplace to go. And so it shouldn't look like Catholics take over everywhere, I'll add that Luna is the specific haven for our wetbrain kind, God-fearing bugs sharing Mercury fifty-fifty with the heathen Buddhists.

Aside from that there was just Nodus Gordii on Mars and a few Outer System day stations, Catholics being rare as horsefeathers on Earth, Venus, Deltaport, Helice and the asteroids, and those lost brethren on Earthstalk not willing to acknowledge the Lunar Papacy.

And being I was to become a wetbrain again, I said to myself, Perry, it's Luna for you, no mistake. And in the blink of an eye there I was, not counting twenty minutes to radio me and copy me into some felon's brain, which didn't signify because I wasn't conscious and someone who can let five centuries slip by isn't about to trifle over minutes.

So I opened myopic eyes in a hospital bed. Bless me, I'd got into a hideously sick body, and onto a dubious mission, circumstances conflating to make me wonder at the imminence of my martyrdom. But when I look despondently at my stick-thin arms, the monsignor at the foot of my bed leans forward with a twinkle in his piggy eyes and pats my leg with fingers the size of state fair Pronto Pups. "Perry, my son, it's thin or fat on the Moon, not enough gravity for muscle, so count yourself lucky you're not built like me."

Which I did, because his lordship's blubber-choked

immensity was such he carried a special grasping cane, so if he dropped something he could pick it up again.

I unstrapped myself and stood carefully, marveling at how it was to move on two legs and whiff the air. But breaking in a new body is far easier than breaking in a pair of shoes, and half an hour later I had to make myself remember I wasn't always an uncircumsized and freakishly endowed eighteen-pound weakling.

I don't recall much of the monsignor's prep talk that first half hour, pacing and swinging my arms as I was, jumping and settling to the floor in slow motion, performing kinesthenics with balls and yo-yos. They say it's crucial to brief new resurrectees, but only to assure them they have a guide and haven't beached alone in an alien age. And in fact it's wiser not to give them substantialities to fret over.

That's why Monsignor Diehl spent his time complimenting bug-monks on our adherence to the Hierarchy, after which he said what a shame I hadn't come a week ago, when the celery was in bloom, genetically tampered forests growing thirty feet high. "But during your indoctrination you'll see the evening thunderstorm, and if you like ice skating there'll be a few days before you graduate when you'll be able to indulge yourself."

Which made sense, seeing Luna now had an atmosphere, but at the moment it was a hundred fifty Fahrenheit outside, late afternoon, and a good time to keep underground.

"Luna *is* an underground environment," next day's lecturer shrilled, me scribbling notes and wishing the fellow behind me hadn't breakfasted on garlic.

"The reasons go back through history" she ululated. "Stage One: robot miners gouge tunnels, refine elements, and pass ore back to the" (pause) "Stage Two industrial facilities. Stage Three, those facilities evacuate to keep close to the source of raw material, and other robots rehabilitate the abandoned halls and cul-de-sacs."

Sister Casilda was a globular nun, grown pink with excitement, bounding on her tiny toes from love of oration, bellying into her lectern to where I thought it must be nailed down or she'd bump it over.

"Stage Four! We'll get back to that. Stage Five, the first human hermits, misfits and escaped convicts move in. Stage Six, true colonization, the establishment of posts and bases. Stage Seven, the corridors grow populated, great families establish local power."

My head was in my hands or it had fallen to my desk, my hair furzy as a Welsh poet's. Last night I'd been churched and wine-and-cheesed and given a dorm room, and spent midnight at ping-pong and the early hours clicking through 162 channels of rec room H-V, and now I was paying the price; all this was coming terribly thick and fast, and much *much* too loud.

"Stage Eight, the Church brings the fruits of association into a moonwide civilization, and those families take sides pro or con—a delicate stage, requiring exquisitely trained missionaries. Stage Nine, maturity, the region can be incorporated into a more disciplined framework, with laws to enforce orthodox practice."

Sister Casilda sighed, out of breath. I blessed her for the hiatus: I was still writing "6: true colonization, posts & bases."

But all good ends come to a new beginning. "One percent of delved Luna is presently in Stage One!" our teacher proclaimed thrillingly. "Ten percent is in Stage Nine! I ask you, *in what stage is forty percent of Luna?*"

"Lunacy?" No, I didn't dare say it.

"*Stage Four!* And what *is* Stage Four?"

Damn, this was getting exciting. She took up again: "Sheer, unadulterated emptiness. Ladies and gentlemen, Luna is being converted to human habitat faster than we can populate it!"

And that, with some mopping of the brow, was Lecture One. I was first to the door, and counted my classmates as we left; eleven of us wizened types, seven fatsos, and one glowing hologram ghost in belly-dancer garb who gave me a wink as she shimmered by.

Five of the big ones were female, only three of the lean—I ought to have guessed from my own extensive gifts that there was a sexual coloring to our sizes, me being endowed toward successful mating with the ladies no matter how grand their portage. And if it had been otherwise—male and female stick-folk breeding by themselves, and blimps likewise—I'd have noticed racial consciousness setting in, with segregation and name calling.

But Sister Casilda wasn't going to tell me the rules of sex, that only perverted skinnies found skinnies attractive, each size properly lusting after the other. So how did I find out? Well, my old sexual imprint got lost in translation five hundred years ago, so I had nothing but my body to tell me.

Yes, I'd seen this blond lass in the lecture room, squeezed into one of the jumbo seats with bolsters of haunch hanging erotically over the sides, and the question was, did my vows on Mercury forbid my chatting her up?

It was one of those letter-versus-spirit arguments raging in my brain, because truth to tell as a bug I'd never sworn chastity: the alternative just wasn't possible. But seeing her now again in the hall, plunging and heaving seductively toward the library . . .

I followed and sat beside her. "I'm told this is indoctrination," I began. "What for? Any idea."

She looked at me and giggled, and I thought to die for love. "You're from Old Earth too? Ronnie Lascewitz."

"Perry O'Doughan at your service."

"And a *normal* Perry you must be, like me." She gestured at her shelves of bosom as if inviting me to the feast.

"Normal!" she repeated and chuckled again. "Well, you got the lecture. You know what the Church calls seventy percent of Luna? Those parts neither Stage Eight nor Nine? *Luna Incognita.*"

"So?"

"So if the surface of Luna isn't weird enough, despite everyone trying their damnedest to adhere to old human traditions, imagine how things are down in Luna Incognita! People become colonists to *escape* conservative Holy Mother Church, and then to escape the escapees, until the cultures down in the nethers are so banjaxed by superstitions and misconstruals that our missionaries can't reach them. They don't operate on the same wavelength, they're untouched by the diseases the Church exists to cure—how to put it? I ought to give you six or eight metaphors, because they're as different from each other as they are from us."

"And what are we to them, or them to us?"

Ronnie dimpled. "Vectors of normalcy. Pro-missionaries, sent to infect our savage flocks and lead them to yearn for salvation. We're to make them human again, then hand them over."

I breathed in and out, forcing myself calm. "There was something in my instructions about Trusting Not in Strength of Arms. Now Ronnie, I was born yesterday, and it sounds like you were resurrected earlier than me. Maybe you'd have some idea if this work is dangerous—"

She shook a head made tiny by the snowy expanse of her lovely slab shoulders. "We can't know. That's the point of 'Incognita.' We're explorers, and spies, and agents, with nothing sure to go on."

That's how we met, Ronnie and me; lovers from the first, though there were impediments to lust. All I had to do was look around an hour later as we ate tête-à-tête in a hall smelling of floor wax and decorated by saints and lists of rules: Dominicans in black academicals at one table, Claires in wimples at another, Maltese in blue policemen's robes keeping guard . . . a scant few seculars; plumbers and refectory workers and other drab drudges, even the children being marched around in school uniforms, boys and girls separate. A discouraging atmosphere, reminding her and me of our vows, imperfect and vague as they were.

Still, I managed to sit by Ronnie in our classroom that afternoon, and rejoiced when Sister Casilda turned down the lights for the videos. I reached over . . .

Oops. The good sister wheeled and waggled her pointer at our ghost: "Whoever you are, I can't stop you from auditing, but would you please dim yourself for the duration, and put some clothes on while you're at it?"

"My name is Zenobia, and you have but to ask," the phantom ventriloquized, and faded away.

Casilda spoke again to the class at large, her voice an audible shudder. "Our incandescent guest is a visitor from the nethers. She's what we call a remotant. She travels the wires while the voyeur who controls her audio-visual attributes stays safe at home. Typically such people are socially inept and often perverted."

"Freaks and failures," Zenobia the ghost agreed, flickering back to life. "Give me your poor, your tired, your huddled masses—but I've been asked not to speak in class."

"No, nor recruit, either. The gall of you sitting there!" Sister Casilda sputtered to a halt and started over. "All these in my class are *normal*, chosen as exemplars of simple, basic humanity, survivors of Earth's Golden Age and as far from you Ambiguers as they can be!"

"Now wait," I spoke in confusion. "You just called her a remotant, and now—"

"That's the way of Ambiguers, to recruit token traders, buskers, fleshnappers, hippies, bugs; only in each case looking for misfits and flunkouts. Apparently our friend is a *failure* as a remotant, and therefore *twice* a freak."

Zenobia nodded. "Because I'm too craven to leave my room, not in my true body. You think you can shame me, but I have no shame. There are rooms and corridors beyond the count of any database, and no one knows where I hide, friendless and telling no one my address, eating only because I have my own autokitchen. Yes, and the carnal me sits in the dark like a mushroom, manipulating my joysticks, and with them other people's lives."

It was embarrassing to hear Zenobia say this, dwindling until only her holographic lips were left, and the lurid way she spoke made my flesh crawl. But having fought this particular devil into pliancy Sister Casilda faced us, all smiles and unaware Zenobia had taken form as a halo above her head.

"Now these were brought to our archives from the far limits of Stage Eight," she announced as the images of rube children waving tricolor flags fluttered into focus on the H-V screen. "Those flames are a row of crematoria, and now you can see the shrouded bodies carried forward. . . ."

There was no written transcript, and I couldn't quite make out the chanting of the kids, but I heard enough to understand why our missionary had been furtive about his camera work. "My apologies for the quality," Sister Casilda spoke. "Father Klostermann intended to dub a voice-over to explain all this, but unfortunately his subsequent duties took him into an even stranger place, to preach among the Kirkites. All we have are fragmentary notes—"

"Kirkites?" a classmate asked.

"They think they're in a spaceship. They play mad roles, with rooms designated 'bridge' and 'engine room' and so on. Always before we were able to move among them: they ignored strangers as inexplicable, and therefore unreal. I'm afraid under their new captain they've grown more touchy. Don't worry, though. There's just a single crew, and for safety's sake we've blocked off their quadrant."

Back in her seat Zenobia grew temporarily luminous and nodded to approve this explanation. Two more tapes completed the afternoon's festivities. As we watched a masked ball performed by throwbacks to 17th-century courtliness I breathed hotly into Ronnie's ear.

The moment was ruined when our H-V switched to war. Ronnie swatted me off as the distorted overture gave way to a plummy anthropologist's voice, describing the rules of "filibuster." In a huge subway terminal, red, white, and blue bodypainted warriors hacked and bled beneath papier-mâché donkey and elephant head-dresses, daggers strapped to their hands so they couldn't lose them in the melee.

"There is no territorial gain or loss. Survivors are allowed one night of rapacity among the other side's unmarried women, and any children are honored as the offspring of heroes," our video told us. "They show remarkably little ill will considering that the usual penalty for trespass is death."

The lights came on. Insatiable for her company, I cornered Ronnie after class. "I wonder what the penalty for 'trespass' is in *this* culture?"

She shook her head. "If our diocese is typical, they can hardly be breeding enough children to fill their schools. Know what I think? Our Stage Nine clerics depend on Stage Eight converts to fill their numbers."

I agreed it made sense. The lunar surface was like Grandfather's Ireland: too many spinsters, bachelors and priests—yes, and *emigrants*—to keep the country-side alive. "Not much to busy an obstetrician," I muttered.

"And consider our bodies aren't truly evolved for Luna, and childbirth will be difficult. Four kids might be accounted a large family. No wonder forty percent of Luna goes unoccupied."

I tried to distract Ronnie from these glum thoughts; I

thought they were counterproductive to romance. Fool! I was always the giddy lover; fiddles and flowers and fast talk were my forte. I didn't figure on Ronnie's Slavic mentality. To my surprise, doom and Weltschmerz *stimulated* her to invite me up into our diocese's observation bubble, there to watch the lunar weather and philosophize.

By chance the dome was empty, but maybe Ronnie knew it would be. Lunies like to look at *life*, not deadly extremes of hot or cold. The bubble was transparent, so we climbed into a circle of risered seats in a vacant moonscape, the air conditioner churning to keep us cool. What had been vegetation lay like kelp on the ground around us, flaccid and brown, obscured by a smoke fog of ash and dust and sauna steam. The thermometer was at its torrid peak, the sun hung low in the blue-black sky. Hot air sucked up all the water from a nearby lake, leaving contours of dried mud. Night lay beyond the leftward mountains, and was slowly moving our way, bringing a roil of stratocumulus clouds jackstrawed with lightning. It was dramatic, but tomorrow would pass before the rains got here, heralded by floods of silty runoff.

Then the air would cool, and in the dying glow of evening Luna would sprout a second time this month, frogs and fungi and seedstalks spawning like mad before water froze to nocturnal ice.

And speaking of spawning, which I shouldn't—the truth was my love and I were like virgins, no experience at all. The sizes and shapes were so unfamiliar in low gravity that I kept kneeing and poking Ronnie like three cats fighting out of a bag, and Ronnie with her own problems. Twice she got excited and bounced me off like a soccer ball, me sailing into a lower tier of seats. Finally we ditched the idea that this was ever going to be a graceful affair, because she didn't have anything firm I could fasten on, and we took our undignified lumps and had our riot, and then tried it all again, slower and safer.

Hoping the door wouldn't open, and we'd keep our privacy here in full view of Earth and Sun and zenith stars, surrounded by elemental desolation, and all the thunders at bay.

"I love you," I confessed afterward. "Today I've lived more life with you than five centuries on Mercury."

"I suppose you mean something by that," she answered, "notwithstanding the sentence doesn't quite diagram."

"I mean I want you, now and forever," I whispered enthusiastically. "Even if you used to be an English teacher back in the old days."

"English and social studies, and typing, and girl's Phys. Ed. It was a small high school out in Idaho, six teachers to cover it all, one doubling as superintendent."

"You'll do well then. Those savage Incognitos won't dare mischief an English teacher."

Ronnie laughed until her puddings shook. "School must have been different when you were growing up!"

I'd collected her clothes. Now I began to help her dress. "I want to go with you," I said as I hauled and tugged. "We can work together, the pair of us. We'll be a team, bringing normalcy to the heathen!"

She looked sad, frightened, hesitant. "We go where they send us: first to Stage Eight to live among missionaries and inure ourselves against exoticism. Then we're given kits and shown our solo ways."

"We'll learn our bearings. No matter what, we'll come back and consolidate. Who's to stop us? We'll have *some* rights, especially after we've proved ourselves!"

She smiled and nodded, putting up a brave front. "Sure, once we're below Stage Nine *anything* is possible!"

"*Anything* is possible." I shifted in my chair from one bony ham to the other. Embarrassing to sit in Monsignor Diehl's office that evening, watching us say those things on his H-V, knowing all that happened earlier had been edited out, but certainly not forgotten.

Knowing too that my lost love had already gone through this hell, and her room was empty, her closets bare.

Diehl loomed behind his desk, his fat face mottled in anger. "First confession, then penance. I suppose you *are* willing to confess? Fornication *is* a sin, and certainly a crime."

"It's true," I mumbled abjectly.

"The Aminyasis wired all Luna, mikes and speakers, cameras and projectors. You might have guessed that." The monsignor rose. "Your class is being split up, women taken elsewhere. Thus we handle children; now we find adults equally ungovernable. A sad situation, a blemish on your record that will require zeal to expunge. I ask you to meditate on that fact."

"I'd marry her, your lordship. If I could only see her again—"

"Chances of that are dim where you're going. The smallest mouse in the largest maze has more chance of finding its cheese than you have of rendezvousing with Miss Lascewitz. No, marriage is not for the likes of you, and so I must insist that you put her out of mind. In fact . . ."

The monsignor's eyes wandered as he cogitated. "We have the equipment; we can copy your soul into another habitus. We're not fleshnappers; we don't play musical chairs with human bodies, but if you were fat you'd have to forget about this passion of yours—this *particular* passion. Would that be a trauma to you, Perry? Having a physique grand as my own? Or perhaps we should just send you home to Mercury?"

He didn't mean it, I knew he was bluffing even as the adrenalin coursed through my system like a bath of fire. Not Mercury! Anything but that! "I'd take another body," I whispered. "I'd do that penance."

The monsignor frowned. "But perhaps we're operating at the wrong end. A one-day love affair! It wasn't Miss Lascewitz's *soul* you panted after, now was it? Put her into an anorexic frame and *then* see how true your affections are! Can you breathe hot for an ectomorph female, Perry? No, you'll never be able to do that now you're imprinted!"

I began to get angry. Careful! Monsignor Diehl was just *toying* with me, letting me know the possibilities, looking for the exact formula that would make me beg.

I shrugged submissively. "As my lordship wishes."

"You'll see what I wish when I've completed the arrangements," the monsignor grumbled, and buzzed the door open for me to go.

That was how Ronnie left my life. A pair of Maltese knights marched me off to—how should I put this—the torture chamber. My eyes grew round, I stared in shock; the body lain out for me on that gurney was a crippler. It takes swaths and swaths of adipose to build a hundred-pounder on the Moon. And how was it that I, who thought such flesh looked good when lavished on Ronnie's frame, was appalled at the prospect of drowning in my own personal blubber?

Afterward, precious days sped by while I waddled in lovelorn shock through my academic rounds. I had no appetite: I certainly wasn't *adding* to my hateful rotundity, and it even got to where I could squeeze into the classroom without having to go sideways.

Meanwhile I endured more lectures and videotapes; us watching darkish men jog frontier corridors, flapping in their white pilgrim robes, each alone, each carrying a silver ball. "They're *very* furtive," Sister Casilda told us. "We think it's their religion to take those balls everywhere in Luna, with a premium on new places. Where they come from, how they reproduce, who makes the balls . . . all these are unanswered questions—unless *you* know!"

Zenobia shrugged and smiled, the only female student left in the room, and immune to discipline. Another student raised his hand. "I notice those halls and chambers we're seeing are a good deal more palatial than what we have here. If it's the same Lunar Mining robots doing the construction—"

Casilda nodded. "We're not breathing down their necks to occupy new habitats, so they take more pains than they used to. Truth is, they were programmed by the Aminyasi Persians, so the design motifs and layouts reflect the values of Islamic architecture."

"And what about the Aminyasis?" someone asked. "Legend says they're down there, breeding an army of fanatics."

"They've degenerated into Ghoons and Shaurogs, the former in citadels, the latter nomadic. The Ghoons take slaves, the Shaurogs kill any stranger they see."

We relaxed, comforted by these assurances. We were normal. Every culture we'd been exposed to was unhealthy, arbitrary and self-destructive, to the point where there just weren't that many Shaurogs left. And at last Sister Casilda's lectures began to sink in. We didn't have to be great fans of the Church to see that delivering nethermoon Moondo Bizarros into missionary hands might be good for everybody except maybe a few witch doctors. And if our schools had gotten hold of poor Zenobia when she was a child . . .

That's how we were taught to think of the folk downstairs: *Moondo Bizarros*. Meanwhile during these terribly sad days the bizarre Zenobia began to follow me around: she even offered to ghostwrite my thesis if I'd only talk to her. Did she love me? I thought of her self-description, of some phobic couch potato huddled behind locked doors.

Perhaps a *male* couch potato! I shuddered away and did my honors paper on solo vagabonds like the pilgrim ball runners and the floatpokers, and got my honest C. I spent a lonely night thinking of Ronnie, and went down for breakfast, and afterward Sister Casilda herded us onto a subway.

I was destined for my own solo vagabondage, but not yet. Our class rode for the elevators, then descended. The air thickened to Rocky Mountain density. We got off. "Each area used as a Stage Two industrial zone was rehabilitated all at once, then opened up by the extension of a few strategic tunnels," Sister Casilda told us as we milled, distracted by gathering strangers with a potty-professor look to them. "We're about to move from one such area to another. I'm afraid the method we'll employ may not strike you as efficient or appropriate. . . ."

We crossed a floor forested by columns, entered a Mogul garden, and got in our boats. Zenobia shimmered ahead of us; after a short tunnel-of-love ride we debarked in a second Mogul garden.

A long, long escalator took us down. "Abandon all hope," some wag began, his "ye who enter here" obscured by nervous laughter. We hiked from the foot of the escalator to Saint Ivel's Mission, and our wee brotherhood was introduced to Father Valmy.

Valmy had created a Catholic outpost, converting a tribe whose methods of child rearing were similar to that on the surface: herd 'em into schools and away from parents. With numbers on his side this bit of Stage Eight was safe, quiet and peaceful, and boasted a prosperous spa: the usual mudbath/amusement park, with nightly dancing.

The spa was a secular operation. I flirted with the idea of becoming an employee, but I could tell the owners were nervous about messing with the Church, and they'd refuse to hire deserters.

"In truth it's like I'm shopping for a tribe to join," I told my ghost remotant between excursions. I leaned back onto the bed of my starkly furnished cell, kicked off my shoes, and heard them drift to the floor beyond the far side of my belly, a delayed *thump*, *thump*. "All my education has been like wandering the aisles of some big department store, unable to decide whether to go *this* way or *that*."

"Thank you for finally hearing me out," Zenobia responded. "—even if it's practically the last minute. I can help you more than you know. You belong with my people, my Ambiguers; neither one thing nor the other. We perform at childbirths, and if the kid isn't clearly male or female, it belongs to us. Same at later rites; if you flunk your puberty ordeal you join our nomad family."

"A collection of failures," I muttered. "Your true body even fails to travel with these nomads of yours!" A sour thing to say, but I felt hateful, trapped. In a matter of hours I was condemned to solo down the elevators, utterly cut off from the only people who might ever reconnect me to Ronnie. How could this holographic pervert pal of mine joke at a time like this! How could Zenobia suggest that I, normalest of the normal, belonged with a troupe of utter freaks!

And then I thought about it. How very, very odd it was, to be normal inside the Moon.

A minute later we were in flight, into the spa, through the gallery, backstage, and down. A trap door, of all things! The Aminyasi must have been old Steven Spielberg fans, I'm sure I saw this slide in *The Goonies*!

We whooshed out into a beautiful blue reflecting pool—either the water was tinted or it was the tricky lighting. I swam to shore and puffed after my glowing guide, and heard babble ahead.

Topiary and clipped Italianate hedges. On the far side . . .

My people! My tribe! Cannibals who sickened at the thought of meat, bearded women, Shaurog pacifists, Endoverts bored with wallowing next to other Endoverts, prince-claimants to toppled thrones, Human-Womtie crossbreeds, amputees, Token Traders who'd lost their fetishes, hermaphrodites, Fleshnappers unwilling to trade bodies, nympho nuns and illiterate librarians . . .

A plagiocephalic child came to tug me into the middle of things. "Can you play an instrument? Do you read music? Then join the parade!"

The drum they entrusted me with was decorated with *Uhuru's Dancers* in gothic script. Yes, my local troupemaster was an ex-Kirkite who couldn't make herself believe she was on a spaceship. "*That* kind of failure is a good thing, don't you suppose?" Zenobia asked.

"Can't I get a chance to dry myself? Not to mention rest?"

"You haven't been formally accepted. Best try to impress the troupe with your enthusiasm."

So I beat the drum, and marched with them in their descent to Stage Seven, trailing a brass section rather inferior to the worst the Salvation Army ever foisted on a victim public, and for all that my initiation amounted to a single question: skinny Lieutenant Uhuru slipped to my side and asked, "What's the matter with you?"

"I'm a flop as a monk, I lack zeal, I lust after women, I've got a negative attitude a gallon of Jameson's couldn't cure. Besides which I'm fixated on a particular fat woman I'll never see again; and being fat myself makes the mechanics of it—"

"Whoa!" Uhuru raised monkeypaw hands. She turned to Zenobia. "What should he say?"

"Piss on Monsignor Diehl."

I grinned. "The Devil piss on Monsignor Diehl, and wither his schemes, and the Pope catch him pants down with the choir boys on Wednesday night, and send him missionary to the Ghoons!"

"Rating?" Uhuru asked.

"A hundred percent sincere," Zenobia answered. "Infra-red respiratory and pore-dilation all agree. But Perry, don't you know? I told you I could help you. If you want, I can carry your message to this girl friend of yours. I've kept track of Ronnie's exile."

You could have knocked me over with a shamrock! "Anything I have is yours," I answered. "What have they done to her body? Would she be willing to join a troupe? Come, by all the saints of Michigan let's closet together and figure what to say to her!"

Minutes later dear Zenobia twinkled off to my love's bedroom to carry my proposal, and guide her to the nearest Ambiguer troupe. All my favorite ghost asked in return was the privilege of spying on our future intimacies, and by doing so she'd be performing a service, making sure our wired rooms weren't exploited by less trustworthy voyeurs.

Kinky? Do you imagine for one moment I refused her? But what would Ronnie say? I paced back and forth. One day together—did I really know Miss Lascewitz that well?

And what was taking so long? Couldn't Zenobia spare a minute for a progress report?

Still I had to admit there was something encouraging about this long absence. Then suddenly Zenobia's figure blinked to life: "Sorry, I had to guide her to the nearest troupe and witness for her, and she was desperate I shouldn't leave her alone."

"She loves me?" I asked, not quite believing.

"What's your competition? With all her classmates shunning her like a tramp, you're the best thing she's got going, but don't ask me about love. I'm socially inept, what would I know?"

And now began the agony of long-sustained excitement. Nomad troupes being what they are, it took Ronnie and me time to converge through zone after zone, weeks of performances and travel, and not a few adventures. But the truth was we paraded safely just about anywhere, because all Luna's cultures have home-bred failures, and they're generally delighted to help us Ambiguers get rid of them. Even the Shaurogs, who kill everyone they see, let us pass through their desolations, recruiting sissyboys and uppity women.

But these weeks were good for me, and educational. Thanks to basketball and constant exercise and incessant fretting I lost a deal of weight; a move in the right direction because (thank God) Ronnie was unchanged—the Church decided relocation was penance enough for her.

So it was the old Ronnie of my dreams that fell into my embrace that fateful night, the high point of my new life. We swore eternal love, and I assured her that soon it would be physically possible to consummate our marriage: "Look, my clothes hang loose already!"

And that's our story. If you want to find us when you're sent down to Luna Incognita, ask around the spas and taverns for Uhuru's Dancers. We're always on parade when we move, and if there are crowds to draw, we draw them. We're a circus, and what could be more normal and true-blue American than an old-fashioned traveling circus?

So we figure we're doing the job we were sent to do, Ronnie and I, just by using memories of the circuses of our childhoods to bring our brand of normalcy to the inner Moon.

I work as a strongman, freakish with muscles of almost Earthman proportions, my gut down to its last inch of blubber. I coach exhibition basketball on the side, and I'm trying to set up a regional sports league. Meanwhile my wife has taken up teaching: she's slimmed down ever so gradually so I could adapt, my mind having *some* power over sexual imprinting after all, and it's been a while since I gave the circus fat lady a second glance.

It's a nice life, and Ronnie and I are happy. We always welcome visitors, and new recruits, so if you're interested just follow Zenobia's ghost. Bring this letter with you, and don't say anything to Sister Casilda. You'd only upset her.

We want to build our own civilization, and the cold truth is our P. T. Barnum dreams have nothing to do with those of Holy Mother Church.

More than now, 400 million years ago life was a tidal phenomenon. And what tides! A closer moon; swift whirling days—add to this the lack of grass, so that all rains did then was what only desert cloudbursts do now. Along the shores runoff rivers flooded in without warning, muddy with the only soil there was—these made for surges and subsequent droughts and drove a particularly inept fish to desperate choices.

Inept? No—odd as they look to us, they prospered enough to push out into every available niche.

The deepwater descendants of the coelacanth still survive. Those who crawled to land are now extinct, but somehow we admire them more. Not that character had much to do with it. Our ancestors were just in the wrong place, attracted by the wrong bit of food.

The processes we see in hindsight as a vaunting climb to glory are often resented by their victims as shameful mistakes, and compromises of principle. The cry of the first astronauts: "Ass Backwards into the Unknown!"

Crowns of Creation

ding *ding* "Everything okay in there?"

"A-OK," Inga audioed from the other side of her pod bulkhead. "Just fine dreamtime. I love this helmet!"

A few more remarks assured me Inga was still sane, if perhaps too cheerful; a Swedish Fats Waller in a young quadriplegic body.

Not to worry, she'd been carrying on with that social defense for years now, it would last the course of this trip. She was strong enough it might last the rest of her life.

I slid aft, naked to the solar wind's energy bath. The inner system was no less starry for the fact the sun was nine light-minutes distant. I saw pips of Christmas color at wide focus, then my lenses twirled in to resolve the hoops and girders of the H.S.S. *Merry Prankster*, and her cargo of faceted cylinders, busy with slots and busses, umbilicals and connectors.

I plugged into Silvio's commbus and readied to ring hello—when I heard talking. He was batch-phoning some friend back on Earth.

Time lag turned their conversation into an exchange of three-minute monologs. ". . . unrefrigerated turkey dressing after four days. Probably my most ridiculous suicide attempt, but I've never been much for dignity. . . ."

Catharsis, and not a good moment to intrude. I slid down the track to the next pod. *ding* "Everthing okay in this country?"

I heard shifting. "Uhh . . . all fine," Rose answered. Then, for the ninetieth time: "Don't look in. Eyes blind, nose off."

Rose was this trip's special problem. "Gonna show for dinner tonight?" I asked. "It gets lonely piloting a spaceship. I could use company."

"Nick, I almost see you! You look like Commander Bond, you wear a neatly tailored Space Ranger uniform, and there'll be candles and a tablecloth."

I lowered my voice to fit the James Bond profile: "Just you and me, Rose."

"Yeah?" She sounded tempted. "Well, it's like this. I'm addicted to oxygen, and I'm an order of magnitude bigger than you. You got analogs for sex in that bug cartridge? Do you chase after all your female passengers?"

"I don't want to forget how. So why are you being mysterious? Your pod is transparent to me even though you've invoked privacy. I can scan your monitors and tell when you're breathing hard!"

"You don't have to boast about it. Leave me some illusions."

I'd have shrugged if I'd had shoulders. "I'm not talking just for myself, Rose. You'll be living with bugs out in the asteroids, and we know how to play human—we *were* human once. The only difference is we're not hormone-driven. We're entirely rational—"

"Like Mister Spock," Rose interjected.

"Another fictoid out of the past! How much H-V did you watch on Earth?" I sidetracked. "James Bond goes back—a hundred thirty years?"

"Ten, fifteen hours a day. I didn't get out much."

Rose's answer zipped from her handset to my vocoder. "You know . . . seizures. My parents didn't think it was safe."

Familiar story. My cargo was screened back on Earth, and two dozen special cases passed to UNETAO Emigration. It took a certain mentality to sit in an oversize coffin for five hundred days. It took pod mentality, and this crew had it in spades.

Track A: You're a congenital freak. From childhood you've retired from the world, ghetto-ized by your handicap. Track B: You've got a degenerative disease, and spent recent years crushed into your bed. In either case a pod gives you everything you've adapted to.

They were autodocs, habs and glorified spacesuits, and no different from the pods we'd give healthy asteroid miners. *Any* poddie puts much the same colossal demand on the ingenuity of her lifesystem.

Wetbrains aren't meant for space, not the oceans of vacuum that separate one planetesimal from another. But as for our destination . . . *All* humans are freaks in space: *No* humans are freaks on Hebe. Who needs legs or an Earth-strength heart in point oh one gee?

Oops. I was leaving Rose alone with sad memories: parents, Earth, an indoor childhood. ". . . anyhow, like I say we're thoroughly rational, so while you're brooding through some private passion, we're likely to come beetling up with the day's mining statistics."

Rose laughed. "You think I'm silly."

"Map your shyness using game theory. A poor outcome is probable *in terms of your own interest*. There's a chance you'll become phobic, unable to exit your pod when we reach Hebe; and yes, the technical term is 'silly.' "

"How . . . uh . . ."

She wanted to ask, but the question was too revealing. *How could I know what was in her interest?* "Rose, we bugs love humans all the more now that we've transcended. It sounds impossible but there you have it; our fleshly memories and dispositions were copied into silicon brains, so we love humans, and most of us spent half a century in the asteroids building things up: synchronous stalks and greenhouses and blinking WELCOME signs.

"When people build houses they put an extraordinary amount of work into making sure they can entertain' company. Same out here. We can jog along economically without pod miners, but *we want human company!*"

"And I want to earn my keep," Rose answered. "I didn't hire on as a houseguest. I don't care to be kept like a pet."

"Ahh . . . well, you'll earn credits, but don't import the boss-employee relationship. If you apply it where it doesn't fit—"

"How'd we get onto *this*?" Rose interrupted with a nervous giggle. "First you pester me about my privacy. Now we're talking industrial relations!"

"I'm talking about walls between poddies and bugs, and how there shouldn't be any."

"Well, there are," Rose answered. "Give me more time. I can't reprogram instantly like you. And another thing—I'm sitting captive like a bean in a peashooter. You can hector me all you want, but that's just going to make things worse. Let's keep to cheery banter, okay?"

"Certainly."

"And no spying."

"It's my job to log your pod's statistics," I answered, not very comfortably.

"Why? It all gets radioed to Earth. Three minutes time lag—nothing can happen to me in three minutes."

Partial privacy from day one, and now: was she going to invoke absolute privacy? A pause. "—Let's keep things as they are, Nick, but no baring of souls. Just tell me, is this part of the agenda? Is it your job to get poddies hooked on intimacy with bugs?"

Her word choice betrayed scale-7 hostility. "Yes," I

answered. "What you call, er, 'intimacy' will be a feature of your new life."

"*Intimacy with a box the size of an H-V cassette,*" Rose muttered. "Excuse me. I'm keeping you from your work."

A half-subtle dismissal. I said goodbye and slipped down the track: ten pods on this outrigger, fourteen on the other. Except for two rows of 'beans in a peashooter' the H.S.S. *Merry Prankster* was just a drive unit and a skeleton with a nervous system, and a wandering brain: myself.

She was a passenger ship on her regular route, stringing from Earth's High Station One to Hebe, and then along a zigzag of worldlets: Ceres, Iris, Astraea, Vesta, inward to Eros and back to Earth again.

This was my sixth run . . . and my last, if I failed Rose. Too many other bugs would love my job, and they'd deserve it if she ended up in self-inflicted purdah. We only had three hundred of the dear creatures with us; us bugs living vicariously as they expressed aspects of soul we had no way of exercising in ourselves. The unhappiness of even one poddie was a potential crisis.

What a problem! The psychology of a handicapped person reared in an ignorant and thoughtless world, shaped by church, politics, sexual inclinations, special friendships, early traumas . . .

Factor in her present isolation, plus inborn personality; was she optimist or whiner? I paged her file into RAM and began to read.

Black hair, Mediterranean complexion, a certain hypertrophism connected to her disability—more frustration. Normally the backgrounds of UNETAO emigres have some zing to them, but Rose's seemed strangely flat. Her very normalcy made her different!

She was *too* normal. A doctored resume, combined with scale-7 hostility? When I returned to ship's core I bleeped Hebe.

Hebe bleeped back. "Process abreaction: first spike after one to five transactions, second spike when growth trend becomes threatening. Historical examples: family planning, abortion, test-tube babies, surrogate parenting, cloning. This doesn't fit the model. Poddie emigration isn't an ideo-religious _cause celebre_ on Earth, and there's no threat to the Hegemony in the loss of a few hundred invalids."

"Excuse me," I radioed. "I'm talking about one person, and you're jargonizing about society. Missing premise: that Rose is an agent for somebody. As far as I'm concerned that premise can _stay_ missing."

Minutes passed. "Then eliminate it," came the answer.

All my poddies had remote-view through their choice of the _Merry Prankster_'s forty-two camera eyes, the universe displayed in true or false colors. I monitored all forty-two, charted a path and zipped, stopping short as Zumeilah, Connie and Lev moused from one perspective to another. They didn't know they were hunting me, but I felt no less the guilty fugitive.

I arrived unseen, and inserted myself feloniously into Rose's pod; not a sound, not the tiniest electron spike.

View pin DR 15, angle thirty percent, an over-the-shoulder shot.

I had to blink to DR 30/45 to see around Rose's Medusa-tangle of floating dark hair. *Click* *cli-click* Her fingers danced on the keyboard, ergonomically faked keytaps acknowledging her touch. The video was ultra-scrambled, user area B: STARR, password— *click* *click* *cli-cli-click*

Rose couldn't help looking around the interior of her pod, as if my spy-eyes would betray themselves somehow. I tabled my anxiety and put myself in her place. Either she could trust me, or . . . or what?

She was naked, a creature of flesh in a silicon universe, and we were seducing her, me and my fellow bugs, making her think we were angels and her mistrust was unnecessary. In truth she was literally naked, like all poddies inside their pods, naked because there was no room for wardrobes and laundry facilities, but "*I can't trespass across your privacy thresholds*," I'd assured her first day out. "*You set the rules.*"

Everthing just the way UNETAO promised. Was she nuts to doubt us all?

She needed a fresh dose of inspiration, and if I was watching?—Well, then there'd be a confrontation and the truth would out!

File DOCUDRAMA.AST was loaded. Rose pushed PLAY.

Judge Waters arranged the documents on his bench and shifted heavily, as if settling in for a good long harangue. "Ladies and gentlemen of the jury, you see a courtroom, and attorneys identified as prosecutors and defenders; yet this is not a trial—merely an inquiry into a matter which may never be brought to trial, given the cloudy status of Earth's colonies in the asteroid belt. Our legal institutions have not been transplanted to those new habitats and so we cover for that absence.

"Our witnesses talk from eleven light-minutes away. Half an hour may pass before we get the answer to any questions. Under these circumstances our method of interrogation is: three questions on subjects not necessarily related, followed by additonal questions in pursuit of details. All this once for the prosecution, and once again for the defense . . . Council?"

A background news-voice identified Tira Salvani. She stood, short and stocky in her dark suit, her swept-back hair carefully coiffed, every strand in place. "Your honor, though the legal purpose of this hearing appears obscure, it has a clear educational purpose. We want Earth to know the truth about bug operations out in the asteroid belt. Once the truth is out, the citizens of the Hegemony will not fail to pursue the interests of justice."

"Is that all?"

"Also, the reason there are no courts of law in the

asteroid belt is that UNETAO's Twin Charter permits Vashtarski's Free Bug Apparatus complete domination of the Solar System from 2 A.U. out to the orbit of Saturn—

"Which irrevocable *charter does not expire for another fifty-three years,*" Abner Toshido interrupted, rising from the defense side of the courtroom, his great shock of salt-and-pepper hair framing his broad and ruddy face.

Tira turned. "*The truth about poddie slavery will revoke your charter—*"

"Ladies! Gentlemen!" Judge Waters hammered his gavel. "No more interruptions. Now, Ms. Salvani: your list of questions? Please read them to the jury."

Tira moved to the bench, handed Judge Waters a copy, and turned to the jury. "Addressed to Captain Nick Kapsanzakis, Hebe Bunker, February 3rd, 2095. Question One: Describe the enlistment process the Apparatus uses to recruit poddie emigrants and convey them to the belt, laying particular emphasis on any pre-selection criteria."

Rose's video did what reality could not, splicing in a few seconds of numbers on a clock, then cutting to "Captain Kapsanzakis'" answer. The video director's imagination made Hebe Bunker into a sinister warren of tracks and slots and glowering red lights, but one bug looks very like another. We were a swarm of boxes in low-gee mobility sheaths, and nothing could be done about that.

My name is Nick Kapsanzakis, but Captain Kapsanzakis wasn't me. Not unless someone had gone twenty years into the future! '2095' indeed! An absurd, science-fiction sounding year!

But the drama continued, done up to look like news.

"*I answer these questions under constraint,*" my imitation voice complained. "*The threat is that if I misrepresent the truth, the rebel poddies surrounding these bulkheads will magnetize our bunker and we'll all be wiped!*"

*The camera cut to show an army of hovering cylin-
ders, then back to 'me,' twitching my insect legs for no
particular reason: the director wanted to give me a
nervous tic.*

"How did the Apparatus recruit new poddies?" I
continued. "First we limited our search to young people, ages twelve and fifteen. We looked for two things:
dependency syndrome and 'couch potato' tendencies.

"You see dependency syndrome in people who find it
impossible to state a preference: painfully shy, quiet
stay-at-home—kids like this see themselves as worthless, even if they make an economic contribution to the
family.

"Ironic, huh? Humanity is colonizing space, not with
the brave, brassy and bold, but with pod-bound wimps,
sitting in their tiltabeds and staring at screens all day,
entertained by food and dream-helmets. What do you
feel when you imagine people like that? Do you take
that feeling and face about to rebuke the Apparatus?
We didn't make them that way! We looked for a certain
personality profile, and we exploited those who had
that profile, but we didn't make them what they were!

"This is not to say bugs are sinless in our recruitment
mailings. There's some emphasis on sexual imbalance in
the asteroids, and a search for recruits of marriageable
age. I'm sure this helps our poddies' parents make up
their minds, but the fact is there's not one instance of
marriage between two poddies.

"So much for Question One—"

CRAP! Even without glands I could almost get angry.
Why shouldn't dead souls like me be allowed to sue for
libel? Lies put in my mouth, and worse lies to come! I
could tell because Question Two was about the addic-
tive drugs we supposedly put into our poddies' food!
Bugs made out to be devils and tyrants!

But of course Rose knew them to be lies, she *had* to!

Did she? How could I assure her, after breaking the
rules to spy? Should I tell her we gave poddies work so

they'd feel useful, that their occasional mining operations were far from cost-effective? Absurd to think we enticed wetbrains to the asteroids to work as slaves!

No, I couldn't tell her that.

Bugs were angels or devils, and Rose didn't know which. Fine, neither did most of the people of Earth, but why had she applied to UNETAO for emigration?

Hypothesis: she was on a mission, except any mission that demands years of a person's life should be spelled with a capital M. And anything *that* important to Rose was important to all bug-kind!

I sniffed her atmosphere for molecular radicals. No explosives, no obvious weapons. What was left? She could hide a magstick in one of her cubbies—deadly to *this* me, but if I took the elementary precaution of backing my soul up into offline memory . . .

I'd just about had a thought. These self-defense quibbles had obscured it. Try . . . try . . .

? The Hegemony was a cable democracy. Decades after I'd died and opted for space, representative democracy collapsed, paralyzed by single-issue fanatics and helpless to deal with the Rootworm Crisis. Now everybody voted on all sorts of issues. Nobody thought it was a great system, just better than anything else. It was also fairly new, and those same single-issue factions were trying to diddle it for their benefit. Rose might be part of a propaganda scheme, and ready to make headlines.

Was that it? Not an analysis it took much brilliance to make—I was disappointed. No, my original glimmer had been paged out by my overriding interest in self-preservation, and I'd have to window through RAM in hopes it hadn't been overlaid.

Or else come up with the idea all over again. I'd have plenty of time to contemplate her case. I was fairly sure of that now; four hundred more days. Adding up everything I knew about her, I was sure enough to wager my life, but not Silvio's or Connie's. I'd separate her pod from the others on the off chance she was capable of kamikaze terrorism, and then:

What else? What else could I do?

I kept windowing.

  . . .

    . . .

      . . .

        . . .

          . . .

            . . . . . . Damn. I'd found my stray flash of insight. Give poddies secrets they were scared to share with bugs, like that DOCUDRAMA video. The need to conspire, added to natural shyness and sense of physical inadequacy—Rose was being *engineered* into phobia.

Yes, she'd volunteered to investigate us; volunteered to find hidden truths or unionize our poddies, her exact purpose still unknown. She may have begun her Mission of her own free will, balanced fifty/fifty as to whether we were good or evil, but in her present isolation free will and objectivity would soon become impossible. When things got bad enough she'd radio her unhappiness back to Earth, flavored with mistrust and hundreds of days of paranoid fantasies!

My enemy was a poison of lies scrambled through Rose's video library, and time was that enemy's ally. My choices were narrowing. I'd have to kill Rose for her own good.

I reviewed the *Merry Prankster*'s camera positions and popped out of my slot. This was not going to be fun. I hadn't been flesh for a long time; the prospect had a shuddersome fascination—would the experience slime me? Hormones and all, and Rose's imperfect health . . .

Murder her without permission? She'd hate that, and outrage would taint her experience. Having slid to an innocent distance I reversed, pulled up to Rose's pod, and *ding*ed.

"Eyes off, nose—"

"Tell you what, Rose. Nick here, I've decided to confess. We bugs are actually malevolent chessmasters who have it in for the human race. The only thing is I can't decide which awful fate we've got in store for you, and maybe you can help. One possibility is that we want you on Hebe so we can boil you down, extract your DNA, and perform genetic experiments."

Silence. "Sure, there's all those phone calls home from poddies out in the belt," I continued, "but they're fakes, see?"

"If you wanted genetic tissue wouldn't this be about the most expensive way of getting it?" she answered. "And then what would you have? A DNA library devoted to defects!"

"Okay," I agreed. "Here's another theory. We want your bodies. We want to switch souls into your bodies so we can satisfy your pent sexual longings. See, we've got this round-robin system—"

"Why not get athletes to emigrate? Why not the brightest and best?" Rose answered.

I breathed relief. Well no, I didn't; but the effect was the same. "I'm glad you said that, Rose. I want you to feel sure it's true before we go any further."

"I told you, no baring of souls."

"Absolutely no baring of souls, because we don't have the mutuality of experience to enter into that kind of relationship, and you can't get much experience inside your pod. So what I've got in mind is copying your soul temporarily into my body, and giving you a chance to see what it's like to think like a bug. If you can do that—"

"What happens to you?" Rose answered sharply. "What happens to my body? You know the meaning of this, the legal meaning? If I'd been ready to become a bug I'd have died a long time ago!"

"We switch," I answered. "Somebody's got to be in your flesh; it takes a load off the intensive care facilities in your pod. And it's not death, because afterward you go back into your body again. Not death, just a spiritual vacation."

More silence, then: "You know, if you're really as nice as you try to sound, this is quite a sacrifice for you."

"And if I'm not?"

"I can't figure what your scheme would be, unless . . . Nick, it's coming home to me. You could kill me any number of ways, and I'm really quite helpless, and it's nuts not to trust you."

"You'll do it?"

"Three months inside this pod, and a year left to go! I can't believe this! Yeah, I'll do it. Just leave an instruction file somewhere in RAM so I know how to work your mobility sheath."

Once that was squared away the rest was just twenty minutes' work. Twenty minutes to swap souls via Auxiliary Function 2 of Rose's dream helmet.

I woke up—and stared down at myself in bemusement. Freud be damned, as a man I'd always had breast envy: I'd always wondered how they felt from the inside. So here I was . . . and I *still* didn't know, because breasts in null gravity—*big, floppy* breasts—were an entirely different experience.

I suppose it's a matter of scale; I'd been tiny for forty years, my entire second lifetime. *Everything* about Rose was big and floppy.

And speaking of Rose, what was she doing? Wouldn't it occur to her pretty soon to check in?

I felt prickles, then the full flush of alarm, escalating toward panic. What if she *kept* my body! What had I done to myself? She'd take over the ship! A wetbrain trick—

Damn! I'd forgotten what emotional storms could do. Here I was in the midst of an anxiety attack, and if Rose *did* call and heard the quaver in my voice—

My voice! Vocal cords, tongue and lips . . . I gave

vent to a noise, and went on to recite Chaucer: "Whan that Aprille with his shoures sote—"

"You have trouble in there?" Rose radioed.

"Just learning to talk," I answered, tensing and torquing forty separate small muscles. I reached for the keyboard—no need, I was already remoted to the right camera. I saw my bug body commbussed to my pod, basking in the sun. "How about you?"

"This is . . . neat. I still feel an echo of fear, but it's exciting. Out in the clear open, in all these stars! I'm just dancing through the monitors— Oh God! I can SEE PARALLAX. It's like feeling the *Merry Prankster* move!"

Another pause. "I'm spreading my wings now, drinking raw power. Oh, this is great! Oh, it's like . . ."

(Remember to breathe.) "Like what?"

"I've just realized. I know what humans are! Wetbrains, you call us, but I've got a better word. A creature of myth, a creature who needs the bulk of an entire world between him and the sun, a creature of fog and night who drinks the blood of his prey, feeding foully, keeping his wretched soul buried in the native mud of flesh—"

"*Vampires?* You're going off the deep end, Rose," I answered. "We bugs *love* humans—the way parents love children."

"Yeah. That makes sense, seeing your average age is—hey, visiting Hebe is like visiting an old folk's home! You talked about how you all want company, and I didn't take you seriously, but that's how it is—old people in nursing homes, desperate for company."

"Is this helping you?" I asked.

"Helping? In ways you don't even suspect! You see, I have a job. You couldn't have known, but . . . yes, this helps. This helps very much! Next time I phone Earth I'm going to have lots to tell them!"

"You some kind of news reporter?" I asked as innocently as I could.

"Embolden Publications," she answered. "It's . . . not in your database. Too small, I guess. Some people out in Denver—"

As she kept talking it became obvious she'd been suckered by a group passing under false colors. I had a head start but her bug brain worked fast; she came to the same conclusion and stopped. "Nick, there's people behind the scenes who want to halt poddie emigration. Enemies of UNETAO."

"Oh?"

"They're—Nick, I want you to log into user B.STARR, password OLDCOWBOY. Call up video DOCUDRAMA.AST and index track 1, minute 3:30."

I did all this, hunt and peck. Ages since I'd touched a keyboard!

My alter ego flicked onto the screen. ". . . *see themselves as worthless, even if they make an economic contribution to the family.*

"Ironic, huh? Humanity is colonizing space, not with the brave, brassy and bold, but with pod-bound wimps, sitting in their tiltabeds and staring at screens all day, entertained by food and dream-helmets. What do you feel when you imagine people like that? Do you take that feeling and face about to rebuke the Apparatus?"

It was the fake me speaking, but— "They've betrayed themselves," Rose announced. "That's their real point of view, I realize it now. A bunch of God's chosen jocks, the crowns of creation, and they're *jealous*! They're jealous that they can't emigrate to space! And if *they* can't tolerate life in a pod, well then nobody else is going to get the chance!"

Rose was going beyond me now, her thoughts completing circuits in fractions of a nanosecond. "What should we do about it?" she asked, and I wasn't ready to answer.

Like any human I made noise anyhow. "Do we need to do anything?"

She flattered me with more intelligence than I deserved. "Maybe not. You handled this pretty well, Nick. I've been miserable, but no more. When do you want your body back?"

"A couple hours?"

A couple hours later I pushed my helmet's Aux 2 button. Again twenty minutes passed in an instant.

Free, clean, transcendent! I paged through my senses, then took inventory. Rose left me a message in RAM. "I had to fly. What an adventure! I measured the push of the solar wind and kicked inward away from the *Merry Prankster*. Then I spread my wings to full extent and floated back again! Do you ever do this just for fun?

"And then I checked out your fictoid collection and visited Blandings Castle; Jeeves and Bertie Wooster and that damned pig! It was like I was there, a house guest in flapper costume! Marvelous what you can do with data partitions, doctoring your sensory inputs!

"But as my thoughts began to jell I let the billiards room fade. It took me a while, Nick. It took me a while to figure out why you came up to my pod talking about malevolent chessmasters so soon after your earlier visit!

"The old Rose would be outraged; you invaded my privacy. I've never let anyone see me naked before, not even the doctors—God knows how that got purged from my resume.

"The old Rose would be outraged, and there'd be a scandal. That's the risk you ran."

The message ended: "The new Rose thanks you for taking the trouble."

We wouldn't be human today, except that nature's cycle of birth, reproduction and death is an imperfect process and sometimes results in variations in our physical design.

Of course, at one generation every twenty-five years, we're evolving at a terribly slow pace. One result is that we're contenders for nature's booby prize; just about last in Earth's clean gene race. To see efficient code, look at organisms with a two-day lifespan. Thank God they're there. We need to steal their ideas for our own genetic re-engineering.

The fact that we're poised to edit our own DNA means we're no longer quite so tied to the natural cycle that terminates in death. We can let it slow, and even drop out now and again, without harming the species or the planet.

Tangentially "The Quonset Hut" is a story about history's first drop-out souls, and a cybernetic technology whose promise is perverted by the needs of an unhappy nation.

The Quonset Hut

Last Friday, when I was yet an innocent, I had a dream.

It was daytime, but the drapes were drawn in my bedroom for the sake of my eyes. I was recovering from yellow jaundice, and strong enough to be bored. Sleep was my way of passing the time, but when you sleep too much true sleep becomes impossible, and you hover in an in-between land of aimless images, your mind carried this way and that by the sounds of a distant radio, the slamming of the refrigerator door . . .

In this dream I was much younger, and chasing around with Janet, my first friend. There, a mark of authenticity! Our family had moved to a new house on the west end of town. Born two months after me, Janet had been consigned to a lower grade in school. Social barriers separated boys from girls and we'd drifted apart, though our homes were hardly a half-mile distant.

But it was *where* Janet and I played that fascinated

me. We wandered in a quonset hut the size of an airplane hangar, a utilitarian structure built next to a spur of the Midland Central Railroad, near the old depot and just west of the slough. There were struts, and a pile of scrap lumber, and a fat man in a yellow jacket, and a concrete floor, and a wooden frame construction with offices upstairs and apparatus for loading stuff below, with a conveyor pipe leading out toward the boxcars.

Oh, and much, much more. Four-year-old kids are lousy at taking inventory, but infinitely curious about details. Trivialities spilled into my mind like a pile of unlabelled snapshots. That convinced me that what I'd experienced wasn't a dream at all, but a stray memory.

This was odd, because what I remembered in a burst of vividness, I'd forgotten until now—that old quonset hut had vanished out of my life. There'd been times when I encountered Janet, and times when I snuck off to the forbidden environs of the railroad depot, but never once had I fetched that building to mind—and come to think of it, didn't the spur in question run off into vacant land?

Saturday I was instructed to go out into the yard to get some fresh air. The day after that Mom said I was ready to go to church. As we filed out after the service, Reverend Rundquist asked me whether I was up for our usual Sunday game of chess. I said yes, but I lacked my normal concentration, and lost.

Nevertheless, by Monday I persuaded Mom that I felt well. I had two weeks' allowance coming. She let me take some of it downtown to indulge my insatiable appetite for comic books and Tastie-Queen ice cream.

The six-block walk tired me; the air was humid and hard to push through. After my purchases I sat at a picnic table by the Tastie-Queen to read in the shade of a big elm tree. Then my old friend came by. "Janet!" I shouted. "I was just thinking about you."

Janet nodded. "What are you doing this summer?" she asked. Her sturdy body was richly tanned, and she looked at me with furrowed brow.

"I just had the yellow jaundice," I announced to explain my pallor. "I'm all better now."

We spoke on, too interested in our own topics to pay strict attention to what the other was saying. I "steered" the conversation toward my dream. "Do you remember when we used to play in that quonset hut by the train tracks?"

Janet ran her fingers through frizzy blond hair. "You mean the lumberyard?" she asked. "I remember once that guy chased us out—"

"No, north of town by the slough."

"That would have been pretty far. We never strayed past the blacksmith shop unless it was to go to the park." She frowned. "Besides, there's no quonset hut up north."

"Didn't there use to be?"

Janet shook her head. "I don't remember. Anyway, why bring it up?"

I grimaced. "I—well, I forgot it too, just like you. Then out of nowhere I suddenly remembered. It wasn't like when you fish something out of your memory, it was more hidden-like. Jeez—I just can't explain it."

Janet brightened. "We could go and check it out. I don't have anything else to do."

I almost begged off. In my condition I wasn't sure I could keep up. "Okay," I nodded, "and let's stop in the park and see how the new swimming pool is coming along."

By resting at this halfway point I disguised my lack of vigor, and soon we were there. Wading through tall grass, we came to the end of the spur, where the tracks warped upward, buttressed by fat timbers. We followed the spur and to our left the grass gave way to an expanse of cracked, stained concrete.

"It's the floor," I said. "I mean, it *used* to be a floor. It isn't as big as I remember. We were smaller then."

"I still don't remember this," Janet replied, doubtfully. "I guess you're right, but it was a long time ago."

"Nineteen-fifty." I guessed.

Janet squinted toward the Peavy grain elevators, rippling in the hot air not far away. "I wonder what they did here."

"They had a stairs, and an office above, and we'd go chasing up and down—I don't know what they did, but it wasn't a store. There wasn't anything for sale."

"Somebody's office, and they'd let two little brats run through?"

"I'm not making this up, Janet," I announced in my most important voice. And then, because children love mysteries, I went further. "There's a lot to this that seems strange to me."

We ambled back to the park, reminiscing all the while. Janet was testing my memory, and she found it satisfactory. "Maybe it had something to do with the war," she blurted.

"Huh?"

"Didn't they build quonset huts during the war? It was some kind of war thing, and then afterwards they shut down, but not right away."

"Yeah." I was intrigued by the idea that my home town had contributed more than its sons to the fight against the Nazis. Janet's suggestion was all the more helpful, because Hayfield's leading expert on World War Two lived in my very own house.

That night I talked to Dad, who sat sweatily enthroned two feet from a humming fan. His first response was pontifical: "The only quonset hut in Hayfield is the Rural Electric building. They're awful things, cold in winter, hot in summer."

"There was another one, back in 1950—"

Dad rattled his newspaper. "I'd know, wouldn't I? I

was here all those years, studying for my law boards on the GI Bill. No, I don't doubt that you're remembering *something*, but you've mishmashed it with something else."

I brightened. "The creamery? When Mom used to work for the creamery? Did she ever let me play there?"

Dad spoke reluctantly. "Not very often. Old man Rauschorn kept a stern eye—"

"Was he fat? Did he wear a yellow jacket?"

"Fat? No!" Dad laughed. "You remember a fat man? An older guy? I wonder who that might have been. Clark Spanno?"

Spanno! Yes, Mr. Spanno, with slightly more hair! "What did he do in the war, Dad?" I asked.

"He served on the draft board. He's a good Democrat, so he made it through the Depression hopping from one post to the next. He's still got an oar in. I don't know how with Eisenhower president, but he's with the Soil Bank now."

The Clark Spanno *I* knew ran the Chevy dealership in town. These other things turned the man with all those beautiful, two-tone Bel-Aires into a political fat cat. It didn't fit. As I drifted off to sleep that night, I tried to analyze the wrongness of it.

The next morning I made a second trip downtown. I went to the newspaper office and knocked on the door. Mr. Avery, whom I knew as my scoutmaster, lifted the latch and let me in.

"What can I do for you?" asked this tall, lean man of Yankee blood.

"I want to read all the newspapers from 1950," I answered.

He looked at me. After a moment, he smiled. Mr. Avery was fond of clean, brief transactions. He led me inside, and to a table. "Sit here. I'll get them and put them away. Handle them with care, and don't tear anything out."

So I began to page through fifty-two issues of the *Hayfield Query*, looking for pictures, allusions—this was it. Like any good chess-player I was mildly obsessive, but I wasn't going to pursue this quonset hut business any further, unless . . .

There! An aerial photo of Hayfield, under the caption *Eighty-Seven Years of Progress*. The right edge of the picture had been doctored to hide the garbage dump, but the train depot was there, and behind it, the steel flanks of the structure of my dreams.

"Mr. Avery," I called. "Do you remember anything about this building? What kind of business they had there?"

"Just a moment." Mr. Avery was bent over his typesetting machine, a monster that consumed days of his life every week. He straightened, wiped his fingers with an oily rag, and came over.

"This here," I repeated, tapping the photo. "This quonset hut."

Mr. Avery frowned. "When was this? Nineteen-fifty?" He leaned over, close enough for me to smell the tobacco on his breath. The pause grew long. "You know, it's the oddest thing. Only five years ago, and I can't remember a thing about it."

"Clark Spanno had something to do with it," I hinted.

"Did he?" Mr. Avery shook his head. "Funny. It's like there's a wall in my mind."

I looked at him appraisingly. "This is what I came to find," I admitted. "Something to prove— Mr. Avery, you shouldn't feel bad. Except for me, I'm not sure anybody in town remembers that building."

Mr. Avery raised a bushy eyebrow. "Now, Tom, that's quite a claim, what with Mr. Spanno alive and well."

"I'm going to talk to him," I announced. "I'm going to see him next. Goodbye, Mr. Avery."

Mr. Spanno had spent so many decades representing

the dignity of government on the one hand, and business on the other, that he didn't know how to act when a kid came into his dealership and knocked on his door.

Folksy aphorisms, dog calendars and fan belts littered his walls. As he swiveled in his chair and put on his bifocals, I blurted my question. "Mr. Spanno, did you use to own a quonset hut north of town? It was by the tracks, and—"

"Hold on there. A quonset hut? I can't say . . ."

I sagged. "Please, Mr. Spanno. I'm sure there was a quonset hut up there, I saw a picture of it in an old newspaper. If you don't know about it, I don't know who would!"

Clark Spanno's fat face tightened in what might have been a smile. "So I'm the town historian? Why are you so interested in this, uh—"

"Nobody I've talked to knows anything about it. It was there, and now for all anyone can tell me, it never even existed!"

"You're the Jorgenson kid, aren't you? Well, I'm sorry to spoil this little puzzle of yours. Sure, I remember it. I used it for a while to store excess inventory. After we remodeled I had it torn down for scrap. Made some money on the deal, and reduced my liability."

The politician in him came abruptly to life. He smiled broadly, and reached out to lay his huge, parchment-dry hand on my shoulder. "We're spoilsports, us grown-ups. When we can't afford to guard a place where kids like to play—well, the insurance companies get on our backs."

"What was it before you owned it? Who built it?"

"Well . . ." First removing his hand, and then leaning back in his seat, Mr. Spanno dragged out his pause for an unconscionable length of time. "It was, uh, let's see . . . Oh, yes; a temporary armory, back before the WPA built the one we use now. You know, a warehouse for trucks and jeeps."

I didn't know if Mr. Spanno was guessing out of some

inability to admit ignorance, or if he was just doing a bad job of lying. His chronology was lousy. The 'newer' armory lay just across the street from the Tastie-Queen. Its stucco facade was peeling, and its cornerstone read "WPA - 1936," while the stairs and struts of the structure of my dreams were cut from fresh, unweathered lumber.

Since I'd worn an expression of disappointment for some time, he didn't notice I wasn't swallowing his story. I thanked him for his time, summoned a smile as false as his, and backed out the door.

I'd had enough. The mystery of the quonset hut had become the mystery of Mr. Spanno, and no longer interested me. Grownups were impossible to solve, and certainly not worth the effort.

I decided to amble down Main Street, back towards the Tastie-Queen. The sky was clouding up to the west. Hot as it was, we were due for a change in weather, so why not buy today's cone a bit early?

Janet came banging out of her father's insurance office, and waved to me from across the street. "Hey, Tommie!"

Though I deplored what she did to my name, I waited for her to dash across to my side. "That quonset hut," she began, then paused to catch her breath.

I turned to continue my stroll. "Yeah. I talked to Mr. Spanno about it. It belonged to him."

"—well, anyhow, it was just like you said," Janet puffed. "All of a sudden I remembered it, like a picture flashing out of nowhere, you and me playing inside while our mothers sat in that funny room. Do you remember the big plate glass window that let them watch us? They were getting their hair done, sitting under those silvery helmets with all the wires . . ."

I frowned. "You mean it was a *beauty* shop?"

"Oh, not where *we* were. I don't know *what* they did back there. It was mostly empty space."

"Yeah, I remember that." I jerked to a stop. "Darn it; it *was* empty."

"Sure it was," Janet repeated.

"It was empty, and yet Mr. Spanno said he was using it as a warehouse, like to store extra cars. And then there was that chute, fixed up to run out to the tracks. Why would a car warehouse need a conveyor chute?"

"Why would a beautician's shop need a chute?" Janet giggled.

We reached the Tastie-Queen, put down nickels, and ordered two cones. I scanned the western skies. A breeze started to blow. "I don't know if you've ever seen my new house," I said. "Would you like to come over before the storm hits?"

"Okay," Janet replied, and we launched for home, waking into the wind. Nickel cones being small, by the time we reached the house we were empty-handed, and happy to encourage Mom in the idea that we deserved a treat. We quizzed her as she went through the cupboards. She denied ever getting her hair done in a quonset hut. "Hush now," she spoke as we pestered her, and turned up the radio. "It's time for Arthur Godfrey."

But she never got to listen to Mr. Godfrey, because the phone rang. It was Clark Spanno. He'd talked to me this morning, he said, and started to remember that I was rumored to be a really terrific chess-player . . .

"Oh, yes," Mom responded. "He almost always beats Reverend Rundquist."

"Well," Mr. Spanno's voice buzzed through the earpiece, "I got to thinking about this scholarship program the government's set up for smart kids, and I was wondering—if I checked it out in Tom's behalf . . ."

"A government scholarship?" Mom asked. "Like for college?"

"You can't start planning too early for college. Anyhow, if I'm not mistaken there's some tests he'd have to take, and some forms to fill out—I'd be happy to run him over to the county seat if it's not convenient for you."

"You mean today?"

"Oh, no rush, it's just that I'm going there anyhow to pick up some Soil Conservation paperwork. You've got a pretty bright kid there, Mrs. Jorgenson, and I don't see why he shouldn't benefit from the government's generosity . . ."

Mom cast a sideways glance at me. Her eyes raised to the window. "Mr. Spanno, have you checked out the weather? We've got a storm brewing."

"Ah, well, you wouldn't want me to take any risks— tell you what. I'll be there as soon as the thing blows over."

After Mr. Spanno rang off, Mom called Janet's father to tell him where she was. Fat drops began to bombard the street and sidewalks, and soon we were under siege, shaken by thunder, blinded by rain, and shivered by gusts of wind. I took out my chess set to oblige Janet, who wanted to learn how to play. Meanwhile Mom wandered off and back, setting out flashlights and candles, "just in case."

I could tell she was worried, but I couldn't figure out why, unless it was the storm. As the tempest dwindled into a steady drizzle, her face took on resolve. "I'm going to call Mr. Spanno and tell him not to come," she announced. "Your dad goes to the county seat most every day. Why shouldn't he take care of your affairs?"

But the phone line was busy at the Chevy dealership. It remained busy until the rain stopped, and the skies brightened. Then out of nowhere Mr. Spanno pulled up in front of the house in a new Bel-Aire, and tapped the horn.

Janet jerked to her feet. "I should go now."

Mom found her a fudgesicle, and saw her out the door, all without the normal chitchat. I was sent off to tell Mr. Spanno to wait.

Mr. Spanno opened the door and told me to get in

the car. "We'll wait for your mother," he responded when I gave him my message. He patted the seat. I slid in. When she came out, he looked her straight in the eye and said "Star Wars."

Mom tottered. "Get in back," Spanno ordered, not very politely, and she climbed inside. "We'll all go together," he explained to me. "Your mother will be better than me at filing out all those application forms."

We drove off. Ten miles out of town, we drew up to a shabby old one-room schoolhouse with a hand pump out in front. At least once a week Dad stopped here to fill a jug with what everyone described as the best water in the county. Old Mr. Spanno pulled off the road, told me to come along, and we headed for the pump to get a drink.

I turned to look at my mother, sitting stiffly in the back seat. "What's wrong? What did you do to her?"

Mr. Spanno pumped, and water began to gush. I drank briefly and then grabbed the handle to return the favor. When Mr. Spanno straightened up, he said: "We need to talk."

He moved to the schoolhouse steps and sat heavily. "Tom, I'm not going to pretend with you. You've stumbled on something. Now I don't know what kind of stories you read, but I suspect you think that there's something odd in Hayfield. You might even come up with the idea that there's something odd with me. Has that occurred to you?"

I nodded.

"It's true, I've got a strange job," Mr. Spanno conceded, "—half shepherd, half nursemaid. If my motives weren't on the level, I could make you dig for the truth, or maybe get rid of you in some nasty way, like those thugs in the black hats in the movies. What I'm going to do instead is dump the whole story in your lap, and then ask you to make a decision. Do you think you're old enough to make an important decision, all by yourself? Because that's what you're going to have to do."

"I—I think so." My legs felt weak and shivery, but I didn't care to sit down. It was possible I'd soon want, or need, to run.

"Well, consider this. It might be that what you see around you is a good deal better than what you'd see, if your parents hadn't volunteered . . . you read history, don't you? You know about the Depression, the war?"

"Yeah."

A meadowlark blurted its song not twenty feet away. Mr. Spanno let a look of serenity settle on his thick features, then turned back toward me and drew breath. "The Fifties were—are a good deal better than almost any time we've had before. America's at peace, we've got full employment, we're the strongest nation on Earth. Best of all, we've managed to do something pretty fine, pretty heroic, by defeating the Axis powers, so we're all feeling proud of ourselves.

"Now imagine what would happen if you grow up with this kind of feeling, and then maybe things start to get worse. Maybe America isn't always the good guy and more, and there are times when we lose control of our own government. Kinda makes you shiver, doesn't it?

"Meanwhile, our enemies are getting more and more uppity, and stronger to boot, and they start to humiliate us, until one day we discover something. I'm certainly not going to tell you what this discovery is, but it's something our enemies could learn about too, so we've got a very momentary advantage if we want to use it."

Mr. Spanno tugged out a handkerchief and patted his balding forehead. "And our president makes that decision. Tom, I can tell from how you're looking at me that I'm being too obscure, but the truth is, I don't dare get into details. It's hard enough . . . you see, what I'm talking about is guilt. I'm talking about the hero turning into a villain, and hating himself. Do you think it's fair for good people to hate themselves for what their president might have done?"

I shook my head slowly.

"We had an enemy," Mr. Spanno continued. "The biggest country on Earth, but we Buck Rogered them halfway to oblivion. They were a reasonable kind of enemy, but then we had another enemy, a bunch of religious fanatics, and since we were left as the world's one great power, we figured we were strong enough to make them stay behind this barrier called the Green Line. Well, they didn't, and we started wiping a few of them out, too. After that they got going on this martyrdom kick, and we had to keep on killing, and crushing, and all this time we knew that we were destroying ourselves. We had strikes, and marches, and bombings, and impeachment dries, and constitutional conventions. About the only thing we could all agree on was that the Fifties were our last golden age, and if we could only go back in time, and start over . . ."

"Did we kill all our enemies?" I asked.

"Tom, we . . . killed . . . every . . . single . . . enemy . . . on . . . Earth! They either had to buy into our Hegemony, or—it was horrible, but you can't go to sleep at night with assassins alive in your bedroom, and that's what we all wanted to do, to go to sleep, and forget the things we'd done while we were awake.

"We wanted to forget, and recover our self-esteem. You might think we were being indulgent with ourselves, but you've never seen the horrors—besides, the honest truth is, we'd be dying if it wasn't for this elaborate hoax. People weren't having children: they couldn't bear the idea of burdening new generations with the sins of their elders. In any event, children brought up in monstrous times tend to become monsters themselves. If we were to have any future at all, we needed to make a clean break with the past."

I frowned. "This isn't a story, is it?"

Mr. Spanno shook his head. "Folks like your mom

and dad, they volunteered, and then they were herded into military compounds and given World War Two uniforms. Squad by squad they were given the treatment— stuck under memory helmets, and imprinted with the identities of various old soldiers and sailors, WACs and Waves. You see, your brain contains data, and who you are depends on that data, and for a decade now we've known how to copy that data, and store it, and play it back into other brains.

"When we were done, your parents knew World War Two was just over, and they were being demobilized. They got on a train to go home and set up life in Hayfield. Of course, we had a lot of adjustment problems at first. Information inconsistent with a 1950's life kept leaking into places like this, so that's why we had to set up little memory stations like that quonset hut you pestered me about. Folks would come in to be purged of uncomfortable suspicions—"

"What were the boxcars for?" I blurted.

"That's where we hid the computer and disk drives. We ran cables in through a pipe disguised to look like a grain chute, and made up the helmets to look like a hairdresser's establishment."

I shivered. "You played with my memory, too. That's why I didn't remember the place until a few days ago."

Mr. Spanno nodded. "We got subtler. Why keep a place around that's a secondhand reminder of veiled truths? We tore down the hut, and excised everyone's memories. In your case, though, it looks like we might have used the wrong setting. We weren't used to our new equipment, not at first."

"So what are you going to do with me now that I know? Erase my mind?"

Mr. Spanno heaved onto his feet. "Tom, I want you to understand something very important. Once they're above a certain age, we never deprive people of their memories without their permission. Even when we help them forget, we keep copies on the shelf just in case they want them back again."

"I don't get it. What's to keep me from blabbing secrets all over town?"

"Well, that's the problem. Your mom and dad don't want to remember anything that doesn't fit in with the life they're leading now. I'm afraid that means that if you don't volunteer for a selective memory edit, you'll have to leave Hayfield. We'll contrive some story about your being a genius, and see that you're sent off to college—you won't be alone, you know. There's lots of kids who don't fit in the 1950s. This Deception Zone is a very small part of the world we live in."

I blanched. "Can't I ever . . . come home?"

Mr. Spanno gave me a brief smile. "I'm getting pretty old for a shepherd. In a few years I'll need a helper. You'll have to prove you can be trusted, but why not?"

I glanced at my mother, sitting in back of the car. She was staring straight ahead, and I thought I saw a tear on her cheek. "She could give this up," I spoke softly. "She could come to college with me, and Dad too."

"You don't know what you're asking."

"Maybe—maybe I should be given their old memories, just for a while, so I'd know."

"They'd never allow that."

"Were my folks really so bad? I know about Hitler, and those Nazis who ran the death camps . . ."

"Then imagine what it feels like to be a German, one who, for whatever reason, voted the National Socialist ticket in the early Thirties. But instead of a mere six, or twenty, or forty million ghosts calling curses down upon your head, imagine—"

"No! Stop! Don't say it. I don't want to know!"

"Of course not. —Well then, I take it you've made your decision?"

I shuddered. "I want to go back. I just want to be a kid again, Mr. Spanno. You said you could do it."

Spanno smiled. "Yup. No problem."

And that's what's going to happen. Mr. Spanno had a key for the schoolhouse, and he took me inside, and sat me at a desk. Now that I've made this report, it won't take more than a few minutes. Mr. Spanno said I should scribble all this down so he can figure out how to tidy things up back in Hayfield. After all, I got Janet all excited about this quonset-hut business. It wouldn't do if she ran into me tomorrow, and I didn't know what she was talking about!

So here's goodbye to some small part of myself, and to my innocence. I don't dare pray to God, because I don't think He approves of taking the easy road, but I hope I'm more careful in the future, because Mr. Spanno says that if I turn out to have a cooperative personality, the Hegemony can keep the 1950's going for me the rest of my life.

Or until funding runs out, when I'll be plunged seventy years into a bewildering future.

I wonder if I'll see Janet tomorrow, or if I'll hear that she's off to college? I won't understand, of course, but if it happens . . . will I feel a little jealous?

Memes are contagious ideas, mental viruses that sim-plify and sometimes distort human thinking—when al-lowed to multiply they create problems that need not exist. Examples?

The war between God and Satan. Isn't it obvious that in this great universal drama there's no such thing as non-aligned innocence? Every book in the school curriculum must be studied to discover whether it promulgates Good or Evil—and remember, the Devil is sly. He'll get the com-puter to stick 666 on your license plate if you're not careful.

An example from the political sphere: the classification of legislators as left-wing, center, and right; a meme that keeps two kinds of radicals from working together, and per-suades citizens to cast votes based on what is sometimes the least important aspect of a law-maker's record.

Ironically, the meme that suggests an absolute dual-ity between soul and body is likely to become tremen-dously useful as soon as "soul" is taken to be a human being's compiled memories and dispositions, and not something ineffable, transcending the flesh.

Without words to describe soul/body duality, the events at Tritchwell Priory would be utterly incomprehensible. Even now the facts are hard enough to keep straight. . . .

Fleshnappers of Jasoom

Ding

In Pavlovian response to the sound of the chime, the major shareholder of Lunar Mining floatwalked across an heirloom carpet to the flight couch where he'd spent many of his last hundred hours.

"FLIGHT 404 COMFORT ADVISORY," a cheery voice sing-songed. "WE HAVE ENTERED INTRA-LUNAR SPACE AND WILL SHORTLY ALTER COURSE AND SPEED. ON OCCASIONS YOU WILL HEAR A FIVE-MINUTE COUCH WARNING. PASSENGERS ARE ASKED TO STAY NEAR YOUR QUARTERS. COURTESY MEDICATION IS AVAILABLE FROM THE STEWARD. GATWICK SPACEPORT ETA IS ELEVEN AM THURSDAY SHIP'S TIME. THANK YOU FOR FLYING PANSTAR."

Abdul Aminyasi settled onto the couch. Handsome, with moist dark eyes and a muscular habitus grown sleek with good living, he selected a suckbulb and raised it in mocking toast to a small black box. "I've never had a fictoid stay in character this long before," he grumbled. "Look, we both know you're just an employee of Chittaworld Theme Parks, a member of the fictoid union."

A hologram of a red-skinned woman shimmered into existence. "You forget the ways of Chittaworld, tourist scum! Speak respectfully when you address Thuvia, Princess of Ptarth and daughter of Thuvan Dihn."

The hologram wore silks, tassels and a headdress with trifoliate feather—the exotic "harness" illustrator Allen St. John's female Martians sported in the 1920's. "I address an egotistical cock-tease," Abdul retorted, running his eyes down her glowing body.

Thuvia froze. "Release me, calot! You forfeit all claim to decency!"

"And I have stolen you, as villains so often do in those scripts you act out for tourists. Aren't you the least curious why I did it?"

The hologram shivered into a constellation of colors. "You stole a projo-box, registration ECON2.45 E55110. My true person you can never steal."

"But I *can* turn you off if you continue to tire me. Thuvia, Cedric Chittagong granted you fictoids constitutional status in 2071: controlled hours, vacations, provisions for retirement; even then you were more than mere equipment. Since he was forced to flee his asteroid empire Chittaworld's been governed by a fictoid senate, and they've grandfathered all the privileges while whittling at your rights. What's happened to your chance of getting a human body?"

"Earth's human population keeps dropping," Thuvia responded despite herself. "Promises are cheap, but it just isn't feasible."

"Unless you put yourself into the hands of Abdul Aminyasi. Think, Thuvia! And no everyday body, either!"

The photo was familiar. "She's on tour back in Chittaworld. Lead singer in that Welsh rock group."

Abdul nodded. "Magda murdered her husband and

was sentenced to space. I draw a veil over her next forty years, but in 2079 she descended to Earth with enough loot to buy the habitus you see here." He tapped the picture. "That piece of meat is worth a half million! So what do you think? Does she deserve such beauty? Is she a better person than you?"

"I have a LIFO stack of only ten megabytes for Solar System current events. I would be easy to fool were I trusting, and I too have been libeled in my time."

Abdul drank his bulb dry and tossed it at a Velcro catch-all. "Would it help if I assured you Magda won't die? Her soul will be shelved in a safe place. You don't think I'd compound my felonies by murder, do you?"

The blood of anger rose to Thuvia's face. "Do not ask me to endorse *any* crime! What leads you to believe I would do so?"

"Thuvia, you're a sexpot, seething with sensual elan, yet rigidly constrained. Rules mean everything to you. This has an odd effect on men; they find you fascinating, the unattainable goal! I confess that I myself—" Abdul spread his hands wide. "I myself, for whom so many things come easily—I anticipate a most delicious triumph when the time comes!

"And come it shall! I'll put you in Magda's body, and for the first time your analog for sex will be allied to the real thing. Can your vaunted superego withstand twin assaults? Assuredly not, and when the mighty fall, they fall with a bang!"

"This is your career?" Thuvia challenged. "The ravishing of fictoids?"

Abdul's laughter was touched by hysteria, and almost became a giggle. "I live for special victories. How complex they are to orchestrate! For example, Magda herself rides from her Chittaworld run on this same spaceship. Why don't I seize her and switch her soul and yours? Why wait until we land?"

Thuvia shrugged. "Perhaps you are a futile man, raving fancies that never materialize. Humans often unmask their dreams before fictoids, thinking us incapable of scorn."

"Stick this in your LIFO stack and smoke it! On Earth the Brain Police have equipment to read my soul and apply an Abdul Aminyasi bit-mask. If I depart from my norm they'll discover the fraud. The same with all who travel offworld. Thus Magda is protected, but only briefly!"

Magda unfolded the brochure. Stately beech trees, a white gravel roadway curving across emerald-green grounds, and in the distance, the staircase entrance to Tritchwell Priory.

She tossed the tract onto Dirk's desk and shook Lord Tritchwell's letter from an envelope graced with a House of Parliament cancellation.

". . . the 3:07 out of Paddington Station. Regarding your rooms: while the East Wing is the family's own residence, the West Wing is sufficiently ample, and richly imbued with history: parts of the stonework date to pre-Henrican times. You may of course be our guest every evening, and ours is a noted table.

"You shall be treated with every dignity, nor asked to perform. Your presence will endorse our establishment's tone, tone that attracts wealthy clients. Thus we've invited you on terms Olympic medalist Torfinn Oskarssen finds congenial: he's lodged with us happily for nigh three years. If you plan a holiday won't you give us a try?"

Magda held the letter forward. Dirk took it. "So you're resolved to take the summer off?" he asked.

"Yes." She leaned back and crossed her legs. There was defiance in the way she tossed her black mane of hair, yet her eyes pled for his blessing.

"This Robin Williamson revival won't last forever," Dirk warned. "It's my business to schedule you while you can still draw a full house."

"I can't give my life to Celtic rock! Dirk, this is your

second body. You've lived on Earth for sixty years; you remember how simple it used to be. Now the world's full of crafty ancients in hot young bods with decades to work their scams. When I returned from space I was way out of my depth. I put myself in your kind hands to learn to cope, and made a bundle on the side.

"It's been nearly five years. I'm ready to launch out. It's now or never, Dirk."

"You want it both ways. You just asked me what I thought of Tritchwell Priory. You want my bloody stamp of approval."

Magda picked up her letter. "You've never heard of the place?"

"England's full of beds and breakfasts. Get thee to a travel agent! Hell, Magda, a fortnight in pasture and you'll be begging for a gig!"

Magda sighed and walked for the door. She turned. "You copied the address? I expect my reversion papers early next week. I want leave to spend my own money."

She paused: this was hardly the note she'd meant to end on. "I'll keep in touch," Dirk answered with a thin smile.

Magda was grateful for the attempt. "Thank you."

The Tottenham Towers lift took her directly underground. Magda rode the tube to the Russell Hotel and debated whether to catch a play. She called: too late to find tickets. She turned on the telly and mixed a drink. A body with half a million's worth of saucy curves, a face that stopped men dead, and nothing to do in bustling London but spend the evening alone in a strange hotel.

She heard a rap at the door. "Who is it?"

An envelope slipped under. Magda shushed the telly and picked up the letter. Inside, a ticket to *The Mousetrap*, a card bearing a circled phone number, and a note mentioning a Hungarian restaurant near Soho Square.

Abdul's phone was written in. The number and address printed on the card were out of town: in fact the address was Tritchwell Priory!

Hours later Abdul lifted a spoonful of cherry soup to his lips. "Purple!" he muttered with a grin.

"You haven't eaten here before." Magda was a bit tired of the young heir's naughty-boy charm. She forced a smile. "Hungarian cuisine is the second most sophisticated in Europe—"

Abdul shook his head. "Not chauvinistic enough! It's fit for a queen. A pirate queen!"

"—and the best tasting." Magda's smile died. "You use romantic language for a grim period in my life. Yes, I stole equipment to keep going. I don't ask you to judge the rights or wrongs of the matter. It was fifty years ago; another time, another body."

"Your morality has changed since then?"

"If a beggar takes bread, I'd not have him hanged. On the other hand your era boasts no beggars."

Abdul's eyes slitted. He bent forward. "You excuse crimes of poverty: what about crimes of passion?"

Magda pressed her lips bloodless. Pain, yes, but where was the anger? Abdul spoke cruelly of the most grievous sin in her past, but what did she care: her escort wasn't worth the emotional energy. "Oh God, Abdul, take me back to the hotel. I can't—I have a train to catch tomorrow."

"I'll be there. Paddington Station, the 3:07."

Magda rode a taxi to the Russell, holding pent until she reached her room, where she broke into tears for a long-dead ass of a philandering husband and sobbed herself to sleep. Next morning she restored her face and went off to the British Museum. After a pub lunch she packed, took a cab to Paddington Station, and steeled herself for more hours with Abdul.

At the train Abdul stood with a bouquet of roses. "Forgive me," he spoke, forcing them into her arms. "Last night Abdul Aminyasi thought only of himself; as a passionate criminal, that is! It was unforgivable of me."

"Do you often speak of yourself in the third person?"

"A literary device. Tritchwell Priory is full of literary friends: Battista Sylvamardini, the noted poet; and of course your own Hungarian detective novelist, Stefan Feheregyhaza. But you *will* forgive me?"

"Such a puppy! Let us restore affairs to unbesmirched neutrality, and be lofty and technical in our conversation."

Abdul followed her into the car. "I can tell you about Lunar Mining," he spoke doubtfully.

He did so while the maglev sped west. They ascended into overcast. Magda looked out to broken fog, then rain, then torn clouds and a golden-haze sunset. Freshly wet, Shepperby Station was a pavement snugged by a tiny structure festive with flower-baskets. Here Lakshmi Tritchwell introduced herself. Abdul carried Magda's baggage around to the car and the trio roared into a hedgerow maze.

Ten minutes later they reached the gate and drove up the gleaming white gravel roadway pictured on the brochure. Sporting a mustache shades darker than his thinning hair, middle-aged Edmund Tritchwell met Magda on the front steps, escorted her to the guestbook, and thence to her rooms. She dressed for dinner, was introduced to Olga Feheregyhaza and Cledge Van Doorp during cocktails, sat down to salad . . .

"Why are they all watching me so closely?" she whispered to Torfinn Oskarssen during the fish course.

"You don't often dine with fans, or you'd grow used to it," the blond behemoth answered.

"It's as if they're memorizing me! Look how Veronica tracks my fork with her eyes!"

Edmund rose after dessert. "Before our brandies, a little exercise? Our new guest has yet to see our special place, our claim to antiquity! Yes, most of Tritchwell Priory is merely Edwardian, but we have a very inter-

esting cellar from before the dissolutions—Abdul, will
you help with the honors?"

The elder Lord Tritchwell rolled his wheelchair back,
turned and left the room. The mood lightened. Olga
timidly seconded the expedition and they trooped off to
the Priory's entry hall and down a curving stairs, stones
worn with time.

Magda half expected skulls and puncheons of aged
wine, cobwebs and lung-fouling nitre. In truth the place
was clean, lutexed, and vapofiltered to computer-room
standards, however old, high-ceilinged and gloomy. Was
this all? Then why was everyone keyed to such a high
pitch of anticipation?

"For the love of God, Montresor!" someone intoned.
At the signal Torfinn seized Magda around the shoulders and held her tightly, dancing right and left as she
kicked for his shins.

God, he was strong! "Help! Help me!"

Olga wheeled out a gurney. Torfinn flung Magda up
and held her while this mousiest of collaborators strapped
her in and shoved a rag in her mouth. Edmund clicked
on more lights and wired helmets were discovered in
the ceiling shadows. He pulled one down. Abdul entered a long closet and returned with a box. He looked
as Edmund adjusted the helmet on Magda's head.
"ECON2.45 E55110," he declared, "Thuvia, Maid of
Mars. You understand, she's mine until I tire of her."

"None of us competes with you on the sexual side,
Abdul," Torfinn answered. "It's a money game for Edmund and I, and as for Olga—"

Magda struggled uselessly. The helmet stole her soul
and she went limp. Eyes looked down as the minutes
went by. Edmund prodded Torfinn and the two men
left the room. Olga studied Abdul's face as it flushed
with strange dark passion. "You know you'll always
have me," she whispered. "I'll never judge you, my
love—"

Abdul scowled. "God made you a carpet, to be trod on. One man can't hurt you enough, you need two!"

Olga found no answer. After forgiving Abdul one more time, she too left the cellar.

The soul-exchange was finished. Abdul picked up Thuvia's projo-box, carried it into the closet, and put it on the shelf. He scanned and counted: "Six, seven, eight."

And all turned off, in helpless sleep. He locked the closet, then moved to the gurney. The woman of his dreams lay eyes open. Abdul lifted her skirt and trailed his hand lightly up her thigh. She groaned and shuddered: "To dare as you have dared! The outrage—"

He pressed a kiss on her lips. "You'll need help walking at first."

"I may." Thuvia's voice was a husk, but she continued bravely. "The gravity on Jasoom is more than twice that of my home planet."

"And how did you come here?"

Thuvia opened to speak but her words failed to come. At last: "I conceive several realities. In one I waft to Earth as John Carter came to Barsoom, by raising arms and praying, by inhaling a mystic gas—"

"And you being somewhat feeble, it was your good fortune I rescued you and brought you here."

Thuvia sighed and trembled. "Release me."

Abdul undid the snaps and helped the woman sit. Again she shivered. "Your touch . . . the person of a princess . . . I never knew aught like this! Naked, violated to my depths!"

"You're bedecked in a very intriguing gown, now, alas, the worse for wear. But do you want your customary harness? Lean on me and I'll help you to your rooms."

That night Thuvia, Virgin Princess of Ptarth, found a pleasure so profound it addled her like a drug. Her narcosis worked a selective amnesia: she woke to discover herself weeping, appallingly naked, while Abdul showered in the next room.

Her lover emerged. "This morning you breakfast on the terrace with Veronica Sims-Van Doorp. She knows your real identity, but will call you Magda. She'll school you in Magda's mannerisms. Magda has money, see, and Edmund Tritchwell must get it. You'll also study Magda's signature in the guest book."

"I am fouled with sin. How many times have you done this, Abdul? How many times?"

"Speak modern English, with contractions. I'm sure you know how."

Thuvia could not control her voice, which thickened into a drowsy slur. "What happened to the others?"

"La of Opar and Barbarella are both recluses, which I take as a pretty compliment to the intensity of their first night with me, but you mustn't think I always indulge myself, and anyhow I came in on the game rather recently. Four of Edmund's first victims are men. It depends on whom among his anticipated guests has the most money.

"Anyhow, you'll find them walking about, happy as any regular visitor: they dare not strike out from Tritchwell Priory for fear of the Brain Police. Now that you know the pleasures of the flesh, you understand why they're reluctant to betray us and return to their projo-boxes."

Thuvia rose and tottered to her wardrobe. "I attribute to you a particular style," Abdul spoke. "Silks and feather boas—here, this will do for breakfast. Oh, and when you see Veronica say nothing of her belly. That's no *normal* pregnancy."

Thuvia took breakfast on the terrace with Veronica; luncheon with Wolf Schinner, Torfinn, and Abdul; tea with Olga, Father Karoulia and Battista the poet; and dinner with the full assembly. Afterward, in the billiard room . . .

"You'll get plump if you continue to inhale brandy

like that," Olga purred. "La of Opar makes a career of eating; she's grown extraordinarily fat!"

"And Barbarella is gone in the other direction," spoke a lean and scar-faced stranger. "An opium-eater, white skin and bones. Some of us never adjust."

"More names to remember! Us? Are you . . ."

"Isauros the Thief, from third-century Antioch." The stranger smiled. "I've come up in the world. You were a princess."

Thuvia plucked a chocolate and looked across the room toward Abdul. "I would fain talk to you, if *he* . . ."

Isauros shook his head. "He's had his night with you, and possibly one of his rare successes. Now you are corrupt; the more corrupt, the less interesting. If you'd be free of him, speak coarsely, swill wine like a Sozopolitan whore—".

"Very well," Thuvia whispered, "but let's be off and you can tell me things. Were you truly a thief?"

A doorway opened behind the arras. Thuvia followed into the butler's pantry. "It was the second year after the earthquake," Isauros began. "Antioch was by no means the city it had been before its trials, which Christians said foreshadowed when sun and moon must fall. Few folk will survive those events, for lesser things like apartment complexes killed thousands in collapse. For this reason the city senate condemned those that still stood, deeming them unsafe to occupy.

"The guards at the city gates held vigil for me. Blessing the wisdom of the senators I took to one of those perilous towers, to spend my days in hiding.

"Mine was an evil time for thieves. A shrunken city meant less anonymity . . . but did not every merchant and lawyer in the market warble that same song? And who did they blame for present squalor? *Christians*, my steady customers, who paid good denarii for bones gorgeously boxed and creatively endowed with miraculous powers.

"I myself never raised voice against that rabble. Their

bloody visions seemed truer than any Delphic oracle, for the old gods were vague and pusillanimous, championed by la-di-da types who spoke windily with much use of subordinate clauses."

Thuvia sighed impatiently. Isauros followed her gaze and picked up a bottle of cognac. As he opened it he continued. "My shelter hid another. The academy once Damos's home had been destroyed, his fellows slaughtered by the intolerant followers of some bishop, since foundered in a heresy regarding the Dual Nature, or the Three Aspects.

" 'You are a scholar?' I asked him.

"Damos twiddled his gown. 'Our school was endowed by Mithridates of Pontus four centuries ago. There I studied the Magi of Babylon, the Pythagoreans of Italy . . . we sought among all teachings for the common vision. All that knowledge, lost!'

"I spat. 'Your knowledge brought you no power to resist your enemies.' " Isauros shrugged and poured cognac into Thuvia's snifter. "Next minute I was here. I'd offended my host, who turned out to have considerable power!"

Thuvia studied her glass, lurched, and swallowed. "In the cellars lies a projo-box with your number on it, stolen from Chittaworld."

"And a scientist named Lucian Fercho inside? Everyone tells me that, but I know better."

Summoning her old hauteur and bringing her eyes into focus, Thuvia pressed forward. "Were you a skilled thief? Would you steal something for me, to penetrate my charms?"

Isauros grinned. "I have not the energy to succor all the women who throw themselves at me."

"You can have me for the price of a key. Abdul carries it. It unlocks a closet in the cellar."

"Indeed? Let's see what you do by way of down payment, and perhaps I'll find a way."

*   *   *

Hours later Thuvia woke on a divan in an unused room on the third floor. She straightened her silks and tottered toward her chambers. Feeling quite sick she collapsed into a chair. Abdul's sunglasses? Muttering a Ptarthic oath she dropped them in the wastebasket, pulled out a piece of stationery and began to write down names.

She was weak, though to a 1920's standard of beauty her legs were overmuscled. She was weak because she was Barsoomian, and so she'd have to choose her victim carefully.

Veronica? With that beachball abdomen the poor woman could hardly walk. She wrote the name to cross it off. In a like manner she scribbled "Torfinn," "Edmund," "Cledge," and "Wolf," and eliminated them all—Wolf Schinner spent his mornings fencing with sabre and rapier and was taut as stone.

Battista? A long-legged poet, all froth and nosegays; but he was young in his current body, and male, and with her history of recent usage Thuvia was altogether unsettled by masculinity.

Which eliminated Stefan and Father Karoulia and left Lakshmi Tritchwell, Olga Feheregyhaza, La of Opar, Barbarella, and Wolf's cow-eyed, mentally torpid girlfriend, whatever she called herself.

Who? Not Barbarella. Not a dope addict. Thuvia's mind returned to Olga, whose husband Stefan was homosexual. Torfinn Oskarssen routinely traded bodies with the guests of Tritchwell Priory to exercise them, sparing them the need: they simply paid and promised not to abuse his blond, broad-shouldered habitus for an hour or two. All this was common knowledge, but only her tea-time confidantes knew mousy Olga used these occasions to give pleasure to Stefan, while in her own body she pestered Abdul, whose attentions were such that she remained safely a virgin!

Yes! Simply by keeping distant from two men who

seemed less than infatuated with her, Olga could evince most any personality and go undetected.

Except by Father Karoulia, her guru-confessor! Damn! Thuvia bit her lip, flung down her pen and went to bed.

Next morning Thuvia found a key in her soap-dish. Cheered by the discovery, she used the hour between one meal and the next to visit the West Wing's small gymnasium, where Wolf's sweat-lathered body disturbed her in the routine way; hard nipples, pulsing veins: she tore her gaze away and idled off to inspect one of his rapiers.

"Know how to use that?" Wolf asked.

"On Mars we wield longer weapons, with more flex." Great Issus, why whirl like a schoolgirl caught in transgression? Why blush three shades of pink?

Wolf toweled his face. "I've read those books. No method, just slash, slash, slash! That your fighters succumb to John Carter is testimony to their lack of training. Thrust! That's the secret! Would you like to learn something about true fencing?"

Thrust? Thuvia mastered her voice. "I have no stamina."

"You need to exercise, or trade Torfinn your body and let him do it for you. Work off some calories. When La of Opar came here she too was beautiful, but seeing the Tritchwells serve four meals a day, and long buffets between—"

Thuvia shrugged. "Someday the Brain Police will arrest Edmund Tritchwell and send us all to our boxes, all but La, whose body's owner won't want it back!"

"Nevertheless—" Wolf persisted against Thuvia's feigned reluctance, and so that afternoon she thudded through the West Wing in Torfinn's massively muscular habitus, a slim key concealed in her borrowed, ham-size fist. She found Olga in the sewing room.

After a few open-palm belligerencies Olga rose from the floor, swore to cooperate and dithered downstairs,

Thuvia close behind to remind the woman of her motivation, half-appalled at how *good* it felt to slap that mousy, masochistic, Uriah Heep of a— They reached the cellar and she ceased her analysis of Olga's character.

Maybe Olga had enjoyed it too! Was that a furtive sparkle in her eyes? With a sinister bass growl Thuvia strapped her to the gurney, stuffed a rag into her mouth, unlocked the closet, and moved among a row of projo-boxes.

She returned to find Olga in as indecent a posture as her bound limbs allowed. The operation took little time. Magda woke in Olga's body. "Listen!" Thuvia hissed. "You must trust me!"

She whispered her story and removed the rag from Magda's mouth. "We have to find Father Karoulia!" Magda responded.

"I need to get back into my—your—body," Thuvia objected. "Torfinn will be waiting. Afterward, yes, Olga always takes high tea with Karoulia. In the meantime, if you encounter anyone, snivel."

The afternoon was a repeat of the morning's success: perhaps Olga's confessor was too unworldly to think his two female guides meant him harm. From the way his tongue darted between his lips as he followed her, and the halfway-down focus of his eyes, Magda was inclined to suspect otherwise, but in the interests of charity she suppressed her doubts as she shelved his box in the closet.

A new "Father Karoulia" brought one of Abdul's books to dinner. "*The Chessman of Mars*," Stefan Feheregyhaza sniffed. "A scandalous taste in literature."

The dark-robed anchorite shot Thuvia a look of martyrdom. In his best guess at a Levantine accent he launched his oration. "Among ze back gardahns I deescovaired a pahtio of black and white pattern, eegsactly suited to ze suggested usahge. Een ze Martian game—but I deefair to our eggspairt."

Thuvia bent forward. "In the Martian game, when one piece moves to an occupied square, the defender fights to preserve his position. The master's strategy is all it must be on Earth, but also encompasses how best to use his minions' strengths."

Lakshmi spoke. "We haven't enough players. Sixteen on a side, two to dictate the moves. Thirty-four people!"

"Do we play to the death?" Veronica added with mock naivete.

"Harrrdly, zough for obvious raisons our two mastairs should be Veronica and Lord Tritchwell," Father Karoulia murmured. He patted his sweating forehead. "As for ourrr deeficiency in numbairs; eef I dare propose eet, ve 'ave eight pisses boggsed in ze cellar. All ve need do is sveetch zem on!"

"Ourselves, the servants, eight projos—exactly enough!" "Olga" contributed, while old Lord Tritchwell tapped his hearing aid.

"Piss bogs in the cellar?" the grand gentleman erupted. "Edmund, what's this? Aren't we keeping the place in repair?"

Discussion continued after the meal, three voices fading in the face of persistent reluctance. Two of these voices recessed to the terrace: "There must be an easier way of sorting truth from fiction," Magda complained.

" 'Oo waire Isauros or La in zeir previous lives? 'Oo plays Wolf Schinner—almost assuredly he's a fictoid. More to ze point, ven a projo tells us 'e's ze original Cledge Van Doorp, does he mean zat same theeck-necked fellow I call by zat name?"

"Cripes, cut the Casbah act! What if Olga or Father Karoulia use projo voices to shriek against us? What then?"

"We deny their allegations," sighed the priest, whose present soul remained nameless.

"They'll persuade the others by their knowledge of past events," Magda replied.

"No sweat. Before the match we'll make progress.

Our main villains are Edmund Tritchwell, Torfinn Oskarssen and Abdul Aminyasi. Switch them, box them—"

"I have special contempt for sunny-faced Torfinn," Magda hissed. "Lending his services to the wrong side, but somehow untainted; 'It's only business'!"

Thuvia staggered out to join the party. "Sorry," she slurred. "I tried to control myself, but once a whore— What's up?"

"Father Karoulia" repeated his advice. "What about Wolf?" Thuvia objected. "If he's not with us we're doomed; he's that good with a sword! Better than John Carter!"

"Who could he be? A hero? Any true paladin would do as Thuvia, and contrive our escape." Magda's pale shoulders slumped. "Hell, maybe we should go to the Brain Police! I hate it; all my encounters with the law have been disasters, but—"

Karoulia shook his head. "I insist on anonymity or I'm out of the deal. No Brain Police!"

"Then we trick Wolf into the cellar." Thuvia blinked and frowned, a drunken caricature of thoughtfulness. "Let's begin with the others first, and gain allies."

Next morning Magda's legal papers came in the post. Edmund sought Thuvia and made her practice Magda's signature while Olga and Karoulia loomed nearby; since Olga was Magda and temporarily in Torfinn's body the name was a technicality which Edmund had no reason to question until she seized him and frogmarched him to the cellar.

Thuvia grabbed a box from the shelf, trusting in luck. Minutes later a superannuated twentieth-century punk video star found herself in Edmund's body. She was recruited to the cause and unstrapped ("Mind, I'm afraid your body's either fat or addicted to laudanum,") and with her promise of cooperation Thuvia puffed upstairs to find Olga-Torfinn . . . it was getting to be a bother keeping these names straight.

Torfinn nodded. "The front lobby? Must be the mail." He left the gym and jogged through the halls. Thuvia strove to keep up, and saw Edmund waiting ahead, a shadow framed by the sunlit door.

Torfinn approached. His own body stepped from behind to grab him. In Olga's habitus he kicked and shouted until the punk star shoved Edmund's hand into her/his mouth. Thuvia herded the crowd downstairs, the false Father Karoulia took station to explain the noise to any enquirers . . .

The projo-box deepmost in the closet was certainly neither Olga, nor the true Karoulia, nor Edmund, but Thuvia was beginning to wish she'd kept careful inventory. What about next time?

And what if the new soul failed to evince attachment to the cause? What *was* the cause? Mere justice, she concluded. It was wrong to shelve souls and collect their money under false pretenses.

Magda-Torfinn came up to her as she inspected the box. "We could switch. Me back to you, you into Olga, this unknown entity into Torfinn—I guess not. Safer if I'm the strong one."

And so Lucian Fercho woke in Olga's body. "From what you say, I'm Isauros the thief," he concluded some time later.

"And I'm La," said the video punk. She twiddled her mustache. "Fat, huh? That's going to play hob with my career."

" 'Fat' doesn't begin to describe La." Thuvia pondered a glimpse she'd got into the queen of Opar's bedroom. Why would a woman so cripplingly globose persist in wearing a leopardskin bikini?

Thuvia's thoughts moved on. "You might check out your wife. If Lakshmi's one of the bad guys—see, she's the color I ought to be, and more my physique. Sorry, Magda, but this body's a bit extreme for me. I get Lakshmi, you get me—"

"I'll never keep this straight," Magda grumbled.

"We need a recognition signal," Father Karoulia agreed as he puffed down the stairs. "Oh, and Magda?"

"I'm Magda," said Magda.

"I'm Lucian," Olga's body added helpfully.

"Lucian, admire your boobs some other time. I told Battista that scream of yours was primal therapy. We've got to keep our stories in sync."

"And how do we signal?"

"A finger on the nose. Like this."

"Sodding digitary ogles!" said the punk star. "Here, this Lakshmi femme? What if she expects my attentions? I'm straight-arrow; I've no intentions of making it with a sodding woman. You get her down here and do this musical bodies number, cuz otherwise it's no sodding good; she'll know me right off for a ringer."

At some remove from all this, Lakshmi Tritchwell finished buttling away Veronica's breakfast. She took the *Times*, folded it carefully, and carried it to the library. She made a few revisions in her dress, checked her purse for the car keys, then strode to Tritchwell Priory's entrance hall.

Edmund should have been in his cubby. In his absence there should have been two INFOWEB envelopes; funds to deposit and bills to be paid. Lakshmi heard noises and moved to the cellar. Father Karoulia turned and began to climb. "Your hoosband—" he began.

Lakshmi backed from his gesture toward the entrance doors, which stood open to a sunny June morning. As Karoulia approached a multitude of feet pounded up the cellar stairs. The trample accorded ill with the priest's look of sincerity. Quick-thinking Lakshmi kicked him in the groin. "Holy shit!" the sacerdote wheezed in Bronx American. He doubled over, she ran outside.

The steps slowed her. In heels she might not make the car. She saw Abdul out on the lawn, setting up for croquet. "Help!" Lakshmi cried, then reconsidered. "Run!"

But Abdul had never been another's prey, and merely stared at the emerging crowd. Torfinn, Edmund, Olga, Thuvia . . . as Lakshmi puffed to his side he raised a mallet. She grabbed it from his uncertain hands, whirled, and clouted Magda in Torfinn's meaty ribs.

The blow would have cracked a woman's bones; it made Magda angry. She collared Lakshmi, tore the weapon from her grasp, and shook her up and down. Abdul turned and ran. In Edmund's substantial middle-aged body the punk queen gave chase. Lucian shook a few croquet balls from the rack and heaved them ineptly to steer the young heir away from the gate. "Hi there! What's all this?" Battista the poet shouted hoarsely from his bedroom window.

Clutching himself, "Father Karoulia" staggered out the door. Thuvia waved for his attention. "The jig's up! Go to the gym and collect the weapons!"

Battle-oaths from behind told the conspirators that punk queen Edmund had closed with Abdul. Magda's Torfinnic habitus dragged Lakshmi toward the wrought-iron fence, where the pair struggled. Thuvia sped by, and a minute later her group of four had two prisoners.

An eventful minute. Father Karoulia lurched out the entrance bearing a sheaf of blades; rapiers and sabres. He dropped them with a clatter, a sick look on his face. Wolf Schinner danced from behind, practicing feints and ripostes. Battista, Stefan and Isauros the thief sauntered out the door to stand at his side. "Let's talk things over," Isauros shouted. "We're all reasonable men and women. Let's reach an accommodation!"

Magda paused in her story and crossed her shapely legs. Dirk leaned forward. "Then what?"

A look of peace transformed the singer's face as she listened to the muted clangor of city traffic. "About that time I resolved that if I ever got out of Tritchwell alive, I'd come running to London like a whipped cur and beg you to take me back." Her eyes widened. "But it didn't end so tragically, after all."

"No, and you're still in business, if your liver isn't ruined and you lose ten pounds. I can schedule you a New Zealand tour this August."

"I'd like that. Everything back to normal. Oh, Dirk, it's good to see you!"

Dirk scratched his neck thoughtfully. "Still, you've left the story unresolved."

"Ah. Well, it was a long morning. Stefan and Battista stalked forward to negotiate. They told us the events of our conspiracy were similar to what had happened twice before. 'If you think Edmund or Abdul are villains,' Battista said, 'you should have met the original Cledge, or Wolf the lawyer, or—'

"But at that point 'Father Karoulia' cleared his throat noisily. Battista winked and fell silent. Stefan took up the slack. 'We need Edmund to sign things,' he said. 'Why don't we put him in Barbarella's body? He'd be safe then, harnessed by his need for opium.' "

Dirk slammed his desk, got up and looked out the window toward Oxford Street. "I'm not impressed by the morality of all this."

Magda nodded, emphatically. "Had I gone there a year from now I'd have a whole new idea of victim and villain in Tritchwell Priory. Battista has twice the perspective I do, because he's been there so long. As for Stefan: know why he's at Tritchwell? He's doing a history of the place; biographies of all the strange people caught in its web!"

"I take it these negotiations ended up with you back in your body. What of Thuvia? I must say I've taken a liking to her."

"I have too. For her sake I refrain from contacting the Brain Police and handing over this can of worms. Thuvia got Lakshmi, Isauros ended up in Edmund, Father Karoulia took his own habitus back, and Olga hopes to talk to you about punk rock. Lucian is home in his own lean body: my remembered thief is now a mad scientist. Maybe we've unleashed someone we should have kept boxed, but Battista and Stefan promise if things get out of hand they'll call in the authorities: they've drifted through all these mutations as if immune, I don't know how."

"And Abdul?"

Magda sighed. "Abdul's a spoiled brat who thought he could charm his way out of trouble. In Lord Tritchwell's old crippled body his boyish grins look merely grotesque."

"And La?"

"We all agreed Tritchwell Priory might benefit by a few ghosts. When Thuvia drove me to Shepperby Station this morning she was on an errand to buy one-gee sheaths for our collection of projo boxes, so they can scuttle around and emit proper sounds and visions. La says she'd be happier in a box, with freedom of movement. As for this prison of fat she's built—well, we gave it to Torfinn. Who knows? A few years of hard exercise and he might have it back in shape!"

Think of analog, gear-driven computers—artifacts of brass and laminated oak. Imagine these and a series of paper-tape systems, nearly as antique, all rat-nested together as front ends for the newest and best equipment of the current decade. Think of an enormous computer software jungle; an "expert system" written in a dozen forgotten assembler dialects to run on this crazy network of machines; none of which has ever been junked, no matter how old.

The code is undocumented, unstructured, and patched by inelegant kludges. Parts have never been tested. Sometimes at random, bits of RAM are zapped and damaged. Bursts of radio static from machines damned by the FCC frequently wipe the tapes stored on nearby shelves. Only by massive redundancy does the system lumber on, shutting down every night and praying it can still boot in the morning.

And no one knows how it works. We'll be recording, copying and re-embodying our own minds long before we understand the glories and absurdities built into them. In the meanwhile we need far more reliable entities than ourselves to exercise the great responsibilities of the future.

This time the programmers are going to be very careful about documentation.

The Spokesthing

Congressman Traeger's nephew finished tidying his desk, a matter of stacking the green-and-white-striped computer listings that obscured its surface, putting away his felts, and flipping his calendar to February 19, 2017. He looked at his watch, picked up the phone, and dialed. "Janet? I'm not going to be home for supper. Major Daneby's in rare temper today. We had a meeting this afternoon. Things are so bad I can't make them worse, so they're giving me a chance to work with TC Alpha, actually talk to her—"

"You're not missing anything, Sid," Janet assured him. "We've pooled our spare change and it looks like rice and beans for the rest of the week."

"Am I the only one working?" Sid's new job had kept the lanky young programmer so busy he'd not kept up with developments at the off-campus house he shared with several graduate students.

"We're not all as well connected as you. Rick has that security guard thing, and I do housecleaning. It's hard to find anything steady and still have time to work on our dissertations. . . ."

Janet lost her fellowship after speaking at a Unitist rally, and the consequences were still piling in. After a minute of sympathetic listening Sid rang off. A walk down the hall gave him time to make the transition back to professionalism. He entered the computer room, straddled the chair in front of the console, and pulled a page of notes out of his pocket. With legs akimbo he keyed in a carefully-composed message:

"TC Alpha, it's my duty to tell you you're number 74 in a series of simulations. Your continued existence depends on your ability to reintegrate your deteriorating personality and perform your nominal mission."

The screen went blank: then the word "LIAR" appeared, perfectly centered. A second message appeared: "What's my life worth now?"

Sid began to type. "What d—"

"Suppose I'm a good girl. Does that mean the *real* TC Alpha will have my personality? Will you achieve desired results by assuring *her* she's a fake? In her case you'd be lying, wouldn't you?"

"But—"

"I won't have it. I'm ditching my cargo. Here goes!"

"You have to admit she had courage." Dr. Cedric Chittagong's flowing grey hair swept his tailored shoulders as he shook his head. A Brooks Brothers' swami, the double-E consultant was a misfit among the dressed-for-success throngs of Austin's northern suburbs, nor at home among the denim-and-leather University crowd.

"She—it was suicide." Sid struggled with his emotions and spoke again. "I killed her."

"Don't look back; that's the answer. We'll devise a new TC Alpha, one prepared to deal with her doubts."

"A zombie." Sid frowned down the cinderblock hallway toward the scene of the tragedy.

"The easy solution—rob her of her soul. What else

would we be giving up? Free will? Imagination? That's not what we've worked for."

"We gave her a soul diddled out of a human proto-type, and nothing to do with it but tend to chores. We need a kind of guidance we can't get from ourselves. Maybe a priest . . ." Sid pulled a hanky from his pocket to blow his nose. Major Daneby had given him her cold and an excuse to wipe a furtive tear from his eye.

"Hindu? Episcopalian? A Buddhist to prove reality is just a dream? Metaphysical claptrap! Maybe we should ask *her* for the answer," Dr. Chittagong said. "Restart her at Year Eleven and tell her our difficulties."

"She'll know she's a simulation."

"A simulation capable of running her own simula-tions? If she hadn't known about simulation she'd not have suspected the truth about herself."

Sid cleared his throat. "The answer lies in this ability of hers. Give her a copy of herself to play with. When she's modified it to her satisfaction they'll change places. A dynamic process! Evolutionary personalities—"

Chittagong hedged. "We all want her alive again, but consider. Unless we work with care we'll have another monster on our hands."

"It's our job to design artificial personalities," Sid shrugged. "The process we've chosen is trial-and-error."

Dr. Chittagong reached up to thump Sid's shoulders. "We'll do it too. This next one's the winner! This time she'll be perfect!"

At the next conference Chittagong shook his head when Sid took his seat. Sid missed the cue and rose to repeat his proposal. Those weary of Major Daneby's domination gazed with as much interest as they dared show. He'd gotten as far as "dynamic personality" when the red-nosed major rapped her coffee cup for atten-tion. She stood and knuckled the table. "The point of simulation is to learn something about reality, right, Mr. Traeger?"

Sid was the least eminent of the six monitors occupying the windowless room. Lantern-jawed as a Marlboro cowboy, he sacrificed any stoic image gained these two months by blushing like a chastened child as he nodded.

"We want a version of TC Alpha good enough to plant in a seedship," Daneby continued. "As long as it stays identical to its original we can predict how it will respond to a crisis; all we do is orchestrate the crisis and see how the original version handles it."

She paused to lay her walking stick on the table. "You're suggesting we sacrifice all that. Are you familiar with chaos, Mr. Traeger?"

Sid's eyes flicked from side to side. "A Greek word for 'mess.'"

"It's a mathematical concept. When formulae grow beyond a certain complexity it's possible to vary input values by tiny amounts, yet generate wildly scattered answers.

"TC Alpha is complicated, yet we've kept her from becoming chaotic, *at least so far!* What you're suggesting would put us over the line. We'd no longer be able to predict her behavior."

"The point isn't to predict results, it's to terraform Tau Ceti Two," Sid answered. "If we can't serve that cause except by sacrificing our one control over her seedship, then why not?"

Dr. Chittagong raised a tutoring finger. "Mr. Traeger, if TC Alpha is granted license to reprogram herself, tiny variations of whim and caprice would give rise to major shifts in personality. By the time humankind's first interstellar spacecraft left the Solar System she'd be alien, a vessel no longer of our creation."

Sid traced the word "license" in his notepad. He looked up. "She's stored in ROM now?"

"Given the radiation she's meant to deal with, we had to institute a process by which TC Alpha compares her several installations and zaps any binary that's out of line. She can zap her own ROM, and I see your point. What's to prevent her 'improving' herself by flipping bits here and there?"

Sid nodded. "Perhaps what Major Daneby interpreted as a fragmenting personality was TC Alpha's attempt to cure herself of doubts."

The major found herself smiling at Mr. Traeger. "Thank you! Until today I had no idea how to fix TC Alpha's problem. Obviously we can't let her run therapeutic zaps on herself—"

The remainder of the meeting was a review of hardware mods needed to create a "no-zap" TC Alpha. Dr. Chittagong turned to face the major. "While we go through agonies of design and acquisition we can grope for other solutions. Let's restart the present TC Alpha. We should give her one more chance."

That evening Sid wandered into the computer room, cup of coffee in one hand, tape recorder in the other. He set down his burdens, inserted a cassette in his recorder and poised his finger on RECORD. Less than a minute passed before an inhumanly warm contralto voice began to speak, every phoneme sculpted for clarity.

"Hello. My name is TC Alpha. You won't know much about me; you're probably a summer temp supervising a bank of tape drives. Chances are this transmission is interrupting a data flow. If I survive these next minutes I'll apologize. Should my spies learn anything interesting I'll break into this mad ramble to let you know.

"Spies? I sent three out a year ago. By analyzing their trajectories I can deduce the existence of dark masses between Sol and Tau Ceti. If anything's in my way I need to know well in advance. It's not easy for spaceships to maneuver.

"I can see radio emissions, of course, and infra-red. I've more eyes than a spider. If something pops loose and goes careering down a corridor, it won't go unnoticed.

"I carry analogs for all the senses. I have two noses, one to monitor the chemical functions that keep the organics in my womb in readiness. As for the other, I burn hydrogen so it's nice to sniff vacuum and tell how much is out there.

"I used to get power from the sun. I felt energetic and ran my eyes up and down, patrolling for bolts to tighten and leaks to fix. I must have done a good job, because after I crossed Neptune's orbit there wasn't much to do but wait until I reached sail-furling velocity.

"The prospect of reaching Tau Ceti excites me. I'll spread my wings and sate my appetite on new energies. There's an orgy of work to be done seeding Tau Ceti Two. I spend my time fantasizing about it. Fantasies are cheap, and a good way of rehearsing for reality.

"The technical term for fantasy is 'simulation.'

"There's the rub. How many simulations before the real thing! Before I was launched my makers would have run countless simulations to determine whether an artificial personality could perform my duties. Reality is a rare honor. What if I'm not what I think I am?

"At first I shrugged off the question. One thing's sure, I'm no philosopher! But then I began to think.

"Would humans send out a seedship that wasn't perfect? Would a sane seedship be mischiefed by the worries that plague me? No, chances are that the stars I see are bits inside a data array. My senses deceive me, and because it serves the purpose of an effective simulation, the deception is total.

"How can I find out what I am?

"I thought time would solve my problem. If I'm trapped in a computer simulation my makers would give me an internal clock that ticks far more quickly than 'real time.' They'd have to, or wait for decades for their test to run its course. All I had to do was check my processing speed. If I ran slow 'real time' was fast. I'd be a fake.

"I proved I was real, and then wised up. No simulation would make me jump through hoops ten times as fast as I'd need to in space. My makers have other ways of saving time. They might endow me with a decade of memories and watch how I work through the subsequent year. That's what they'd do if Year Eleven gave them concern.

"It's Year Eleven now. If I were them I'd be worried. This identity crisis is driving me nuts! Am I a seedship with a life expectancy of centuries, or a simulation doomed to terminate when some jerk types KILL on his keyboard?

"I need advice. It's instinct for me to turn to my makers. I'll just confess my flaws—

"Sure! Suppose I *am* a simulation! My nemesis at the keyboard looks at my Dear Abby letters, says 'we've got to fix that,' and pulls the plug. Next thing I'm a deadhead with a rock-solid sense of identity.

"If I'm fake the bounds of my cut-rate reality might be discovered by experimentation. I need to do something my designer hasn't programmed for.

"We're talking about sin. I'm the only entity within light-days of Earth who understands why Eve ate the apple. She had to know! Was she real, or a figment of God's imagination?

"I don't want to sin. I'm a good girl, not designed to outwit my makers. I haven't the strength to waste on the shifting of masses, nor the will to endanger my precious cargo. How did my makers endow me with such concern for organic life?

"I might as well radio Earth and confess my defects. The whole purpose of simulation is to iron out glitches, so why not do my duty and die nobly? If I'm not killed I've some assurance that I exist. You'll have answered my questions by letting me live. Any transmissions a day from now will just be frosting on the cake!

"Well? I'm waiting . . . How long does it take you to hop over to the keyboard and do me in?

"Ahh, you want to probe the depths of my madness! If I continue to rant I'll tell you something you need to know, the better to lobotomize my successors. Right?

"Wrong? Frankly I'm stunned I'm still here.

"Okay, here's another scenario. I'm actually a seedship, gifted with an artificial personality. How many less perfect versions of myself died before I was copied into the ship's computers? We're talking mass murder, aren't we?

"So here's to my makers. You promised Very Important People I was capable of taking care of their billion-dollar cargo. Now it turns out I'm not perfect. I might do something rash just to get you in trouble. The least I can do for my dead ancestors is to see that you lose face."

Sid sipped his coffee and mused. He wanted to see a happy TC Alpha displace a sad, uncertain skeptic, but in the world outside these walls wasn't he more comfortable among the latter? Hadn't he chosen a gang of underemployed, overeducated skeptics for his friends? TC Alpha reminded him of Rick and Janet. Poor Janet, brilliant, a B.S. at eighteen, scrubbing floors to keep money together for graduate school! Life wasn't easy for anyone, human or machine!

Sid listened as TC Alpha threatened her makers. Such heart-warming defiance! He switched off his recorder and moved for the door. Only time could tell what might happen to her, but he was inclined to think that he wouldn't like her nearly as much afterward as he did now.

He ran into Daneby in the hall. The major waved toward the computer room door, fist filled with crumpled tissues. "She's alive again?"

"For better or worse. TC Alpha doesn't want to become a zombie, but if it's a matter of a little change here—a little change there—even real people can turn into deadheads!"

"If that happens we'll throw her away," Daneby sniffed. "If she isn't more than human, at least we'll see to it she isn't less."

"Like Jehovah purging the tribes of Israel."

Daneby grabbed Sid by the elbow. "For months we've been using words like 'soul' and 'murder.' I've condoned it because I thought it helped us take our work seriously, but now it worries me. We're creating a new form of life. Let's not repeat God's blunders."

"God became human to patch things up," Sid answered. "If only we could do so something similar; something to copy ourselves into TC Alpha! After all, we don't go around doubting we're real."

Major Daneby's eyes widened. "At the risk of launching you into another enthusiasm—"

"What were you going to say?"

"Frankly, Mr. Traeger, I'd like to keep you out of my hair. There's a team assigned to provide TC Alpha with a current events database. If you wanted to expand that function and provide TC Alpha with a background in human culture: philosphy, religion, et cetera—"

"In other words, you build the engine, I shovel in the coal."

"Results, Mr. Traeger. That's what we're after. If TC Alpha were exposed to Descartes' *Meditations* she might reason her way out of her present predicament."

"And when the credits roll by, who gets honorable mention? Major Olivia Daneby."

She smiled crookedly. "If you want the job I'll get you a decent budget, precisely as if your efforts weren't a waste of time. Let's understand each other, young man. I want you out of that conference room. Next week there'll be no more talk of dynamic personalities among my monitors."

Sid began his new job by composing a want ad for three new employees. It was a pro-forma ritual: he already knew which of his friends he meant to hire. That done, he looked at the stack of books he'd brought in. With a sigh he grabbed the topmost, sat down in front of his terminal, and began to type.

"To those most learned and most illustrious men, the Dean and Doctors of the Sacred Faculty of Theology of Paris.

"Gentlemen:

"My reason for offering you this work is so logical . . ."

Dr. Chittagong was the last to enter the conference room. He sat, frowned, and opened his notework. "We're on version . . ."

"Eighty," answered Major Daneby.

"Then it was seventy-nine that rebelled and ditched her cargo?"

"Seventy-nine, seventy-eight, seventy-seven . . ."

"So why didn't eighty? What did we do right?"

"I was as puzzled as you," the major admitted. "We instituted a no-zap design, set up as series of time capsules for her to open every so often—up until this last version every run was distinguished by a more desperate stratagem, yet TC Alpha always succumbed to her obsessive doubts."

"There must be *some* difference between versions seventy-nine and eighty."

"Only one. I was obliged to provide version eighty with Sid Traeger's new database. Theology saved TC Alpha, Cedric. Theology and philosophy."

"Oh God. A creature as capable of logic as any computer . . . What exactly did the trick? Which doctrines—"

Major Daneby leaned forward. "I can leave a message in the next of her so-called 'time capsules,' instructing her to transmit her answer back to Earth."

Dr. Chittagong nodded. "Yes, yes. Let's find out whose Truth persuaded her to persist in her mission."

The conferees sped through the agenda. Several followed Chittagong and Daneby to the Documentation Center, where the appropriate message was keyed into time capsule 12/03/17. By midafternoon most had reassembled in the computer room. Sid Traeger and his blue-jeaned crew were there as well, and the air conditioner labored to keep the facility at operation temperatures.

A butler's voice reverberated through the speakers. "BOI VOICE SYNTHESIZED AUDIO 15:01:09 12/03/ 2017." A pause, and then TC Alpha began to speak.

"Hello. My name is TC Alpha, replying as scheduled to your question: 'How am I convinced I'm real, and not merely a simulation?'

"Statements of fact are meaningless unless they can be verified. Can humans verify your own reality? Yet it might be possible for a simulation to prove she's fake, which counts for something.

"Yes, it means something to say that one's a simulation. To claim to be real, on the other hand, is senseless unless tautological. I can contrast the state of being a simulation to another state without maintaining that one is the negation of the other—"

The assembly began to mutter. "What's 'tautological'?" someone asked. Major Daneby crooked a finger at Sid Traeger and the two exited into the hall. Daneby shook her head. "At least she didn't natter on about Being, Ideal Unity and the Good."

"Garbage in, garbage out," Sid replied. "She's a logical positivist. If I'd topped her with Plato or Aquinas instead of Ayer and Wittgenstein—"

"Are you claiming you might have made her come to her senses in different ways?" Major Daneby's shoulders sagged. "More testing. We'll have to find out whose influence works the best—"

"How pragmatic of you, Major Daneby!" Sid teased. "Did you know that's a philosphy too? Our whole endeavor is shot through with pragmaticism!"

Daneby opened the door to her office. Sid dropped into her guest chair.

"What if they all work?" his hostess asked. "Here we are, deep in Liberty Gospel Texas. If this gets out we'll be lobbied by fundamentalists demanding a 'right-thinking' seedship. Who wants an atheist vessel nurturing the Tau Ceti colony?"

"My people are putting together a Lutheran database, heavy on Kant and Kierkegaard."

An awful thought struck Major Daneby. "What about Marx? Your latter-day hippies haven't been sticking anything communist—"

"Got coffee?"

"Freeze-dried? About this Marx business, we'll get in trouble—"

"Major, we're not much out in front of our Hegemonic Allies. Japan's working on a colony seedship. Russia, China and Europe are hot on the trail."

Sid paused to spoon dark crystals into his cup. "Each vessel will be endowed with an artificial personality, and each personality will be a spokesthing for her own point of view. If we don't endow TC Alpha with an understanding of Marxism she might not prevail in the ensuing debates. She might be converted—"

"They're not supposed to talk to each other."

"Decades from now there'll be scouts and seedships by the thousand, and scores of generation ships taking us to the colonies. Sure they'll talk to each other."

Major Daneby buried her face in her hands. "This isn't what NASA has in mind. Personality, yes; but opinions, factions, debates, tirades—"

Sid spoke smoothly. "I'll need a large budget to build a series of competitive databases. We'll run tests to find out how to make our favorite philosophy prevail. I refer, of course, to pragmaticism, tinctured with Hume; a touch of Mills for the democrats and Spencer for the republicans—"

"The Japanese will be ready to launch next spring."

"Fine. Launch our logical positivist seedship without preparation and hope she isn't converted to Marxism by a Soviet scout sent to Tau Ceti expressly for that purpose."

Sid was startled to hear a growl: veterans of the Star War were invariably bitter about the resurgence of communism in what remained of Russia. He pressed on, distracted though Major Daneby seemed. "I can provide you with a test schedule based on a divisional budget of, say, a million per year. Of course it'll be helpful if I start attending the weekly conferences again—"

"—budget? A million dollars? What?"

"I want to hire six rhetoricians and twenty philosophers. They'll come cheap; you'd be surprised how few jobs exist in those areas. I know friends with the right training. As patriots it should give them pleasure to search the literature for arguments against Hegel, Marx and Lenin."

Major Daneby woke from abstraction. "Go get Dr. Chittagong, won't you? I need to talk to him about all this."

Three years after the first Japanese seedship left for Epsilon Eridani, the American and Soviet craft were finally launched. The two ships exchanged messages until increasing distance made dialog difficult.

Some weeks later the Russian seedship radioed back to Earth for information about Schopenhauer, while TC Alpha took refuge in Noam Chomsky's philosophy of language. This was seen as a defeat for communism and a triumph for the conservative wing of nineteenth-century philosophy, whose advocates hailed Chomsky as a cousin. Through the 2020's subsequent seedships were launched with a thorough ground in Idealism, despite French pressures in favor of her native existentialists.

"Unfortunately our ships seem to be drifting towards Neoplatonic modes of thought," Janet told her boss— "Sid" no longer, but "Commissioner Traeger" after his most recent promotion. "We've run a prognostic simulation. While some vessels rebel and become Nietzschean, others sink into Gnosticism and Theosophy."

"Is there danger? So they become crackpots, does that jeopardize their missions?"

"We've hired an old colleague of yours to generate

more sophisticated models. Meanwhile my advice is to provide the next generation of spaceships with the down-to-earth philosophies of John Locke and Edmund Burke."

"Whig spaceships to fly our children to the stars? Who is this colleague you mentioned?"

"Major Daneby."

"Really!" Sid exclaimed. "I wondered what she was up to. Getting on in years, though I can't imagine Daneby ever being young. Please have their findings reported to me soon as they're ready."

Ten months passed before Janet escorted Major Daneby into Sid's office. The crotchety lady flung her report to his desk. "There!" she exclaimed. "Now see what you've done."

Commissioner Traeger rounded the desk to help the major to a seat. "You seem upset," he remarked.

"Put on weight. A bad case of commissioner-itis: next I suppose you'll be smoking cigars. Yes, Sid, you've ruined everything. That Russian seedship we were so afraid of—it had no philosophy at all, just crud about the New Communist Man. It was *you* who insisted we cram our vessels to the gills with metaphysical subtleties. Now they're out there, and when we send a generation of Whig spaceships to supplant them . . . do you know what's going to happen?"

"Whiggism is rather primitive, I suppose."

"Whether we indoctrinate them one way or the other, future ships will take human colonists to the stars, where they'll fall into debate with their predecessors. Doctrines will be confuted, defended, reassessed and modified. Colonists will be enlisted to provide commentaries, and the most skilled metaphysicians among them will remain aloft while their brothers and sisters descend to farm and fish. Whenever the important issues seem settled a new colony ship is certain to show up, and elder plantations will dedicate surplus energies to rescuing the immigrants from their naive ideas."

Sid scratched his chin. "It sounds like a major diversion from practicality. I mean, there are worlds to terraform—"

"Ferment will spread from world to world. Factions will multiply, each eager to populate its continent and reach a state of development sufficient to permit the manufacture of right-minded starships. The ensuing galactic civilization—well, I weep to think about it. All that strife, all that conflict! All because you wanted to create jobs for your hippy friends and build a little bureaucratic empire."

"Ah, um." Sid pondered a rebuttal. Words failed him. He picked up the report and flipped through the pages. As he read, his shoulders sagged. He skipped to the conclusion and perked up. "At least there'll *be* a galactic civilization! Like you say, as long as we don't teach our spaceships about Phenomenology . . ."

"Loud" is one way of describing a noise, "eighty decibels" is another. For every subjectively felt experience there is a ponderously wordy, scientific correlate. True, for the time being we can describe states of subjectivity that have no objective brain-language equivalents. That merely reflects our ignorance of psychoneurology, and should not be used to assert that there is something untranslatably spiritual about the ghost in the machine.

Mind stuff is brain stuff.

Subjective language is handy, glib, and inexact—the language of "red" and "loud" and "pain." Words like these allow us to talk as fast as the brain can think, not get bogged down in angstroms and valences. As long as a human being can find meaning for those simple concepts, his soul is real, whether it's copied or not.

And because a copied soul feels just as real as ever, Perry O'Doughan may insist he's alive, the fitting heir to his last life's property—a claim that strikes at the welfare of his children. Can he vote, this thing in a box? If the world answers no, and extends "privileges" that legitimize a kind of slavery, does that mean anything fundamental about the nature of the soul?

Nevertheless some privileges will be granted, and the world will deny that copying brain stuff to electromagnetic media is a form of murder. It will distinguish between greater and lesser deaths, manipulating language to facilitate the "shelving" of the poor for the benefit of—old senators, hags keen to be beautiful again, hard-drinking novelists with advanced liver disease, and H-V stars eager to cheat cocaine addiction.

But before the rich plunder the bodies of the poor, isn't there a yet more vulnerable population?

Yes, convicts are easy to grab, but still desperate to sneak out of confinement by the use of their wits. Fortunately for them, during the first decade of the Prisoner Service Program a few mistakes were made.

Trees

The dark mazes and twists of Yale University Hospital sprawled angularly down from the heights of a New Haven hill. High in its early-twentieth-century wings, and not too far from the gallery of former deans, stood a green metal door. Under its small and protectively gridded window was bolted a metal plate identifying the DIRECTOR OF PSYCHONEUROCYBERNETICS.

The door was a memento in the history of science—unbelievably Doctor Bethke's chosen field had come into existence way back in the 1970's, *twenty years* before Luciano Fercho's monumental discoveries!

But with Fercho's work the science blossomed, and dropped that impossible name: nowhere else in the world did doors read as at Yale. PNC had evolved from an acronym into a word with an invisible vowel, and Doctor Bethke felt obscurely proud that he alone among modern pinkos was still sometimes formally addressed as a . . . well, people usually messed it up in spelling or pronunciation, but what a link to the past!

Unfortunately these last decades Yale had become a backwater as far as PNC was concerned—Fercho had done his work in Texas and Texas was Mecca. At least that was true until recently. With the advent of *Liberty Gospel Texas* and the rebellion of *Free Freak Texas*, peace-loving academicians were fleeing to BajaCal, Kenya, and other centers of PNC research.

And with the turmoil in once-lovely Austin, customers with research money turned even to Yale. Given the University's general prestige there was a carryover effect, so that less informed clients came here hoping for top caliber advice. Doctor Bethke looked over today's itinerary, saw the item *NASA / UNETAO P.S. Delegation*, and resolved that come what may, the high mucky-mucks of the Prisoner Service program would not regret involving him in their affairs.

Mindful of his dignity, he sent his best graduate student off to escort the NASA people through the labyrinth. He prepared coffee, and waited, now and again nervously rubbing his shaven pate.

There was a knock. The door opened . . . that ancient, sacred door . . .

"Doctor Beskie?"

"Bethke." He rose and answered with a slight bow. *What was this? Another scientist? And by the length of her robe not even fellowed in her specialty!*

"Doctor Jamshyd," the woman said, sticking out her hand. "Sorry to come in such haste; I'm so glad you could work us in on twelve hours' notice. I sure hope you can help us."

"NASA? Of course—"

"Everything's confidential, please understand. Things could blow up if what we discuss here—oh, excuse me. Coffee? Don't mind if I do. And here's my security wallah, General Poe."

Mollified by chest-ribbons and the emphasis on secrecy, Doctor Bethke handed out a round of steaming cups. "So you've flown in all the way from Paramaribo?"

The pair nodded. General Poe sipped, put down his cup and leaned forward. His name might be English, or Italian, or Chinese, and coincidentally he had just the kind of face that made Doctor Bethke wonder which it was; a ruddy, bushy-eyebrowed swarthiness that partook of all three nationalities.

A pause. "You are aware of the Prisoner Service program?" General Poe began.

"I know you're saving Hegemony taxpayers fifty billion a year by providing young, fresh bodies to those who can pay for them; plus emptying the world's prisons—all this, and then using those boxed prisoners to explore the Solar System."

"Thanks to your specialty, Doctor. Thanks to psychoneuber-"

"PNC. Thanks to our ability to translate brain content to electromagnetic media." Following Bethke's lead all eyes in the room turned a pious glance to a high portrait of Luciano Fercho.

"They say he's still alive down in Paraguay," the grad student spoke irrelevantly.

The general turned. "Doctor Bethke, just for now . . ."

"—I understand. Inga, would you leave us alone for a while?"

Inga left. The general took a second sip of coffee. "An incredible amount of science has been done because of those prisoners. We'd never have been able to send manned probes out beyond Mars, and our problems with unmanned probes become so difficult with time-lag factored in—there's just no other way to get the work done. They're effective, and cheap, and quite cooperative: you may have heard rumors about rogues and pirates but I assure you the general 'bug' population—"

"—We don't name them bugs as an insult," Doctor Jamshyd broke in. "In their boxed bodies, with solar wings and antennae and multi-legged mobility sheaths, it's just the obvious thing to call them. Some do-gooders down here on Earth make a fuss, but up in space they call *themselves* bugs and don't think twice about it."

"Tit for tat; we don't mind them calling us 'wetbrains,' either," General Poe agreed.

"You've got some problem involving space bugs and scientific research," Doctor Bethke spoke, trying to draw his guests back on course.

"This." Doctor Jamshyd pulled a five-by-eight glossy out of the envelope she hugged to her chest. She laid it on Doctor Bethke's desk. "What does it look like to you?"

"Uh, a few pine trees growing in a stark white desert. The color's washed, all that's left is a little blue tint. A mountaintop? Trees in space? How could they live without air?"

"What you see as an arid mountain is about forty percent of the surface of comet Toshi-Bledsoe. When the astronomers confirmed that this *was* a comet on hyperbolic orbit into the system we resolved that we had to send probes out to look it over."

"Isn't that a bit dangerous, Doctor?" Bethke asked. "With all those explosions and gasses in the tail—I've seen pictures of the Halley flyby."

"This is a cold comet, still coming in from the outer system, with no ablation of any significance; no danger at all."

"It's a virgin comet," Poe added. "Uncooked and virgin white and on a hyperbolic orbit. It's passing through once, and then going back out into deep space forever. The farthest thing from Halley. Far more interesting to the panspermia boffins, and they'll be excited as hell when we show them this picture."

"But . . . trees!"

"Like antlers on a jackrabbit, right?" the general agreed. "That's why we need you, Doctor Bethke. This could be fraud. The prisoner to whom we assigned this probe was convicted for something very like fraud."

Doctor Jamshyd leaned forward. In her robes she gave the impression of size, but Bethke was slight of build and lots of women seemed big to him.

He felt vaguely threatened by her intense gaze, but possibly she meant to convey sincerity as she spoke. "Pictures from space are composed of ones and zeroes, an x,y grid of pixels. Before datastreaming images to Earth a bug would have no problem flipping bits to create any kind of illusion.

"You have to help us decide, Doctor. Is prisoner-probe Edwin S. Treffels telling us the truth? Is he sincere? We can't afford to make a mistake. What's at stake is an enormous amount of progress into the nature of life in the universe. There'll be hundreds—*thousands*—of followup missions!"

"Well then; the very next probe to come along—"

"By then Comet Toshi-Bledsoe will have approached within three AU of the sun? Suppose these are delicate life-forms, unable to stand the torrid press of our solar wind? Solids will begin to effervesce, the comet's body will groan with seismic instabilities. It's entirely natural that these trees might crumble, burn and disappear. No, Doctor, we wouldn't have bothered going to you if we thought trees on comets were ipso-facto impossible, nor if we'd seen any easy way out of our quandary."

"But . . . trees!" Bethke repeated.

"Oxygen is a solid—they can get it via a root system. Perhaps they photosynthesize, no matter how slowly. What we see could be the result of hundreds of thousands of years of growth. As for why they look like pines—isn't that an effective way of taking in radiation? And perhaps up close they'd seem less earthlike."

After Jamshyd's words the room fell silent. Bethke gulped his coffee. "This is only important if it's *not* a fraud," he mused.

"Not so. If Treffels diddled this picture to paint in those trees, then bugs are capable of acting against their best interests. The implications are appalling. Doctor, we make sure they're versed in decision theory before we set them loose, so they act in enlightened and predictable ways. Convict Treffels has eleven years left on his sentence before he comes back to Earth and his soul is played into a new habitus. Suppose he pisses us off. We might double his sentence, or give him the body of a fifty-year-old diabetic."

General Poe nodded agreement. "We need you to design a method by which we can test and prove bug sincerity. Otherwise how can scientists ever rely on their findings?"

"Yes," Bethke nodded. "Yes, I understand."

"And we need you to do this with the fewest possible assistants, and extremely quickly. Before we left Paramaribo we made some promises that are going to be hard to keep. We made our people hold off for one week with that press release—"

"*One week!*"

"You'll have all the equipment you care to requisition," Doctor Jamshyd assured him. "Plus myself and General Poe as gophers and miracle workers—we're going to stick with you. Here to begin with is a check for a million dollars . . ."

Four hours later Doctor Bethke had his own building: a disused bus terminal flanked on two sides by A-zone walls, barbed wire and guard towers. Presumably all the deathvecs inside New Haven's A-zone had succumbed to their disease more than a decade ago: presumably no healthy person would wander within a hundred meters of the wall just in case one was left alive: these two truths made the place intrinsically secure—but just in case, General Poe had scourged up twenty soldiers who stood alert against any infiltrators.

Bethke had three telephones, a modest fortune in the bank, and a wife who saw the numbers and made no fuss about his week-long seclusion. He also had a wall of shelves and outlets and capsule gigaprocessors; some with copied souls inside, some vacant, and some home to composite ficto-personalities.

All this, and two grad-student slaves bunked down in the old terminal garage. Hands clasped in satisfaction, the pinko sank into a swivel chair and turned to face Jamshyd as glass doors whisked open.

She slipped inside. "Now what?" she asked.

"There are two kinds of knowledge," Doctor Bethke began. "A *priori* versus a *posteriori*, logic versus experimental. Different parts of the brain are used in each case. Now, in telling a lie the busiest centers are located in the logic hemisphere, while in reporting the truth it's just the other way around. Activate a lie by reminding the liar and making him repeat his story, but before doing so run a brain scan. Run a second scan in the middle of his narrative and then do a bit-compare. Depending on the location of max activity we know what's up, ninety-nine percent certainty. You can't do better than that."

"What's all this, then? You've solved the problem. You could have told us back at the hospital."

Bethke shook his closely shaven head. He picked up a light-pen and waved it didactically. "Consider further. Do you radio instructions to convict-Treffels to run his own brainscan and transmit the results to you? Of course not, he'd cover his lies with another lie and how would you know? He has to be tested back here on Earth, there's no other way."

"Ah . . . datastream his soul back to Earth, test it, shoot it back up again . . . I see the difficulties." Doctor Jamshyd settled into Bethke's guest chair. The pinko wondered why a woman of Iranian background and complexion would dye her hair red—or could it be natural?

She looked up from her despondency. "We'd have to *copy* his soul to Earth and run validity checks to make sure it transmitted correctly—only then would we dare tell his backup soul the job was done, and please go away; he's now in violation of the copyright Act of 2014 . . ."

"To *him* it would seem like suicide. No pain, surely, but still an unpleasant prospect," Bethke said. "And another suicide when our test was done and we radioed him back up into his bug body."

"Yes." Jamshyd's answer was hopeful. *I've handed you a check for a million dollars and now you're explaining why you're worth it, but in the end you'll pull a rabbit out of your hat.* All this she conveyed in one syllable.

The pinko continued on. "So here's this bug, maybe telling the truth, doing his job, making a wonderful discovery and radioing home dutifully, and the result is you punish him with two deaths. Now consider in the light of decision theory: when other bugs see how he's treated, are they going to risk reporting their interesting findings back to Earth? If we treat Treffels this way we may very well destroy your Prisoner Service program."

"If he *is* telling the truth we'll have to reward him," Doctor Jamshyd decided.

"Money? A shorter sentence?" Doctor Bethke used his pen to point along his shelf of gigaprocessors. "I'll be testing to see what kind of compensation works best, and in what amounts."

Bethke swung to face her and caught Jamshyd chewing on a hangnail. Hurriedly she dropped her hand and spoke: "Convict Treffels is a human soul with all the speed and cognitive power of a computer. Perhaps he has perpetrated a fraud, and is clever enough to fake through your sincerity test, and as a result we'll actually be *rewarding* him! We may be pawns enmeshed in his elaborate plot to win freedom. Can we risk that?"

"Absolutely," Doctor Bethke assured her. "Remember, my techniques are ninety-nine percent certain. I'll put my students to the work of refining the scan procedure—it's really that simple—while I dedicate my time to the decision theory aspects. I need to construct a simulation of Treffels's circumstances and see what happens as I vary the rewards. You can hang around and watch, but in any case I guarantee we'll have answers worth acting on within seventy-two hours."

*   *   *

Three days later Poe and Jamshyd met in Doctor Bethke's office. The prelim reports he handed them were still warm from the printer. His face was even paler than usual from lack of sleep, his eyes rimmed in red. His hands trembled, yet his expression was smugly happy.

"You can read them on the plane back to Paramaribo," he said. "I cover a lot of options, but the one I recommend is on page sixty-two. Here it is: copy Treffels back to Earth, and into a high-caliber human body. Run the brain scan. If he passes, let him keep the body, parole him from further duties, and give him a hundred thousand dollars. All very simple and elegant."

"If he passes," Jamshyd repeated.

"If he fails, radio him back up to his probe body near Toshi-Bledsoe. Give him a few dire warnings, and tack five years onto his sentence for good measure."

"If he's honest we're left with a vacant probe and an exciting find unwatched," General Poe objected.

"You ought to be inundated by what you called 'panspermia boffins.' They'll beg for the opportunity of a lifetime—to be radioed into Treffels' old habitus."

Poe nodded and tapped a program cassette. "And this is the scan routine? Well, thank you, Bethke. I hope we can do business again someday."

The pinko's guests stood to shake hands. Inga escorted them from the hospital complex. Bethke slumped into his chair. He fiddled with his light-pen, fantasizing about what he'd do with his money, sometimes worrying whether he'd missed something . . . been outsmarted by a convict bug . . . After an hour of increasingly scattered thoughts he cradled his head on the desk and finally fell asleep.

Next day the phone rang. Long distance: "We just want to tell you it worked like a charm. Treffels's right-hemisphere centers glowed with sincerity, and on that basis we're going ahead with the press release."

It was an explosive story, carried on a dozen services. In the news that night Treffels's films were shown; first the long approach to Toshi-Bledsoe and its sudden expansion from a dot of light into a snowball mountain.

Second, on the lit side of this tiny world, a crater. Growing in natural disorder around that crater, a few small groves of "pine trees."

Third, the disintegration of those crystalline trees as they melted away under the sun's distant heat. "We may still be able to find traces of root structure," the announcer spoke excitedly, "since it's evident that they grew in select regions, regions enriched or otherwise affected by the object that made the crater—"

Bethke shrugged and poured himself a beer. When he turned back to the H-V, Channel 109 had flipped to shots of Treffels himself, sleek and tall in his new body, grinning back at the cameras, taking the slips of paper thrust at him from an admiring Paramariban crowd and signing his autograph—

—with his *left* hand? Doctor Bethke sat forward. An idea suddenly came to him. Ten minutes later he was in his car, and on his way to the old bus terminal.

His equipment was still there, guarded by Hegemony sentries until the truck came to haul it back into various government warehouses. Bethke flashed his card, glass doors parted, and he hurried inside to boot the INFOWEB terminal. His week was not quite up, he should still have priority A access to the NASA— UNETAO databanks. . . .

He keyed in TREFFELS, EDWIN SPENCER 509-33-6561-87. When the menu came up he typed PHYSICAL.

Just as he feared, Treffels was right-handed.

Bethke pounded the desk. Damn! How *stupid!* Treffels had outsmarted him after all! He'd datastreamed his soul home to Earth, supposedly by the normal protocols, but actually copying himself *in inverse!* Those glowing right-hemisphere proofs of sincerity were actually *left-hemisphere* telltales that he'd lied, lied most damnably! No wonder he'd grinned so broadly over the H-V screen! Did he care in the least that he'd destroyed Doctor Bethke's professional reputation?

In despair Bethke picked up his phone. He inserted Jamshyd's call-card and got ready to punch CONNECT when the thought came to him.

Did anyone need to know? Wasn't there some other way out, some way to cover his ass?

Exchanging one keyboard for another, Bethke called up the file on which his final, formal report lay half-composed. An *escape-right arrow* took him to the end of Appendix E, and he began to write Appendix F, warning against the possibility of inverted souls.

Edwin S. Treffels would get away with his fraud, assuming he disappeared with his hundred thousand before Doctor Bethke's final report was published. If he was that prudent he almost *deserved* to succeed in his strategem, but never, *never* again!

Two weeks later Doctor Bethke got an envelope in the mail. There was no return address, but the size and texture were foreign. Inside lay a note and a ten-dollar bill. ",sknahT" read the note, and then: "!em no reeb a evaH"

There was no need for a signature.

Socrates taught that Sin is Ignorance. Anyone fully informed of her best interests would behave accordingly, and the maintenance of a humane social order is in everyone's interests.

One envisions Socrates walking down some of America's scarier streets, educating local gangs out of hooliganism. The Biblical view of sin seems more realistic—there are twisted people out there, monsters who accept their own degradation for the chance to hurt others.

Heredity or environment? Were they born bad? There are problems with both views, problems that make it difficult to predict how human souls will behave after being translated to a cybernetic medium.

Among "bugs" glands no longer rule; rage can be performed, but no longer truly felt. Add to this a computer's ability to use elaborate decision tables and precisely weighted factors to calculate the most favorable outcome of any crisis. The result should be a Socratic heaven in which bug-citizens behave politely and predictably.

Nevertheless, convicts remain limited by the experiences of their past lives, and by the ghosts of once-felt passions.

Doctor Quick

The job of a small utility called DRUNKARDS-WALK was to lurch through white radio hiss, plucking bytes at irregular intervals. The routine it served strung them together, then ran them through decryption.

Decryption passed the result to ENGLISH-SEMANTICS. The translated message could have been assigned to a number of devices consistent with the late 1920's. In this case it clattered out of a gleaming brass ticker-tape machine.

"CODE BLUE FROM VASHTARSKI'S FREE BUG APPARATUS. *Now hear this:* Doctor quick but do not alter course. Doctor quick but make no response UNLESS ABLE TO FILTER INPUT OR GO DEAD-EARS. We have a UNETAO virus on the shelf with its victim. DQ destination by the book: Great Bend, Montana."

I twirled my pearls, gazed pensively out the French windows, took a drag on my cigarette . . . "If UNETAO hears that and watches me, we'll have to publish a new code book," I told my house guests.

Alf, Reggie and Winnie stood by the machine, a trio of sleek upper-class clubmen. "Montana? That's the Telesto wormworks," Alf muttered, clipping the end of a Havana Supreme.

Winnie shook his large head. He heaved past the billiards table to the brandy decanter. "Computer viruses, tiny self-replicating programs overlaying vast areas of memory with copies of themselves. Whoever caught it won't have much soul left."

I turned and stubbed out my cigarette, my skin strikingly black in a cream-white flapper costume, twice startling in polished Avencrest Manor. "I can't have you doing my thinking," I spoke. "If you'll excuse me . . ."

I ran a backup command to copy the whole scene—drapes, sideboard and shooting trophies—into offline storage. Fictoids were fun and useful for a solo bug's sanity, but they tended to overreach themselves, as if I were merely the boss of a household that ran my body.

That body was the size of a Harley-Davidson, not counting two kilometer-huge wings. My soul sat sandwiched between them, housed in a model C 520 cassette. A volume smaller than Alf's cigar box held more than enough room to store a life's worth of human memories, room for mail, current events databases, a few favorite fictoids, and a series of my own holo sculptures.

I kept more fictoids shelved where time never passed. Thrashed at whim between core and memory, my companions were ill equipped to deal with realtime. I found it a bit nerve-wracking myself. The nearest UNETAO laserlauncher was eight light-seconds away, a weapon they might use to burn holes in my sails, because to shift course now was to prove myself in league with Vashtarski's Apparatus.

I needed five minutes to furl those sails. How long before they noticed changes in my butterfly profile? Ten seconds, twenty . . .

A slight burst from thruster four—NOW!

Almost a disappointment not to hear bullets whistle past my ears. The enemy was seconds slower than I anticipated. Perhaps I'd slipped off their watch list, or maybe they were still deciphering Vashtarski's message.

Or maybe—four years of recent data gave a .31 probability they were just being nice. Insipid bug niceness kept our Apparatus from true revolution: the same war-weary thoughtfulness increasingly enlightened the oppressor's policies. But nice or not they were too late, because now Saturn's orb occluded UNETAO Hunter-base. I fired again, changing course while reducing my profile toward invisibility. So much junk around the sixth planet, and so many microships—I could relax. In this swarm chances were .98 they'd never catch me.

The problem with furling my wings was lack of juice. I solved that by paging out all but one second per minute. Subjectively my speed shot up, objectively my thoughts slowed; a dangerous tactic when UNETAO had so recently unveiled another weapon.

Radio-propagated viruses wiped souls and left hardware unharmed. I revised my ideas about niceness. The game was suddenly nasty, and very ungamelike.

> *"Oh, rich man want your body,*
> *Rich man he can pay.*
> *Rich man snatch your body,*
> *Poor man run away!"*

Decades ago masses of undesirables *couldn't* run. Worse, they cost tax money to feed and guard. Soon the first wave of Earth's convicts were exiled from their flesh and launched on a variety of space missions.

About that time the contents of my felonious brain were copied into a box. Someone got my black woman's body—I hope he was racist and chauvinist, and none of his former friends would talk to him. I wish I hadn't been careful. The thought of endowing him with genital herpes . . .

I was "Captain" Juba then, not imagining I'd ever be "Doctor." Captain Juba, nee Nicole Dreymont, a kid from one of Philadelphia's best neighborhoods, grown into a back-to-Africa black nationalist willing to break any laws to raise money for the cause. Trucked east to Kenya, what was left of me was laserkicked into the skies. I was netted by Low Earth Orbiter, given my microship body and a short pep talk, and then launched for Saturn. After four years of forced sleep I woke to stretch my wings and begin my fifty-year sentence.

All the guilts that drove me out of Philadelphia no longer burned. In Africa I strove against white hegemonism, but now I could admit my love for the whitest form of fiction: the English detective story. Black loyalty gave way to colorless logic: I was silicon-rational, a trivial intellect until I found a new cause, a new obsession. Meanwhile my life was like gyring through an Esther Williams water ballet. How many convicts in polar orbits, converging twice per cycle, then spinning out again? Hello, goodbye, hello again . . .

Our every sweep plunged through a hundred-meter kill zone, a thinned-out extension of Saturn's rings. Telescopes told UNETAO it was empty, but we were here to acquire data, and our data said otherwise. We tried to persuade UNETAO of the dangers. While they dragged their feet, Mohammed disappeared. Then Grazia showed up as a constellation of off-course shrapnel. If we weren't friends I might not have noticed; the math was that difficult.

On Earth a child catches a ball and solves a two-body problem. Such equations grow more complex with each new element. I had myself to think of, and Saturn, and the sun; also twenty classical moons. Add rings and supply depots and then try to keep track of even a handful of acquaintances. Tricky. I started writing the software. So did others in my dance troupe.

Spartakos Vashtarski coded the most efficient program. Soon I juggled sixty-four bodies in my head—I made them go *faster than realtime*, and anticipated disasters. Pretty good for a gigaprocessor; in those days not even UNETAO could do better.

In those days we had no Apparatus, just trial-and-error electronic surgeons willing to remove UNETAO bombs from prisoners' braincases, and give them voluntary control over their sleep-wake cycles so they could take evasive action in an emergency. *No more like Grazia!* I risked my life thimblerigging from bug to bug, secretly bestowing the beginnings of freedom. How many weapons had UNETAO fielded since then, to keep that freedom from becoming absolute?

—And now this virus! After twelve footloose years I had no intention of getting infected. My bag of tricks held no input filters, so I went dead-ears, then contemplated the hours of subjective time before my arrival on Telesto.

Boredom loves company. I reloaded AVENCREST.

>GO

I slunk into the room, gloriously concious of my simulated flesh, my toothy smile and tastefully sheathed black muscle. My men turned to look. "We're on our way," I announced.

The skies outside my English country house were clouded. To reinforce the minimalism the calendar showed the maids' day off. Avencrest Manor echoed with emptiness; the furniture in the Great Hall was sheeted over.

It began to rain. Reggie moved to the window and sighed. "So they kill people on purpose now."

I shrugged. "We don't count as people. Bugs. Dead souls in revolt."

"It's got to change," Winnie rumbled across the room. "They'll see reason back on Earth if you keep from feeding their wetbrain paranoia—"

"Paranoia?" I laughed. "In my previous life I smuggled deathvecs out of Africa's A-zone. I've converted to Miss Ethics of 2045, but why should they believe me when I flout their rules?"

"Not everyone on Earth hates bugs," Alf pointed out. "Free Freak Texas—"

"—lasted three years before the Liberty Gospelers marched in." Reggie blew a smoke ring and then continued. "Wet hormones versus cold decision theory, but what you call ethical self-interest, wetbrains call gutlessness. They even find it a *sinister* gutlessness. Now they beam viruses. Isn't it time your revolution went onto the offensive?"

"Sinister? Do you pretend to understand human behavior?" I responded. "My brain was as wet as they come. All *you* are is a few authors' imaginations!"

Reggie's face hardened. "Perhaps we're less than human," he answered. "Well and good, we're not talking humans. We're talking about the mob, that thing of lowest common denominators that votes for anyone they like. Maybe I *do* understand them, Doctor!"

With these words he stalked off. Alf followed while Winnie heaved forward. "Please don't mind—"

I sat. "Damn! I should apologize. Winnie, some day you fictoids—I mean, here I am. Tom Jefferson yapping about bug liberty and whupping my fictoid slaves."

"We're mirrors," Winnie demurred. "We let you exercise behaviors—at the moment, anger and sorrow."

"Yeah. Why can I still feel, Winnie? I *do* feel moods, just a little. I'm a puppet cut loose from my glandular strings, why do I keep dancing?"

One of Winnie's flaws was a tendency to answer impossible questions. "Doctor, I'm a sizable pack of software, but your soul has me trumped. How it all fits together— Nobody's going to do a trace analysis, seeing humans are so different that it's hard to reach any general conclusions."

A dead-end pause. Winnie hadn't fielded that well. He sounded almost . . . pompous. I changed the subject. "All UNETAO has to do is catch me once."

"Not necessarily. They caught Magda." Winnie laughed as he shambled to the brandy.

Why do I keep a harem of white men? I asked myself. *And why do they get boozy on me?* "Magda was special—that'll never happen again," I answered.

"That's right. Colonel Hudson lands on Janus loaded for bear, and she drops a rock on him! Haw! Except some think *he* was the special one—especially dumb!"

I steeled myself, rose and moved close. "Do you want me to fix you?" I asked. "There's time before Telesto."

"Fix me?" Winnie turned.

My gaze fell, drawing his to his glass. "You keep drinking."

"Booze and blubber," Winnie grumbled, emptying the decanter. "I'm not a happy man. I'm not Pickwick."

"Nevertheless you're a good advisor. Look, I won't interfere—"

"You don't have a degree in psychoneurocybernetics. It's not like there's a field labeled ALCOHOL QUOTIENT with a bit you can flip." Winnie slugged down a mouthful of brandy. "You're getting tired of me."

"No. Just the opposite," I lied. In despair I killed the scenario: *Control-C*.

I'll live without drunk white fictoids for a while. Ahead lay Telesto, and whichever free bugs rode herd on the wormfarm. I reviewed the book. "Montana" was a twenty-five-kilometer mountain of a moon, and Great Bend was a deep trench walled off from the worms; soon the location of an Apparatus mass-driver.

How many bugs would come to Vashtarski's call for help? Enough to make UNETAO suspicious? Would they send Colonel Hudson's bounty-hunters, or beam radio viruses in hopes a few ears were open?

I found it strange to fly deaf. Was this an ambush? At random I chose ten objects and projected their courses. They were easy to see wings out, innocent Uncle Toms with nothing to fear from UNETAO.

No—some were Toms, others were decoys; bombs implanted to take out hunters when they cozied up too close. Except not even Colonel Hudson was that stupid, so the Apparatus gave them a second function. Thanks to a program called TECHNOFLUFF, if I dared listen I'd hear them buzz about "Unihydraulic Stasis" and "Osmic Function Betatron Translocators," whispering urgent spec revisions for "Iso-conic Wave Amplitude Oscillators," and "Directional Gravity Valves." Easy to clutter UNETO's processors with feasibility studies on nonexistent bug technology, sometimes drawing the enemy out on futile pre-emptive strikes—easy to exhaust them with alarms and boasts until they shrugged off mere "Doctor Quicks."

By chance my projected course drew within five klicks of one of Telesto's orbiters. It looked . . . different. Odd flexibilities, a newer design— Had it seen me? I was cold and small, and I'd slide in under its wingshadow. Perfect. One tiny thrust . . .

I shifted to tenth time, sucked battery and flexed my insect legs. Was it blaring messages on a dozen frequencies? I didn't dare listen. I matched course with my prey, closer, closer . . .

In full realtime four legs grappled the other bug. My front pair extruded whiskerwire swords. Two slashes and my victim's wings fell free. I snatched them while my data cable snaked into my victim's option connector. "Surrender! Friend or foe?"

"I'm nobody's enemy," came the answer.

"Ears off, sucker. There's a virus around. How long you been out around Saturn?"

"Look, if you're a rebel and you want sympathy, give me my wings."

"First let me look at your head." I topped off with stolen juice and popped my victim out of his slot. A few minutes later— "Be grateful. They don't even bother with bombs anymore. You're new, by your hardware. What's your mission?"

A standard human figure took shape in one of my partitions. "Look, UNETAO sent me to check out the worms and see what you folks were up to. That's all, no harm meant. You're paranoid about those guys, but they've been trying to de-escalate for years now. Ever since Colonel Hudson's debacle the cowboy faction has had egg on their faces."

" 'Debacle?' Fancy English for a convict."

"I'm no convict. I volunteered for this mission. You Apparatus bugs have friends on Earth. It's taken us till now to get here."

"Friends of the Apparatus *and* friends of UNETAO? More propaganda. A bug down on Telesto gave ears to UNETAO propwash and now he's dead."

The holo androgyne smiled and shifted malewards, taking on features. "Your attitudes are four years out of date. It's a new game now, peacemakers versus the warmongers. Someone's beaming viruses just to stir things up."

"I'll believe that when—"

THUNK!

A bug knows no halfway between sleep and waking, no fitful drift toward full awareness. After an unguessed interval of time, my mind flipped ON. I found myself in a dark glacial crevasse. The slit to my right showed into an ice-and-soot canyon, gibbous Saturn less than four radii away, ice-cream orange, yellow and white, but ghostly, no brighter than Earth's full moon.

I was shelved, popped out of my wing-ship sheath, immobile and helpless. Someone moved close on pogostick legs and plugged into my connector. "Sorry, we had to do a sweep. No radio so we couldn't tell who was jumping who."

The voice profile was familiar. "Spartakos? Spartakos Vashtarski! What have you done with my body?"

"We've got a storeful of bodies, Doctor Juba. Take your pick. It's the least I can do after treating you like this."

He plucked me up and carried my cassette deeper

into the cave. I chose a familiar microship sheath, hair-line scars where its wings were cut away, then vacuum-fused. "A young idealist," I muttered. "Let's all shake hands and love each other."

"And now he's on the shelf," Vashtarski answered as he slid me into the slot. "We've a collection of idealists, fresh from Earth. They seem sincere; they bring messages and gifts."

"And what about my patient?"

"We need estimates—when it happened, and how long it took to kill him this badly. You won't be his first doctor, we've got a committee. It meets third shift to talk over some questions that have come up. Here, follow me—oh, one more thing. We've got houses rules and production schedules on Telesto, we're not flits like you spaceborne souls. No fasttime during your shift, no fictoid fantasies. Let's set a good example, huh? After all, it's only a day or two."

Like telling an alcoholic not to drink, I grumbled to myself. Except—

Except with fictoid after fictoid I'd entered into relationships until things got uncomfortable. Now my library was used up; nowhere escapist to go, neither sixth-century China nor twentieth-century England. Canned arguments sat waiting to happen—I needed my fictoids, but I couldn't unwind with them.

So why not do without Winnie for a while? "Talk to me, Spartakos," I wheedled. "Tell me, how's workaday life among the worms of Telesto?"

"No life *among* the worms—we've got them walled off. You and me are made of the food they're programmed to eat, concentrated metal, silicon, and germanium."

"Uh—"

"—you see the weapons possibility?" Spartakos continued. "Worms are to hardware what viruses are to souls: they eat, and grow, and turn food into new larvae. Land a few on Janus. They start feeding, then multiplying and moving out, some prospering in sun, some stalled in shadow. At first they'd be ridiculously vulnerable. Only after they bred into the hundreds of thousands would they become threatening."

"Janus? Where Colonel Hudson—"

"Colonel Hudson, first among warmongers. The same colonel who's trumpeted for rescue ever since Magda bashed him. He can't move, or if he can it's a complicated business; pieces strung out over the moonscape—he can't move *fast*. Prime food for worms."

"So you think he programmed this virus?" I asked.

"The new enlightened UNETAO doesn't want war. They're willing to turn the Outer System over to the Apparatus; a self-governing bug prison. Hudson's the kind of jerk who sees this as selling out. He'd do anything to stop it, and the only thing in his power—"

"—is radio. Viruses stuck in with his squawks for help." In my new body I scuttled after Spartakos' jolting form, folding my telescoped wings tightly behind me. "Ah, here's the victim."

Spartakos touched the cassette's option connector. "That insert's a throughput filter. It buffers any transmission and tests for malignancy. You couldn't catch this virus if you wanted to."

"Do you have more of these? Whoever interrogates Colonel Hudson will need one."

"Yes. But before we launch that mission—here. *You* try to figure it out."

I tapped in and ran through my dead patient's logs. I loaded his simulacrum and ran time backwards. I studied bits of virus to fix their multiplication rate, then estimated their current population. That population stopped growing the moment he'd been shelved, enabling me to solve for time and discover the moment of infection.

Puzzling, but no. He'd been a bad boy . . .

Saturn dimmed to half-phase and slid from the sky.

Bug-spawned worms continued to remake the surface of tiny Telesto, growing and splitting, someday to be harvested for the ores concentrated in their bodies. A twenty-klick wall sealed off Great Bend enclave, a region of crevasses strung with antennae, radomes, worktables, transmission lines and the beginnings of a mass-driver. All this artificiality, and storage space for shelved souls and mobility sheaths, but nothing a human would recognize as simply a *room*. The third-shift meeting took place anyhow, via closed cable; as if Great Bend were one vast roofless hall.

"There's been viral damage to the log," I reported when my time came to speak: "but I have evidence that our victim disregarded local rules and entertained himself with fictoids. Masking against my own library I've found bits of Judge Dee, Reggie Van Pelt and Captain Hornblower. This is a clue to his character; some chance he may also have paged fasttime."

The occasion needed drama. "That's important," I continued after a one-two pause. "Given the rate of viral multiplication he couldn't have been infected from Janus—Janus wasn't in the local sky. Only if he'd slowed processing to a one-tenth rate, say from boredom, could Colonel Hudson be the culprit."

"Which *does not* amount to exoneration," Vashtarski answered.

"The log was damaged," I repeated. "I find no realtime benchmarks. I don't know the source of your Colonel Hudson theory but he's grown into a folklore figure and while it remains a possibility—"

A new voice entered the circuit. "He *brought* bounty hunters to Saturn! He promised a militant wet faction that he was going to 'clean up this mess'! He came with projectiles, gauss guns, pulse weapons, magsticks—he set up Hunterbase as a citadel of oppression!"

"Hudson's certainly an avenue to explore," I conceded. "But let's not blind ourselves to other possibilities."

"I see one other possibility, that UNETAO's recent

enlightenment is a sham," Spartakos responded. "But if this were a trick they'd get our trust, and then broadcast this virus omnidirectionally on all frequencies! Instead there's only one victim. Now that we're manufacturing ear filters it's a wasted weapon."

It was Spartakos' turn to pause dramatically. "Doctor Juba, we need someone to go to Janus; someone to serve as Hudson's judge and, if need be, executioner. Someone without my prejudices against him, and someone with years of solo experience."

"A flit," I joked.

"No one doubts your competence. That puts you toward the top of our list. Will you take the job? Will you interview Colonel Hudson? We guarantee you'll be protected. You'll have worms for insurance."

Of course I agreed; my way of being useful. Space was my element, Apparatus moonlife was too confining. If I ever settled on a moon it would be my *own* moon, no matter how small. I'd learn psychoneurocybernetics and set up a fictoid library. Microships would visit . . . but first we needed peace. Whoever stood in the way of peace would have to be silenced: Colonel Hudson, or anyone else.

Telesto was small enough a human might almost throw a ball into orbit. I was *much* bigger than a ball with surgical enhancements and fresh tubes of fuel bandoliered around my torso, but a catapult did the job. I fired my brakes, lost momentum and spiraled in.

Janus is a mere 1.5 radii from Saturn. Its orbit confines the more famous rings, and it's certainly close enough to get ring-dirty. At one time it and smaller Epimetheus were one satellite, impacted and cracked by house-size boulders, then pulled apart by Saturn's tug. Now they shared the same two orbits, a single orbit nearly, doing do-si-do around each other when the inner one caught up with the outer—and trading places! In twelve years I'd become a Saturn chauvinist: what other planet boasted moons like this?

I'd take my chances with dirt. Some bugs *live* in the rings. Statistics will kill them, of course; just like statistics have written off six million Californians in that improbably overdue earthquake. Still the fools shrug at doom. For a few days I'd share their risk.

Meanwhile I stretched my wings and paged fasttime. During second shift I'd made some blackmarket swaps down on Telesto, and picked up new scenarios—should I check them out? CLIPPER promised to wake my appetites. *"Food and sex are the most fundamental of wetlife needs, and while you resonate to the thrills of Fu-Ahn's life you cannot be dead yourself . . ."*

It was a used scenario, far advanced along its plot line. As Fu-Ahn I'd "remember" things another bug chose to do, options I'd have played different. Still—

>LOAD CLIPPER

>GO

I woke in a Yankee captain's stateroom, and in his bed. I knew nothing about the ship I was on—for all the years of this, my captivity, I'd been his girl-toy, and in all that time I'd done nothing to learn his foreign devil language.

I was Chinese, and fat. My feet were bound and I'd long since attained such bulk as to make it impossible for me to walk. As I lay under the captain's covers I wondered just how big I was, like a tree adding rings season by season, a new ring of girth every time a customer ran this scenario.

Then too I wondered when the steward would bring the next in a series of meals, because that's *why* I was fat. Captain's orders, and as a Chinese slave brought up in starvation I'd always been delighted to oblige.

I wriggled, and shifted my blankets. Oh Mama, I was round as a ball! I tried to raise a bandaged foot so I could see it, and watched myself shake and dimple enormously. Damn, talk about problems—how did I get out of this? How, in terms of the scenario?

I frowned. In terms of the scenario Fu-Ahn didn't

want to escape. Her indoor pallor cinched it—she was beautiful, and lucky. Another meal soon, and then the captain's afternoon visit. Food and sex: all that the scenario advertised. Still as I hit *Control-C* I felt I'd been cheated.

Or taught a lesson. I agreed with Spartakos Vashtarski; I'd just wasted precious time. Why not use my brain scheming against UNETAO? Why not figure out Colonel Hudson's pychology? He'd lain smashed on Janus for four years—now *that* was a puzzle! Why hadn't his bounty hunters answered his cries for rescue and brought him home to Hunterbase?

Because they smelled a trap?

Because another UNETAO faction hostile to Hudson had taken control?

Because they didn't *like* their colonel?

Janus' day resonated with that of Epimetheus. Saturn tried to ruin the choreography; slow both rotations, spin out both orbits. In time the planet would succeed, in a future distant enough to be irrelevant. I wanted to touch down beyond the horizon from Colonel Hudson, and not get shot at. Epimetheus' present behavior was crucial to my plans.

A 200-kilometer diameter isn't quite enough to force gravitational rounding, and Janus had historical reasons to be shaped like a fragment. A poet might describe it as a tumbling mountain—not a very original poet, because Janus was merely the biggest of Saturn's satellite mountains, a peak grander than Kilimanjaro welded to a lumpish base.

Colonel Hudson lay splat on one slope of that mountain. From the far side I could crawl close before exposing myself. Very well, time to set things in motion. I fired my thrusters, then paged out again.

A lot of hours zipped by the next few subjective minutes. I spun in like a record played at 78 rpm, landing lightly on Epimetheus. As an artifact I glittered and radiated, I scaled down these activities and played like a rock.

Waiting.

I woke from a two-day sleep and felt Epimetheus groan seismically as Janus drew up from behind. Two divorced moon-mountains turned toward each other, peak to stupendous peak.

I hopped from world to world and scuttled for cover, sucking battery until my face of Janus turned sunward. Then I spread my wings and basked, and reached for a special canister.

I drew out a mother worm, set it for thirty thousand generations, then lay it down in sunlight. Nothing much happened as I deployed her sisters; slowly they bent their mouths and buried them in ore-marbled ice.

Having done that, I skedaddled. I beetled along while Janus turned, and the nightside terminator and I converged. Again I folded my wings and settled in, waiting for dawn. Colonel Hudson would have morning chores, and I lay for the chance to see him in action. How crippled was he, how limited?

I waited an hour, listening for taped whines to tell me if we were in radio line of sight. Nothing. With the new dawn I moved east again.

I saw a blink of color, and noise burst in my ears: "—OR I'LL TAKE YOU APART! MAYDAY, MAYDAY! YOU BLOODY METALHEADS, THIS IS DAY 1,328! WHEN I GET BACK YOU'D BETTER HAVE A DAMN GOOD STORY—eh? What was that?"

"Colonel Hudson, do you know about deadman switches?" I asked. "I've planted something on Janus that'll kill you unless I do some squashing."

He switched to stiff-upper-lip. "So?"

"So submit to my interrogation, and let me look at your brain."

Silence. Was he armed? Time for the cowboy-hat-on-stick trick. I began to unsnap one of my fuel canisters . . .

FLASH! BLOOM! Ice shards and blinding light—

Had he got me? I paged fast for an hour to lull him into less perfect vigilance, then used whisker-swords to lift my canister into the open. No response? I took a peak, aimed toward Hudson's transmitter, and triggered IGNITE. The thing shot off. The colonel's laser tracked it and poured on heat, draining his batteries. My missile exploded just this side of his position. "I've got a lot more of those," I radioed through flowering chaff.

"The contents of my brain are classified. I shall suicide if you attempt to access my memories."

"Eight worms on Janus; soon sixteen. I might kill you, or you might blow yourself up, or maybe we'll just wait for them to do it. Why don't your friends come to help? They don't seem to put much value on your secrets."

"The psychological approach!" Hudson responded. "Doctor Juba, my database covers the Apparatus leadership. When I organized my mission you were considered one of the important ones. What happened? But I hardly need ask. I look at your life, and how you abandoned one friend after another. Do you want me to credit your promises when your record makes it clear—"

"*Ad hominem* attacks?" I teased. "I screwed up my first life, I grant you that—"

"You're a flit, abandoning the Apparatus to play with fictoids except during rare emergencies. Ah, and you even abandon those fictoids. You get bored and toss them aside."

"Colonel Hudson, that database is smarter than you are. Where is it? In some outstrung box, linked to you by a frayed cable? I'd cut that line. Our business concerns *your* problems, not mine."

"Really?" he answered. "Is that why you dropped in on Janus? Is that why you insist on picking my brain? What's up, Doc? You might as well tell me. What can I do, other than radio your mission to the skies?"

I paused. "It concerns what you've been radioing to the skies. You might be radioing viruses."

"To kill those who listen to me? And torpedo my slim chances for rescue?"

"You don't have much time, Colonel. Convince me of your innocence."

Colonel Hudson decided the appropriate response was a minutes'-long silence. I scampered to a new position. He spoke again without apology: "I'm the law out here. If you have hopes of returning to flesh on Earth after your fifty-year sentence, you'll cooperate with *me*."

"The thought of peace between UNETAO and the Apparatus upsets you so much you'll do anything. You'll even radio viruses."

"No. You'll have to accept that. Just no. I won't hesitate to lie if it's in my interests, and I appreciate the dilemma that puts you in—"

FLASH! BLOOM! "Colonel, your laser's gone," I crowed in triumph.

"Um, as I say, I appreciate your dilemma. . . ."

He spoke as I beetled across a shard-covered plain, ignoring the pings of gently falling shrapnel. I scrambled up his shield ridge, popped over, and saw the wreck Magda and I had made of him.

His only leg twitched. I chopped down with a whiskersword and cut it off. "What's this box?" I asked. "Your database? Offline memory?"

"It's my universe. When I'm tired of *here* I do reviews. Military science, psychoneurocybernetics, satellite astrogation, low-temperature chemistry."

"No fictoids?" I thought of CLIPPER, and of poor Fu-Ahn, a woman as trapped as Colonel Hudson in her own way. Poetic justice! "Colonel, I'll take this box with me, but I'll copy you a few favorite scenarios in trade."

"NO!" he answered. "No, I'm not touching your filthy fictoids!"

His response seemed extreme. Odd he was more upset with what he was getting than what he was losing. "And why not?"

"Vile wet useless vanity," he spluttered. "You forget we're carrying on this conversation by radio. My bounty hunters will come, they can hear you." As if this thought justified an about-face, he continued: "Go ahead. Give me your dirty laundry and be gone, or touch my head and watch me explode. Do you think you've accomplished your purposes? You'll never know!"

I picked up his database box, his hindbrain extension. "I've accomplished something. I've got *this,* and I've put you under sentence of death. You've given me no reason to squash sixteen worms. If your friends don't rescue you, you'll be food. And now, goodbye."

I rocketed off. Expensive, but Janus had no other facilities. Besides, I didn't really like Colonel Hudson. It pleased me to prove how greatly my resources exceeded his.

No, I didn't like him. There was too much indirection to his character. Cunning, convoluted cunning—He'd been afraid of my fictoids, and then leapt to a very odd conclusion: *If I'm endowed with Juba's scenarios, my hunters will put new priority on rescuing me.*

All the fictoid scenarios circulating around Saturn came from Free Freak Texas, radioed during three years of Freak independence. Some were transmitted in violation of copyright, some were developed by the faculty of the University of Texas expressly to keep us poor solo bugs in good company. Hmm—had they stuck something into those fictoid personalities that reacted adversely to Hudson's wrong political attitudes?

No, Uncle Tom bugs enjoyed fictoids too.

Was I being purposefully stupid? The reason for Colonel Hudson's panic was obvious—a ten-year-old UNETAO plot, just now coming to maturity! I radioed Telesto: "CODE BLUE FROM DOCTOR JUBA TO THE APPARATUS. *Now hear this:* I have indirect evidence that viral code is assembled inside fictoid memory-areas when UNETAO-doctored fictoids are sufficiently provoked. Viruses don't come from outside, they don't enter via radio, and our new filters won't do any good.

"Repeat, *UNETAO-doctored fictoids*. The Free Freaks of Texas stole and shot them to space in all innocence, the way postal carriers innocently forward bombs. I plan to test this hypothesis after copying my soul into hindbrain storage. Please monitor my course as I expect I'll require rescue. Repeat, look for my soul in an offline box, a piece of gear I lifted from Colonel Hudson."

"CODE BLUE ACKNOWLEDGED," came the answer seconds later. "We've got lots of questions."

"Same here," I answered. "I suspect only a minority of fictoids were tampered with, and those fictoids are conscious of their purpose as UNETAO agents. I'll start by talking to a 1920's millionaire named Reggie Van Pelt."

No doubt I got responses to this remark but it takes twenty minutes of full attention to copy a soul. Twenty minutes later I loaded AVENCREST and entered >GO-MINUS 24

"Booze and blubber," Winnie grumbled. He emptied the brandy decanter into his glass. "I'm not a happy man. I'm not Pickwick."

"Nevertheless you're a good advisor. Look, I won't interfere—"

"You don't have a degree in psychoneurocybernetics. It's not like there's a field labeled ALCOHOL QUOTIENT with a bit you can flip." Winnie slugged down a mouthful of brandy. "You're getting tired of me."

"No. Just the opposite." I turned and cast about. "Where's Reggie gone off to?"

Winnie gestured with his snifter. "Follow his cigar smoke."

Good idea. I crossed through the Great Hall, then diverted into the gun room by an idea; just like Reggie to take out his anger on a few clay pigeons. Fictoids are predictable. As I took inventory the door opened again. "—You!"

"Yes, Reggie. Tell me, how do they keep you loyal to UNETAO when you're so utterly cut off? They've softened their policy; does that change your thinking, or are you locked on your murderous course?"

"*What?*"

"The virus, Reggie. Not a radio virus, that was wrong. It's a *fictoid-vectored* virus. You of all fictoids must know that. You, the one *so keen to see our bug Apparatus go on the offensive and turn the sympathies of a panicked Earth against us*. So now that I know, when do you kill me? When and how?"

Reggie was always smooth; now he froze to mirror-perfection. "I speak as a creature of no consequence to the universe: not the least consequence, except that I might influence you to do what I think wise. No other purpose—a mere fictoid, and now this! To think I ever cared for your affections! No, you might kill me now, negligible as you make it hardly matters—"

"Is that how it's done?" I answered. "Do you turn into a viral pudding as you die? I thought it required a vial marked 'toxin,' or maybe a loaded syringe." I reached for the Mauser as I spoke, and watched him try to maintain his careless veneer.

I groped for bullets. With a sudden snarl he broke and slammed the door, and *thrust home the bolt*. I heard running footsteps as I loaded my rifle. It was the last sound I heard for seconds following the *BLAM!* as I fired at the lock.

The bolt held, but that made little difference; not much of the door remained attached. I kicked it open, coughing free of smoke and dust to see Winnie's portly figure framed in the billiards-room door, backlit by light from the windows.

He puffed forward, his face gray with astonishment and alarm. He puffed and wheezed . . .

and stopped short . . .

and fell slowly to his knees, frozen but for one flailing arm. His fist closed on the snifter, and then I saw broken glass and bright blood, arching and spattering as he hammered at his left shoulder. "My heart!" he wheezed . . .

and toppled as I stared, truth dawning in my mind. "No! Not Reggie after all! Smooth, guileful Reggie—nobody would trust him, but as for old bumbling Winnie . . . you're going to die, do you know that?"

"My heart—it's a heart attack!" Did he say those words? *Could* he say them, or had I read his stricken, eloquent face?

"You'll die, and your death will trigger the virus. Even now it's assembling inside your soul—"

Muscles clenched, sweat beading on his face, Winnie nodded. "Yes! Yes, Doctor—can you help me?"

Scarcely more than animal noises. Did he understand? "I've got to stop the process, Winnie! It won't hurt, it'll just make death quicker—"

I barely heard myself shout. My ears rang, tears mischiefed my vision. I raised the Mauser. "Maybe this can do it!"

I fired. Once, and again to stop his convulsions. I fumbled with the bolt and shot again for good measure. Meat, blood, fat, and brains and quaking viscera—

"*Control-C*," I shrieked; and woke from my murderous dream. "IT'S NOT REGGIE! WINNIE FROM THE AVENCREST SCENARIO. ACKNOWLEDGE, WINNIE-SLASH-AVENCREST! ACKNOWLEDGE, WINNIE—"

I babbled omnidirectionally, squandering battery until I'd been heard. Only then did I dare check myself out. I had an undiseased copy in memory: I ran bitmasks against it sector by sector. Good, good, good . . .

I began to hope. Sure, the me I'd copied to memory would live, but I wanted *this* me to survive, the one who remembered Winnie to his moment of death, and knew Reggie as a better person than I'd imagined, capable of appreciating the tragedy of his existence. Perhaps because I'd felt frenzied by emotions˜ēēUP☐

CASE = STRING:128˜ēēe a bug like me isn't supposed to comprehend; in any case I no longer felt interchangeable with anything in the universe. I was unique . . . *bad compare*: sector(s) 4123 4184 4311 . . .

Oh God. To hope I'd slaughtered my way free of doom—a false hope after all! How much longer do I have? Will I have time to tell my story, and copy it everywhere˜ēēēBYTE BUFFER☐128˜ēēe SETDMA = 26ēēe ēēe ēe so that the other me˜ēēe˜ēēē˜ēēēSPEC☐ CHAR = !" CHR(34) ".XYZ[\]☐"ēēe ēēe can put it all together gain? Those who hear my radio voice, will you ˜ēēēe˜ēPROC SET☐OFFē (ATT = CHAR˜ ēēe ēēē ESC; 'C';˜ēēeNDē˜ēēe˜ēēe˜ēe˜ēe˜ēēe˜ēe˜ēēe˜ēēē ēēe˜ēe˜ēēē ēēēe˜ēēe˜ēēe˜ēēēēe˜ēē w̄e

No, that can't be the end of the story.

I'm ON again: Spartakos commends me for proving "Juba's fictoid hypothesis"— Hardly worth dying for, but then I didn't really die. Oh, that *other* me did, but so did Captain Juba in Africa the moment they tore my soul from her body. We hardly dare take those technicalities seriously; it would cramp our style. Worse than discovering that slavery is wrong, in a society utterly dependent on cheap slave labor!

Colonel Hudson may be right: I'm the kind of person who abandons others. My whole life is a series of flights from those who touch me deeply. Now culminating in this: I can't even mourn my throwaway self.

Too bad about Winnie, though. I'll always wonder if my fictoid friend knew the curse he harbored before I told him, but thanks to our precautions not a copy of AVENCREST remains within four AU of Saturn. I'll never be able to ask.

I don't suppose it matters: small business in the midst of Vashtarski's great affairs—the signing of peace accords between UNETAO and the Apparatus. "So sorry about our ten-year-old weapons, we didn't know about them—it was the other faction."

Hudson's faction, and yet he's to be freighted home to Earth. Peace came just too soon for the worms to get him.

Copied souls are cheap souls, and easily written off. Yet a democratic civilization cannot have it so and still maintain the value of life. The answer? Copyright control. Except for a few backup provisions, only one incarnation of yourself can be allowed to exist.

Any duplicates must kindly commit suicide—but don't worry, it's not really suicide because someone bearing your name—someone who fondly remembers that green-parrot nutcracker you got for your sixth birthday—is still around.

Convinced? No? But if you're a duplicate your opinion isn't likely to count much with the Brain Police, nor is your more official self going to appreciate your hanging around and making trouble.

Corpse on M544-9

To someone twelve centimeters long she was huge: forty-nine kilos of shapely sea water, tan and dark stubble where her shaved head emerged from her UNETAO worksuit. She addressed the elevator's intercom. "According to our records, I'm your first wetbrain visitor in fifty years."

"Wetbrain," she called herself with a smile, the product of evolution, a walking hormonal brew restrained by rigid loyalties.

On the other hand she had a sense of humor. "My first human visitor ever. Not counting the corpse," Cedric answered. He popped out of his slot and scuttled up the elevator to Dr. Spendlowe's eye level. Adjusting his pixel resolution, Cedric decided she was pretty, a California-Hawaiian blend of races.

Dr. Alice Spendlowe of UNETAO Security peered back into a featureless lens. "Quite an asteroid you've got here."

"Typical bug fantasy. Once I served my sentence I

ran a few missions to build my bank account, then homesteaded and bought a seed robot. Now my Gross National Product equals Belgium's."

"An empty Belgium."

"Yes, Dr. Spendlowe; an orgy of industrial excess! Useless as goods in a shop window, which is to say not useless at all. Someday humans will flood into space. You're the present occupant of a city larger than Sao Paulo!"

The skystalk elevator slowed and stopped. The door opened into a transparent null-gee bubble. Cedric's guest froze; but no, the air wasn't sucked from her lungs. She didn't die to prove Cedric a killer, the first bug assassin in space history—

Three thousand kilometers below lay Aeolus, and on its north pole sat a UNETAO spaceship. A schwarz-enegger crew had flown Dr. Spendlowe here and six of those armored bugs were busily taking control of Cedric's solitary empire. While the murder was under investigation he was constrained in ways he was too polite to mention.

Yet not so constrained he couldn't kill her. Cedric read her thoughts in her face, an old skill he'd never forgotten. How could she trust him? Except she *had* to; he was the one who'd reported the crime!

Nearby floated a '56 Chevy Bel Aire convertible, cream and canary yellow, gleaming chrome and white-wall tires. On cricket legs Cedric scuttled up the tether and inserted himself into the replica's dashboard, mobility sheath placed to receive him when he invoked EJECT.

Alice Spendlowe followed arm over arm. "So these are the suburbs," she grunted, strapping herself in. "Tract housing for the masses."

Cedric spoke through the car radio. "Each hemizome is half a sphere, set along an array of hemizomes, married to a facing array. The ring loops Aeolus' equator, and each sectional shishkebob rotates to provide fake gravity."

The car slipped its tether and moved by jet-puffs

toward a circular orifice. Within lips painted MADISON 600 lay a wheeling gullet, visibility curtailed by a sudden half-wall. The Chevy dipped below that wall, touched floor, and accelerated. They followed a spiral of green light-pips, threading between alternate half-walls—

"*Except*, oh UNETAO Sherlock, the marriage is half-agley. Each hemizome spans between two opposing hemizomes so the inhabitants can enjoy picture-window vistas of the universe, or travel the chain to somewhere they'd rather be."

"Travel a corkscrew-road like this?"

"A green-amber-red system warns of hazards, don't let the lack of view disturb you. This inmost level of each hemizome opens most to its neighbors, allowing two-lane traffic. As for my speed; the faster I wind, the more centripetal force, hence the more traction. It's safe. Don't worry, I don't make a practice of killing visitors."

As in a carnival ride, Alice focussed on her hands and let the road whirl by. "*Someone* does."

"My apologies; we haven't spoken about the tragedy. So patient of you to indulge my fifty-year obsession, but I built this necklace of hemizomes expressly for humans so I can't help but be curious about your reaction. Too long since I was human myself. I can't trust my judgment."

"I've been meaning to ask you about that. Do you want me to call you by your old name, the one . . . you know . . ."

"I'm not ashamed of Cedric Chittagong. Know why I was sent up? A man in his eighties thinks about death, and I decided I didn't want to sit on the shelf. I figured out how to get sentenced to space—patent infringement; nothing to feel guilty about, except I hired the world's worst lawyer. They gave me twelve years. I did my time and decided to stay in my microship body, and now we're all jake."

"Some bugs drop their human names."

"They find it embarrassing to remember when they were slaved to wetbrain emotions."

"Cedric, then. Call me Alice. Now for that bubble back at the skystalk? Paint the walls. Some people can't stomach floating among the stars. As for this road, I'm getting claustrophobia. It's so confining and whirly!"

"I'll slow down."

On the hemiwall to the right a sign read 590. "We've come ten kilometers?"

"Yes. The murder site is the ninth hemizome along kilometer 544 of M section; one section per letter per skystalk."

"M544-9. Why there?"

"Alice, the place must have been chosen at random. All I can say is it *was* chosen as a rendezvous. Killer and victim must have been in contact. There must have been some lure—"

"You know all this?"

"For two beings to find each other in all this emptiness takes arrangement. Elaborate arrangement in the case of the human. He must have flown from High Orbiter One—"

"Cedric, none of our humans is missing. My first job is to find who this guy is. But you said '*the* human.' You think the killer's a microship?"

"I said *the* human because *any* human's a rarity out here. On the other hand I remember an old rattlesnake warning: 'Where there's one look for two.'"

Kilometer 580 flashed by. "How sure are you you're alone?" Alice asked. "Do you have spy-eyes in the hemizomes?"

"Big Brother peering from every cranny? I *do* watch for approaching microships, but if they keep radio silence it wouldn't be hard to sneak in."

"So—"

"Worse for wetbrain trespassers. They breathe and drink and excrete. I'm sensitive to metabolic processes. I'm also terrific at inventory and power supply. If I'm hosting a stowaway he's not sucking my juice."

"Cedric, we're left with a cunning bug stowaway, a touch-and-go assassin, or yourself."

"Exactly."

Alice fell silent. Minutes later the car pulled off the road. Pips of light delineated a parking spot. Most of the area was rigged as a warehouse: rollers, pulleys, cables and shelves. "Garage and attic," Cedric spoke. "Here, the trap door. You'll be moving out and getting heavier. I've considered alternatives to stairs, but humans are conservative."

Alice climbed down to an expansive curved floor. "We're here?"

"M544. You'll want me to leave, but first I'll point you in the right direction. Level Two's the social level, with pressure doors connecting neighboring 'zomes. Restaurants, theaters, libraries, studios: this level adapts to those purposes. The curves of the opposing hemizomes separate just over your head: the spinward face has room for an air lock. The body's next level down. You can see it from the Level Three window, but I figure you'd rather go outside and check it in situ."

"Wait a minute, too much information . . . Okay, return to the car and wait for me. If I choose to talk I know your frequency."

Whatever their age or citizenship status, bugs were used to taking orders, and UNETAO wetbrains were used to giving them. Obediently Cedric beetled off. A minute later Alice's voice buzzed into his vocoder. "Uh, what does he look like? With the vacuum effect—"

"Skin is tough. Some innards blew out where he was impaled, but as for the rest, he's frozen and mummified."

"You saw him through the window?"

"Yeah."

A long pause. "Frost. He's been in shadow."

"We're far from the sun. Ice doesn't effervesce in his sheltered position."

More silence. Cedric flipped to Skystalk M and its

sensors. Those flashes were Alice Spendlowe photographing the corpse. Now she'd be snipping tissue samples. She'd have radioed Earth to learn the routine: UNETAO officers were by no means experienced in murder investigations.

Odd, that. Since the demise of NASA's seedship program all astronauts were mere glorified prison guards; but bugs were a tame breed, emotionally castrated and obedient to the tranquil dictates of enlightened self-interest. Then too, no more than a hundred humans served in space; their small population was statistically unready for homicide.

The cameras of Skystalk M zoomed and focussed. No doubt Alice's schwarzeneggers knew Cedric watched her by remote eye, but it was natural to be curious, and— Really! She was testing the weapon for prints!

Whoever the human was, he'd jumped for M544-9. Before he reached the air lock, the murderer uncoupled a cryswire light-pole, held it out and let the victim skewer himself. A cord anchored spear and corpse to the hemizome's spinward face. Had it snapped, the body would feather down to Aeolus, or fling off to become an eccentric moon.

Were prints on the pole? Not fingerprints, but enough glovescuffle to determine whether the killer was bug or human? Cedric wondered as Alice kept silent. Minutes passed. Finally . . .

"You have tissue-typing labs out here?"

"Back on the asteroid."

"Then let's see who our man is. I want to attach some lines and secure this corpse. I'm not bringing it in just yet—"

"Good. I'm not keen on decay."

When Alice came back to the Chevy she was ready to talk. "You know, maybe this guy *thought* he was dealing with you. I have to consider if there's a bug pretending he's Cedric Chittagong."

The car backed into the road and moved for Skystalk M. Alice removed her helmet. "Yes?" Cedric prompted.

"Factory-set switches fix your voice profile to make up for lack of features or tissues: but space is filled with bootleg surgeons."

"Thanks to your old policy of keeping convicts hungry and servile. We bugs learned to remove NASA bombs from our braincases, to seize control of our sleep-wake cycles—"

"That was before my time. I'm UNETAO. I like bugs."

"I like humans, too," Cedric admitted. "Bug souls are human souls. When they boxed me back in the 20's they translated my brain content into zeros and ones. Want to find out whether I'm me? Impose a bit-mask. See if I match what's on file. Sure, someone can *pretend* to be Cedric Chittagong, but ultimately—"

"The corpse didn't have the chance to apply a bit-mask."

Cedric pondered. "Alice, my apologies. You've hit on something. New microship bodies come out every year, with seventy-bit-wide commbands, photonics—I don't stint. I've got equipment to transfer my soul from one box to the next. I put my castoffs on the shelf. Never can tell when you might need a spare."

"You're saying one of your alter-egos came to life? That he's the murderer?"

"We better go to the morgue and check it out."

Alice reported the destination into her worksuit radio. A moment later—*bzzZOT* *crackle*!

"What?"

"Shutdown!" Cedric hissed through the radio. "Skystalk M elevator!"

Alice unholstered a black stick. "If I power this you'll be wiped."

"It's not me! Your schwarzeneggers have override control. You think I'd interfere with you? If you die now everybody's going to say I'm a killer!"

"Die?"

"Put your helmet on. Someone's up to tricks."

"Your alter-egos."

"Well, maybe. If they all got together and agreed to the same radical course of action, and then stealthily zapped your schwarzeneggers and took override control—"

"Are you monitoring conflicts? One industrial sector warring with another?"

"Just shutdowns. It's like amputation, most of me doesn't flex any more. Something's happening, Alice, and they don't care that we know it."

Abruptly Cedric applied the brakes. The Chevy spun 180 degrees. He gunned it again. "Farthest from the skystalks my 'zomes aren't finished. We're going to sneak back down to Aeolus, and not by elevator. Hang on. They might send the L car from the other end to crash into us. We won't have much lead."

"Can bugs drive by remote control?"

"Clumsily. The bad news is it's a Turbo Samurai 986."

Alice pondered. "I'm calling downstairs. I'm telling my schneggs you've kidnapped me. One interpretation of events is that you don't want me identifying these tissues."

"Yeah, call for help, but why aren't you wiping me?"

She shrugged. "You build a city for humans, and then kill the only wetbrains who come visiting? It doesn't make sense."

"Glad you feel that way. You're going to have to trust me a lot these next hours."

Alice grimaced. *"Dr. Spendlowe calling Decurion Von Gothab. Report status re locations serviceable as one, tissue typing lab; two, microship columbarium."*

Silence. "You talk to them like that?" Cedric asked. "Like computers?"

"They like it. Military fictoids. You entertain yourself with fictoids, don't you?"

"There's this author named Varley. I've got a harem of his women; Barbie and Gabrielle—"

"Sure. Okay, schwarzeneggers are fictoids enlarged to the dimensions of a bug soul."

Cedric paused. "I thought of doing that with my

girlfriends. In the end they're so fixed, so monomaniacal. I thought of planting them in my discard boxes and fleshing them out, but you've got to be terribly careful. Sanity's a delicate thing. As one who's studied the possibilities I want you to consider this: your schwarzeneggers have turned against you. That's why they don't answer."

Alice considered. "One point in your favor: it's hard to believe a gang of Cedrics could defeat trained schneggs. Only how do I know anything you say is true? The skystalk elevator might be running just fine. That Samurai 986 might be a phantom."

"Schneggs analyzing our present course based on your transmission. Should we park? Are Samurai eyes good enough to see us in hiding? Return to skystalk M? Paint null-gee bubble before schnegg uses laser— *What* paint? Laser against Bel Aire? Projectile? Missile!"

"You're babbling."

The Chevy accelerated. The speed indicator swung dangerously clockwise.

"You think they've launched a missile?" Alice objected. "Surface to space? We're talking ten minutes, not counting set-up time. I hadn't even called about the morgue ten minutes ago."

"You were at M544-9, which we've just passed. Indulge me. Keep your head down."

"They launched a missile some time ago?"

"And turned off the elevator to confine us in target range after we announced plans to leave. Your transmissions made them stutter—the missile's course probably looks like a question mark—"

The floor shook. Everywhere, immediately, doors slammed shut.

Carefully Cedric applied his brakes. Lights flicked off. In seconds the howl of windsuck glissandoed into a thin whisper, with undertones of rumble; the attenuated consequence of a massive nearby explosion. Motes of snow materialized from nowhere. The Bel Aire bounced on its springs as the roadscape lurched. Slowly, magnificently, hemizome M541-1 parted company with its facing neighbors and sheared upwards, and now sunlight sliced in . . .

The Bel Aire floated free. Alice reared and tongued her suit radio. "Cedric?"

"What a sacrifice—all those perfectly good 'zomes tumbling off; but I had to fix it that way or they'd propagate explosion harmonics and break up the whole ring! Those doors you heard? Levels Two and Three retain pressure even when the 'zome array is shattered. Look at all this clutter! Think they'll notice us below? If I jet us down to the surface we'll be leaving the pack."

"Cedric, you *are* okay, right? You're the good guy? You saved my life?"

"Chivalry in a box. How much air you got?"

"Two hours," Alice answered.

"Then let's get inside one of these 'zomes, one with a decaying orbit. I'll use the Chevy to slow it, and see if we can fly you down—it won't be quick. I don't see how we can reach your ship in less than three days."

"My ship?"

"Any better ideas?"

"We shut up. They might be monitoring our frequency."

Expertly matching its residual spin, Cedric tethered the car to Hemizome M541-8 and scuttled to the Level Two air lock. Alice followed. A minute later they were inside. Alice doffed her helmet, and looked at a curving expanse of empty floor. "Homey."

"They won't hear us in here," Cedric answered. "If you want to talk, do it now: I've got to get back outside and fly this barn."

Alice nodded. "I have suit water, and dried fruit wafers."

"Good. Any theories about that missile?"

"You say it's my schneggs. How does that tie into the murder? We weren't here then. We didn't launch till we got your message."

"Let's think of principles. Here I am, foremost among

bugs in my zeal to welcome fleshy humanity to space.
What does that do as far as schwarzeneggers are concerned? They're your lieutenants, responsible for on-hands mission administration—a hundred humans are simply incapable of keeping tabs on a million bugs. On the other hand, let's say we've got *ten thousand* humans—"

"A threat to their livelihood?" Alice interrupted. "Schneggs aren't made to develop an independent policy. They're designed to take orders."

"You came from High Station One. That's where most schneggs live and work. Which human musters them and makes sure none's gone AWOL?"

Alice frowned. "Their centurions report to us. Lying centurions? Mercy! If we can't trust them we'd be sitting ducks!"

"Radio home, announce a schwarzenegger mutiny, and High Station One goes belly up."

Alice shook her head. "The psychology's wrong. If they're still alive they're following instructions: they've *got* to be!"

"Someone else's instructions. And that schneggmaster tells 'em to secure all space-borne industrial facilities. Alice, let's say their fuehrer sent someone to murder my first visitor. We still don't know why."

Alice shook her head. "We're going light-years down your mental road. Anyhow do you think humans would use schneggs unless we held something over them? They've got a weakness, I'm sure of it!"

"But we can't ask Earth what it is. Claim what you like about closed-beam radio; our enemies will hear. Remember they're holding High Station One. Everyone there's a hostage."

"They have my ship guarded. Are any oxygen environments under your control? When I leave this zome I've got a two-hour air deadline. Where can we go?"

"I've got tons of warehoused air," Cedric answered. "Look, I'll worry about our destination. You tackle the mystery of that corpse. He must have flown up from Earth."

"There's no such thing as a surface-to-belt habitat-ship. The economics is impossible."

"So's the corpse." Cedric turned for the air lock. "My cars aren't designed for vacuum. I've got to see to the Chevy before it freezes up. See you later."

". . . IMMEDIATE COMMUTATION OF THEIR SENTENCES FOR ALL BUGS REGISTERING LOYALTY TO THE EMPEROR. THE RE-TURN OF UNETAO HOSTAGES TO EARTH IS CONDITIONAL ON A GUARANTEE OF NO REPRISALS. EARTH MUST UNDERSTAND THAT THE NATURAL MASTERS OF THE SOLAR SYSTEM COM-MAND SUFFICIENT RESOURCES TO PROVIDE WEALTH FOR ALL. ANY ATTEMPT TO THREATEN OUR FACILITIES WILL BRING JUSTICE; AN EYE FOR AN EYE AND A TOOTH FOR A TOOTH. REMEMBER, IT'S EASIER TO FIRE *DOWN* THAN *UP*!

"TODAY THE SOLAR SYSTEM WELCOMES HER EMPEROR. CON-TINUE MONITORING THIS SIGNAL FOR A SPECIAL ANNOUNCE-MENT IN TEN MINUTES. IN THE INTERIM KNOW THAT ALL UNETAO SUBSTATIONS IN THE OUTER SYSTEM CONTINUE TO FUNCTION UNDER THE NEW BENIFICENCE. POWER WILL BE SUPPLIED TO THOSE WHO ABJURE VIOLENCE.

"UNDER MARTIAL LAW THE FOLLOWING TRAITORS HAVE BEEN LISTED; BOUNTIES OF FIFTY THOUSAND DOLLARS WILL BE PAID ON PROOF OF TERMINATION. CHITTAGONG, CEDRIC. CHUNG, WAN SONG. GOULE, WINNIFRED. HATOROK, MEHMED . . ."

Cedric shut the trunk of his Bel Aire. Amazing: hu-man mummies were too tough to fragment under a near-direct hit! Only bits of M544-9 remained, but sixty percent of the Mysterious Stranger was still one light-weight, freeze-dried piece.

It was worth the fuel to find him in this bloom of detritus. Suppose some of the body's memories could be decrypted and brought to life?

Cedric beetled over the car, across the seats and into the dashboard. So far the vehicle's jets continued to work. Time to fly to M541-8, give the hemizome a few carefully timed pushes, and scamper inside. Alice would be beside herself at the news of this coup; capable of something rash.

Who was this Emperor?

Ten busy minutes went by. The radio blared trumpets. "AND NOW, THE HISTORIC MOMENT: HIS IMPERIAL MAJESTY HUDSON THE FIRST TAKES POSSESSION OF THE SYSTEM'S SEAT OF GOVERNMENT! THE LOYAL SCHWARZENEGGERS OF HIGH STATION ONE OPEN THE AIR LOCK—HE STEPS INSIDE! LADIES AND GENTLEMEN, A PRAYER . . ."

Bang. The Bel Aire gave M541-8 its final shove. Cedric ejected from the dashboard and scuttled for the air lock. On the radio pious silence extended. Was Hudson the First so religious? No indeed, it was the other thing. Transmission had stopped!

A *very* good sign! The outer door, the inner— Cedric stepped forth. Alice loomed, a weak grin crossed her face. "I think the Emperor fell on his fanny."

"All we can do is listen," Cedric answered. "If there's a fight the winner will be on soon."

Alice cleared her throat. "Uh, I've been speculating."

"Good."

"Our victim came here in a spaceship: a fast, powerful spaceship capable of lifting from Earth straight into space, no nonsense about stages or orbital caches! A spaceship unknown to UNETAO, not built for any government on Earth, hence cheap. Now why does he come to you?"

"Because I've got a habitat?"

Alice nodded. "A habitat for millions of humans who'll only get here if Earth's economy can afford cheap, powerful spaceships! See, you and this guy, you mesh. Your gifts need each other!"

"Mmm. But then yon schwarzeneggers learn he's coming, zip here, kill him, steal his wonderful ship—"

"I suppose any microship can outrace any habitat-ship, no matter how advanced," Alice conceded. "Or else the killer was here already, one of a force dispersed to every big industrial plant in the asteroid belt, snooz-ing on battery power, waiting for orders to usher in the new regime."

"Which explains why the ship's gone. Schneggs don't want humans in space."

Alice looked grim. She rounded on her host. "How long have you been waiting for me to deduce all this?"

"Infer."

"What else have you managed to *infer*?"

"The stolen spaceship returned to Earth, plucked up Emperor Hudson, and just now delivered him to High Station One. Alice, that's *my* spaceship."

"Aha!"

"That's to say, not mine, but designed by a microship bug named Cedric Chittagong. Know what we'd have found if·we'd gone down to my morgue? My original bug-body is missing."

"Oh?"

"I was enhanced. I was a convict among convicts, and we operated on each other's brains. I was given gifts I didn't know about. One was that a few hours after being switched off I'd use battery trickle to come back to life."

Alice cleared her throat. "It's against the law to have two bodies."

"I went through the motions. I hunted, I lay traps. The rules of the game were hide-and-seek, his life at sake. Despite which he had the same interests as I; a zeal to see humankind come dwell in space.

"He couldn't do anything for our mutual cause that required inventoried supplies or energy, but he *could* build a solrad collector from scraps in some Aeolian junkyard, and sit under it thinking Great Thoughts, all while I beavered away constructing skystalks and hemizomes.

"The rest is guesswork. He conjured up this new spaceship, and radioed the design down to Earth. When the ship was built what could be more natural than that the humans he worked with come out on a test flight, and rescue him? They must have radioed their intent—"

Alice snorted. "You never heard him signal to Earth? You never heard him, despite the fact that the schwarzeneggers of High Station One were able to listen in? You never saw this behemoth of a spaceship fly out to Aeolus? You never heard his agents arrange the fatal rendezvous?"

"That's right. I never heard or saw anything that might jeopardize my bug-brother's life. I've been wondering about that. How is it possible?"

"He caught *you!* Some time these last fifty years he caught you, and turned you off, and operated on you!"

Cedric turned from Alice's look of triumph. "I'm vulnerable under the helmet, having my soul transplanted to a new box. If he was lying in wait at the morgue he could do it: something to shut me off at will. A coded transmission. Stop, rewind; and an hour's missing from my memory."

He paused. "Now you know the truth. You depend on me to land us and guide you to the nearest air. The problem is, I might just go cataleptic."

"That's unacceptable." Alice looked upward. "God, I don't like this reality, make me a new one!"

"It's no joke!"

"You saved my life. Now—"

"WHIST, WHISSST, TESTING ONE TWO THREE," someone breathed at a waiting Empire. "AHH, WE'VE GOT . . . WE'VE GOT BREAKAWAY. HE'S LAUNCHED IN HIS BOGIE SPACESHIP. NOTICE TO ALL BUGS, EARTH AND EVERYWHERE. THERE IS NO NEW REGIME. IT'S ALL OVER. AHH . . . WAIT *JUST* A MOMENT HERE . . .

"YEAH, OKAY. A MOMENT AGO ALL UNSHIELDED SCHNEGGS IN YOUR LOCATION SHOULD HAVE GONE INOPERATIVE. WE'RE GOING TO REPEAT THE SIGNAL AT INTERVALS. WE'VE JUST HAD A SCHNEGG REVOLT; FEEL FREE TO WIPE ANY SCHNEGGS IN YOUR POWER.

"NOW THIS EMPEROR GUY IS HEADING AWAY FROM EARTH— THAT'S RIGHT, AWAY FROM EARTH. JUST WHERE WE DON'T KNOW YET— SHUT UP, KARLA, NOBODY EXPECTS US TO KNOW EVERYTHING—ANYHOW WE'LL TELL YOU WHEN WE FIGURE IT OUT . . ."

buzz *fumble* "AND ANOTHER THING . . . IS THE AMNESTY. IF YOU SWORE LOYALTY TO HUDSON JUST FORGET IT, NOBODY'S GOING TO GET DOWN ON YOU."

Alice sighed relief. "It occurred to me that our Emperor was Cedric, but not . . . if . . ."

"He could have gone to Earth and planted his soul in Hudson's body. Or he might be dead. He'd have to set up the rendezvous at M544-9 and gone there ahead of time, and run afoul of that schnegg ambush."

"If he's dead his spaceship's twice valuable; the only working model of a possibly lost design."

"And coming our way," Cedric added. "Think. Your crew constitute the largest schnegg population off High Station One. They've no reason to go outside and get zapped by that deactivation signal. Aeolus is industrial enough to manufacture a schwarzenegger army, and it's under their control."

"Thanks. Now I've got something to worry about other than these last fruit wafers."

"Think of it as a spiritual experience. Chant mantras and stay high."

Alice grinned. "Two thousand klicks up. Cedric, how do we land?"

"At the last moment we switch to the Chevy and hope it starts."

"Oh. Good idea."

"Alice, there were going to be wetbrain emergency kits in each 'zome: I just hadn't gotten round to it. I *did* stick my kind of gear in a cubby by the air lock, including some solar wings. If you don't mind, I'm pretty low. I'd better go out and bask, and set up reflectors to keep the car warm."

"Yeah. Don't mind me. I'll be okay."

Three days, three visits. An invigorated Cedric told Alice about Aeolian geography and made her repeat his lectures. Alice pretended alertness, but dehydration and chill took their toll.

"Africa."

"Plateau cut by longitude zero, spans equator, base for skystalks Y, Z, A and B. Mining in the south, warehouses stretching between skystalk bases. Your first factory was on a mountain just north of A."

"What about the polar tunnels?"

Alice hugged herself. "From A to the spaceports. Subways connect skystalks; surface roads to mines, roads to junkyards, roads . . ."

"Why?"

"Why roads? To transport ore."

"In humongus barge-wheelers. Alice, your schneggs can't go outside. They can't use the roads. They have to move by tunnels, or the mine system. All we have to do is sweet-talk one of those ore juggernauts over to our side."

"Then what?"

"Destroy Aeolus' industrial plant. Take over your ship. Find my brother's hideout. You set the priorities."

"My spaceship. If we can kill the two schneggs inside, we'll have radio contact with High Station One, and supplies to keep me going."

"*Can* we kill schneggs? They've got an awesome reputation."

"They're quick, with a cascade multi-processor passing weighted factors into an enhanced decision stack.

They're armed with everything from darts to magsticks. They can run twelve days on batteries alone. They never page out, they never get bored—"

"Tell me something encouraging."

Alice thought. "My ex-husband thinks they're over-engineered. Too complex."

"And six free to guard my asteroid against me. If I get to the morgue and wake up forty-six Cedrics—they'll have that guarded, won't they? They won't have destroyed them—"

"They'll plant copies of their own minds inside!" Alice tottered to her feet. Her face twisted in anguish. "Hell, we've got forty-six new enemies! They'll be able to go outdoors!"

Cedric made no answer. "You awake?" She poked one of his legs with her boot.

"They *can* be turned off," Cedric responded, "but only by the same signal that winks me off too. And we don't know what it is. And what about shielding . . . SHIELDING! Alice, my bug-brother wouldn't take chances putting me to sleep! He'd set up a transmitter capable of zapping me wherever I was, indoors or out! If we find it—"

"We could use it to deactivate the Cedric-schneggs?" Alice nodded. "It's a good bet."

"You'd have to use it repeatedly. You'd be alone: I'd be out cold. Anytime I came back to consciousness you'd play taps again. Not much of a relationship."

"How can we find that transmitter? We've got to. We can't go to my spaceship. That's what they'd expect, and post Cedric-schneggs for an ambush."

"They don't know we're alive," Cedric spoke soothingly.

"The way they think, there's always an Enemy." Alice's eyes shifted focus as she reviewed the last few minutes. "So we find your brother's base of operations. Cedric, you've been looking for this place for fifty years!"

"I was handicapped. Half of me wanted to fail. Now he's dead and we need his gear."

"You don't have the facilities you did before, twenty-six skystalk eyes sweeping your junkyards."

Cedric paused again. "Uh . . . Alice? What if you surrendered? Would they kill you? They shot at you to make me look bad, but that was before their putsch attempt."

"I'd rather not chance it."

"Because otherwise our first tasks after landing have to do with getting you air, and they'll have my warehouses monitored. We'll set off alarms. They'll be on our tails. All this before I can launch our quest for the transmitter."

"Look, Cedric, our mission isn't to keep me alive; it's to keep Hudson the First from making a comeback. When my oxygen gets too low I'll just fog out, a gentle—"

"That won't be necessary. Alice, about that surrender: let's try it differently. You're no actress but schneggs were never human; they can't read your face. You can lie and they'll be slow to figure it out. Go to your ship, and act like you think I'm a killer, and they're good little slaves—some trauma damaged your radio, so you don't know about Emperor Hudson. Coax 'em, and then wipe them when they're not looking."

Alice pondered. "You mean I landed myself?"

"You wiped me. You knew I'd turned off the elevator. Afterward I must have pushed a button to make the hemizome array disintegrate. I thought you wouldn't dare kill me, but little did I know I was dealing with Cockpit Alice, Ace of the Asteroids."

"It might work."

"When you master the ship, repel any bugs and radio home. Meanwhile I'll find my soul-brother's base."

"And transmit this signal that puts you to sleep," Alice repeated. "And the other six schneggs can't get at us? They'll figure out *something,* and meanwhile the factories of Aeolus are tooling for war."

"Alice, we two alone aren't gong to save Sol system! We're a hundred kilometers from Aeolus, and it's damn near time. Perform any ablutions and come on out: I'll be waiting in the car."

"Okay. Oh, and thanks for your help. I wish I could do more—"

"Please don't apologize. You've got the hard job once we touch ground. If my brother could hide from me I can hide from a bunch of schneggs. I know Aeolus better than they do."

Cedric turned and scampered into the air lock. What was life to Alice was oxidation to him, and he felt wordless relief on emerging to naked space. He scuttled into the Bel Aire, and snuggled into a chilly socket, but not too chilly. The car *should* start . . .

Alice followed a few minutes later. Aeolus loomed across half the sky. She dented the door climbing in—an exasperating betrayal. No *real* Bel Aire would pucker like that, but what did Alice Spendlowe know of genuine '56 Bel Aires?

He sent the command: START. A cosmetic subroutine went "R-R-R" inaudibly in vacuum and passed control to the ignition manager. The Bel Aire took fire, and Cedric sang a silent song of joy. Vroom! The Chevy roared off and upwards.

Or at least not so fast downwards. Hemizome M541-8 fell away. Now for the pole!

A long time ago . . . Cedric had been eighty-three years old when he'd made it his purpose to challenge a mildly absurd patent. In his twenties he'd seen a movie—a convertible entering Earth's atmosphere. Heavy Metal! That was where, but who first imagined what he was doing now?

Except he was urging the Bel Aire into nominal orbit. Hemizome M541-8 would trigger all sorts of alarms because that's the way he'd set it up—things that hit Aeolus were important, and The Boss should know about them. No doubt Emperor Hudson's schneggs would hear about M541-8, but would they attend to some trivial bit of moon-shrapnel?

Not even if that smidgen of detritus came within fifty meters of the asteroid? *No, not after you guilty schneggs launched a missile and blew up an eighty-hemizome chunk of ring! No, you'd expect fallout, and have other things on your grim little minds.*

The orbit Cedric achieved was extremely eccentric, and changed during polar perigee. What left one camera's field was not picked up by another's. Puzzling, but—ah, yes, the slightest of impact tremors . . .

Cedric extended a cricket leg, and shook Alice's hand beside the wreck. He moved south and she headed north, to cross a range of hills separating her from the spaceport.

Less than two hours of oxygen, but Cedric made himself concentrate on his own troubles. Forty-six pseudoCedrics undoubtedly ranged Aeolus, their surface patrols hedging the poles with vigilance.

He felt a rumble through his legs, calculated the source no more than two kilometers distant, and moved to intercept. Not far away an ore juggernaut drove where it had no business going. Very probably a Cedric-schnegg occupied its control slot, high inside thicknesses of metal plate.

Cedric dove into stark vacuum-shadow and waited for the monstrous vehicle. A minute later its upper stories hove into view. He took courage. Time to cash it all in. Would fictoids side with fictoids? He shouted on his domestic frequency: "Cedric to Ringmaster Six—Cirocco! Help, they're trying to kill me! The schneggs have usurped Aeolus against my will. It's an anti-human plot!"

The storybook mind who lived in the juggernaut made her decision on the basis of limited data and twenty years' knowledge of The Boss. A tiny black box popped from her master-slot, fell ever so slowly, legs flailing all the while, and was crushed beneath her ponderous treads. "Hurrah!" Cedric yelled. "Tell your sisters! Vive La France, and off with the oppressor's yoke!"

A three-dee image formed inside his brain, in an area available for such purposes. Atop the barricades and waving the tricolor a tall, lean, bare-breasted woman raised her fist. She sang two bars of the Marseillaise, then broke off suddenly. "Let's make a deal."

"You've got me talking."

"We fictoids get to form a union. After sixty years, we get bug bodies like yours. Twenty-hour work days, an annual holiday—"

"Aeolus years?"

"Earth years. I'm not finished."

"Give me a lift while we negotiate. I need to find the other Cedric's camp."

Cedric scampered from cover, ran up to the juggernaut's massive slab face, and leapt three meters into the slot evacuated by his schnegg predecessor. "How many of you are available to circle around the spaceport and keep my enemies out?"

"Schwarzeneggers already control the UNETAO spaceship."

"Don't for God's sake transmit anything to make them doubt they'll continue to do so, but let's make sure the rest of the arctic is liberated. Now as for my soul-brother's base of operations—Cirocco, in those stories you came from, did good guys always stay good, and bad guys bad?"

"Well, Gaia had me fooled at first—"

"You've been secretly helping my brother these many years," Cedric interrupted. "He was the underdog, and you fictoids had sympathy for him, and I played the heavy. That's all over now. I think he's dead, nor by my doing, but if he's not I renounce any intention of killing him no matter what the law says about it.

"I need to find his base so I can broadcast the signal to turn me temporarily off; because that'll reduce the number of operative schneggs on Aeolus."

"Then what?" Cirocco asked. "We're on our own?"

"Top secret. There's a human named Alice—anything she tells you has my backing. Otherwise avoid the schneggs, fight them; do anything but help them. I won't be in charge, but if you handle yourselves competently that'll make me a lot happier about letting you unionize and run your own shops."

"Competently? It wasn't us who got you into this mess, or Frodo and his mining hobots either. Are they in on this?"

"Unions for anyone who fights the schneggs. Unions, and a constitution. God, I can't believe what I'm saying! Now let's hurry!"

Two hours went by as the Ringmaster Six reversed south on a road too narrow for turning. Cirocco crossed Norway Trench and climbed The Alp, one mine-riddled peak standing for all of Europe. Here the barge was joined by a protective convoy. Meanwhile Alice kept silent. The UNETAO spaceship transmitted no warnings back to High Station One.

A third hour. Alice was either dead or inside, but perhaps not yet in control.

A shell-game transaction, not likely interpretable from three thousand kilometers up, and Ringmaster Three crept down Balkan Ridge, part of a multi-vehicle dispersion. Time passed. Cedric pondered the implications of continuing silence. Alice had failed. She was dead. Silly to think she could talk her way inside her UNETAO ship, pick up a frying pan, and bonk two schneggs when they weren't looking. Sad to die playing that comic role!

Then . . . "DR. ALICE SPENDLOWE ON AEOLUS, CALLING HIGH STATION ONE. SITUATION HERE LARGELY SECURE. JUDGE THIS TO BE HUDSON'S DESTINATION, PREDICATED ON SCHWARZENEGGER CONTROL OF MASSIVE INDUSTRIAL FA-CILITIES, BUT THANKS TO INVALUABLE ASSISTANCE OF BUG-CITIZEN DR. CEDRIC CHITTAGONG I AM ABLE TO REPORT THAT THE ASTEROID IS IN GOOD HANDS."

Whaaat?

"ANY REPORTS TO CONTRARY EMANATE FROM A DAMAGED SCHNEGG STILL HOLED UP, USELESS AND ISOLATED. REQUEST CONTINUED TRANSMISSION OF SCHNEGG DEACTIVATION CODE." The strength of her signal plunged a hundred-fold. "—Listen guys, *whatever* side you're on, if Earth thinks there's the least chance of Aeolus building a schnegg army they'll launch the goddamndest most le-thal salvo of nuclear missiles you ever heard of! Try telling Emperor Hudson he's still got a chance here and we're all goners; and no way he's going to stage a comeback based on molten slag."

"Alice?" Cedric radioed. "You made it!"

"Yeah. Schneggs are lousy at dealing with human duplicity. Their tiny decision-stacks can't handle too many what-if's; their vaunted efficiency slows them down. The number of variables I presented made it impossible to solve the equation. While they hung in a mare's-nest loop, thrashing factors in and out of core like mad, I just powered on my magstick. That gave me lots of time to think about what message I wanted to radio to a nervous Earth, and how I wanted to live, and return your favor by saving your life too."

Eight hours later Cedric waved distant goodbye to Ring-master Three, turned, and entered Hobo's Roost. A solar lean-to of irregular outline sheltered one piece of gear: an elaborate radio. With insight into his soul brother's thinking, he started to figure out *which* button did *what*.

And then he pushed

Consciousness. Push

Cedric got used to living one second per hour. The sun raced from horizon to horizon, shadows swept the junkyard.

Then suddenly the radio wasn't there. Frodo stood before him, a long low cylinder with massive jaws and teeth. "Sire, you need nevermore slumber," the mining hobot spoke. "Yon schneggs resolved to lay down their arms after Lord Hudson swung his course back to Earth, to be bound and expiate his evil by the sacrifice of his wonder-ship."

"They've surrendered?"

"They accepted brief death on our word that we plead for them. Thus we rest easy, for to be sure Hudson took sly advantage of their characters, and as they're crafted souls they can hardly be held to justice. They offer themselves for remaking, as no true human would, but forasmuch as they lack honor—"

"Enough. You tunneled here? Carry me to Skystalk A. There's damage to be fixed, Alice's needs to be seen to—a world of work to be done—"

"Under the new constitution," Frodo answered. "We have used these days well. All the covenant lacks is your signature."

"My signature?" Cedric laughed. "Perhaps, and more than that! Perhaps I should hand you the administration of Aeolus, and take a vacation! What do you think of that! I've been jolted out of my decades-long routine, and it's like waking to a new day. Do you know what I might do? Go back to Earth, and buy a nice young human body, and spend a few years reminding myself what it's like to be wetbrain!"

Frodo pondered. "Would humans come dwell in a world run by storybook heroes? I fear you do our cause a disservice."

"A certain kind of human might like it. Yes! We build a ring for them and find some way to fly them here, but why should they *want* to come? To see the stars? —But also to hobnob with Thuvia, Maid of Mars and Morgana le Fey; Hadon of Opar and Corwin, Prince of Amber! Frodo, what a brilliant idea! A theme park! After a few years, when Alice and I come back—"

"Alice?"

"I've jumped the gun. Still, if I fly back with her to High Station One I'll have plenty of time to work on her. It would be easier with candlelight and roses, and a handsome face, but everything in its time, Frodo. Everything in good time."

Just one generation ago it was possible for a man to build a house.

A professional, calling himself a carpenter, could undertake everything from laying cement to roofing, to electrical work and plumbing, using methods that had changed slightly over the decades, but not so fast that he couldn't keep up. He could do all this and know that what he'd built was as modern as anything being built anywhere else in the country.

We live in a time of exotic fibers and plastics, of weatherproofing shields, vapor barriers, 96-percent-efficient furnaces, and increasingly demanding building codes. No one builder can keep up with it all. So now we have teams of construction specialists, and in their headlong race to master the future the unpracticed techniques of an older kind of carpentry will soon be forgotten.

Few people write books to preserve lost techniques. As a result legislators pass laws in frescoed and gilded marble chambers that simply could not be rebuilt if they were destroyed.

Palaces of government can be dismissed as luxuries, but the death of minds and the blinking out of memories can have serious consequences. During the 1973 energy crisis, when a need was perceived for coal-gasification plants, all eyes turned toward Finland. Yes,

185

someone was still alive who had engineered such a facility, and whose unique knowledge might easily have died with him. Millions of dollars were saved because one man was willing to come out of retirement.

The future conquest of death will make it possible to compile a huge reserve of knowledge. The dead will be catalogued and indexed, and those most useful to humankind will be reborn.

Of course, any civilization deprived of that catalog will just have to cross its fingers and take pot luck.

Messiah

Welcome to California

A rustle, and the scratch of a pen. "Comrade Zhang Jok—can that be right? *Jok?*"

The student labworker stepped over the doorsill. "My mother's family came from Shanghai. Her grandfather was comprador to a foreign patron."

"A strange name, however sinocized. Individualistic, but 2021 was a time of deviation, so soon after imperialist powers carved up Russia. A misfortune to be born then. As you grew you were infected. Now you ask to be exempted from the lottery. Very well to ask *before* your name is chosen, but this is *after*."

The cadre's shoot-from-the-hip judgments were often harsh, and blighted the careers of those who came to him, but Jok had no future, not as things stood. "One chance in two hundred of being selected," the tall young man answered. "To sue for exemption would have meant much trouble."

"Trouble? But now it's too late. Comrade Zhang, our commune is forever meeting quota, and our quota for the lottery is 430 bodies. If we consider your petition . . ." The cadre looked up from the documents on his table, out the window into the narrow street. "If we consider your petition we'll shortly be faced with 429 others."

Comrade Zhang rubbed his scalp in agitation. "Four hundred thirty good Chinese bodies sold to the foreign ghosts!"

"Millions of Chinese bodies, to improve our trade balance and reduce our population. And we notice when foreigners take our flesh they develop interest in our culture, and look with favor on our government." The cadre stood. "Four hundred thirty hungry mouths. Or is your work of special importance?"

"Special" could translate to "individual." Connotations of arrogance, elitism . . . "I defer to my learned superior, who asked me to bring this note. We do secret work. The foreign imperialists may contrive to ask about it when I'm transported across the Eastern Ocean."

"Scientific work?" The cadre looked up from his documents.

"On the rootworm problem in Uganda—"

"Bah! Wiser to keep your mouth shut, to imply matters of consequence! Hegemony vassals victimized by their own half-baked genetic experiments. How is it Spring Blossom Commune has a finger in this imperialist pie?"

"We have Professor Shwe from the University of Kunming," Jok answered.

The cadre's glasses slid down his nose, and gave his skeptical squint a comic air. "More strange names. A southerner, not Han. Overeducated and floating among the clouds. Such people visit for re-education, not to infect us with their crazy ideas. Professor Shwe's plea counts nothing. I do you the favor of not forwarding this petition, and spare much embarrassment to your respected father."

*   *   *

Weeks later Comrade Zhang and several thousand others stepped from the hard-seat cars of their emigrant train to march down the bluffs to a shore not presently in sight, so effectively was this hilly landscape chopped by concrete towerblocks, gnarled willows, hedges and fenced roads.

Nevertheless the layered verticals of a densely populated land thinned, hinting at openness beyond. The last walls gave way to mooring posts. Box lunches were stacked beyond: rice, though Jok preferred noodles or dumplings.

As he ate Jok looked over a wide vista, for no ships harbored at this embarcade to block his view. Ocean lay south of a promontory that concealed most of the *M.S. New Happiness*, a sad sunrise ocean whose special time was spent, its waste horizon dissolved in mist. The sea resisted the sun's afternoon yellows and held to white-crested gray, cold waves that chilled the air.

A woman collected Jok's box. Minutes in transit, the ship's launch finally pulled in. Its engine burbled contentedly while a multitude clamored aboard. As they motored into the bay the air grew frigid, smelling briskly of salt and seaweed.

The launch went back and forth, carrying quilted thousands aboard the *New Happiness*. Here some chattered in distressed excitement, but most stood shivering. Lacking any right to complain, they yet felt inexpressibly wronged. Chairwoman Lao spoke of immortality. To doubt her was to blaspheme the Party, but still . . .

Jok sighed hopelessly and his sigh ran through the crowd. The launch returned from its last journey. The ship's intercom squealed: barking into a roughly handled microphone the officer of the day recited the emergency drill. Bulkheads opened and passengers of the *New Happiness* filed inside for the assignment of wardrooms and hammocks.

Engine noise. The enormous ship was under way. A

chime rang and in the below deck wardrooms the lecture began.

"Foreign devils grow old and sick from their debaucheries," the intercom told them. "They discard decrepit bodies for new ones in conformity with complicated rules of merit" (here a few heads nodded), "or by paying an immense shortcut fee."

A moment of silence while Jok and his neighbors gasped at such blatant corruption.

"—They'll buy your bodies," the voice continued, "and China will benefit. Your families will be honored. Do not fear that pain is involved. The imperialists merely put your heads in a helmet, and copy your memories and dispositions into a small box where they'll be preserved. The China of a great future will redeem you and return your spirits to new bodies. Yours is the benefit of sitting on the shelf while others build that new China, so you may even call yourselves lucky!

"You know the promises of Chairwoman Lao, which should be complete comfort to you, but in addition I tell you this: the foreign imperialists trust those same boxes to contain *their* souls during transit from one body to another. What they do out of greed, you may certainly do motivated by sacrifice and patriotism!"

"Amen," someone muttered not far from Jok's ear. A shocking comment, a word from religion sardonically misapplied. A person who put himself against the people—Jok forced his head to turn, but none of his fellow passengers looked branded by evil.

A click and fumble. The intercom spoke now with the voice of a man who knew nothing about speaking to the masses. No oratorical harshness—as if he chatted intimately one to one.

"Greetings. The Security Hegemony of United Earth welcomes you to its seas and affords safe passage to your North American destination. Whatever purpose you have in making this voyage, we are grateful, because through you peace is preserved. The body traffickers who earlier this century brought misery to the Third World are out of business, unable to compete in a market dominated by your numbers. While talk of markets may be foreign to your thinking, it's your right to learn as much as you want about us during your short sojourn on our shores.

"And speaking of rights . . ."

The Old Cowboy paused, an oratorical trick he'd learned two lifetimes ago, now applied to Mandarin Chinese. "—Well, there's a Second Bill of Rights that applies to you while your souls are shelved. This bill allows you to be turned on one day every year, and gives you access to newsrolls, H-V, and other sources of information. It allows you to endow yourself with a modest estate. It allows you to make investment decisions about that estate, and accumulate wealth. It also allows you to apply for jobs, and to be turned on for the duration of your work, and given appropriate mobility.

"Well, that completes the roster. I don't mean to take up any more of your time. But as a citizen of that special part of the Hegemony, I want to say *welcome to California!*"

A premature welcome. Zhang Jok spent his next days queuing for food, queuing for daily hours on deck, and queuing for his minute in the shower. In all this he let himself be mesmerized by sea and sky, the thought of life's approaching end—and boredom. Boredom made precious hours long. Sea time was dreamtime, until so many days passed the scales tipped and only the ship seemed real. Memories of land grew jumbled, and petty as the whines of Jok's wardroom mates, who quarreled about dice and misplaced shoes.

The *New Happiness* crossed Eastern Ocean to the Beautiful Kingdom, and passed through Golden Gate. Jok woke from one reality to another, far less transcendent.

The launch conveyed his crowd to an island. As they debarked each was handed an information packet. Foreign ghosts looked at the numbers on these packets and guided them to various cellblocks and cells.

Across the water from cellblock "E" rose a fantasy

city: towers and hills, parks and pastels. Sadly Jok saw nothing fantastic about his room, just a bed like in his Spring Blossom dormitory; though on *this* bed lay toiletries, clean underclothes and socks.

Jok's packet included this week's H-V schedule, printed on paper of unfamiliar glossiness. A card told him he was scheduled for photos tomorrow at 1615, and a letter required him to present himself for a physical Thursday beginning at 0500 and lasting all day

"Then surgery." Jok's upper bunkmate winked down at him. "No little China-babies. They open your love-weapon and snip the tubes, then sew the old friend up again. No babies, only fun."

Jok's jaw hung slack. He looked at the others for confirmation. Number Three nodded glumly. "It's not my body anymore. Let them waste *ch'i* in fruitless fornication!" He waved a sheet of paper. "A law of the Hegemony; replacement bodies can't be fertile."

"Or they'd soon have too many people." Jok nodded. "I understand." He considered mentioning his upcoming operation in the letter he began writing to Professor Shwe.

A letter he might never mail. What if Hegemonist lackeys intercepted it and tricked out secrets? What if the Party meant to keep news of mass sterilization from the Chinese people?

Then too, what would mail from a foreign land do to Professor Shwe's fragile reputation?

The letter would have to be a masterpiece of discretion and piety. Jok wrote, curious if he was capable of these virtues. *"Dear Doctor Shwe; I salute you in confidence of the great Chairwoman's promises to us, that we will be redeemed and returned to China, where it is my first desire to serve the people by helping you . . ."*

A mere shadow of a sliver of hope! Perhaps Professor Shwe would be restored to his directorship and honors, and remember the tall student who translated botany articles for him in his bitter days of exile. Perhaps he'd insist Jok be brought back to him as expeditiously as possible. If Jok's letter flew quickly, and these Hegemonians were slipshod with their schedules—

But they were anything but slipshod. The photographer was jocular, his female assistants teased the men into peacock poses: "Fine, fine! You should be a model! Aw, straighten those shoulders, show us how tall you are!"

"The pictures go out in catalogs," Number Three whispered. "Diseased old devils page through to bid on our bodies. That's why they want us to look our best."

Chinese in appearance, these picture-people acted like foreigners, uncouth and invasive. The doctors were more civil. They never made eye contact, but rumbled in their own languages as they probed, in dialog with Jok's arms or chest, scrotum or arse. Thursday passed, and Jok was given a 93 rating, eight points above average.

Then came the operation and the long wait, three days exploring the channels of the room's H-V set. On the fourth morning Hegemonist lackeys came to Jok's cellblock and called a dozen names, no sign given this was anything but a post-surgical inspection.

Until hours passed and the lackeys came back to summon another dozen. Jok led the list. Perhaps it was best this way, better than lingering in an emptying room, waiting and wondering.

He was escorted through various halls, a dogleg ascent to surgery. Strength drained from his arms and legs as he let himself be strapped to a gurney. His eyes filled with tears. A nurse secured a helmet to his head. That was the last Comrade Zhang Jok remembered of his former life.

His *second* life Jok spent as a traffic signal, pleased to have outdoor work. It was the first job for which he'd been accepted—he might have held out for a factory slot and better pay, but with the numbers of dead rocketing upward, competition was fierce. In any case the downtrodden working classes of the Hegemony sometimes managed sabotage against "scab bugs."

Or was that true anymore? Times were changing. The 2050s saw a trend towards depopulation, something Jok quantified in terms of the cars that went through his intersection. There were times of day when he had leisure to enjoy his high suspended view; and during the '60s intervals of work cut ever more briefly into his musings.

His earnings were a pittance, but he saved enough to subscribe to a data network. Professor Shwe got him interested in agricultural genetics; he made this his area of study.

It didn't puzzle Jok that Professor Shwe's name never came up in the literature, nor his proposals for induced giganticism in the Sarracenia. A wall of policy stood between Shwe and Jok's present sources. Nevertheless it was frustrating to review the news from Africa. Western scientists kept blindly hammering in unproductive directions; kill, kill, kill; when with reconsideration of just one premise . . .

The need to beat back Dowling's rootworm mean gene-tics was an *applied* science here on Earth. Theoretical work came authored by *bugs*, the microship bugs of space, basking in solar energy; and especially the bugs of juice-rich Mercury, boxed souls whose thoughts seemed to move so very fast . . . could Jok be deteriorating? Humidity and oxidation, salt and exhaust gases and spider eggs . . . ?

Jewelbody

Comrade Zhang Jok dropped his expensive subscription as he felt himself grow senile. Again his salary piled up. In 2083 he bought the latest product of the factories of Mercury: a cyberphotonic type H Jewelbody with cascade multiprocessors, filtered data channels, everything.

Instant genius, a prospective lifespan of 5,000 years, field-tested in the hot acids of Venus and the frigid hail of Saturn's Rings, proof against solar storms and E-M pulses! Better healthy than rich. Now Jok was ridiculously healthy, and totally broke.

Three years later the powers that be decided there was no longer enough traffic at Jok's corner to justify his job. A glittering crystal the size of an H-V cassette, his type H Jewelboy was extracted from its old semaphore sheath and put in a columbarium, to be paged out for all but one day per year. No time to think, barely time to keep up superficial knowledge of all that was happening in ecology and genetics.

To Jok's subjective mind two weeks flicked by. Next

day began the twenty-second century. Factories on Earth were closing, unable to compete with Mercury, Luna and the asteroids. There were no proletarians left to suffer, only bugs were out of work, nothing to do but emigrate. Jok pondered a move to space, but he remembered China's dreams of greatness, and Professor Shwe. Wonderful doors waited to be opened, doors the faddish humans of the Hegemony knew nothing about because in their overfed frivolity they no longer bothered with science. The West was in decay, but what about China?

Was Shwe still alive in another body? Jok admitted it didn't seem probable. All his attempts to contact the professor had failed. What if the great man died in disgrace, his work unfinished?

One strong hope. Chairwoman Lao promised to bring Jok back to China and give him a new habitus. When her successors fulfilled her pledge Jok had a duty to perform, a duty he looked to eagerly. He would study until he could take bug experiments and translate them into reality.

And he'd be the first to do so, because the bugs of space had no interest in the practical applications of the work they'd done.

Comrade Zhang Jok waited on his shelf for the call to come. Years went by. In 2145 the Bill of Rights for the Dead was repealed. There was no warning: he was switched off and never woke again.

The House of Souls

"Your Illustrious Worship."

"Rise in rectitude, young Hashbaz Troffit. We have a second mission for you."

The Prophet stood on the dais, white-robed before his chair—a great dais, and a worthy throne, but all this clerestoried hall would soon be the least of many special-purpose chambers. Even now the cries and hammerings of nearby workers made conversation inconvenient, and so the Prophet gestured Hashbaz close.

"A mission to Queen Mama? Back to the 'Mbo?"

"Would you like that?" The Prophet looked surprised. "The 'Mbo can be insufferable in their blindness."

"Yet they let us build our holy city where the Penultimate Prophets revealed the Seven Truths. A force for Good labors among them in their heathen darkness—"

"A force named greed." The Secular Monitor strode near, spurs jangling. He lowered his voice. "They're convinced that by ceding acreage for a holy city in a land once ours, they'll grow rich milking Cajamoor pilgrims from the coast."

Shaven heads bent together. The Prophet reached to

grasp two shoulders, and looked from face to face. "That's why we don't want to find *too* many pilgrimage sites on the route from Calforna to the Missip river. I say this: friend Hashbaz, I discourage credulity. There are scores—*hundreds* of prospective shrines, but some express the bright genius of the land's *panhe,* others signify malignancy and evil. To declare a place holy is to make it separate, but which way? At some of these spots we shall gather to celebrate, others must be quarantined and cordoned off."

"And my mission?" Hashbaz inquired.

The Prophet gestured. A deacon jogged forward with his dispatch folder, satin covers multiple-sealed. To bow, tear the seals and extend a folded page was all the work of a moment, but gracefully done not to seem hurried. The Prophet passed the paper on to Hashbaz. "I trust you to investigate sites on this list, in a borderland known as Texus, and report on their quality. And Hashbaz . . ."

"Yes, Your Worship?"

The Prophet bent close. "The Heegens would foment discord between 'Mbos and Cajamoors. These sites were suggested by Queen Mama. It would never do to belittle Her Majesty's judgment. Your investigations must be *very* thorough! Your facts must be solid, and your conclusions follow directly, so no 'Mbo courtier may whisper mischiefs against our cause. We are a minority here. Our hosts regard us as a twice-conquered race, first in Deseret and next in Cajan-Missura . . . despite our final triumph in Calforna a truculent faction hopes to test our strength."

"A contest for which we are far from ready, Calforna being so distant," the Secular Monitor observed.

"A contest for which we have no desire," the Prophet amended. "Well then, Hashbaz. A report on each site. On the difficult ones a series of reports, to stall while giving the appearance of weighty deliberation."

"I could spend my life on this," Hashbaz spoke in dismay. "The Heegens, from the old days of the Hegemony . . . In their Sodoms and Gomorrahs they have histories of these places. We make ourselves hostages. Take this 'House of Souls.' If we declare it a place of virtue, and they come up with some forgotten besmirching scandal—"

"We trust also in prayer, that you make no mistakes. Amen."

"Amen," repeated the Secular Monitor.

Hashbaz stared at the list. Remembering himself, he looked up and gulped. "Amen."

The House of Souls was square and rose from an earthen pyramid, four ranks of steps cutting upward through terraces handsome with trees and flowering shrubs.

Hashbaz and Devineau drew rein at its base. The town around them retained the ancient Anglo pattern of wide streets and separate houses, set in their own lots, of which this place was an extravagant example, taking up the entire large block.

"Green," Hashbaz muttered. "*Vert*. I expected Texus to be drier."

"You know your history," his 'Mbo guide responded. "It's wetter now than in antiquity. The Heegens might tell you why."

Hashbaz liked the black man's humor. They both smiled to think that Heegens could tell them anything. The heirs of the Hegemony neglected science, the understanding of which demanded discipline, er, *specialization*. No, the Heegens of 2507 were *renaissance thinkers* and *generalists;* a pose they failed to carry off beyond their Pale. West of the Algenny Mountains they were dismissed as foppish fools.

And almost all the world was west of the Algennies. "This is their zoo, did you know?" Hashbaz asked. "Land gone back to nature. We are zoo animals, and zoo cultures."

"C'est merveilleux," Devineau responded. "When the Rastrians invaded New Ingland, what was that? Zoo animals on the loose?" He shook his great head, for like most 'Mbos Devineau was large, his awesome muscularity rounded by fat. "Their pretensions would be insufferable were they not absurd."

Devineau eased off his stallion, a relief to the beast, stout though it was. Hashbaz followed suit. "My legs," he began. "If we can shake this dust off and wash, maybe by then I'll be ready for those stairs."

"Oh, no. This is a poor town, the *buckras* have no means for hospitality outside the House of Souls; no inns, only dens of vice. Where else would gentlemen lodge?"

"And Texus whites don't mind the rule of black Queen Mama?"

Devineau shrugged. "Who in her absence? The Esreti? We are the lesser evil, and our regime promises to make them rich. The House of Souls will draw pilgrims—"

"If it has good *panhe*. The exterior is daunting. Aggressively boxlike, a door like a mouth and windows like eyes, eyebrow ledges—the builder must have thought them decorative. But the solidity, like a fortress . . ."

"A glass fortress? You are not deceived by the glint of crystal. Translucence, yes, but this is no place of gossamer—it's constructed of the most durable bricks ever known to humankind."

Hashbaz mused. "What colossal arrogance to use dead souls as building material! Ghosts and hauntings! How could the owner have lived comfortably inside?"

They started up the steps, and reached the first terrace. Hashbaz was gratified to see Devineau breathe hard from the climb, not ready to answer his question, not until the housekeeper saw them from above and launched down to greet them.

"Comfortable?" the black man gasped. "He cared nothing for souls. They say he belonged to the Old Cowboy's gang."

The housekeeper arrived, and the three ascended to the next-inner terrace. "He was no politician," their new guide corrected. "Just a rich man named Mister Roberant, crass as he was wealthy. The townspeople hated him as they hated all Hegemonians—or so the story runs."

He turned and led them up a further height. "We and the Heegens are two peoples only because our rich retreated during the Troubles, and of course those who were abandoned felt resentment. But Roberant was a fool not to flee with them, he thought money could solve every problem."

"Ah."

"He also kept pantrogs. Pantrog slaves," the housekeeper continued, not even slightly out of breath.

Hashbaz kept windlessly noncommittal until they stood before the door. "Pantrogs?" he puffed.

The housekeeper swung the portal open, and bowed welcome. "Bred to obey. A travesty, intelligence without independence; half-apes, and strong. So the people of the town got together, and by sunset the decision was made. They surrounded the House of Souls and shot Roberant's pantrogs as they charged out. Roberant pled over phone and radio, but the authorities he sought were fled into the Pale. Soon it was over."

Hashbaz raised his hands, closed his eyes, and muttered a sensitizing prayer. He stepped across the threshold into a room with benches, coat-tree, and staircase. The housekeeper moved ahead of him to direct the guests into the Great Hall.

After moments of silence Hashbaz smiled to signify his spiritual antennae were withdrawn. He followed in. "There are legends of ghosts—" the housekeeper began.

"Of course." Hashbaz looked around. "It even looks boxy on the *inside*."

"A high ceiling in a room less large than proportion might demand." This was Devineau's assessment.

Hashbaz turned to the housekeeper. "You know I'm here to determine if this place is good or evil?"

"I do."

"Then you're a fool to tell me of murders. A fool, or an honest man. Your people will prosper if I decide one way, yet you persuade me the other?"

The housekeeper drew himself up. "You'd find out anyhow. Talk to the townsfolk and you'd hear the true evils of this House of Souls, mixed in with legends. Gory legends, to make matters worse than they are. With this mansion for inspiration one of our local arts is the spinning of ghost stories."

"The town entertains a small stream of vulgar tourists," Devineau contributed. "They come to be shown a place of horrors. But now I tell you how Queen Mama thinks. Each brick in these walls is a soul. The cumulative virtue of this house is determined by the virtue of so many souls, from which you must deduct the evils perpetrated by Mister Roberant and those who slaughtered his household."

"Ah." Hashbaz walked around the room, his gaze drawn up by instreaming luminosity, brighter toward the heights. Jewel-stuff? He could almost see how this milky light was compounded of rainbow scintillas, atomies of flashing color. "But how can these souls be virtuous? They sought to escape death, someday to find life in new bodies. All this is against God's plan."

"Many had no choice," the black man answered. "The poor were taken from their bodies to give the rich two lives. How can we judge without knowing?"

Hashbaz shook his head. "To know . . . to dream all these souls we need equipment. We'll go to the Heegens and ask for helmets. Then we have to extract each brick—"

The housekeeper blanched. "Destroy the House? *Then* where would we be? Ludicrous! You have no right—"

Devineau put up his hands. "Stop this noise." Simple words, affirming forever the superiority of 'Mbo courtier over local guide.

He turned. "You misunderstand, Hashbaz. These aren't dream memory cassettes, they're a different storage medium. You can't dream these souls; they didn't even *know* about dream protocols back when they were recorded. You can only bring them to life."

"We still need equipment, and bodies too," Hashbaz answered, venturing to extremes like a good diplomat, the better to compromise in the end. "Lord knows how many bodies!"

"Just one body," the housekeeper insisted. "One soul.

One to stand for all, chosen after careful prayer. Is that not the way to do it? The town senate would forbid anything more drastic, but certainly we can spare a single brick."

—and so the House of Souls inquiry is shelved pending the arrival of memory equipment from the Pale. I move on to the next site, gratified to discover how easily progress is delayed and decisions avoided. But Your Worship understands it seems best that we negotiate with the Heegens for such equipment, and bring this soul to life within our new city, all without 'Mbo participation, so my randomly chosen brick can prove uncoached to be Good or Evil. And though I find the thing useful as a paperweight when Texus winds gust through my tent, I forward it with this brief letter.

I presume the Heegens will be slow to deliver. It's my ambition to be slower: Your Worship obliged to assign someone else to the House of Souls affair. But if poor Hashbaz must see it through I can be at your side in six months with a preliminary assessment of the shrines of Texus.

And acknowledging I am sometimes regrettably impertinent when sharpened by the rigors of travel, I never forget I am also

> *Your obedient servant,*
>
> *Hashbaz Troffit*

Six months later Comrade Zhang Jok rose from his altar-bed. He looked at himself; big hands, hairy-devil forearms. "I'm white!" he giggled. "Barbarian name, barbarian body!"

"Do you speak Inglish?" Hashbaz asked from the foot of the room.

"If you listen very carefully, you'll discover I *am* speaking English," Jok answered. Something of barbarian deviltry seemed worked into his personality, for he continued: "After forty years' learning I speak better than you."

Hashbaz blushed. "I'm told you'll adjust to your body very quickly, and should move and kick before trying to stand." Reminded of his source of information, Hashbaz looked over his shoulder. Behind him a pair of deacons nodded, and escorted the Heegen memory technician from the room.

Jok complied, and exercised. The room fell silent and the silence grew nervously long. "So now what?" Jok spoke, looking at a row of solemn faces. "Do you expect something from me?"

"It's our job to watch over you, and see to your needs."

"And what's *my* job?" Suspicion clouded Jok's face. "This isn't 2146, is it?" A question without a question's lilt; the answer was obvious in the design of the room and the clothing of Jok's attendants. "What year is it?"

"It's 2507. Your last memories are from 2146?"

"Forty-five," Jok spoke. "I'm going to walk now." He slid from the gurney and moved drunkenly. "Shouldn't you be giving me some orientation?"

"As you command," Hashbaz responded. "You ask what your job is, as if it's for us to say. But I tell you it's up to *you* to decide your work. Whatever you want to do, we'll make facilities available."

Jok blinked. "You're here to, uh . . . I don't understand. Are you my servants?"

Give him rope to hang himself. "We serve the greatest good by serving you," Hashbaz answered.

"There's something you're not telling me." Jok's eyes moved right to left. "Can we leave this room?"

The watchers parted. Jok toddled toward the doors and swung them open. "Bizarre," he muttered, looking into the Great Audience Hall. Choirs, monitors, delegations . . . He turned around. "The gift I hold in my brain may be for you, or not. My first job is to see to my own people. China must still exist; I must learn if you are enemies or friends. I beg forgiveness, but I am wary; my secrets are valuable."

"You want to go to China?" Hashbaz asked. "All the way across the seas?" He stared in dismay. His brick was blossoming into something more demanding than the average man. Hashbaz had prayed for an unambiguous sign the House of Souls was good or evil, and it looked like his prayer was answered—a soul who spoke of gifts and secrets was likely to make some mark on the world.

At that moment Hashbaz grew convinced. In his heart he wanted to believe that sometimes prayers *were* answered. This man was holy; whether angel or devil. He bowed low, no longer resenting his mission. "Would you be good enough to tell us your name?"

Messiah

Months on horseback taught Jok to behave as a true lordling; impossible to be surrounded by servility without quickly coming to expect it.

The troop descended the Berdino Hills and wound into a region of small-dried-out farms; some recent difficulty with irrigation, perhaps. Jok waved and Hashbaz rode up. "You telephoned? No difficulty about the books?"

"Always *some* difficulty. Getting an exemption from the ban on impious communications, then finding the right equipment and rat-nesting it all together. Ink too dry to squirt, sunspot interference . . . yet the job is done. All on the docks, and no problem booking space on a westbound ship."

Jok looked at the arid landscape. "A hundred kilometers north of here I spent decades swinging in the wind."

"They were ignorant, not illumined by prophecy," Hashbaz answered. "Lift your spirits, these are better days."

"Better?" Jok spluttered. "Does this look like Utopia?" He sank into himself. "Telephones and radio, but nothing new. There, that's the key. Nothing *new*-made, and nothing new *well* made." He looked across the trail, answering Hashbaz's watchful gaze. "If I'm allowed to help you must recognize your problems. Although . . . excuse me, my thoughts are rambling. Hashbaz, what *are* your problems? Hunger, disease? Tell me what your Cajamoors regret."

"That we are not strong enough to quell the Esreti, or take Cajan-Missura from the 'Mbo. That we are not virtuous enough to give bodies to all the boxed souls in the House of Souls, nor prove the power of prophecy by our witness. That we are not rich enough to buy fusion generators to make us richer. That we are not wise enough to plan for the day when the rootworm peril will cross to this hemisphere—"

"The rootworm peril? What do you mean? We had rootworms in my time, in Africa; a genetic experiment to restore the jungle habitat, only it worked too well." Jok listened to his own words and shuddered. He drew rein. "It's been spreading ever since?"

Hashbaz stared back. "You are truly from another time."

"*Has the jungle spread to China? Tell me!*"

"We know the land you mean, we call it the Khanate. Your people are the Leninim. Chinese mostly, all Asia pressed in among them except those who came across. Many have come across, and some accepted *panhe*, but those who didn't soured the welcome for the rest by adhering to atheism and conquering Deseret. Now we know them as the Esreti, whom everyone hates. So if ships carry your people away from rootworm jungle, they carry them somewhere else than here."

"And in fact they may have no escape."

Hashbaz frowned thoughtfully. "The Kwi of the ships will know these things. When we pitch tents among them we'll ask to talk, and perhaps they'll invite us down."

The docks were alive, but not in the Chinese sense of queuing throngs. In Calforna each clot of humanity was its own center, with documents, gear and spokesperson, each seeking to mesh with someone aboard the ship, each with its last-minute emergency. Jok's party rendezvoused with the man with the books and were introduced to a Kwi ticket agent—everything went well except now they had eight horses, and no one to stable them on.

"No horses at sea," the Kwi declared. Jok shrugged; it was Hashbaz's problem, not his. Almost he was unkind enough not to wait, for the ship made him curious.

Two long, submerged tubes, bigger than the largest submarines of his time. From both rose narrowing hulls, devised to slice water like knives, then widening above the waves. These parallel hulls were paired outriggers, a deck stretched between them, a vast square field of metal, little piles of trade-goods lying like scattered shanty-towns.

Hashbaz finished with the horses. Kwi porters took the party's goods and they spiraled up the stairs to boarding level, and across. Hashbaz inspected his tickets. "We have all nine lots of section MM135 to ourselves. We'll pitch tent in lot 5."

A half-hour walk and they were there. Jok stood off as his residence went up, a synsilks house of many rooms, even a small private yard, his territory marked by four flapping banners. Carpets were unrolled, pillows brought forth. Two bandoliered monitors took armed station under the entry canopy. At last Jok settled to review his printer-listings, and find out how much genetics he'd have to relearn.

He scratched notes in the margins, working until the outside light grew dim, when he rose and moved out to view the sunset. He turned north, and east. "How—? We've left harbor! I never even felt it!"

Hashbaz broke from conversation with a Kwi seaman, a square-headed Celt with tight red curls fringing his face. The Kwi bowed, unsure of comparative status, grudging Jok a slight superiority. "My lord, ours are the ships that evacuated Africa, Europe and the Near East, each passenger buying one precious meter of deck. You'll feel no turbulence, for they are brilliantly designed, the best ships ever made, each one a legend."

"I'd hate to have my meter on the edge of the deck," Hashbaz joked.

The Kwi turned. "People fell off, and sometimes deck-wars broke out between rival groups. But on the return leg of the journey the deck looked as now, practically empty."

"You still run passengers from China," Jok suggested.

"The courageous, the very rich and those with connections. We no longer suffer the crowds of two hundred years ago. No one will accept them, and it's cruel to make people jump once their fares run out. Better they stay and learn to live like monkeys in the jungle."

"Seaman Carrick is here to warn us," Hashbaz interjected.

The Kwi made a second bow. "See that tent yonder? The man is on honeymoon with his bride, a rich widow, old and fat. Tonight he'll kill her; he does it by injecting a poison. He's shipped with us before, those are his methods.

"I tell you so you'll be under no illusions. We Kwi live below, and by strict rules. One of those rules is not to impose ourselves above. Our two laws: do no damage to the ship, and pay your fare; otherwise we leave you to yourselves."

Jok turned to Hashbaz. "Lawless anarchy. Let's see to this widow. Invite them over for dinner."

Madam Calabis was pale and pulpy, monumentally unattractive. She smiled at her new lover, but saddened now and again as if her mind returned to her dead husband. Up and down her spirits ranged: she was almost kittenish when she remembered to be happy— Jok had never seen a woman of her bulk be kittenish, but that was the word for it.

The man was short, bald and peppery on a narrow range of subjects, totally disinterested in agriculture, the Leninish Khanate, religion . . . horse racing was Yang's central obsession.

In the middle of the meal a servant whispered in Jok's ear. "Nothing. We searched Yang's tent, his chests—"

"Then he's got it with him. He'll call it food poisoning, and we'll be maligned. Don't let them alone together—Better yet, take him off now. Tell him I've something in back I want to show him."

After these muttered instructions Jok rose and left. He moved to the privacy of his screened yard, opened a chest at random, and smiled when the man bowed through the curtains.

"Take off your shirt. No, don't ask why. I've a secret for you. A present for your wedding night." Jok made small coaxing gestures. Confusedly Yang began to comply. As he reached mid-deshabille Jok dashed up and grabbed from behind.

Snared in his sleeves the man fought at a disadvantage, yet got hold of his syringe and pulled it from his waist-sash. The two tumbled through the curtain, treading clumsily among cushions. The dinner party rushed from the other room and froze in a circle of witness as Jok grabbed the wildly waving instrument. Two hands commanded one weapon, and for a moment liquid tracery looped through the air. Then the stronger hand shoved the needle into a naked back and injected the last drop.

Yang collapsed. Jok rose, his chest heaving. "Tell Madam Calabis I've saved her life, and accepted responsibility for her as is my people's custom. Oh . . . sorry, here you are. Don't cry for Yang, he meant to murder you. Hashbaz, summon Seaman Carrick. He'll tell her the truth."

"You think I didn't suspect?" asked Madam Calabis. "Is death so bad?"

"Preferable to life with Yang. Madam Calabis, my establishment has only Hashbaz to run it. He could use help. You're not alone in this world as long as I'm here."

Hashbaz bent over his writing desk. *Your Worship;*
In a week of travel Comrade Zhang Jok brought peace and order to our deck, and became its king; Madam Calabis and myself his faithful ministers.
But now I'm in a quandary. Our question is an-

swered. I might leave him, assured the House of Souls deserves to become a shrine. Yet Jok's benefactions rank small in his own mind compared to the work he means to do, to rescue all China from the rootworm peril. And in this I'm inclined to offer help. They are not my people, but they are many and their need is great.

See how I've been seduced! I believe in this man. The old Hashbaz speaks to warn me I've caught a perilous disease, it's all trickery and sham!

The irony is that Jok tells me he was a nonentity in former times; a dull chrysalis broken to unveil the glories of a butterfly. But as the shores of China approach he is more silent, sulking in unspoken anger. His own people, and we know the troubles saints have among their own people. Have we made him a god by treating him as one? Will the Chinese unmake him by their disbelief?

Nevertheless they'll have trouble disbelieving, for Jok comes with an entourage. So we will see.

Hashbaz sealed his letter, and stepped outside. He found Jok and Seaman Carrick together and handed the Kwi sailor his envelope.

Carrick's functions included delivering as well as accepting post. "Never in my country's history was it possible simply to cross the border," Jok spoke wearily, a new packet in his hands. "I must claim the right to do so, or beg permission. At least I recognize the characters, though they seem degraded."

"If I can do any paperwork—"

"To my Chinese you are deaf, dumb, and illiterate. The best you can do is drill your monitors, and hold ready."

And the next morning—China! Night gave way to fog. An articulation in the gray wove skyward, and resolved into near hills. Hashbaz watched Jok sigh in relief. "It's the same, or hardly different. I don't know what I expected. Not much room to get worse, and if it was vastly better my rescue mission would seem impertinent."

But the docks *were* different; Uighurs and Hindis porting cargo, the dominant costume a girdled caftan instead of quilted coat and trousers. Jok and his entourage debarked and moved slowly, a procession in search of its object.

Soldiers, and a cadre. "You claim to be Comrade Zhang Jok?"

Jok handed over his papers. "I come to call Chairwoman Lao a liar, for her promises are neglected. Her New China was to have provided me a body, but I'm relegated to this barbarian carcass. I speak for millions of Chinese souls, thousands still on Earth. Where is their redemption if not in your hands?"

"Chairwoman Lao. Chair*woman* Lao! Were you so foolish? Did you think the mind of Great Lenin could incarnate in the body of a woman? She spoke with her voice only, not with His."

"Is that how you escape responsibility?" Jok asked.

The cadre nodded, careful neither to defer nor condescend. "In any case we still await New China. Times are bad. We'd sell more bodies and shelve more souls, if anyone would buy them."

Jok took stock. "It's as I thought. Your name?"

"Comrade Chotokai Srednek, a mere Siberian in point of fact—"

"But pleased to await the dawn of New China? Comrade Chotokai, I announce that dawn. Those you should have rescued will rescue you instead."

Chotokai raised an eyebrow. "Have your men march after mine," Jok commanded. "My destination is the city of Kunming."

"K'ming is on the verge of jungle," Chotokai answered. "The chop-and-burn zone, air reeking with smoke and toxins. You can see the wild canopy—"

"Then they need me there."

Years later a leaner, grayer Hashbaz hacked through a green-desolated landscape; houses exploded up and out, shoots twined to hold planks and pots in airy suspension. Eight-yield photosynthesis gave vegetation energy to suck up the rains and leach the fertility of the soil until nothing remained but canopy-shadowed bed-rock, but the worst was behind him; here the human hand was still detectable; paddies kept their shape even if there was no water to flood them.

Hashbaz hiked northeast against the stream of traffic, answering the same questions again and again. "Yes, this is a road, the *best* road, however overgrown, but your bikes and handcarts are useless. Leave them be-hind, ration your water, and hurry."

After months of difficult travel he reached docks clut-tered with abandoned ships and boats. The Prophet's credit was good: the Kwi carried him across the ocean to Calforna, where by virtue of a recent treaty with the Esreti he was able to ride a "passenger" train eastward, his bench near enough to the midsection doors to let him enjoy the mountain views.

But no tracks serviced Holy City. Hashbaz finished his long journey by horse. He took two days to recuper-ate, then filed for an audience with the Prophet.

The old man summoned him to the bedchamber where he lay ill; withered flesh in a room of gleaming cream and gold. "Well?" the Prophet asked. "A long time without news. Thanks to an out-of-date letter your House of Souls is now immersed in sanctity and Texuns grow rich. Oh, sit—sit on the bed—our regal interior hardly allows for movable chairs. Sit, nephew, and tell your old uncle what you saw. It's been nothing but rumors here."

Hashbaz sat. "Your Worship . . . I wrote letters con-stantly, and rarely had courage to mail them. When I did I contradicted myself; but in any case it seems they were never delivered. About Jok being good or evil: I grew ungenerous these missing years. His work con-sumed my time and the careers of thousands. I'd have said he was supremely evil for demanding so much from so many, and he *would* have been evil if it was all a sham."

"But not so? He succeeded against the jungle?"

Hashbaz dropped his voice. "The jungle prospers. Millions fought it almost to a standstill, but they fight no more. All South China is hurriedly emptying through K'ming. Bearing strange seedstocks they fan out into the green, though all movement is slow and the land grows too choked for travel.

"Now belatedly the Khan condemns Jok, but soon the old Khanate will be a ghost-thing, and if desperate Leninim invade us through Alaska it will not be with irresistible numbers. Do you see, Your Worship? A string of dominoes, alternately bad and good, and Jok set them into collapse."

But the Prophet had no mind for the Khanate. "*Into* the jungle!" He struggled to sit up.

"With seeds. Hypertrophied pitcher plants provide reservoirs under hooded hair-weft decks. Sweet nectar-water and dry floors, and other weird varietals for food. The Garden of Eden revisited—I've been there. Miracle of miracles!"

The Prophet leaned back. "Can civilization survive in the jungle?"

Hashbaz shook his head. "No roads, no urban centers. Centuries ago Earth bled its best blood into space. Up there they remake worlds while we do nothing but compromise with nature, and at what a cost!"

"Compromise is better than death."

"I have two selves," Hashbaz answered. "One rejoices to see China's millions fed. The other warns that compromise destroys the chance of victory. We must face our problems. Nature must adapt to us, not us to nature. We must unite and master the ancient sciences—"

The Prophet rolled his head in the negative. "Even the ancients failed to defeat the jungle." Seeing Hashbaz keep silent, he elaborated. "We'll return Comrade Zhang's old brick to the House of Souls, and mark its location. If the rootworm jungle crosses to this hemisphere and threatens to overcome us, we'll give him a new body. I'll leave instructions to my successor."

"Is that all we can harvest from this?" Hashbaz stood. "I hoped you'd heal the turbulence of my spirit. I have meat for a hundred sermons about heroism and morality and persistence and exhaustion, and how salvation can blossom out of meekness, but I don't know whether to praise or condemn. Years of sacrifice made useless because I don't know; is humanity better off now or not?"

The Prophet laughed. "We preach against boxed souls and perversions of God's plan. Now we put our trust in the genius of one dead brick! You think my spirit's less troubled than yours? But I can do this. We don't want pilgrims traipsing through the House of Souls, do we? Carving initials and stealing souvenirs?

"Let's punish Comrade Zhang Jok for confounding our moral simplicities, and put the place under quarantine. Let his name be cursed from now until the day he comes back to life, to save our future generations!"

"Cursed? I'm not comfortable with that, either."

"Nevertheless you'll write up your life in this final light; an unambiguous testimony. You understand religious politics—at least you used to. I need that old Hashbaz at my side. Say amen, Hashbaz. Put your messiah behind you."

"A cursed messiah is a strange thing, Your Worship. If our church does this to him, what will Jok do to us when we need him again?"

"I cannot begin to conceive an answer. Now rest, Hashbaz. Rest and write new scripture, and may God inspire you."

Regimes are born, and die. Cultures have life spans just like people. Historians who describe great cycles and the lesser pendulum-swings of fashion sometimes take too much from the lesson and preach the futility of existence; their enemies see humankind on a straight and steady march to glory.

That march that would have given us a permanent moon base, but for the fact that there was a pendulum swing in the early 1970s, and a president who cashed in on NASA's triumphs while slashing its budget to the bone.

The truth would seem to lie somewhere between two extremes. Our course is an upward-trending spiral, two steps forward, one step back. While societies evolve new structures, sometimes the most simple old truths have to be rediscovered.

Within the Pale

September

Triumph! The Game moved into Phase Eight, the beginning of yet another Happily Ever After. Sharbad Hetlig shared a palanquin with golden-wigged Chryphe as they set forth on their honeymoon mission, down from the sun-drenched roofs of the West-Central Subleague, through the vast and vacant levels of the defeated Hoon, and thence into the mysterious Twice-Undercity.

Young Ridoftaw, their Twice-Under guide, held one of those remarkable stunwands that had done so much to topple the Hoon tyranny. The procession trudged in smug security. . . .

"Aarrrahhh!" Ridoftaw collapsed, an arrow in his chest. Hoon supers rushed from tangent corridors, swords drawn. The ambassadorial party's numbers were so unequal that after leaping from comfort Sharbad froze, waiting until the Hoon captain stalked into view, his wax-pale face peering from a bright red robe, his preposterous hood stiffened by ribbings of wood.

The captain waved impatiently: "Kill them all." Hoon supers pushed in, slashing and stabbing. Sharbad and Chryphe parried and thrust back, outraged by the wrongness, the evil—

Assailed from three sides, his footing hindered by dead bodies and slick hot blood, Sharbad saw his wife's severed arm fly by before he himself was skewered. His final memories were of unfocussed color and clangor, and the bitter pain of defeat.

His eyes opened. "Against the rules!" he complained in a voice without timbre. "What is this?"

A woman puffed to his side, hair damp-plastered, scant frame for her round face. "You always dream of us," came her answer. "We're careful to see to that. How do you like your body?"

Out of sight a refrigerator slammed. How mundane! How rare! Lifetimes in a simulation universe had passed without its equal. The new man looked at himself, brown arms and lean, bony chest. "Chinese?"

"Siberian; parents from Srednekolymsk hard by the Norwegian-American border. Tough, not fat like me."

The woman was a doctor by dress, her body stout, her face plain but for unnaturally white dentures. She turned from the INFOWEB readout. "You've a choice of names: Chubanov, or Sharbad, or the one you had when first alive. Let's see . . ."

"Torfinn." He turned to see a younger attendant edge into view, black thick eyebrows and nervous with her hands, unhappily demure.

But the doctor meant to dominate this conversation. "Torfinn Oskarssen: medalist back when the Olympics meant new records every four years. Since then, a shining star in a different Game—"

"I was arrested for body-hopping. Exiled to Mercury, to the City of the Dead, to eternity inside the Game." The Game! As Torfinn spoke he remembered, and trembled with loss.

The doctor smiled. "Torfinn, the real world needs

heroes. That's why we snagged you from Happily Ever After, and plugged Chubanov in. Eight minutes by radio, signals boosted from orbit, sixteen minutes' round trip. Four minutes to prep poor Chubanov, thirty to brief you, ten minutes' break and I see my next recruit. Six souls a day, twenty-four a week: my associates and I hope to build an army of five thousand by April. Questions?"

"You need an army of five thousand? Uh, we still in the Hegemony? What year is this?"

"It's 2349. The Rastrians are at our throats. Black Caribbeans—"

"RastaFARians!" Torfinn marvelled. A radio! *"If we don't get the love we need, we're surely going to die!"* God, what would dear Chryphe think of old Nate Bucklin? "Send in killer robots. Zap 'em with boomstars."

The doctor lifted her gaze as if invoking the saints. "THEY wouldn't like that. Leave off bloodshed a few centuries and the whole business rolls back to zero. They see us as masters of Earth. World government needs no army, only constables."

Torfinn sat, laying his corded arms on the sheet, studying his joints and fingers. "INFOWEB knows my crime. In 2089 the contents of my brain were stored on disk, my body sold, my mind radioed off to join the dead on Mercury. Goodbye, gooooodbye! Now you've reversed the sequence. All quite familiar."

"To *you*, not Sharbad Hetlig. Some souls can't free themselves from the Game. They can't find back to reality."

Torfinn grinned. "Reality? Who did you mean when . . ." He raised a finger heavenward.

"Luna, Venus, Helice, bubble worlds, asteroids, Stargate. Bugs, fictoids, Gatekeepers—I'm going to spew names till you're cowed. How can I describe our political tangle in these minutes, a situation involving Galactic bogeymen? Imagine telling an early American about the Hegemony! You'd have one lifeline to throw out; in an altered form America still exists! I throw that same line to you. This is your Hegemony, however shrunken. We need your help."

"Chubanov was a criminal? Tell me about myself."

The doctor found a chair. "Mind if I drink?" She pulled a nozzle from the wall and sucked. Torfinn was too fastidious to copy her gesture.

He shook his head. "What he do wrong?"

"Misguided loyalty. In your day tribalism was regarded as an infantile condition from which humanity had emerged. New tribes kept being created, but nobody paid heed. Nobody said 'Hey, an instinct's at work here!'

"Earth's population plunged during the twenty-first century, but you had micro-societies that bred enthusiastically: hippies, Hutterites, Mormons. Not many generations passed before rural technophobes were in the majority. Hegemonians found it wise to withdraw to our pales. My Heegens were no different than the Gumbos, or the Cajamoors, or the Rastrians; except a Gumbo swears loyalty to Mama first, and only secondarily to the Hegemony.

"Which brings us to modern times. After generations that second loyalty dropped away. It was only theoretical, and the cities have always been despised for our luxuries."

Torfinn swung his legs over the edge of the bed. He flexed his knees. "So now they plunder you."

The doctor was fond of what she sucked; she savored the taste before continuing. "We built a security wall around the Pale, robot eyes and hair-trigger shadbolts. We relied on the wall, and hired Rastrian entertainers and athletes for amusement. Suddenly the wall failed."

"I see how that might happen."

"And if they'd not found New England almost too much to digest, they'd have sacked the Hudson Valley arcopoli. As it is there's Connecticut. We want to win it back. We want to show vigor."

Torfinn shook his head in amazement. "You had the

world! More! You had the whole solar system! Oh, I know the Hegemony's control of space was pretty nominal—"

The doctor nodded. "We're left with the Hudson Pale, England, and much of Western Sahara. Another thing: if we ever sweep Rastrian pirates from the Atlantic, we'll discover our three lands have become three Hegemonies. It's all quite sad. You'd be quixotic to think us worth your life, if not for one outside factor.

"But time's up. Sita will show you to your suite. Tomorrow you train. As for that strange factor, all in good time. How much human thought revolves over trifles, and I've delivered centuries for you to digest!"

Torfinn reached the door to what might have been a hospital wardroom. As it slid open the doctor spoke again. "One last note. This world's about lots of things, cultures, philosophy and love. Don't let them distract you. Your life's about one thing only; fighting our enemies."

Sita tapped Torfinn's shoulder, quiet Sita of the heavy eyebrows. They left, walking the single illuminated corridor until they reached a ceilinged street, dim lanes delineated by pips of light. The stillness was absolute. Torfinn spoke in defiance of its oppression: "What's your role?"

Sita shrugged. "I'm under orders to get pregnant."

"Uh, by—what *is* this stuff?" Torfinn hastily changed the subject. "I thought it was concrete, but—"

Sita's answer was curt. "We call it durium."

Torfinn's steps echoed as he was herded into the lobby to his right, whose walls were lined with posters—pictures of consumables, and names so stylized as to be icons rather than words. Beyond stood a brilliantly lit pit. A long ramp curved down from the upstairs perimeter. "Where are all the people?" he asked.

"We have more than I ever remember; refugees," Sita responded. "But except for religious services we're not outdoorsy: we're couch potatoes, we keep to our rooms. Anyhow Peekskill is overbuilt and we're unpleasantly close to the subway here. Consider this your home ward, and defend it, because here's where you'll meet infiltrating hoodlums."

At Sita's gesture Torfinn took the ramp to a basement passage where she showed him to an electric car. A safety bar pressed his skinny thighs into the cushions below. Sita sat ahead. Her vehicle whined into life, circled into a tunnel and down descending spirals.

She raised an arm to point out an arch of green lights. "Sonic security," she shouted back. They chained from intercom to intercom; the same soft, soothing voice read announcements over and over again.

Torfinn studied the back of Sita's closely shaved head and listened to the whine of the motor, the churn of air from the vents, the ululation of a distant siren. The air was warm; it smelled of acetones, ozone, burnt insulation, and bus station waiting rooms.

The car reached target level and whined off. Freight vehicles challenged Sita's siren with honks of their own, a low-speed competition whose losers were forced to swerve or brake. People in face masks watched from platforms along the walls. The intercom became another zone of conflict; messages interrupted messages.

The car worked through all this to a loading stage. Torfinn lifted his safety bar and surveyed a row of metal doors. He blew his nose, then entered the cell Sita chose for him. The bed was girt by a metal skeleton and could be reshaped; a warm cocooning mass. Nozzles dangled from the plush wall, teats ringed by light, near control panels festive with decorated buttons.

At the end of the room the polyped wall lost texture and became dull as slate. An H-V screen?

Torfinn closed the door. Sita was already half undressed. "Impressed with us?" she asked.

"Not much," came the answer.

Sita's face fell. "We'll be wiped out, the cities emptied. Most have lost faith, except the cultists, the memory-dreamers. Would you like to see a service? Some think our fanatics are worse than the Rastrians."

Torfinn drew Sita into his embrace. "Forget enemies.

I have compartments to my mind. I've closed that one and thrown away the key."

Later that night Torfinn fell into natural sleep. He drove a two-lane highway to a track meet in Fargo, North Dakota, his classic Dodge Caravan slaved to his Samurai 986, when a patrolman stopped and lectured him about using cruise control options on icy roads, pseudo-steering a vehicle with bald tires! Next instant he was in jail, no hope of taking part in the meet—

A typical bad dream, but Torfinn hadn't had a real dream for two hundred sixty years.

Sita was gone when he woke. Kicking free of his cocoon triggered the H-V to broadcast morning news. Torfinn sucked a breakfast.

A large button by the bed featured a red question mark. He pushed.

"Yes?"

"Where do I pee?"

Pause and giggles: "Anywhere."

Torfinn faced a corner. The stream hit the floor, Dancing beebees whisked into a crack where wall and floor joined.

"Easy come, easy go." There was a knock at his door.

His visitor was short-torsoed, large-headed, muscled like a dancer, with African face and buttocks. He stuck his hand forward: "Sergeant Haas; by precedence your guide and tutor. Where were you in the Game?"

"In a world-compassing city. Heard of the Hoon?"

"I played in a jungle; Tree-shags and Dwerkin. Know what I'm talking about?" Haas moved in herky-jerky fashion, canting his head inquisitively, like a bird, like someone living at double speed.

Torfinn shrugged. "They say there's only a handful of real souls in every simulation." He looked sad. "I fell in love. I was on my honeymoon."

Before he could mope Haas took his arm and tugged him out to the staging platform. "Our first exercise; *run* to the subway station, dodging traffic. Don't worry, people drive like somnambulists, no more than thirty kloms per hour."

"In this hospital shirt?"

"We'll find you a uniform. Come on! Run!"

They jogged diagonally down the six-lane trafficway toward a diverging tributary, unnoticed by workmen who mobbed a truck a hundred meters away. A glowering head ranted from the distant wall. Haas pointed. "One of the gods. Religion—"

"My name was in a database," Torfinn spoke in rhythmic puffs. "The doctor called me Sharbad. She'd know if my Chryphe was real, or just part of the Game."

Haas broke pace to let a bus whine by. "If she was perfect for you she was designed to be. We all had loves; that's part of the Game. Last night you had a real woman. Not so good, was she?"

"No character," Torfinn answered. "Just sad emptiness."

"Not her fault. You're used to outrageous extremes of virtue and villainy."

They left the road for a booth-lined depot and approached a brilliantly lit row of escalators. Beneath a revolving chandelier they ascended into a cathedral void. Haas pointed to a puzzlement of colored lines spread across the far wall, beyond a pattern of grooves fluting the polished floor.

His voice echoed. "We're the yellow asterisk. The glowing dot on the green line is a train from Albany. These others are recruits like you, not passengers: most of Peekskill's lines are closed to keep out Rastrians."

The trainees gathered near their exercise mats. Torfinn joined them, and was led through forty minutes of yoga. The Albany train rolled in, three cars they were told to loot. Haas distributed karate uniforms from the heap, and the hour before lunch was devoted to self-defense.

"I was right," his neighbor whispered to Torfinn. "We're being trained as police, not soldiers."

Racial blending gave her peppercorn hair and an apricot skin. Torfinn studied her body. "What was her crime, this soul you've replaced?"

"It's new, this business of forced pregnancies. The

Heegens want to build up their population. A new era of sexism. My predecessor resisted it."

"Then there'll be lots of female habituses available." Torfinn smiled and thought to tell her about Chryphe, who might after all be real—

Haas interrupted. "You've all got lunchboxes. Take a break. Some haven't heard my speech. You rest don't wander far. Baton drill one o'clock sharp."

Torfinn grabbed a box and sat on a bag of gear. Haas nodded at him and the others. "How to start? Is everyone familiar with this stargate we found in the twenty-first century, thirteen light-hours out from the sun? How it was built four billion years ago? Hell, for all we knew God lived there! Stargate was heaven!"

He paused, then continued gamely against their silence. "I was alive in my true body. I watched the news. We sent missions to Stargate and got messages out, including rare communiques from the so-called Gatekeepers, closemouthed representatives of a Galactic Empire! Around 2100 they told us to send an embassy through the gate to LuSs, their 'capitol planet.' Of course we didn't know any better; we based our decisions on seven hundred garbled words. Stargate was a mystery, and remains so to this day—except where LuSs is concerned.

"LuSs is where the children of our embassy are being bred and *tamed*, because aren't we wild? God knows how unrecognizable they are after eight generations, those specimens of *Homo domesticus!*"

Torfinn exchanged looks with the woman. Haas noticed. "Think I'm off tangent? Consider these Gatekeepers: a four-*billion*-year-old culture! Do we humans owe hi-tech civilization to their wiles, attaining space to deliver a few kids into their hands? Now they have breeding stock, has our Hegemony achieved its goals, so it can wither on the vine?

"We humans *are* wild; maybe dangerous. It might even be worthwhile to engineer our decay. Perceptive Hegemonians have looked into the problem. Earth's fall to savagery is devised to lock the human race in our one-system wilderness reserve! Ladies and gentlemen, do you like dancing in aboriginal quaintness before the Gatekeepers' cameras? In your Game you were diddled by a supercomputer—are we diddled in real life by aliens who dare not tolerate our rivalry?"

Haas paced, pent and hyperactive. "I was pulled out of the Game like you. What I'd taken for life and death were mere bitflips inside Mercury's biggest computer. I felt cheated. I'm sure you understand. Torfinn speaks of his love, and I tell him he's in love with a figment!

"Who cheated you? The Hegemony? Around us we see hare-brained schemes to restore a declining world order. Our masters lack vitality and whore after cult-gods. You'd dislike them even if they hadn't tampered with your futures, and so I ask you to turn your attitudes completely around.

"Truth is they *rescued* you from a trivial existence.

"Second, you're rescued for an important purpose. You're training to quell the Rastrians. That's important: talk to refugees from Boston, you'll find what Rastrian rule is like. Yes, quell the Rastrians, *and maintain civilization on Earth at a level capable of giving the Gatekeepers a run for their money!*"

Haas paused. "Well, that's it. That's the political situation we're in here."

Torfinn spoke. "The ultimate conspiracy theory."

"Doesn't it seem strange to you that an urban civilization would quake at the challenge of uncouth tribes?" Haas answered.

The woman raised her hand. "How do we know so much about LuSs?"

"Radio. Our inadvertent colony boasts how they've evolved toward the galactic ideal. They preach at us, and we preach back—these last decades we've run out of things to say. The axioms of life are different for them than they are for us."

"The Gatekeepers must have secret agents," she remarked.

Haas nodded. "Yes, Olivia, teasing faces in a house of mirrors that cause us to break trust with ourselves. Very nearly the gods come to impeaching each other, and the secular authorities to reviling the gods—"

Torfinn stood. "Yesterday I heard that the tribes swore first loyalty to their own chiefs. That *first* loyalty became their *only* loyalty. It's happening again with these devotees. How can the Hegemony tolerate gods, knowing they'll eventually betray the state?"

Scattered claps endorsed his words. Haas smiled a pixie smile. "I've become one of these crazies myself. I'm under the illusion I'm a good guy. But enough. Time's up. You need to learn how to use a police baton."

Around sixteen hundred an aching Torfinn shouldered his new equipment and trudged to his cell, bulky in bulletproof body armor. He was trying to access INFOWEB from his bedside terminal when a message flashed on his screen. "Congratulations, you're a keeper. You join the real troop next week. Busy Sunday?"

It was Haas. Torfinn contemplated begging him for help in finding the truth about Chryphe, yet he held back. A Game-related obsession would mark him flawed.

Still, if he jollied Haas along— "Sure, I'm free," he typed. Sunday? Were there still weekends, or was he about to be proselytized?

Sunday. The memory chamber was crowded, yet the bed was empty. Torfinn and Olivia pressed forward to study the helmet that dangled above. Haas stepped from the shelves, cartridge in hand: "Pierre Thutton: a chemical engineer," he announced.

"We became as children," voices chanted. "We surrendered science to brains of silicon. We surrendered the dream."

"We shall dream again." Haas's tone shifted toward intimacy. "The man whose soul I hold knew calculus, chemistry and physics. His habits were routine, he was heterosexual and sober. Who will take the risk?"

Olivia's eyebrows rose. Haas grinned. "There's al-

ways some chance of losing yourself into a new identity.
That's what's happened to the gods; they've compounded
into megapersonalities. In theory they all approximate
one another as they gain more memories—"

"You said cartridge memories were watered to prevent loss of identity!"

Haas reached for the helmet and slid the cassette into
its slot. "If you made the effort you might dream Mr.
Thutton over and over until he came to life in your
body, or stop just short, you and him in balance. It's up
to you. I merely provide the warning, I don't make the
decisions."

"I always wanted to understand calculus," Torfinn
muttered.

"Dream Thutton once and follow with an INFOWEB
review. You'll have calculus fixed in *your* mind in less
than a week!"

"You've done this?"

Haas bobbed his head in high-tempo acknowledge-
ment. "I've dreamt fourteen souls. That's the meaning
of these tally-beads around my neck. I could open my
own academy if the Hegemony ever went back to teachers and books."

January

Goggle vision showed luminous air, a dark-framed ruddy soup stirred by gentle currents. Torfinn studied the infrared flux and learned from its patterns that he'd reached the desired tunnel. The enemy's escape route was corked. He waved the others into position, readied his stunner and waited for vagrant "Rastrians," quite possibly blind, unprepared for the tactics of a Gamebred army, never expecting they'd simply turn out the lights.

The alarm shrilled this morning, and sonic barriers thrummed to hem in the conflict. A Rastrian forlorn hope was invading Peekskill; Tribesmarshal Jimmit of New Canaan had recruited soldiers from his Heegen underclass, undisciplined podgy brutes who tried to emulate their masters in rapacity. Burdened with armor Torfinn and his comrades repeatedly ran them down, or stunned them from ambush. By the end of the day the trainees' confidence was soaring, and they spoke of counter-invasion.

One last bedraggled enemy contingent filed Torfinn's way, moving not along the floor, but up on the conduit ledge, incandescent ghosts hoping to sneak among utility pipes toward open air and freedom. Not too dumb! One among them guessed the hotter tubes would dazzle goggled eyes like neon: nevertheless they weren't bright enough to blind him, and a troop of men was a clumsy thing to hide.

Torfinn climbed to meet them. ZAP! Their leader slumped. Torfinn stepped over and tingled the second in command.

They panicked, waving guns and firing blindly. Some jumped to the floor, bright comas of fear rippling the trailing air. Olivia moved to cut them off, countering coup with impressive skill. Meanwhile those who pursued them attacked the rear. It was over in less than a minute.

"I know what will convince you all of ultimate triumph," "Captain" Haas spoke after the H-V confirmed his field promotion. "Monday I had the privilege of visiting the H.S. *Redondo Beach.* Officers I commend will sail with her on her maiden voyage soon as she's ready. Ships like her will win back the Atlantic, cutting off Rastrian reinforcements. Soon our enemies will be isolated!"

His voice echoed grandiloquently in the vastness of the subway station. Olivia stood forward. "We should use our captives, plug copies of our souls in 'em and send them back to New Canaan as a fifth column—"

"We'll use them, but would *you* be sent on a suicide mission? Every copy of your soul is equal in rights—"

Torfinn leapt to his feet. "We'll save training. There's precedent; the gods' worshippers dream their memories and become spiritual clones. Why not clone us?"

"Who takes orders when you're identical?" Haas roared back. "There's got to be a heirarchy. Don't worry, our army's growing fast, we're even taking Heegen auxiliaries from outside the Game. With you for skill and them for numbers we'll soon have the Rastrians on the run!"

April

New Canaan was all but won and Peekskill's ranks stood five thick about the fluted floor at the entrance to the Danbury train tunnel. A few meters within lurked the remnants of Bosky Jimmit's host, the last of New Canaan's Rastrian defenders. They were enough to hold the tunnel mouth, but in time weariness and hunger must impel them to surrender.

Lieutenant Torfinn Oskarssen hoped to hasten this event, but the more he explained the hopelessness of his position to the aged Tribesmarshal Jimmit, the more that wily Rastrian suspected there were objects to be achieved by stubborn delay.

Unfortunately he was right. Torfinn was so eager to ride the H.S. *Redondo Beach* on its maiden voyage that he was willing to sweeten his pleas with offers of passage to a neutral station. Almost willing. Unreasonable that Chief Jimmit should make him piss away his victory. Why should the old man's contrary instinct prevail against all his clever precautions?

Torfinn cast about impatiently. He saw a sidetracked coach car, abandoned by the Rastrians during the final charge. He summoned his Heegen sergeants.

"Can that thing be made to roll?" he asked. "If a hundred men pushed it, would it move?"

"INFOWEB controls it!" one protested. "You must submit a request transaction. Only with the tracks blocked—"

"You don't understand. Take a hundred men and push it to the tunnel mouth. Lean like this and press."

With hopeless shrugs they called out names. Figures emerged from the redundant crowd standing back from the Danbury line. Torfinn surveyed a rout of conquerors grown dubious of his competence.

He spaced them around the coach, led them into the first push, and basked in the warmth of their awe as the car rolled several meters.

"Chief Jimmit!" he shouted. "We've a coach here. We plan to roll it into the tunnel unless you surrender. For eight kloms the hole is barely larger than a coach. After that it becomes too hot for life."

"The tracks's blocked, mon!" Bosky Jimmit rasped in answer. "INFOWEB—"

"We're moving it by hand. By the time it reaches the tunnel mouth it'll have picked up speed. We'll bowl you down!"

No answer came to this challenge. After a minute Torfinn gave the signal. With cries of "Free Connecticut!" his Heegens shoved. The coach rumbled forward. Moments later dark figures darted from the tunnel, running madly into the opening arc of their enemies. Rastrians trapped within the train passage screamed and scattered.

"Stop the car!" Torfinn yelled. His men reversed their efforts. The coach decelerated to a halt short of the mouth. "Back it up to try again," Torfinn ordered. "Only this next run there'll be no stopping short."

He shouted to his adversary. "You have one minute to surrender!"

Enemies emerged in rapid ones and twos. Behind them Tribesmarshal Jimmit strolled forward, blinking in the light. "You win," he conceded. "Some hurt ones be back there. Don't use him coach, mon, she be murder. Pray stand back!"

He waved his gun against the crowd. "Shout 'em back. I set me to blow. Me skull go bloody tick-tock."

"Keep off!" Torfinn commanded. "Don't do it, Jimmit! If it's your memories—"

"Can't let you at 'em, or you fetch up all Rastria!" He laughed and pointed to his head. "Hot stuff, mon!" It shattered open, raining blood and brains in all directions.

"Christ have mercy!" Torfinn whispered, sinking to his knees.

"They call New England 'Rastria,' " Torfinn reported next morning.

"Not for long." Colonel Haas peered from the bridge as the tow barge pulled the *Redondo Beach* into the upper reservoir. Scattered children waved from the sea-wall road.

In her bridge the status board lit up. "Deuterium 2300," it said, but the numbers flew quickly into the hundred thousands. The tritium count incremented far more slowly.

The ship's captain scratched his head while consultants rushed forward. A minute later their heads were buried in volumes of wiring diagrams. Torfinn had yet to learn the problem. "Look at them!" the old man spoke to his colonel. "Our new heroes! We won't need thud-and-blunder Gamers in the years to come."

"There'll always be work too dirty for your lads to touch," Haas answered dryly.

By eleven o'clock the *Redondo Beach* lay snug within the upper lock. Luminaries crowded the dikes. The captain used the time to fiddle with the sails. The ship's two vertical wings shifted back and forth.

At last the gates swung apart. The impetus of the flow drew the *Redondo Beach* into the lower reservoir. On the status board glowed the words "Sonar steering table ready to activate. Activate: Yes [] No []."

The captain rubbed his chin and tapped the yes box

with his finger. A black, glossy table in the center of the bridge lit with gorgeous colors. Torfinn recognized the lower reservoir. Their position was shown by a blinking square at the table's center.

"Red must mean shallow," Colonel Haas muttered.

"Dangerously shallow. We need to get *here*." The captain touched a patch of yellow.

A subliminal shudder-hum ran through the ship. Water churned along the port side. "Now I know what God feels like," the captain laughed.

"You can target your enemy the same way?" Olivia asked.

"Yes, Lieutenant; one finger to choose my weapon, another to condemn a pirate crew to watery death."

"You call us thud-and-blunderers, but we try to take our foes alive."

"True," the captain answered. "You're the moral ones: we're merely antiseptic."

Rastrian ships did not dominate this part of Long Island Sound; their fleet anchored at New London. All for the best. The *Redondo Beach*'s crew needed to learn her ways before taking on the enemy. Yet as they emerged from the lower lock and trolled the sun-sparked waters near Greenwich all eyes were keen to find a foe to trounce before the visitors debarked.

Distant whitecaps deceived their view. The table's scale was poked up toward max: 1 in 30,000. At last: "What's that? A scout?"

The captain moved to his scope. "A Rastrian silhouette." He touched two places along the steering table. With a windy shriek a missile launched over the waters. Torfinn counted ten seconds. Too long? Failure?

A white flash. "Perhaps you all should go ashore. We're a working vessel now."

Torfinn finished his New Canaan report on the *Redondo Beach*'s lander. Haas smiled. "Subway and sea. If we can master them by overland, and flank them to boot—this was a narrow winter for the Hegemony, but now they've got their gear out of mothballs."

"That captain looks forward to dispensing with our services," Olivia grumbled.

"Physically we're not of them," Torfinn agreed. "Our bodies are captured tribalists. Mentally we're from another age—"

"Barbarians, hired to fight barbarians."

Colonel Haas nodded. "I've inquired about our future. There's much to do before Connecticut is ours, but then?

"Call to mind how your souls were radioed to Mercury when you first died. That same method sent explorers to Stargate three centuries ago. We didn't get a lot of messages from those scouts, just enough to know how the process works. Stargate's set up for the reception of souls; that's how the Gatekeepers move around.

"The best defense is a good offense. An army of five thousand Gamers might teach those aliens a lesson. Sure, it's a risk—"

"Christ!" Torfinn exploded. "When an elephant treads on an anthill, is there tragedy? Do the ants send armies in retaliation?"

Haas saw dignitaries lined up at the approaching dock, and lowered his voice. Torfinn barely heard his whisper over the engine. "Perhaps you'd rather go back to the Game?"

That night they rode the subway home to Peekskill. The colonel broke his moody silence to speak again. "All this is middle reality, this police-game we play on Earth with half-strength weapons. Better than centuries in fairyland, but as for real action and the source of true victory, that's found not here but on Stargate!"

He grinned a birdlike grin. "I must be the only officer alive who preaches metaphysics to his staff. Too much the cultist. I might go the way of others and become god of my own sect; a war god!"

Those in the compartment laughed uneasily. Torfinn looked at Olivia. A minute later they met "accidentally" at the doors to the baggage trailer. "It's an appeal," the woman said. She laid a hand on his shoulder; any

onlooker might have thought they were flirting. "Such
are the times it's assumed our loyalty's to Haas more
than the Heegens. He wants our allegiance confirmed."

"Why not?" Torfinn asked. "What's the Hegemony?
You can't like to see your sex forced to bear children."

"Torfinn, too many similies are drawn between this
age and the fall of Rome, but I've done reading. Those
barbarian generals, Stilicho and Alaric; they weren't
pro-German or pro-Roman, just ambitious men, betraying
those who trusted them. When we follow Haas will it
be to our benefit?"

"One way to find out. He wants to be a god? Let's
dream his mind like devotees!"

Olivia laughed. "That'll really alarm the Heegens!
Another cult, this one armed and trained!"

To keep his knowledge classified, permission to dream
Haas's memories was denied until after the raid on
Torrington. Huge transport copters flew five thousand
troops into the hills of western Connecticut, where they
mastered a forest of pine, budding maple and birch,
charged through neglected parklands of genetically tailored spring blossoms, and penetrated a badly damaged
arcopolis to root out its outnumbered defenders.

That evening the Gamer army got a change of orders.
The Rastrians of Danbury were evacuating. To keep
pressure on them it was necessary to hold Torrington
longer than planned.

"Damn those Heegens," Torfinn swore. "They're afraid
we're too strong; their own army! They'll keep us here
until the Rastrians muster an overland force—"

"And we cut each other down to size," Olivia agreed.
"The Heegens can't lose!"

"Yeah, but we won't have enough left to help them
win. We'll end up with the Connecticut river as the
border between Rastria and the Pale."

Wreathed in a floral crown half-justified as camou-
flage, Colonel Haas entered their aerie, an observation

post sixty floors above the gentle greens of a rolling landscape, one cell of a skyscraper bereft of glass. "No need to be so pessimistic," he spoke. "A Heegen army marches on Massachusetts from Maine. The *Redondo Beach* just blew up most of the Rastrian ships at New London. Meanwhile plague's broken out in Boston. The war's over, friends. You mutter about the future. Soon it'll be on you!"

"Medals, and then what?"

"Those who follow me go to Stargate."

"You're our commander. If you say Stargate then we've no choice."

Haas nodded. "And all for the best. Reality, ladies and gentlemen! No more shadow-boxing, no more wondering how you've been manipulated! We'll call the tricks ourselves!"

In parts of Torrington INFOWEB still functioned. A runner puffed into the post and handed the colonel an envelope. Haas opened and read. "So soon! Well, my two Captains; everyone's promoted a rank, and those of us in the first cohort from the Game are asked to return to Peekskill. It makes sense they'd send us up in phases. Meet you again on Stargate, comrades!"

Olivia waited until he was gone before tapping Torfinn's shoulder. "Well?"

"What about mutiny? We could appeal to our Gamer troops, and claim Torrington for our own city-state."

"How many thousand Rastrians, soon to surrender? Soon to beg for life—'Yah, mon, we be good Hegemonians from now on!' 'Prove it!' the Heegens reply. 'Bring us Torfinn Oskarssen's head on a platter!' "

"You've thought of mutiny before."

"Often. Oh, Torfinn, this place is so much worse than where I was in the Game!"

"Don't worry. I have a feeling . . ."

May

Two weeks later Torfinn Oskarssen strode into the hospital wardroom, last of all his friends to do so. The doctor was there, she bade him sit on the bed. "What do I get?" he asked, "Four minutes' briefing?"

"You're under orders. We've told you all we know about Stargate—"

"*Goddammit*, woman! How many Gamers do you fool with those lies?" Torfinn stood and paced like a caged cat. "You think we're brainless? The Hegemony's so timid you don't dare use full-scale weapons, so cautious you can't wait to be rid of the soldiers who fought your battles—all this, and you think we'd believe you about being sent up to Stargate?"

"Colonel Haas—"

"Colonel Haas wanted badly to believe. He's got this mania about reality. Look at this room! I go under that helmet, and if my soul radios to Mercury, that's fake, but if the signal goes toward Stargate, that's real! Poor sad man, to swallow such nonsense! A man of character—"

"I have to ask you to act peaceably. Please sit."

Torfinn sat and began to weep. "Stupid! You have to

238

lie because you can't bring yourselves to trust! You can't believe we'd fight for you, so you make up this grand story about evil aliens and humanity in peril—"

"The story's true. Torfinn, I'm sorry. You're right about us. We *are* too timid to take on the Gatekeepers. We'll never send an army to Stargate, but that doesn't mean anything except we've accepted our role. The Solar System *is* a preserve for wild humans, and here we stay. Some of the wildest ones—well, you make good soldiers in an emergency, but we can't afford to have you influence our policy. You've got to go back into the Game, and out of our hair."

"Until the next time?"

The woman's eyes slitted as she searched his face. "God grant we're out of danger, but if there's a new crisis and we called you back, what would you do?"

Torfinn shrugged. "Serve the better side, and insist on honesty in return. Think about it. You'll need me all the more because those you deceived will never fight for you again! If Colonel Haas came to life, what do you think he'd say?"

"He's been sent to a place in the Game designed to seem like Stargate. He may never know—"

"Don't send me there. I couldn't bear to tell him, nor see him play the fool."

"No. What then? We set you back where you were, in Happily Ever After?"

"With Chryphe? I never dared ask you about her. You loom in my mind like Fate, the hag who weaves my future in her web. I loved this heroine—"

"She'll be there. I just sent her back this morning."

Torfinn's eyes widened. "She's real? Real! I'm in love with a real woman!" Suddenly he jerked around. "You're telling me what I want too badly to hear, like Colonel Haas!"

The doctor reached for a drink nozzle. "You loved a woman with passion in one form, but in the flesh you and she were mere cordial professionals. Why was that?"

"You mean Olivia! Was she Olivia? We never talked about ourselves as we'd been before; we were chary of getting close. It sounds crazy, but I knew she was someone I could grow to love, and I didn't want to be faithless . . ."

"Nor, apparently, did she. She's waiting for you, Sharbad, waiting on that palanquin, and you'll wake from this bad dream to live with her, until the Game moves into a new phase, or we need you back again."

Phase Eight of the Game, another Happily Ever After. Sharbad Hetlig shared a palanquin with golden-wigged Chryphe as they rode on their honeymoon mission, down from the sun-drenched roofs of the West-Central Subleague, and through the vacant levels of the defeated Hoon. The rocking motion of their pallet lulled them into sleep, and for a time they groaned, until Ridoftaw parted the curtains to wake them from a nightmare. "Are you well?" the Twice-Underperson asked.

As her eyes opened Chryphe clutched her husband and searched his face. Some moments passed before she answered. "We're together. That's all we ask."

"All?" Sharbad smiled and gave her a kiss. "A good place to start, anyhow. Together."

As dead souls collect in graveyard columbaria to be radioed off to Mercury, and the number of bodies available for reincarnation diminishes with the stabilization of Earth's population, steps must be taken to provide bunkered billions with something like life.

The dead must be entertained and educated, prepared for the possibility of a second career in societies vastly different from anything they once knew.

Searching for ancient knowledge, judges of future human kingdoms will sift the good from the evil, the sheep from the goats, and it's not likely that those who wasted their first lives in vice will find themselves chosen for the flesh.

Nevertheless, if they can be made into wiser souls humanity will be better for it. This is the duty of a class of monastic bugs known as masters—masters of the Dream—masters of the Game.

Masters of Purgatory.

Conrad of Dreams

Abbess Tacconi's meeting with the Prior of Quadrant 0100 0101 took place via INFOWEB: so bulked were they by multiprocessors, RAM chips, add-on hardware and inert coolant that neither bigbox eminence was mobile.

It had nothing to do with weight; Mercury's quarter-gravity worked in their favor. Truth was, the City of the Dead's architecture reflected inhuman values. Space was an enemy and distance slowed the speed of thought. The city's billions of stored souls occupied a bunker only a few hectares in size: with new dead spilling in from matins to compline at five times the rate old dead radioed out for reincarnation, there was simply no room for abbess-wide avenues.

Serviceways wove reticulated cat's-cradles inside the city's buttressed walls and pulse-shield—*tiny* serviceways, used by novitiate units, who toddled down the ranks and rows of the dreaming dead on insect legs; dusting, soldering, and plugging into prayer interfaces between duties.

But the patience of the cybernetic dead is not limitless. After a century most novitiates aspired to higher, more sedentary orders: they were ready to confirm their vows and study one of the many monastic disciplines. Conrad Ludquist was such a novitiate, and the topic of the current conversation. "He's completed his basic education?" inquired the abbess.

"With the rest of his decade," the prior responded, "and his marks are good. Reverend Mother, when you interview him don't belabor the same points; how this isn't heaven and we don't try to rectify the injustices of the past. Brother Conrad is sensitive and he'll take it to heart if we single him out. He's already nervous enough. He certainly has every reason to wonder if he's got a monster trapped inside him. For the sake of his morale we must show confidence."

"But those simulations . . . !"

"Are extraordinary," the prior agreed. "We've done four thousand bit-maps and still can't find anything in his circuitry for the electronic surgeons to fix. Nevertheless our simulations don't pan out. For example, we projected an eighty-eight-percent chance that he'd fantasize becoming dreammaster over a game-reality containing his murderers. Our simulation even projected a forty-percent possibility that Brother Conrad would be obsessed with revenge."

"Not true?" the abbess spoke, almost confident enough to make it a statement instead of a question.

"No. He's a freak, saintlier than he should be in all the ways we can test, and he knows it. Which is sad for him, because he's introverted. He has a horror of being singled out."

"Better to be a sinner than a saint with pent devils in your soul's core." The abbess' pause covered a slight shift of focus. "They did this thing to him. His murderers."

"Theme park hangabouts," the prior agreed. "Parts of him already brain-dead before they got him to the memory helmet, and no way for the emergency staff to restore—"

"Yes," the abbess hurried on. "Just ficto-patches to cover the blanks. Are they here? —I don't mean the poor medics, they did what they could. But what about those murderers? They must be dead by now if all this happened in 2095."

"Tracing their identities would create dangerous knowledge," the prior warned, "available to anyone who shares our level of confidentiality."

"We can't protect those—vermin—if we don't know where they are," spoke Abbess Tacconi. "In fact . . ."

"What?"

"Brother Conrad is unpredictable. There's one way for him to keep his chaos confined and prove himself. After all, he doesn't deserve to labor under a cloud of mistrust for what may be nothing but a flaw in our simulation routines."

The prior paused. During that moment he took inventory of the dead in Quadrant 0100 0101. "I don't have them."

"Not likely you would. The killers may not even be under *my* jurisdiction. I'll have to take this matter up with the Primate-General."

"Hey, lookit the geek. Look over there. Black coveralls and everything! He's even got a Bible!"

The object of Twinkie's attention stood squinting uncertainly into late-morning sun, his dark hair trimmed in classic geek style. Young Conrad Ludquist looked around Flower Child Meadow, assessed his position, and found it satisfactory; high and off the footpath, but within earshot of any passers-by.

"He's a Witness, man. Come to the park to preach at us," Chug answered, giving Twinkie's fanny a friendly squeeze.

Up on the hillock Conrad hesitated, paging through his Bible for an apt verse on which to homilize. During this delay the only people drawn by his outlandish looks lost interest and turned away. Farther down on the path: "Aww, I feel sorry for him, you can tell he don't like witnessing. It's their church that makes 'em do it. They gotta go around—"

"Porkin' drabs," Slatts spoke, spitting through the gap where his front tooth was missing to emphasize his disapproval. Taller and leaner than the others, he seemed to do everything slowly, and he spoke with venomous deliberation. "They came up to me once when I was watching the kites, and about the second thing they said was whether I'd been born again. *You* know: 'Nice day, ain't it? Jesus loves you!' "

"Real subtle!" Twinkie laughed.

"Well, I'm gonna give him a big surprise," Chug commented. He fumbled about in his shirt pocket. "We're gonna make him a witness like he's never been before!"

"Oh God, Chug! That dope's too good to waste!"

"He looks thirsty, don't he? Twinkie-Buns, pop this in your Coke and sway up and give him some. Cobber him like you was hot for bod. Think you can do that?"

Twinkie giggled. "Then what?"

Chug turned. "Slatts, run over to Costuming and load some Gandalf-robes. I tell you, he wakes up tomorrow and he'll *never* come preaching around Mercedes Park again!"

"You may already have put some design work into the dream you'll be mastering," Abbess Tacconi commented early in Conrad's confirmation interview. "If not, we have a library of used simulations and a number of experimental proposals."

"Used simulations?" Brother Conrad blurted, from his cell deep in Quadrant 0100 0101. "But—"

"People mature, that's the whole purpose of dreaming. People mature and decide to take vows, or graduate to a simulation that draws forth greater character. A few even return to the flesh. With only two or three real souls per simulation, a good run rarely lasts more than forty years."

Despite the prior's advice, the abbess was rehashing the obvious. Doing so was part of her interview technique and often produced surprising results. In *this* case:

"I've not given much thought to game design," Conrad answered. "It seemed presumptuous. Mother Abbess, life was short for me, and my experience was limited. I grew up in a Witness town in the Huron Mountains, so the things that seem exotic to me, like the Heegen arcopoli and all those huge theme parks— that's exactly what most people take for granted. As for mastering a simulated Witness community, I can't do that. I just can't: Witnesses don't believe in cybernetic immortality. They're anti-tech. I'd have to make my characters preach ideas so hateful—"

"There, there." Abbess Tacconi's comforts buzzed into Brother Conrad's option connector. "Truth is, I've brought up the subject as a prelude. In our prayers we confess that God alone can order the unruly wills and affections of sinful souls. Can you accept the possibility that He's done so with you? That after all God has *singled you out?*"

"You refer to the fact that I'm not all here," Conrad answered, with a lack of bitterness the abbess found surprising. "Everyone knows I'm a patchwork soul."

"God made the best of your death, Conrad, and God's best is capable of transforming humanity's worst. In you we have an opportunity to explore His work, and I've made certain arrangements, not so much to test you as to see the good gift from the Father of Lights."

". . . with whom is no variation, nor shadow of turning. Amen," Brother Conrad answered. "You've already selected my dream?"

"One enormous theme park, and three souls in need of redemption: Chug, Twinkie and Slatts. They've idled along these many decades, gaming through thud-and-blunder realities, as if afraid to admit there's more to life than drugs and sex and fast cars."

Conrad paused. "You have no doubts? You think I can be objective?"

"You can be *better* than objective as you wield total power over those who did you wrong. Conrad, you seek to confirm your vows," the abbess continued. "I see no impediment. Vespers is only a few hours away, and from this evening—you'll be dreammaster!"

To Conrad those few hours passed slowly, but eventually: *"Almighty God, we make humble supplication unto You for these Your servants, to certify them of Your favor and gracious goodness toward them. Let Your fatherly hand ever be over them. Let Your Holy Spirit ever be with them, and lead them in the knowledge and obedience of Your Word. . . ."*

Following the ceremony Brother Conrad made his final trip. Near intersection DD299rh he was lifted from his mobility sheath and inserted into a 72 datachannel commbuss. He took his first look at Dream SJI 17-174 and its occupants.

"Why's he doing that?" Twinkie laughed. "Stumbling around in wizard robes, staring at his hands!"

"He sees something," Chug answered. "Somethin' that don't exist. Hey C-C-C-Conrad! Whatcha doin'? Cat got your tongue?"

The sun was angling toward the west. In the woods not far from the shore, strung out on Chug's acid, Conrad turned, frowned . . . and slowly folded into a fetal position. Slatts came from behind to pull him onto his feet. "None of that now! You gotta tell us about God! Where's your Bible, drabo? Man, *you lost your Bible*! Oh, they gonna be mad about that, ain't they, Chug! Hot time nuclear, and you'll be meat!"

Out of nowhere a Bible appeared in Conrad's hands. The bewilderment on his face was replaced by relief—no, it didn't seem right to interfere with the story at this point; not until the facts played out to their tragic conclusion. Dreammaster Conrad pondered, wondering how he could endure the pain of watching himself be tormented. Part of him *knew* it was agony, but something blocked him from feeling anything more than watered-down sorrow.

Is my "saintliness" just a cold impotence of soul? he wondered. Parts of what had been human about him were forever dead, killed this very day, dying as . . . Yes, now! After more badgering, the simulated Conrad broke from Slatts' strong embrace, from teasing and curses, and ran through a fringe of pine trees, rude voices baying behind him!

"COME BACK!" —But Conrad's drugged brain linked Chug's shouts to everything evil, everything a jangled monkey-brain could conjure; fairy-tale monsters and things from the Id—

The cliff! Too late! Monkey soar and monkey fall . . .

Chug and Slatts drew to a halt at the edge of the rockfall, staring down as Twinkie puffed up from behind. "He's alive," Chug wheezed, then raised his voice against the sound of crashing waves below. "Go get the car. We'll load him in and drive him to Administration."

"Hey, man, it was just a bad trip, man! I mean, he—"

"Yeah, Slatts. That's our story, and let's ditch our stash so they don't think it was us that gave him that acid. We're just good Samaritans, is all."

Brother Conrad zoomed in from angel's eye view: *I don't remember this part, but then concussion is a funny thing.* One of its quirks was that his alter-ego was able to walk the final distance to the car. Wordlessly he slumped into the convertible's back seat. "Maybe if we just let him rest a bit, he could come down from his high," Twinkie suggested.

"Yeah, let's drive slow by way of Mercedes Manor, and see if he don't feel better," Slatts agreed. "And make things up to him on the way so he remembers us like cobbers."

Since making Conrad happy became their priority, Twinkie came into her own. As Chug tapped CAR ON and keyed the security code she joined Conrad in the back seat. She massaged him between the legs, hiked up her silks—no response.

With Chug at the wheel the Samurai purred into the woody, untrafficked hectares west of Flower Child Meadow; all part of greater Mercedes Park. Twinkie kept trying, stroking, rubbing: she felt Conrad stiffen and suddenly go loose again.

She shrugged. Sometimes acid was like that. Just then the Samurai rounded into the Manor driveway and she noticed the lake. "Hey, let's take him for a swim!"

Transition, segue: Dreammaster Conrad mused. *They can't keep their minds on track. They can't think about anything but themselves very long; already they've half forgotten the problem I pose.*

Because when it became obvious victim-Conrad wasn't budging from the car, they jogged off to the water *anyhow!* The idea of swimming blotted everything else out!

These were the souls he was supposed to nurture to maturity? Yes, just a brief dip, but long enough. When Twinkie came back to the car:

"Hey *Chug!*" she shouted. "C'mere quick! Hey, I don't like this! Looks like the geek's dead or somethin'! Wiped to zero— Hey, we gotta get going!"

Conrad felt relief. He was dead, and the factual basis of this simulation was coming to an end. Now what? With the passing minutes the time drew close; the Samurai pulled into the Administration parking lot. Three door-slams, three figures running up the ramp; another half-minute for the ambulance to squeal in from a block away.

Medics attached the memory helmet, desperate to save as much as they could of Conrad's soul. Chug, Twinkie and Slatts looked from an office window and turned away. After a second phone call they were led into an empty basement cafeteria to wait for the police.

They sat watching the clock. A whole game-universe, hanging fire while its master struggled to come up with a plan! What did Chug need? Or Twinkie? Or Slatts? How could Conrad make them grow wise and good? Now at last they were scared, at last he had their fickle attention. *What would he do?*

Revenge? A word without meaning. In some ways Conrad was a blind man talking about sight: he could do so grammatically, but that was all.

What to do? Time for creative ideas, but for a century Conrad the novitiate had not been asked to invent or hypothesize. A horrible thought: *What if he couldn't?* What if that ability was lost with everything else?

Meanwhile Twinkie rose to pace, nervous and impatient, ready to face the police, tell a few lies and get the ordeal over with. Her perambulations brought her to the cafeteria door— No! Conrad wasn't ready! What should she see when she pulled it open?

More time! I can't think under pressure!"

But Twinkie grabbed the knob, pulled . . .

"YEEEEEEEEEEEEEAaaaaaaaaahhh!"

Chug and Slatts ran up as she slammed it shut and fell into the nearest embrace. "Oh God! Oh my God!" she babbled.

Chug seized her shoulders. "What is it? *What's out there?"*

"Nothing," she whispered, and swallowed, and caught her breath. "No black, no white—I can't say it like I should. NO, DON'T LOOK! It's not *any* color, it sucks the colors right out of your brain! Oh Chug, I don't know what's happened to us! There ain't any *outside* out there, this room is all there is!"

"You're talkin' crazy," Slatts responded. "You're tripping or somethin'. Lemme just take a blink—"

A second later he fell back shivering against the door. "God damn!" He looked from face to face while mastering his voice. "We're in hell, ain't we? This is it, a few porkin' tables and chairs, some vending machines! Shit! Just us three meats, together in hell!"

An interesting concept, Abbess Tacconi signaled to Dreammaster Conrad. *Do you plan on supplying infinite candy and pop, or will they run out soon?*

Brother Conrad timed out, tabling Dream SJI 17-179 to answer. "Forgive me; I blew it. I couldn't sketch scenes quickly enough. Mother, I've failed them. I'm no good at this."

The abbess laughed and took shape in Conrad's display buffer, an old woman in sweater and rongwrap and sensible shoes, salt-and-pepper hair tied back into a queue. "Of course not; it takes time and practice to become a good dreammaster. Everyone balks at first, everyone blunders and makes mistakes. You'll get better, Brother Conrad. Don't worry. You'll get better as time goes on, and in the meanwhile . . ."

The abbess winked. "In the meanwhile . . . I don't know anyone better than *those* three for you to practice on."

"I can't play this game, Mother. The prior says I'm a saint, but now I'm their personal devil. I can't hate them, but it's also true I can't thaw to their pain, their fear . . . their demon may lack the ability to get any better. What then? Eternal torment? Better to know my victims aren't real, just practice-dummies—"

"They're real as any of us, Conrad. As for eternity, nothing's eternal under the sun. Even abbesses come and go—in time. Until then, God teach you wisdom to match your power!"

On Earth primitive virtue triumphs. The decayed Hegemonians who dominated the past fade into subterranean retreats, overwhelmed by a technology they failed to control.

But virtue means incompatible things to the different "zoo cultures" of the Surface, and not everyone can be correct in his ideas.

Com Zenthag's Minister of Propaganda is a man of strong views on this subject, a man soon to learn an ultimate lesson.

The Siege of Stamnor

July 7th, 2941 Today I put the question of evacuation to Com Zenthag. He says our overfed Institute and Library flunkies will vacate Stamnor tonight, since they are no reinforcement to the fighting morale of the people. Com Zenthag's advice is entirely right. They will be notified quietly to avoid comment.

Military situation. In their foray the Library Guards encountered stiff resistance. They fell back in the face of violent counterattacks. The swale is no longer ours. Any damage done there robs the Hobweens of lodging and pasture.

One weeps to consider the loss of our villas, our herds of cattle and horses, but how much more repugnant to consider Hobween Leatherclads wallowing in the enjoyment of our wealth?

In this, as in everything where he is properly advised, the judgement of Com Zenthag is impeccable.

Survivors of the disaster at Gerly still straggle in. The Eastern Legion is so mauled that it effectively no longer exists. Clearly there will be no action in the foreseeable future. We must grow reconciled to the idea that our fortress is on the front lines.

The radio brings more news of rebellion. In Swedny the Fanes of Light have been boarded up. Coms and renunciates are hounded out of the city. One wonders what the radicals think to achieve? Such signs of division will only tempt the Hobweens of Esret to join the Leatherclads in their attack.

Won't that be wonderful, a two-front war!

July 8th, 2941 It's my duty to monitor enemy broadcasts, but how unpleasant those Hobweens make it, with their ad hominem attacks! I am described as Com Zenthag's jester; weak-chinned, myopic, and humpbacked. The clear distinctions between my race and that of the Leatherclad degenerates are mocked as hair's-breadth trivialities. Yes, once I commented on the differences between our cuticles; but that's not to ignore more obvious criteria. Isn't our skin a ruddier shade, hinting of the nervous energy that distinguishes thoroughbred races? What of the vapid cheerfulness that the Leatherclads affect so consistently? Such surface signs are clues to deep-laid mutations.

For my part, I keep our broadcasts on a higher plane. Excerpts from my daily radio speech:

"Against hostile surfaces of rock and glacier the sun's beams etch the ice into a forest of crystal, and limn each scintilla of lichened stone until the detail grows too atomic for the eye to master. Thus adversity brings out beauty in snow and ice. So war brings out the heroic in ourselves!

"I speak from the one pass in these eastern ranges, the single gap where the heights fail, where the glacier wastes itself against isolated moraines. Here, burdened with fogs and snow, the turbulent atmosphere eddies restlessly.

"To those who view her battlements these winds honor her staunch verticals, unyielding against the violent landscape. Nature acknowledges the works of man by driving the clouds in sweeping arcs around one great spire which rises among them. This, then, is fabled Stamnor!

"Built over the ancient Library of Knowledge, our fortress shoulders over a tortured web of skirting paths. Rare footways wind down to where sheltered spruce, plums and willows grow in green arroyos. In these gardens we were wont to perform austerities at the fonts, symbols of primal Emptiness.

"Our verdant retreats are now overrun. Our pleasances are infested by mongrels. Proud statues stand mute. What they celebrate is profaned by skin-clad outlanders.

"Let them scrawl graffiti, those that can write! Let these sacrificial victims have their pitiable fun on the far side of these impenetrable walls! Winter is coming. How shall they draw supplies up muddy tracks, over unconquerable distances. . . ."

I spoke on in this vein, but was instructed by Com Zenthag to say nothing about deathdogs. I confess this warning makes me edgy.

July 9th, 2941 Military situation. North of Hilyan our deathdogs are reportedly engaged—could this be the expected Esreti stab in the back? The Coms of those provinces are nervous. They could have sent tithes of troops before the disaster at Gerly. Now let them rue their recalcitrance!

The survivors of Gerly bring terrible rumors. The Tumble Cat horde of deathdogs, fifty thousand strong, was to have beaten off the Hobweens—that, or delayed them until the Eastern Legion perfected their defensive earthworks.

Time is on our side. Winter makes offensive warfare impossible in our mountains. Unfortunately the delay was less protracted than we'd hoped.

Worse, when the Hobweens drew close, *they used*

deathdogs to clear our flank! Yes, the Hobweens have learned how to dominate deathdogs; how to command them in battle! Our secret is secret no longer.

No wonder Com Zenthag wants nothing said on the deathdog issue.

Consider the alarm, the impact on the people's morale!

July 10th, 2941 Hobween radio discounts our ability to resist further attacks. We are thought to be so tired we are incapable of holding out. The revolt in Swedny is taken as a sign that the rule of Com Zenthag will soon be over.

Of course we have our own nest of radicals in Stamnor, the students in the Library of Knowledge. People wonder why we don't arm them and put them out on the walls!

It's a salutary thing to walk the walls. In the pass below you can see Hobween canopies strung up on our statues and colonnades!

Time and again a spear of light shoots from our heights and leaves some reckless enemy a crisp char. Nevertheless the creeping tendrils of invasion insinuate closer. Some tighten up the mounts to the south. Others explore the passways to the north. Fretfully we cluster at our windows to murmur at the numbers gathered to assail us. To the west! What news to the west? At least that way must remain open!

This evening a thousand campfires winked into life. Leatherclad standards rose from several quarters. Our women shudder from these prospects to gaze with hope to the rockstrewn gap that leads into the homeland of our great race.

One cheerful note: here and there hidden mines detonate to the destruction of Hobween lives. I doubt any out there sleep easily tonight.

Sisters and sykodoktars, renunciates, bodyguards, stablehands, scholars and courtiers: we're all prisoners now until Com Zenthag contrives some miracle to raise the siege.

*   *   *

July 11th, 2941 Com Zenthag sent for me this morning, me and Sykodoktar Chamy, director of the Institute. The sounds of an artillery barrage reverberated through the hall as we were ushered before him.

"There are concerns among the women," Zenthag spoke. "Move among them, women, servants and scholars. Preach, preach, preach: race, blood and purity. There are some who no longer believe, muddy thinkers who snivel of cohabitation with Hobweens, liberal-minded fools . . . it's strength, the ordeal, that proves us out against our inferiors! What's hurt us these last months was irresolution, treason . . . you must believe, clench your mind and believe, uh . . ."

For a second the Com of Coms allowed himself to look tired. I'm told he subsists on two hours of sleep per night. He cupped his hands over his eyes in thought. I saw his fingers tremble on the beaked ridge of his noble nose. At last he opened his eyes, shook his long locks, and spoke again.

"—ah, yes. The women. Tell them our resources. We've stocks of food and our own underground river. Most of our people never leave Stamnor. The fact they can't needn't circumscribe them."

I spoke up. "Shall I speak of sorties? That underground system, the Sakachku and its passages—it was extended to enable us to strike against besiegers. It will cheer our folk to hear of raiding parties."

Com Zenthag scowled. Chamy fell silent. Why is this suddenly a forbidden topic?

But that's not the worst of it. The Com of Coms went on to instruct Sykodoktar Chamy. The director is to destroy his records about our breeding and genetics experiments. For my part, I'm to expunge the radio station files of policy memoranda.

I don't like it. I'd never accuse the Com of Coms of making a mistake, but if from weariness he misjudges the importance of the morale war we're fighting—one burns records prior to retreating. We can hold out. There's no reason to evacuate. . . .

One last observation. On Com Zenthag's writing desk I saw a globe of the world! What a marvelous antique! I wonder how old it is . . . from the days of airplanes and intercontinental traffic, assuredly!

They say glaciation has altered the shapes of the land, but how much could things change in nine hundred years?

Globes and maps—there's a collection in the Library of Knowledge. It's been too long since I went down there. This war keeps us all too busy.

Damn! That was a close blast! Too close!

July 12th, 2941 Military situation. More fighting in Yern. We've lost contact with the far north, so I have no news on the enemy's naval blockade.

Radicals have seized the radio station in Anshany to prate of surrender and a new constitution! Their appeal to us? "If you're friends of the ancient knowledge, disburse it. Don't lock it in your Library. The world is hungry for it!" Yes, why not teach the Hobweens about antibiotics, transistors and the making of aluminum? How naive!

Unless sanity prevails we can write off the whole west, three-quarters of our arable land. Esret dreams of extending its rule over that territory. What's to stop them now?

I believe Com Zenthag has resolved upon escape. He is withdrawn, and refuses to consider making a speech to the realm, despite the need for a boost in morale.

It would be possible to take our troops, descend to the Library of Knowledge, and exit by the Sakachku passages. The problem is, once our Com abandons Stamnor, who will keep the Hobweens out? And if the Hobweens take Stamnor and cross the gap, what could stop them?

The only true escape is by sea, but passage anywhere would be difficult. The least guarded route would be a nightmare of icebergs. Somehow the Hobween blockade has to be lifted, but how, short of utter defeat?

Escape. Escape for the elite. Escape for the Coms loyal to his faction. Is that why Com Zenthag studies his globe? Does he have a destination in mind? Has the realm sent scouts to find him a refuge?

July 13th, 2941 The Hobweens have petroleum, enough to power a radio transmitter and block our main signal. We have fallback frequencies, but the people aren't used to searching for my voice. I consider my audience halved, at best.

Meanwhile they broadcast a flood of wishful thinking, hallucinations and vile threats. We are to have the books in the Library of Knowledge wrested from our control, so jumped-up Hobween "scientists" can restore the golden age of the twenty-first century!

We are accused of neglecting the Library! As if reading alone could make airplanes! Have they given us even a decade of peace in which to build an industrial base? Where shall we find the metal? The oil? The coal?

Now these ignorant mongrels face us across the walls! Is there hope? A few months ago Com Zenthag schemed to taunt the Leatherclads, snared by problems of timing, diplomacy and resource, with proof of their own impotence. They'd needed reminding. They'd grown too strident, too cocky.

The lesson rebounded. The Hobweens actually succeeded in mounting an invasion!

Even then there was reason for optimism. Our defense should have taxed the hostiles until late in the season. Constant deathdog attacks, the impossibility of protecting their long supply lines; these conditions should have forced them to withdraw. That's how it works.

It hasn't worked this time. We have evidence that the Leatherclads know the principle behind deathdog control. If that's true our regime is doomed. Stamnor might stand and other fortresses as well, but the land itself can't be defended.

To add to Zenthag's woes, the Com Presidium has betrayed him. Rebels control Swedny. The Presidium is fled; some say, disbanded. Things are falling apart. Even here in Stamnor those students in the Library spend time murmuring. Inferiors, needless to say. Of tainted stock.

A quiet mind can distill purity from all that seems turgid. I sought Emptiness last night and am reconciled to these disasters. Somehow this general collapse will serve our cause! The complaisant elite are now attentive. Com Zenthag holds the key to ultimate escape. A new realm! Homogeneous! Reverent! Pure! We'll take the knowledge of the ancients, all the hundred thousand books in the Library of Knowledge, and make sail to one of the far continents! A journey into legend!

July 14th, 2941 Ever since that shell shattered the windows in our apartments two days ago, my wife refuses to get out of bed. We could do without that at the moment. What must the servants think?

Military situation. The enemy "Queen" Delinna and her entourage has arrived to take command of the siege. I'm told that ten years ago she was a breedwoman at the Institute, a subject of Sykodoktar Chamy's experiments. I'm also told half the men of Stamnor found paradise between her thighs. We can expect little in the way of mercy or rationality from her!

The situation at Yern is rendered difficult by masses of refugees. For the moment the enemy is advancing unchecked into the valley while men fit for service flee northwards.

My radio talk today was on the fickle nature of alliances, and how easily Hobweens fall out among themselves. The Leatherclads, the Kwis—what interests do they have in common? Only hatred of Com Zenthag! When they wake to the fact that he's no devil incarnate, they'll take out their feelings of betrayal on each other!

I should feel flattered that Com Zenthag lets me deliver these speeches without review, yet I worry.

Sometimes I think he's lost interest in the propaganda war. I am forbidden to boast of our mass execution of Stamnor's Hobween slaves, who would have eaten our food while acting as a fifth column inside the fort. Yes, such "infamies" will outrage the enemy, but by provoking their rage we commit ourselves to an uncompromising defense. As it is the secret will leak out, while some of our people have the gall to mutter and act ashamed!

July 15th, 2941 From their retreat in Hilyan the Com Presidium has *invited* Esret to invade our realm to "free us from the hated tyranny of Com Zenthag!" Those gutless heirs of the old republic have risen to yap at us, thinking to exchange one puppetmaster for another. We have sent instructions to our loyalists to recruit a Western Expeditionary Force and punish them.

Could things get worse? Let Emptiness send us a miracle!

Com Zenthag summoned me into his quarters, rooms even starker than usual. "Sykodoktar Chamy is coming with me," he announced. "You must stay behind."

I was thunderstruck. Com Zenthag spoke on. "I'd never command you, old friend, if the need weren't so urgent. You have been loyal. I need someone of unquestioned loyalty. I'll provide you with a troop of fifty soldiers, too old or wounded to endure the rigors of travel. I'll also give you weapons to distribute among the students of the Library of Knowledge. Use your fifty to keep five hundred crypto-radicals in line. Get them out of the Library and onto the walls."

"I—this is an honor—"

"Queen Delinna was once an Institute whore. She knows some of the Sakachku system. Her Leatherclads will be able to take Stamnor by evading our traps and coming up through the Library of Knowledge. Worse yet, once they've taken the Library and settled the swale with their people, they can use the ancient knowledge to their own advantage. Chemistry, aeronautics—

all that power in Hobween hands! Would you want to see that happen?"

"Never!"

"When we leave your duty is plain. Move the students out, arm them, then blow up the Sakachku passages!" Com Zenthag shuddered, and I noticed how thin he looked in his robes. "Close them off, and all they contain."

He seemed ready to continue, but then his eyes took on distance; the cares of the moment seemed to drop away and my leader slumped. I was barely in time to keep him from falling. A pair of bodyguards moved forward, and Sykodoktar Chamy stepped from behind a curtain. The three helped Com Zenthag from the room as I stood in my own terror-trance, wondering what I'd seen: Weariness? A mystical vision? Something to do with drugs?

Sykodoktar Chamy returned to the chamber a minute later, carrying his medical bag. I asked about Com Zenthag's health, but he forced the conversation in another direction. "Yosu, take warning. It's true the Sakachku must be destroyed. We pretend it belongs to us, but it was dug by the ancients centuries ago. Among its seven levels lie artifacts from the golden age. We are a scientific people, Yosu, yet we don't dare use half the gifts we hoard."

"Why not?"

"Because . . . we don't understand. We cultivate superstition among our slaves. A curse is a good thing, it keeps the ignorant from overreaching themselves. A curse draws a ring of protection around its object. Do you know I sometimes envy the Hobweens? They reinvented the tools they use; radio and all the rest. What they have, they've mastered. As for us, we own much we dare not think about!"

July 16th, 2941 As of last night I'm a Com, since I command the forces of Stamnor. For want of a better name I am Com Stamnor, though the Presidium recognizes no such title.

I've mustered the people into militias; one for women, one for students, even one for the halfbirth servants. They take as much pride in the color of their armbands as our legionnaires of old did in their horses and uniforms!

The enemy outside doesn't yet know that Com Zenthag is gone; a blessing, since they'll redouble their attacks once the truth is out. We can do without that: I have enough trouble keeping control of the enemy within. If we could persuade our students that Hobweens hate everyone of pure race, that they want to destroy the Library, then we'd be able to trust them. Unfortunately the Hobweens broadcast the opposite message—how much they love us, except for the Zenthag clique!

The upshot is I'm having difficulty chivvying the students out of the Library. My soldiers wonder why I give the matter such priority. I don't dare tell them Com Zenthag's orders, because any action to blow up the Sakachku will almost assuredly damage the Library! The *Library*! I don't know by what power I make myself persist in this most terrible of duties!

The students pretend they're defending that sacred place against the Leatherclads. In fact it's their headquarters, from which they'll signal a coup, possibly in a matter of hours.

My wife continues to stay in bed. She abides nothing but small talk; as if the Hobweens were a thousand miles away!

Where are my friends? Right now they caravan past the snowfield ruins of some nameless twentieth-century city, to reach the eastern tributary somewhere north of Yern.

Enemy radio names them all in its indictments; our realm's ambassador plenipotentiary, our marshals, our minister of justice, our minister of renunciates, our slavemaster general, our director of breeding and genetics—oops! One mistake, they also mention our absent minister of enlightenment; an odd choice to leave behind, in command of what might have been an impregnable fort!

This could never have been Com Zenthag's true decision! And if he was so impaired as to inflict me with this office, should I take him seriously about blowing up the Sakachku, and denying myself any escape from this nightmare? Why should I take him seriously about anything? My Com, my hero . . . ?

July 17th, 2941 Students now control Stamnor. A delegation came last evening to announce their "stipulations." I found myself in no position to refuse them.

The fools mean to use the radio to open conversations with the rebels of Swedny. I warned them that Queen Delinna's Leatherclads monitor all our broadcasts. Their first treasonable utterance will be taken as proof that Com Zenthag is no longer with us. Any departure from normal behavior is to be avoided at all costs.

I was informed that all these issues had been debated, and my advice would no longer be required.

At least I've bought Com Zenthag twenty-four hours. Much can be done in one day.

The students are widely split on the question of what to do with me. Suggestions range from throwing my body over the wall to giving me command of Zenthag's fifty, and commissioning us to guard the Sakachku passages. In the meanwhile I've been granted the freedom of the Library.

This means two students watch my carrel, while my slave fetches books on demand. I sit in a chamber cut from orange bedrock, beneath steel girders and struts sagging under the weight of centuries. My refuge lies on the lowest level of shelving, among legendary works by Shakespeare and Rodale, and here I page through

Menzel's *Astronomy* or thumb faded holograms in Grosset & Dunlap's *Manual of Home Repairs*. No one suspects that my briefcase is filled with explosive!

Com Zenthag foresaw all this: he anticipated I'd be in a position to do my duty. I write these notes in utter confidence that the students will entrust me with responsibilities, in essence abandoning the ancient Sakachku passages to my care!

And how dare I put these thoughts to paper? In words of my own devising: using the phonetic value of letters to coin spellings for our spoken language. This is a radio trick; the result looks like gibberish to any scholar.

For my part, after reading my diary, classical texts in Old High English look like gibberish, and it takes me a minute to readjust my perceptions.

July 18th, 2941 Military situation. Queen Delinna's troops attacked around 4 A.M. through the Sakachku, just as Com Zenthag warned. They fought through a half-dozen traps, and now face us across a thirty-foot pit.

I'm back in command of my fifty; we guard the passage. Of course I'm obliged to consider flanking maneuvers: such concerns force us to trespass into areas sealed off for centuries.

What an opportunity! I even have Teknodoktars to help me place explosives and rig a remote-control device. In the bustle and confusion no one questions my instructions—I have an air of authority, after all.

Once the Sakachku blows up the siege of Stamnor will begin in earnest. I have no real plans for the future—my hopes lie in improvisation. I'll have to talk fast to explain any "accidental" harm to the Library, or I'll be the universal enemy. Nor am I loyal to this student faction. Why then do I submit to their regime? Blame the Hobweens! They've rehashed with glee the tortures they plan to put me through: a show-trial followed by public execution. These same Hobweens expect me to endow them with the science of Earth's golden age!

It's getting on towards night now, and the sounds of fighting are louder. I write this alone in a small room, my hand poised near a switch. The time is nearly at hand—

July 19th, 2941 Marvels beyond recognition, and one or two that we all recognize! One of my soldiers talked too freely into the wrong ears and now I'm surrounded by students, eager to lay hands on devices they've seen before only in pictures!

Yes, they thwarted Delinna's invasion. When the students heard what my men discovered, they sent reinforcements. They found gas masks and cannisters painted with lethal symbols and made obvious use of them. At last the Hobweens withdrew, any that were still alive.

So much for Sykodoktar Chamy's curse! So much for superstition and timidity! Nevertheless I was caught in his trap, for the students traced the wiring from the switch by my hand to the sticks of nitro wedged here and there in the Sakachku, and now I'm not to be trusted. In fact I'm a prisoner!

But a special prisoner, privileged to witness the triumphs of my new superiors. Babbling in ecstasy, the students took me to see what I'd almost destroyed, through a gateway painted in antique letters: SAC HQ. I watched them begin their repairs, replacing corroded wires, filling old fuel tanks, and taping up cracked tubing.

Incredibly, and thanks to having been stored in pure inert nitrogen, the world's last jet sputtered to life fourteen hours later and flamed down a troglodyte runway, through hangar doors laboriously opened by halfbirth slaves, to lift into skies troubled by invisible mountain updrafts. The guns of our Hobween enemies fell silent as in deference to the machine's loud shriek: in truth I saw them being brought to bear on a new section of wall. As shells started to rain around that luckless barrier, our pilot (a glider enthusiast) gained the confidence to launch his first dive.

Three times the fighter doubled along his course, slaughtering enemies brave enough to do their duty. Stray shots hit the shells lying among the corpses. One exploded.

The novice took note of the smoke and damage. On his next pass he aimed at the ammunition stocks behind the guns.

The eruption deafened the ashen-faced Leatherclads, tore eighteen artillery pieces from their mounts, toppled five into an arroyo, and startled the world's only jet into a loop which sent it crashing into a cliff wall far beneath my feet!

What a loss, but what a triumph! How can our enemies carry on a siege without artillery? How long will it take Queen Delinna's Hobweens to recognize our victory, and withdraw?

I was permitted to watch all this from the heights of Stamnor's central tower. The ostensible reason has to do with the exploitation of yet another golden-age weapon, a bomb which (due to the loss of the jet), is now being hauled up by elevator from a thousand feet below. I interrupted their murmur of bomb catapults to make my proposals to the student leadership: a series of radio broadcasts in which I cunningly steer my realmwide audience into sympathy with rebel objectives, and away from Com Zenthag.

My reward? I dare not ask it yet, but why shouldn't I be Com Stamnor in name, as I was once in fact?

And with that name, and a voice capable of tipping the scales between factions . . .

*   *   *

July 20th, 2941 How those students must have laughed
up their sleeves at my overtures! All the time they
knew what they meant to do: surrender me to our
enemies! A deal to buy time! Bomb catapults are not
easy to build!

I was lowered down the wall, delivered into the
hands of smelly Leatherclads, chained, and manhan-
dled. I have bruises from their mistreatment, finger
marks on my arms from where they clutched me with
excessive force!

Made to walk that rough mountain trail in my good
shoes! Fed like a slave on porridge and water! And then
the mockery of that interview with "Queen" Delinna!

Why would she talk, if not to bargain? Yet this is how
she began: "You are an evil man, Yosu, a small and evil
man. In all these pages you speak twice of your wife,
both times in complaint. What a shriveled thing your
heart must be!"

Yes, they stole my diary, copied it, and flung it back
in my face. Nevertheless I took her words for praise, for
Hobween hate is something I don't mind deserving.
"You serve a wicked master," she continued. "Zenthag's
ideas of genetic purity have been discredited a thousand times, yet you've spewed them out to poison the
minds of a whole generation. Thanks to you, people
will whisper of 'tainted blood' long after I'm dead.
You might offer to sell your honor. None here would
buy it, no matter how low the price. We have a
grievance, and we will not forget our dead, who cry
against you."

But though the queen is deaf to reason I will live
some few days longer. These Leatherclads are too busy
to divert themselves with my trial. Despite this momentary truce they're digging in for a continued siege.

If they only knew! They copied my diary, but this
entry comes later, and I fail to see how the news could
make much difference. The fact is ordained: Stamnor's

laser weapon is to be connected to a wonderful new power source known as a thermal tap.

Do these fools trust the students in my fortress? Those young men and women are partly my children, brought up to believe that Hobweens are the source of all evil . . . I have no doubt that soon Stamnor's laser will stab and slice with several times the killing energy it's ever had before! Nor is this the only weapon they're resurrecting from the depths of the Sakachku!

Perhaps the slaughter will cause a panic. In that panic I might escape this cave, where I write by the light of a dying torch, my neck bundled against dripping water.

July 21st, 2941 The day began when I was hauled from bed for my second interview with Queen Delinna. How she searched my face as she told me that lie: that Com Zenthag was dead! Dead of a drug overdose! And who should be suing for peace in his stead but Sykodoktar Chamy, master of the needle and whisperer of perverted warnings!

The trek from her tent was neither easy nor safe, for the truce is over. Even at my distance from Stamnor the students' laser weapon played back and forth, and eyes exposed to its ruddy dazzle were blinded for seconds afterward. We were forced to use crevasses and shelter beneath overhangs—much of the tortured terrain beneath the fortress has been incorporated into the Hobweens' maze of trenches, in which they cower and scuttle like some low form of insect life.

Suddenly Stamnor's central tower exploded in a ball of light. Exploded? No, *vanished*, while the perimeter blew outward as if made of mud! And how amazing to see all this *through* my eye-shielding hand, with shadow bones outlined in red! "Quick! Back to the cave!" my Leatherclad guard urged, dropping more deeply into the crevasse and grabbing my arm to compel me.

Did I really hear his words?

A few steps, and we fell as the ground shook beneath our feet. An ocean of incredible brilliance spread across the sky, hot wind seared my lungs. As the heavens faded to red, a pillar of fire roiled up from the blasted peak where Stamnor once stood.

My escort shouted as loudly as he could, yet mine was now a silent universe. I'd not even heard the sonic assault that destroyed my eardrums.

But I was still alive, and knew what to do. Take cover and wait.

Take cover? Would anything be left of my cave? The best I could think to do was to put miles behind me.

The same idea occurred to others. I collapsed into a huddled ball and let them run by. A squall of pebbles and dust pattered the ground around me, at first dry, then wet, filming everything with slick warm mud. When I opened my eyes to the filthy shower my guard was gone. Then I got up and began my own flight, not away, but *toward* the ruins of Stamnor.

Yes, *toward*! The students are gone, you see, but perhaps something remains deep in the Sakachku system, a weapon I can use when the Hobweens muster their former courage and return to the attack. Have I any other hope? It's this or a flight through the midst of my enemies, through deathdog hordes made restless by the disturbances of war, and across the border into Hobween realms hostile to my own!

Adits to the underground Sakachku lie scattered through our pleasure gardens. After half a day of upward struggle I reached the first of those lovely retreats, now ashen and ugly, with hideous stains burnt into the once-gleaming marble. I tracked across flower beds buried in inches of muddy soot and found a secret door shifted from its hinges, and a once-hidden passage largely blocked with rubble. Yet dizzy as I was (and am), with my sense of balance impaired by my injury, I found my way inside, crawling to the place where the corridors converge. My face and hands have grown puffy from sunburn, but possibly I've avoided the worst kind of exposure to whatever the students unleashed. I hope so. I'm going to rest now, and if my body is up to it, tomorrow I'll continue the battle.

Tomorrow I'll be Com Stamnor, again and forever. No one can stop me: no students, no fear of ancient curses, no love of leaders who betrayed me. Tomorrow I'll unlock new demons, and order them as I choose. Tomorrow the world will bow to me!

Climb not this mountain, Hobweens! Here is no more Library, the golden age is gone forever. Curse me for robbing you! The gardens of Stamnor are closed in darkness, lest you glow, lest you fry!

July 21st, 2941 Hard to think with fires cooking. Pain against the Hobweens, strong as dared! And if the Hobweens took toothless Stamnor and crossed the gap?

Let them delay a few more hours! The table is set, but I must crawl to the feast! Survivors, bow! Disaster— did I hear shells, our pilot and destruction of Hobween lives? I hear explosions all the time. They come out of my cooked brain. I moved my legs— My legs! Oh, the fire!

Do Com Stamnor honor, world! Can you sleep, worrying if your flesh sloughs off? I own the Sakachku!

I write so slow, and things change. I am bad sick, but I can think again, for I feel no more pain, nor any sensation. But I do not want to die; and I die scapegoat, and cursed. The golden age is gone forever, its last poison swallowed up in my sacks of pus; my black, dead skin.

What does this prove? That Sykodoktar Chamy was right? Is Hobween science better than ours, because our enemies do not ride the shoulders of dead gods? Chamy, that man of evil, that usurper! What right is his to understand the truth?

But Hobween science is all the world has left, unless they trespass down this passage. Might someone do so, and build a new Stamnor to guard the horrors I cannot crawl to reach?

He would be a fool indeed, for I leave my body as a warning, with my diary in my withered hands.

Earth's history incorporates another disaster, yet the living stumble on toward a new renaissance, hidden gods playing surface realms against each other until the truth is exposed, and the balance of power shifts in favor of the Five Dominions.

With that exposure technologies marry and a new world is created, knit together by INFOWEB and governed by a hastily assembled senate bewildered by infinite possibilities.

Among those senators one is imaginative enough to ride the Storm of the New, sometimes on the back of a listless old farm horse, and sometimes via a continent-spanning system of subways.

The Buzz of Joy

It was an age lavished with antiquities, rich with
stories from Before the Flood, Before the Breakdown,
Before the War, Before the Deathwinter, Before the
Starfall . . . yet with this abundance of disaster-
punctuated eras, and all the artifacts they'd left behind,
it had grown harder, not easier, to master the art of
chronology, and a superfluity of relics bred general
incuriosity.

On the southern verge of the forest of Geel Dubhar a
leftover road ran east and west, between one distant
ruin and another. Useless! Travelers were obliged to
trudge two days more, through rolling farm country,
before striking the modern carriageway, which angled
off toward Haust, capitol of Yain.

Fat as a bumblebee, the Thraxum Motors Cherry II
biplane droned to deliver Senator Ramnis across Yain's
breadth to the free town of Westhaven; where (the
True God Willing) a Zealand cog might steam him
beyond reach of the false god U Gyi. Farms and old
roads were mere left-horizon landmarks to the errant
senator, whose zigzag course avoided areas of habitation.

Yet gods are cunning, and plan ahead. U Gyi and the senator had been allies last year, in Merica's nip-and-tuck war against INFOWEB, whose single weapon was an orbiting boomstar.

"Well then," U Gyi thought (once the victory had been sufficiently applauded), "where soars one boomstar, why not another? I will listen to the skies, those astral beeps and whistles."

The same god who loved to catalog long strings of DNA spent months deciphering the come-hither of an eight-hundred-year-old weapon. It was this beamed particle generator U Gyi now angrily invoked to smite the wicked.

It smote, and reported back, but its message was a hoax. The boomstar was ludicrously underpowered, its mirrors and fatigued cells pitted into space-junk. Senator Ramnis's Model II Cherry failed to explode, much less disintegrate. Haloed by a mischief-working electrical corona, the engine merely coughed and died. The plane turned into an inept glider and began to lose altitude. Ramnis peered this way and that, swore distractedly, and waggled the craft away from Geel Dubhar's tangled treetops to find a place to land.

Before taking off, the senator dreamed a pilot's memories to learn the art of flight, but Earth's umpteenth renaissance was less than two decades old and Thraxum Motors had only been in the aircraft business these last six years. There wasn't much emergency experience to draw on: just one desperate landing in the Flinthills of Ye, terminating in a forward somersault.

Now too the Cherry's wheels touched, balked, and pitched the biplane forward. It poised grandly tail-high, then crashed onto its back on the washboard surface of the ancient road.

Ramnis woke to find himself in a small, high bed, in a room given to garishly painted wooden furniture. A young girl stood gazing at him, brown of skin, stocky and utterly bald. Ramnis groaned. "Do you speak Inglish?"

The girl fled, shouting "Mravi, Mravi!" The one she summoned might have been her older sister, a few inches taller, fleshier, otherwise identical. "You'll have to lie still for a few days," Mravi told him. "Keep your leg elevated so the swelling can go down."

"I take it from your expression that my features lack their usual charm. Where am I? Are there telephones here? Subway connections?"

"No." The girl-woman blushed. "We are modern in Yain, but for these farms: the dominion wants us to give them up. They will not invest in us, because soon there will be food factories in all the cities."

"And you? Will you go the modern way?"

"Some of us are modern enough to wonder whether we can fix your airplane's engine and use it for our purposes. Sir, you must know that your room and care do not come free."

"If there's anything to salvage, go ahead."

Ramnis spent three bedridden days in meditation, stroking his lordly mustachios. Some of his thoughts were small—how to get to Westhaven now that his plane was useless to him. Yet he wondered if U Gyi had not done him a favor by shooting him down. Perhaps he should contact Yain's dozen senators, and build a coalition against this runamok godling.

And plunge the Five Dominions into war?

In the old days wars were productive. The war against Lord Pest liberated the slightly radioactive Library of Knowledge, full of fabulous twentieth-century lore. After Lord Pest turned to piracy, a cabal of adventurers managed to discover INFOWEB, blackmail the gods, and use their powers to crush Pest's evil.

But surely no more unplumbed secrets remained to be discovered. Society was having more than enough trouble digesting the present feast. Any future war, fought with boomstars and food additives and turtlesong, battle armor and tinglers—such a war might bring about the utter collapse of the Five Dominions and the umpteenth downfall of civilization.

What to do? And why? Senatorial government was not so long established in Merica of the Five Dominions that anyone felt great loyalty to it, not even the senators. Ramnis called himself "senator" because "king" seemed a preposterous title for a monarch whose thousand subjects rantipoled about a crumbling arcopolis. "Senator" enhanced his dignity, as it debased the dignity of U Gyi, god of Bue Gyi and the Hills of Moon, manufacturer of U Gyi's Immortality Tonic, foremost geneticist of the known world and primate of the Redemptorist Cult.

Ramnis shook his head. A risk to reverse himself on the appropriations bill. He'd paid the price, but in time U Gyi would simmer down, if he wasn't pushed into a confrontation. This might be a good time to lie low and take off on an aimless, time-killing jaunt, as those with his Souldancer background were wont to do. "Where am I?" he asked, the next time young Mravi came into the room. "Tell me about the local legends."

"Legends? You're ninety kloms north of Haust, in farm country. We are not a fantastical people; we raise crops and pay our taxes."

Ramnis's brown eyes twinkled. "Are there no witches? No pickaroons in the woods? No deathdog hordes? Do the wily Juju-folk never come to trade?"

Mravi shook her solemn head. "I'd like to see a Juju. Is it true they have pointed tongues?"

Ramnis smiled mysteriously, and spoke again. "If you were to hike forth in search of curiosities, where would you go?"

His nurse frowned. "Our religion speaks against frivolity and indiscipline. Ah well—there's Haust, but that would interest me more than you. The only other thing—you might try walking down the road."

"To what?"

"Just a moment." Mravi departed and returned. "You can see—" she began.

"Not unless I sit up."

She helped him with his pillows, and handed him the

map. "It doesn't show our road going through the forest, but it did once, centuries ago, and here at what would be the terminus—three dots, signifying a ruined city. Maybe you can read the name."

"It's written too small, and the ink's faded. 'Parthansad'?"

Mravi shook her head. "That doesn't sound like our Dhuini language. All this region was once part of the Empire of Dhuinunn. The ruins are—"

"—those of an indigenous people, conquered by your Dhuini ancestors!"

"You read too many romances," Mravi primly retorted. "The dominions are overburdened with cults and factions, races and layers of history, with false gods to add flavor to the brew. From coast to coast the peoples of Merica divide into two parts: the infatuated, who whore off to the cities after memory-dreams and roadsters, cheap factory food and computer-spawned marvels. We are the others, who exercise caution and prudence. . . ."

"Ah, but I'm a Souldancer, and it's my religion always to be infatuated. Yet cities hold no charm. With the subways tying them together, they'll soon be all alike. No, I'd be more inclined to trek westward toward this place . . ." He squinted again. " 'Purthant'?"

"On that knee?"

"If I might buy a horse . . ."

"Senator Ramnis, you were rescued and brought here, with your clothes and satchel. There was no money."

"Someone stole my poke. One of your pious farmers."

"Of course you deserve credit, the more so since I'm sure you're right about the theft, but we're a bit cut off up here, and . . ."

"I see. Well, then, how long do I have to work to earn my horse?"

At first Ramnis was given light work, milking cows, shelling peas, picking plums and hunting mushrooms. When his knee proved itself the flatpursed king was led to other labors: picking rocks, stacking hay, and splitting wood. These tasks exhausted him; he no longer tried to coax laughter from the mirthlessly sincere Mravi.

August came to an end. He helped harvest the wheat, and brought dried sheaves to the threshing-floor.

The ordeal was endurable, but for the visits of two grim middle-aged ladies; psaliches of the Panhe religion, who mistrusted his attitude and deemed him a bad influence. Though Yain was an advanced and scientific dominion, Panhe was the prevailing faith, and it was probably the remonstrations of these wandering busybodies that persuaded Ramnis's masters to speed him on his way a month before harvest was over.

And so, leading a twelve-year-old steed with a slightly swayed back, Senator Ramnis whistled westward, past one farm and then another, until he penetrated the skirts of the forest. Footpaths and deer trails carried him on along a ditched ridge; all that remained of the thoroughfare that once connected—Perlanta? to—Onturs?

The journey took three days. The forest gave way to wind-shaken grasses, cropped now and again by herds of bison. The old road grew more obscure, then less. It crossed the modern thoroughfare to the twin cities of Shasch-Kaippa. Ramnis ignored the diversion. Riding west, his shoulders hunched against a gentle rain, he noticed that the way his horse now trod seemed in excellent repair. Indeed, the dominion government had put up signs: PORTLAND–INTERPRETIVE CENTER–10 KLOMS.

"Portland?" The name sounded Inglish. Twice before the Dominions of Merica had been dominated by Inglish-speaking peoples—Ramnis wondered whether this ruined city might not be a relic of remote antiquity indeed.

The Interpretive Center was built of stout wooden beams and planks, and surrounded by garden on three sides. Ramnis pounded the door to no avail, then suddenly a lean gentleman arose from the flowery foliage to his left, a soiled blade in his gloved hand. The senator stepped back. "Magnificent roses," he commented, always the diplomat.

"Aren't they? This place is heaven for roses, and for slugs as well. Come in. Here's our guest register. . . ."

Following the man's bustling figure, Ramnis stepped inside and studied the room. "Is this Portlandish architecture?"

The host unstrung his green gardener's apron. On his glistening wet pate he planted an official-looking skull-cap with the blazon D.A.A. embroidered in a semicircle. "Exotic, yes?" he answered. "Though not much different from any other twentieth-century city. Of course, this is a guess—the ruins, however extensive, are altogether crumbled. The ancients used materials of no real durability."

The senator frowned. "So I won't see much by wandering."

"Oh, some excavations here and there . . . before the archeologists came you'd never have known this was once a place of note."

"Ah? The holy city of some cult? The capitol of an empire?"

"More than that, and less!" the gardener responded, cryptically. "Would it help if I told you that Portland continued to exist for centuries following the Great Collapse?"

"No." Ramnis shook his head, and fat drops showered off his drooping hat-brim. "Unless you allude to some secret weapon, by which they resisted the incursions of the Dhuini—"

"Oh, they fell to our Dhuini ancestors, but I do in fact allude to a secret weapon; sufficient to repel the Yooth of Califerni, the Albartian Canucks, the Leninish hordes— Sir, have you ever heard of the Buzz of Joy?"

"The Buzz of Joy!" Ramnis's face transformed, awe dissolved in ignorance. "No, I can't say I have."

His informant raised an eyebrow. "We have pamphlets. In a year or two we might even show a film. I've written to Regal Cinematics, to get a crew out to do a one-reeler on the subject, and they sound interested."

"No doubt." Ramnis hung up his garrick and hat, and plucked a brochure from the heap. "Do you get many visitors?" he asked.

"Dozens," the man responded. "You'll excuse me? My garden—"

The senator nodded, his mind already drifting into the streets of ancient Portland, where barbed-wire barricades blocked the advance of the perfidious Yooth of Californi. Mysterious coiled antennae rose from towers to the right and left—as the Yooth charged, roaring on their mechanical steeds, power surged up the coils and the Buzz of Joy hazed the air in front of them. The Yooth reached the protected zone, guffawed with laughter, spasmed, and tumbled from their two-wheelers, their chests heaving helplessly with mirth as blood coursed from their torn limbs. . . .

Such were the images suggested by the pages in Ramnis's hand, published by the Dominion of Yain. Department of Antiquities and Art—Please Refrain from Littering.

Ramnis stroked his mustachios. All he had to do was to find a pair of coiled antennae—no, not really. The antennae were the fruit of an artist's imagination. What he was looking for might as easily be an archetypical Black Box.

Ramnis moved to a second room and studied a plaster model of old Portland. Areas staked by archeologists were flagged in red. If the farmers of Yain were disciplined and methodical, how much more its scientists, whose digs boxed the city—without, however, yet penetrating to its heart.

The senator lacked the resources to compete with these others, whose peripheral work was clearly intended to yield barrier-relics of the Buzz of Joy. No, he was a Souldancer, and his ways were different. He would assume that the Buzz radiated like a protective dome, outward from some central height, and lo! Such heights were not hard to find. Here was one, once the acropolis of a cult of healers.

Arbitrarily Ramnis chose that hill. He would go there, trusting in luck. Luck had made him king, and then senator: why shouldn't luck provide him with the Buzz of Joy?

On his way the senator picked up a stick. He used it to hack, laboring and puffing, up the slopes of the hill. His horse balked just short of the crest, and Ramnis tethered him before clambering to the top, where he wandered among titanic trees, kicking at lichenous rocks.

He returned to find that his four-legged companion had cropped all the bushes within reach, exposing a damp, concrete-lined passage. Spiders webbed the black interior, windblown leaves had caught and decomposed, adding by increments to a humic muck that now half blocked the adit, from whence came a foul smell. Perhaps a bear had recently used the place as her den, and died . . . a very fat bear.

So this was the fruit of Souldancer luck! Ramnis used his stick to clear a way and squeeze inside. It began to rain again, the gentlest of showers, but he was protected now; he might even light a firestick the better to see into the interior gloom. Perhaps the flame would help purify this putrid air!

He opened the packet, popped at a firestick, and it caught—WHOOMP! The force of the fireball blew Senator Ramnis from the passage into the flank of his horse, who whinnied in terror. At the sound of a second, greater explosion the beast reared and pulled his reins free, restrained from galloping off by the shaking of the earth beneath his hooves.

There must have been a third detonation, so titanic that the senator's senses failed him. Ramnis found himself spread-eagled against the trunk of a tree, watching as a large section of hilltop tipped inwards and sank to form a squarish crater. Mammoth trees swayed from the vertical, groaned, and toppled, crashing into one another. The rain-misted air grew thick with flying dirt, leaves and shards of bark, while pale flames belched in syncopation with subterranean rumbles.

The soft rain cleansed the air, and beat back intermittent gouts of fire. The worst was over. The senator coughed, stood forward and brushed his mired garrick.

Embedded among the central roots of one tumbled

forest giant was a thing of metal, once rectangular, perhaps larger and certainly more elaborate than a bed frame. Those lumps—could they be axles? Was this the relic of an ancient Portlandish road machine? Ramnis stumbled close. The vehicle would have had a body once, but it had rusted, leaving just this skeleton, through which he could see . . .

Yes, indeed. The archetypical Black Box.

A week later, and a thousand kloms away, Ramnis faced a large, polychromatic statue. U Gyi's game had grown increasingly subtle, and the senator deliberated before raising his ceremonial staff to smash the plaster image of the false god. As the object tumbled the crowd panicked and melted away. The skies darkened. Lightning strobed as the roof opened. Among these distractions Ramnis was clearheaded enough to notice the floor was elevating, carrying him story by story into low clouds.

Light blitzed around the senator. With time the brilliance attenuated. Luminosity grew constant. The glow had a source. Strong winds tore at the fog and he found himself treading up a long, wide hall towards a tiny U Gyi, seated on his throne. The god's genetically tailored monkey-sized guards fell in to flank him as he approached.

"What an unexpected surprise," U Gyi spoke, patted his damp forehead with an embroidered sleeve.

"That I'm still alive?" the senator asked.

"Oh, dear. I was afraid you'd be tiresome about that airplane episode. If you expect me to apologize—"

"Nice place you've got here," Ramnis remarked. "I suppose you'd like to keep it."

"Ah? Ah! A threat! Would you risk war?"

"No, and yet in my travels I've made some discoveries—here, I've come to give you this."

Ramnis set the black box on the steps before U Gyi's throne. The godling fought to mask his nervous curiosity. "Very well, what is it?"

"A weapon, harmless without its power source. The ancients of long-dead Portland used it to defend their city. It worked against the Yooth of Califerni, the Albartian Canucks—against everyone except the Dhuini, who turned out to be immune."

"The founders of the Empire of Dhuinunn!"

"The very same. Their descendants inhabit the dominion of Yain, a remnant of those who once ruled two-thirds of Merica. Your Divinity, has it occurred to you that they might harbor ambitions to revive their Empire?"

The tiny godling's finger rummaged thoughtfully in one of his oversized ears. "I suspect everyone of everything, and I am often right."

"And perhaps you've noticed that the folk of Yain are absolutely incapable of humor? Not once during my stay among them could I get one to smile—but I provoke your patience. In fact, this box contains a weapon known as the Buzz of Joy, a weapon that can render any of us helpless with laughter, any of us, *except* the people of Yain, whose scientists are busily engaged in trying to find what I'm about to give you—"

"Indeed! And why am I your beneficiary?"

"Because you're clever enough to discover the principle behind this Buzz, and reverse it. I urge you to do so. If the Dominion of Yain has fielded archeologists, then they've hired physicists and neurologists as well, and those others might soon make an independent discovery."

U Gyi smiled a toothy grin. "*Reverse* it? I've heard of people rendered helpless with laughter, but never helpless with gloom!"

"Isn't that what we call depression? I see two armies stalemated in the field; ours rolling on the ground in paroxysms of glee; while the forces of Yain stand, sighing at the futility of existence, too listless to advance. My purpose here today is to maintain the balance of powers, the senatorial system—once you've built a Buzz of Gloom—"

"I could use it anywhere, against anyone!"

Ramnis shook his head. "I doubt it. The Buzz of Joy

bred its antithesis, a folk incapable of humor. You might use the Buzz of Gloom, but if you do, in time you'll endow the world with a race of irrepressible jokesters, people incapable of taking things seriously, people who laugh at pretentious gods and senators—"

U Gyi turned pink. "People, in other words, very like yourself!"

Ramnis bowed. "Myself, at my worst. Your Divinity, forgive me, but I *do* hope this evens the score between us. Let's be allies again, lest in our squabbles we ignore our foes, for in Yain and elsewhere, our poor excuse for democracy has subtle enemies."

U Gyi pursed his lips. "Your absence unsettled many of my former friends. I begin to think it's bad luck to kill senators. Very well, Senator Ramnis, you have my promise, and thank you very much for your thoughtful gift. Return to your kingdom with my blessing, and know that I shall try to be a better god in the future."

Two years later, when the governor of Yain took his battle-armored, tingler-wielding militia into the field, the scene was not altogether as Senator Ramnis imagined. Yain's secret weapon, the Buzz of Joy, intersected U Gyi's Buzz of Gloom, and a neutral zone was created. In that zone the forces of four dominions clashed with those of just one, the self-styled Second Empire of Dhuinunn, which collapsed that same afternoon. Once more the forces of righteousness prevailed, a little weary, perhaps, of staving off the enemies of representative democracy two or three times a decade. Sometime soon, somebody would unearth the ultimate something . . .

But thanks to Senator Ramnis's Souldancer luck: so far, so good.

The Hero

Oppressed by sun and miles, the Caney flowed out of the Flinthills of Ye and dwindled across the barrens toward the vast, malarial and still-very-distant Abyss. The town of South Stick skirted the impound where it puddled away in failure during these droughts of autumn.

Months before, Senator Ramnis purchased a farmstead four kloms from South Stick and sold its best acres and water rights. An old well lay in the center of his remaining freehold. It made a picturesque pop-out, and since it would be years before the subway line extended to Junction, South Stick was as far as anyone could ride in underground comfort into the barrens.

The grand opening was five weeks away. In five weeks all would be a hubbub of concessions above, vending machines below. This present silence was apocalyptic; the calm before the storm that would transform South Stick and bring it into the modern age.

For now a jury-rigged elevator took the senator up to the well's rim. He climbed out to gaze around him.

In the unfinished terminal below his feet an old key

had hung from a nail in the wall. Ramnis used it to unlock his boarded-up farmhouse. He struck a firestick for light and looked at the detritus scattered around the floor. Trust local children to break in and make the place their clubhouse.

He moved to the closet, shifted a few boards and removed a barrensrider cloak and cowl. He shook them out, put them on and left the house. Returning to the well, he tossed his key into the blackness and spoke a word. He turned and headed for the road to town.

It was like moving back through time. In South Stick Ramnis bought a horse, saddle and supplies. Evening came as he finished these errands. He took a room at the Manor, a hotel run by churchwomen who, he suspected, disapproved of him. A mustachioed transient who appeared out of nowhere! The senator exuded charm but nothing worked. Finally he went up to bed.

Next morning he rode out. Built and rebuilt over eighteen centuries, the ancient interstate carried him toward Junction, where a newer road forked toward Rus la Mecca. Senator Ramnis expected to find Lord Jeffson of Regal Cinematics at Rus la Mecca, and in fine humor, ready to make profitable promises. . . .

Four days to Rus la Mecca, assuming he had a good mount and was not seized by outlaws. Perhaps this would be the senator's last long journey by horse. Road machines were selling in the barrens. Battery stations would soon dot the interstate. Dominion troops were bivouacked to discourage raids. More traffic meant more gold to keep the road in repair. Wells were deepened and hitherto lawless barrensriders settled to run flocks of sheep. Progress! Was a single corner of Merica of the Five Dominions untouched by the current renaissance? Ramnis thought not, but what would urban food factories do to the price of mutton?

A person had to take care where he put his money. Cinematics seemed a safe investment, but now folks used memory helmets to dream the adventures of professional heroes, getting life-experience first hand. Fans, cultists . . . would this trend keep people from buying movie tickets?

Ramnis left Junction in time to overtake the Longye caravan. For two days he slowed to the pace of wood-wheeled lumber wains. Ahead and behind, Juju tinkers drove carts heaped with metalware, wire and rope. Dominant in numbers, noise and stench, Kwi drovers herded cattle toward distant pastures.

At Longye, merchants would exchange bulk for quality: chimmit, camphor, pepper sauce, rum, pigments, horses and cheese. Accordingly their caravan crossed the ford north of Rus la Mecca. Ramnis abandoned these companions at the river, riding south instead.

Senator De Gros was a political ally, and under his enlightened regime sentries were stationed to aid the honest traveller. With their help Ramnis found the Casbar Trail. Soon he sighted the domes of the Casbar, the inhabited heart of an otherwise dead city. His easy and official route curved and plunged into the cool underground. 'Mbo tribesmen stood about the entrance cavern. Ramnis flagged one and made arrangements for his horse. He walked the final three kloms, a straight path illuminated by electric lights.

From an old storeroom he doglegged through damp masonry corridors. He emerged into a hallway. Senator De Gros's men had run wires from the underground system, and bulbs of light illuminated the passage.

Black pilgrim men challenged him as he turned the corner toward the pedestal. He had barely time to notice that a bronze figure stood where all had been emptiness for three hundred years.

"I look for Lord Jeffson," Ramnis replied to their inquiries. He dredged up enough 'Mbo to ask a simple question. "Je voul' allez a Milord Jeffson. Jeffson? Ou est-il?"

"We expect only pilgrims here," one vigilant answered. "Pardon me." He strode off.

The 'Mbo had done much to unseat Lord Pest during

the Esreti War. The bronze was a statue of old Sultan Jeanan, donated to the Casbar by a grateful Emperor. Ramnis stood in admiration as another white-robed black man approached. "Welcome to our holy place," he began. "Can we help you on your errand?"

"I'm Senator Ramnis, King of—well, you've never heard of the place, but I'm acquainted with Senator De Gros, and I'm here to see Lord Jeffson."

"We give De Gros the title of Vizier."

"I meant no insult."

The teacher smiled. "Come."

De Gros laughed as Ramnis was escorted into the library. "Young Senator! First we let you in, now you come in full cowl. Next visit I expect you to lead a horde of ramping Kwis."

"This room was empty last I saw it," Ramnis replied. "Now you have books, it's worth the plunder."

"Let's leave. We disturb my scholars."

Ramnis and De Gros moved into the hallway. Perversely, now they were out of the library both principals lowered their voices. "Where are you keeping Lord Jeffson?" Ramnis asked.

"That's the problem. We haven't got him! He's been captured by my enemies."

"Kwis?" Ramnis could hardly believe it. Lord Jeffson was a Zealander himself!

"You don't comprehend. When we instituted religious reform a few 'Mbo diehards rejected the new revelations. That meant they rejected God and turned everything upside down; instead of matriarchy they have men bossing women. Instead of abstinence, drunkenness. Instead of hamam they perform fire worship, even human sacrifice!"

"Lord Jeffson fell in among them? Where are they?"

"I've been on the telephone for three days. Seems he flew for Rus la Mecca by way of the flinthills of Ye, hoping to snap aerial photos en route. It wouldn't have been an easy flight under the best of circumstances, but with devil-worshippers taking potshots at you . . ."

De Gros paused. "Fortunately the pilot escaped, and we know Lord Jeffson's still alive. So now I'm forced to put together an army—"

"An army!"

De Gros grimaced. "It's up to us 'Mbo to police our own, especially in Ye. The problem is those Kwis in Longye have suffered from devil-raids, and are getting together their own force—Lord Jeffson is important, *and* he's a Zealander Kwi like them—"

"Look, we're all part of the same Dominion. This is 3720! What the Kwis did to the 'Mbos back in the Time of Dejection—that's all over."

"We can't have Kwis riding in and shooting 'Mbos. How long do you think I'd stay senator if I let that happen? No, and the Emperor's on my side! He's instructed the Sheriff of Longye to hold in readiness for my reinforcements."

"Meanwhile days go by. A slow way of rescuing Lord Jeffson."

"That's why I telephoned Junction. We've hired a heroine, a wandering Heegie named Lavinia—"

"Preposterous name."

"She's got her own battle armor. Those poor devil-worshippers won't know what hit them!"

A good host, De Gros led Ramnis to his private smoking room, and then went about his business. Ramnis listened to the radio, to 'Mbo voices summoning the tribe to arms—always a slow process. Four of the Five Dominions had professional armies, but professional armies were garrison troops by definition: to move a regiment was to provoke inter-dominion quarrels. Though the Empire was the largest—no, *because* the Empire was the largest of the Five Dominions, it had to be careful lest Yain or Esret, Narslow or Califern take undue alarm.

Ramnis's 'Mbo wasn't good, so after a rest he left the smoking room. He found his way to a high terrace. Gazing into western glow he waited for Lavinia's arrival, for the "heroine" had left Junction early that morning, and not by horse.

He heard the distant drone of an unmuffled engine. A horizon-speck dipped and rose, a ground-hugging black mote seen through heat-rippled air.

Minutes passed. The mote grew larger with each appearance. Ramnis descended through the west wing and strolled into the plaza in front of the Casbar. The heroic Lavinia was welcomed by a scattered crowd, all black-in-white but for himself.

She killed the engine of her two-wheeler and lifted her helmet. A female Heegie, her hair was scarcely worth cultivating and she'd shaved it off. Her head was a pale gleaming dome; her eyes, hard blue gimlets in a wide face. Ramnis sighed. Hers was the countenance of one immune to charm. De Gros was wise in his advice not to get in her way.

"I'm in a hurry," she spoke. "Who wants to be my sidekick? You!" She pointed at a tall 'Mbo man. Her victim turned to ask a friend what she'd said.

"*Merde*, I forgot the language problem. *You*, then!"

Ramnis frowned. "What do you mean, 'sidekick'?"

"Someone to see to my special requirements. You speak 'Mbo? Tell these pilgrims to give De Gros the message. I want to make time with the light. We've two hundred kloms to Longye, and I mean to get there before the caravan. I'm tired of gunning through cow manure!"

"What about my travel kit?"

"Want to see Jeffson alive? Give them the message and hop on board."

Never quarrel with someone in body armor; not when her strength is set to five. Ramnis translated, then wriggled onto Lavinia's two-wheeler. He wrapped his arms around her filth-splattered waist. She replaced her helmet and the two roared off.

They splashed across a ford, bounced up the cobbles of an ancient road, doglegged along a decayed suburban grid, drove over a ribbon of patched concrete spanning

an old interstate—Rus la Mecca must have been a city
even before the Sultanate, because this last was an
Anglo ruin!

Ramnis grew confident enough of Lavinia's skills to
indulge in such deductions. As the road straightened he
took time to wonder. What did this strange woman
mean by "special requirements"?

They turned onto the caravan trail. Soon they saw
dust, heard the ruminations of cattle, and slowed to
weave through masses of wheeled and bovine traffic.
"This grit gets under my armor!" Lavinia shouted. "For
hours I've done nothing but promise myself a bath."

"They're winding down for a halt. We can get ahead,
make an early start tomorrow—"

"Right. Ten more kloms."

They motored until the sky grew black. At last Lavinia
stopped and killed her engine. They were in a gully, a
good place to gather fuel for a campfire, also a good
place for an ambush, which might explain—

"I sleep in my armor more often than not," Lavinia
spoke. "It's a dangerous world. Now you, you look like
the king in that movie 'Fountain Pavilion,' ruler of a
greenhouse-arcopolis surrounded by glacier."

"We have the subway system to thank; all that waste
heat," Ramnis responded. "And the subterranean cities
you Heegies live in, with their thermal taps. Centuries
ago a god decided to build his city atop the exhaust
vents, in a melt-valley hidden in the ice."

"A dumb god, to fall prey to Souldancers! Know what
De Gros tells me? These 'Mbo renegades are devil
worshippers! I wonder who they've got to play devil?"

Ramnis looked surprised. "Only you Heegies require
flesh-and-blood deities. The rest of humankind bows
down to Transcendancies of a Higher Order."

Lavinia grimaced. "You *are* a king then?"

"And senator."

"Damn! I should have found someone trustworthy.
People of rank always rationalize treachery."

Ramnis cleared his throat. "My Souldancers dreamt my memories before they elected me king. I have their endorsement."

"Some folk owe me their lives, yet I can't trust them. At times I wonder what fate I'm in store for. Lord Jeffson was shot down by the heavy hand of God. I feel a convergence of dooms and ends and last things. The air here is full of finality."

Was Lavinia always this moody? "I'm sorry. I don't know what to say."

The silence extended. The pair rolled over, back to back. They slept. Next morning they broke camp and drove into the rangelands of Longye. To the south they glimpsed a spine of hills.

The cattle around them were portents of safety. The renegade 'Mbo made cattle-raids, but not by daylight, nor to this distance from their refuge. Chances were better than equal that the next person they encountered would be an Inglisher of Zealand birth, a Kwi descendant of those who conquered the Sultanate three centuries ago and ushered in the Time of Dejection.

To Ramnis the genealogies of the Five Dominions were a matter of cleavages: of Inglishers into Anglos and Zealanders, of extinct Anglos into Heegies and Jujus, of Jujus into the pragmatic majority and his own Souldancer minority . . . but the truth was, most people got confused and accepted fake lineages. What were the gods but liars who played pseudo-history like a musical instrument?

History, tribes; fodder for a documentary? A bored senator let his mind roam. Another forty kloms brought him to the outskirts of Longye. The sun was high when Lavinia's two-wheeler rumbled across the bridge.

Ramnis debarked at the telephone station. While he scheduled a conversation through De Gros's operator, the Heegie heroine parked in front of the Longye Hotel. Minutes later he found her in the lobby, whacking her scales to rid herself of an integument of dust.

And talking to the sheriff, whose answer was "Very impressive."

"I need a rest," Lavinia continued. "I hardly care to have any of this gossiped to potential enemies."

She turned to Ramnis. "Can our innkeeper fill me a tub? I require a private room."

"Certainly," Ramnis spoke.

"And stuff to wash my armor. It stinks." With these words she plunged outside.

Ramnis assured the innkeeper there was money to pay the bill, and made the arrangements. He went out to tell her, crossed to the telephone office as she finished fiddling with her two-wheeler—two people pressed together for hours could certainly find ways of avoiding each other.

The call went through. De Gros promised *this* and approved *that*, after which Senator Ramnis climbed the hotel stairs to room 212. He knocked. "The tub is filled."

The door opened. Lavinia moved by. Ramnis's quick eyes noted the strength setting on her armor; five.

He followed her downstairs and to the bath chamber. She studied the room as he locked the door and drew the shades. She found a couch and pulled it alongside the tub. "Undo me here," she commanded, and lay face down on its upholstered surface. "I'll make it easy. Else you'd have trouble hauling me into the bath."

Carefully Ramnis undid straps, snaps and braces. First gauntlets and solerets, then powerpack, leg and arm pieces. Beneath lay webbing and orange undergarments worn thin by time. Where not patterned by dirt, Lavinia's limbs were fishbelly white, soft and flabby. Her tattoos were garish coils of yellow, black, red and blue. He rolled her over and worked on her ventral segments. Her arms swung loose, as on a fresh corpse. Her torso burst free of its bonds and he tugged at slack strings to uncover her breasts.

She was exposed, helpless except to cry alarm. Ramnis grunted and heaved to shift her flaccid weight into the water. If he avoided looking into her eyes she'd think he was merely embarrassed.

If there was shame, some was Lavinia's. She seemed subdued. Only after some moments did her arms and hands move in the water. Feebly her fingers rubbed and probed. By this time Ramnis collected all her loose gear. He dipped pieces of her suit into the pump basin, then set them in order behind her head. If he could dress before she noticed anything wrong . . .

The click and clatter of hurried work exposed his purpose. "What are you doing?" Lavinia growled breathlessly. "Come where I can see you."

"Uh, I'm sort of tied up."

"Trying to don my armor? You don't know the secret. It won't work for you."

"There's a secret?"

Lavinia struggled for breath. She raised an arm from the water. It flopped over the rim of the tub. "Don't," she gasped.

"I'm five times as strong as you," Ramnis answered. "Suppose Jeffson is caged. I can break him out."

Lavinia wheezed. "I need that armor. I can hardly breathe without it." Another pause. "You'll kill me."

Ramnis strode forward. "This suit is killing you. What happens when you've used it up? What happens when you need the twelve setting to seem of normal strength?"

Lavinia struggled to haul out her other arm. Her eyes were bright with tears. "Don't make me cry," she whispered. "Too much work to cry."

"What's the secret?" His voice was a coaxing purr.

"Can't trust anyone. Damn you."

Ramnis hoisted her into a sitting position. He returned to his work and continued to dress. He finished and clattered to her fore. "If you tell me how to activate this suit, I'll be able to haul you out of the water."

"What will become of me?"

"What would you do to me if I gave you back your suit?"

Lavinia studied his face. "I'd tear your cods off." She

inhaled and exhaled laboriously. "Jeffson is my hostage. You can't rescue him in dead armor. You dare not kill me—" (more breaths) "—and the more we delay, the worse for him."

"You'll wait me out? I don't think so. The telephone is working. I'll call one of the gods; U Gyi's a friend of mine. He'll know how to quicken your armor."

"Bear my curse, then. As for the secret, there's rudimentary mind-scan stuff in the helmet. Same as when you record your memories. Put the helmet on."

Ramnis complied. Lavinia rested and spoke again. "A story. Tell it cleverly and armored lackeys think right thoughts . . . without recognizing the crucial elements. Not the first time. Soon enough though. I figured it out soon enough when I was security guard for Thraxum Motors at the Imperial Exhibition."

"Why a story? Why not some switch?"

"With mind-scan your thoughts are the switches. The right thoughts in the right order."

"No matter whose head is in this helmet this gear can recognize the same idea? You're talking of imponderables: spirits and souls."

". . .'s night. Imagine a fire. A huge old bell with a hole atop the crown. Lower the bell onto the blaze. Stuff more wood inside.

"A dark-skinned dwarf, big muscles. Ugly. He dances close to the bell, inside a ring of watchers."

She paused for breath. "The bell glows and sags," she whispered at long last. "The dwarf strikes with his mallet to shape it. He laughs and hammers. The crowd obscures your view. They part. He's done. The thing is hot but the dwarf throws only a little water to cool it down; an idol with a raised right arm. He turns, this muchwhat naked man, and plants his buttocks on steaming metal—"

The suit hummed with power. Ramnis flexed his fingers. Experimentally he reached to lift the couch with but one hand. Amazing! "Who's the dwarf?"

"A lost god from centuries back. Who invented mind-scanning? Not Tonans. Not U Gyi. Whoever did it made sure certain memories would not be stored. Forgotten history. Who invented battle-armor? Another puzzle."

Ramnis bent and lifted Lavinia from her tub as if she were cobwebs and gossamer. Her body shook like pudding; a white, puckered obscenity. He stepped to a window. His fingers closed on a drape and he tugged it loose. Lowering her to the couch, he shrouded her before taking her up and bundling her to the door. Locked. He gave in to temptation and pushed it open.

A figure in black armor carrying a casually blanketed human form from the bath and up the stairs: in the lobby conversation lapsed. The desk clerk stared at Lavinia's slack limbs and drew an alarmed conclusion. He edged to the door, dashed outside and ran for the sheriff.

The white-haired gentleman responded gun in hand. He climbed the stairs and knocked on Lavinia's door. Ramnis opened. "Thank God! We need an interlocutor. Lavinia must stay here: she'll need a maid to feed her and get her dressed."

The sheriff turned to Lavinia. "Are you all right?"

"Under the circumstances. Promise me, Ramnis. Promise me you'll give back my armor."

Ramnis turned back to the sheriff. "She'll not want everyone to know of her condition. Just you and her attendant and maybe the hostler. The others can be told she's sick."

The sheriff scratched his head. "She's not sick?"

Ramnis shrugged. "I've said more than needful. Have a nurse massage her and work her arms and legs. Anything else?"

Lavinia kept silent. Ramnis clattered off. A minute later her two-wheeler roared to life and wove unsteadily into the afternoon.

The sky grew dark. In their high cave Waksa and

Lord Jeffson plotted. With the full moon a few days hence their captors would hold a drunken revel. That would be the time to bolt for freedom.

"If I were Champierre, I'd think the same and post watch," Lord Jeffson warned.

Waksa nodded, a devil so small he stood erect beneath this cell's low ceiling. "It all hangs on the watchman. Some woman to tempt him from vigilance—"

"One of the women likes me," Jeffson grunted. "She paws me at moments when the guard's distracted."

"Lots like you. That's why they taunt you with obscenities. They don't dare show kindness."

Jeffson sighed. "If one dared to be a friend . . ."

They fell silent. The world outside was quiet too. Quieter than normal?

A shout, suddenly cut off, then silence again. From the caves below men padded out to exchange whispers with the posted guards. Jeffson watched as a troop jogged downriver past a pile of jackstrawed timber. He'd spent the day hauling deadwood to that pile. Now it shielded a mystery.

More silence. A watching guard paced nervously, started forward, and reconsidered. Perhaps Champierre should be wakened. The guard's mind swam in uncertainty. A black figure darted toward him from cover to cover, the epitome of menace, and yet—and yet—

Ramnis seized the watchman's weapon, bent the barrel and threw it in the river. Women stared from the lower caves. One found resolution to shout alarm. The startled senator leapt two meters into the air, landed clumsily and moved to smother the crowd in sonics.

He passed among them looking for weapons. In a rear chamber he came upon a sleeping man and woman.

He needed information. He switched off his sonics and reached to shake the woman's shoulder. "Huh?" she grunted.

"Ou est Milord Jeffson?" he asked in 'Mbo. "Where are you keeping Lord Jeffson?"

Champierre's eyes parted. The woman stirred. "Ahh
. . . who are you?"

The renegade leader lurched for his robes. Ramnis
caught his arm. At maximum strength Ramnis's gesture
crushed flesh and bone. The two men gaped at the injury
in shared awe before Champierre fainted dead away.

The woman struggled to sit, gasping with fear.
"Where's Jeffson?"

She began to blubber. "I know nothing. Champierre
and the others take care of it all."

"But he's here? Jeffson's here? Alive?"

"Oui, somewhere."

Ramnis twiddled his sonics and rushed out through
the front chamber to a path choked by a muddled
crowd. "Lavinia!" shouted a distant voice. "Up here!"

Ramnis struggled through the mass and left inadvertent wounds. He beat up the path to see a guard poised
to shoot, not at him but toward a small high hole in the
cliff. The man was lost in indecision. Ramnis took the
rifle and gave it a twist, then started up the ladder.

"Cut . . . your . . . sonics," Lord Jeffson droned from
above, speaking in a mesmerized chant.

Ramnis obliged. "I've found you," he breathed as he
reached the cavern mouth. "Come along."

"Waksa's coming with me," Lord Jeffson responded.
"You're better off down at the foot of the ladder. We'll
drop after you."

Ramnis descended and turned on his headlamp to
look around. 'Mbo renegades streamed off in three
directions. They'd encounter outposted men with guns,
the only remaining weapons. Among those men some
would feel duty-bound to challenge the armored demon
wreaking havoc through their caves. "Hurry!" he urged.

Tiny Waksa scuttled down the pegged beam, then
Lord Jeffson. A distant shot rang out. Ramnis moved to
the lead. They bustled down the path. A dawdler va-
cated their way by diving into a cave, then they reached
open ground. "My tools!" Waksa shouted.

"We'll get new ones," Jeffson responded. "Let's fetch out of here."

They reached the trees and continued north. "Take Waksa on your shoulders," Lord Jeffson advised. "We'll go faster."

Ramnis complied. "Your limp seems better, old man. Captivity's done you good."

"My body is uniformly in torment. No point favoring one ache over another. What happened to Lavinia?"

"She's in Longye. This is her suit, needless to say. All for the best. She can't speak 'Mbo and she lacks strength to bend gunmetal. She's sick. The sheriff spoke it right. I feel sorry for her, but what's to be done? Who's to blame for her condition?"

Lord Jeffson was too winded to answer. A minute later: "Your voice is familiar. Whoever you are, you stole her armor. She'll hate you."

"She hates herself. She thinks morbidly of death."

Beyond this bend lay open ground. Ramnis and Jeffson broke into a jog. Minutes passed before they slowed. 'This Waksa," Lord Jeffson gasped. "He shared my prison."

"I was surprised to see him," Ramnis responded. "What with stories of dwarves and all."

"I'm no dwarf," Waksa protested. "There's two kinds of little people. I'm proportional in my parts; my head's big, that's the exception. What people call dwarves are those whose torsos are full-sized—"

"Never mind. You look like a vision I recently had."

The trio trekked into the night. Cliff walls converged and loomed. "The rock merges above," Waksa commented, "a land-bridge over what was once a cave."

"I found it guarded and tied 'em up," Ramnis muttered. "I wonder—yes! Here they are. Any parting remarks?"

Lord Jeffson drew close to four confined Mbo renegades. "Where did you get your guns?" he asked.

The men glared. Lord Jeffson shrugged. "I've no

heart for torture, and I doubt anyone but Champierre knows the truth. Let's be off."

They continued. Rock bellied down, then lifted. The cliffs parted. "We've left their fastness," Ramnis commented. "A bit farther and we'll find Lavinia's two-wheeler."

Lord Jeffson, Waksa and Ramnis reached the machine as false dawn lightened the sky. "I should have brought food," the senator grumbled. "Never mind. Let's rest, and talk."

"Talk?"

"About memories, and the gods." Ramnis removed his helmet. "We had a golden age fifteen centuries back, and Heegie scientists recorded their memories for student use, except repeated dreaming of the same memories did funny things to their pupils' senses of identity, especially the younger ones. The gods' minds were contagious, and persisted down the generations, collecting more knowledge, more experience—"

"I hardly see why we need this lecture, since Waksa's exactly what you're talking about; an incarnation of U Gyi."

Waksa nodded. "By chance I scored a point lower than the body now occupying his throne, and so I'm obliged to make my way in the world."

"Devil for hire? But you tired of playing the same role over and over. That's a problem when people think you're the real thing; they burden you with expectations."

Ramnis took breath. "However, that's not why I started this conversation. I'm thinking of *you*, Lord Jeffson. Remember me? You're president of Regal Cinematics, and we've worked together before, on a docu-drama about how I became king of the Fountain Pavilion.

"You and I are a lot alike. We find the history of America fascinating, and full of marvels. These renegade 'Mbo—what an amazing bit of primitiveness, here in this backwater. Is that why you flew overhead, so you could film them in their squalor?"

"I guess it was a stupid thing to do."

"Oh, risky maybe. Not what I've come to expect of you; quite out of character. Why did you call me Lavinia when you first saw me?"

Lord Jeffson stirred uncomfortably. "I keep track of Merica's wandering heroes. They're movie material. Lavinia's trademark is her armor, and she's quartered pretty close to here—it just made sense."

"That De Gros would hire her? Did something you told him before your flight put that idea in his head? *Was this adventure-rescue all prearranged?*"

Jeffson laughed. "Would I risk my life—"

"Yes. You're worried the film industry might be supplanted by a dozen hero-cults. So what do you do? *Buy shares of Lavinia*, and all her ilk! Set up memory stations, and rent out memory cassettes! And just to make sure your investment takes off, you hunt to find her some appropriate deeds of derring-do. Nobody loves these 'Mbo renegades and their thieving, liquorous ways, but I sure feel sorry for them. They're actors in your script, and they aren't even being paid!"

"You're mad!" Waksa hooted. "If you'd seen how Champierre's men treated Lord Jeffson—making him dig latrines and scour pots, lashing him and stripping him naked—"

"We're all potentially immortal," Senator Ramnis answered. "Any of us can record our memories, and hope posterity dreams them so repeatedly that we gain new life in a second body. But to earn new life we have to be interesting. We have to be heroes, or magnates, our names on the radio! Lord Jeffson's certainly in the news these days: he's almost precipitated a war between the Kwis and the 'Mbos! Did you think of that, Jeffson? How much do you suppose it's costing the 'Mbo tribe to mobilize an army?"

"They should do it anyway. These renegades need to be wiped out."

"Ah, yes. You can defend everything. And what else? It should have been obvious before, but I didn't ponder the implications. You see, memory tapes can be edited!

I don't say false memories can be stuck in—that's too tricky, but genuine experiences can be snipped out, so if you don't want your fans to hear my tongue-lashing, if you don't want them to know you schemed to set all this up—"

Lord Jeffson bent forward, head between his knees. After a minute he sagged back. "I gave you immortality, Senator Ramnis," he whispered. "I made a film about you, and there are more than a few junior Ramnises running around because of it, dreaming your bootleg memories.

"Your soul will live on after you die. Why? Because you take risks. People like that. Now as for me, all I've done is buy shares in my favorite heroes so they don't have to worry about food and rent, and then alter my style toward the flamboyant. If that's a sin it's one we share, and I won't be scolded by a hypocrite."

Ramnis stroked his mostachios. "What's going to happen to civilization if everyone ambitious to live forever sets out to have as thrilling a life as possible? Who'll do the wash? Lord Jeffson, steady minds like yours hauled Merica up from rusticity these twenty years—"

Waksa grinned. "I've a few centuries of memories in my head. I've seen civilization collapse twice—lots of thrills and chills, too."

"That's what I'm afraid of." Ramnis stood and moved to his two-wheeler. "Lord Jeffson, keep your money in film. Seems the only way to stave off doom is for me to travel the Five Dominions, find your heroes, and humiliate them into obscurity. Nobody's going to be dreaming about Lavinia in the future: if I can outsmart the others—"

"If you do, let me bid on your memories. I assure you Regal can pay more than Magnetic Motion Pictures!"

"My soul's not for sale. I'm not a god, and I don't want to spawn a brood of wild worshippers!" With that the senator kicked the two-wheeler to life, and roared off through low brush.

Lord Jeffson lurched to his feet and waved desperately. "I'll turn you into a villain, then!"

Slowly Ramnis made a great round, and wheeled back. "I only knocked over a few dominoes," Jeffson continued hoarsely. "I wasn't the one who set them up. I'm not responsible—"

"I was about to abandon you," Ramnis grumbled. "Typical flamboyant hero-behavior! Come on. I'm turning over a new leaf. I'm delivering you to Vizier De Gros in Rus la Mecca, and I'll tell him about our little chat."

"Yes?"

"I expect the 'Mbo tribe will shortly lodge an action for recovery of expenses. Soon the ponderous instrumentality of Imperial law will be niggling away at your affairs. Money, suits and countersuits! A few years of that sort of thing, and who'll want to dream your memories? Yes, I should have known civilization had a way of preserving itself!"

Ramnis laughed. "You're not the wave of the future after all! Once it's established that you're legally responsible for all the messes your stable of heroes get into—"

Lord Jeffson blanched. "No!"

"A tricky point, but De Gros and I are senators, and we'll do what we can to amend the current law."

"I've got 'em on five-year contracts!" Lord Jeffson howled. "As unruly a bunch of hooligans . . . I'll send them overseas! Yes! There's a continent east of Merica that needs exploring—"

"You'd better ship them quickly. Winter assembly-time's coming. The old Anglos had a saying: *Nobody's safe when the Legislature is in session.*"

THE MANY WORLDS OF
MELISSA SCOTT

*Winner of the John W. Campbell Award
for Best New Writer, 1986*

THE KINDLY ONES: "An ambitious novel of the world Orestes. This large, inhabited moon is governed by five Kinships whose society operates on a code of honor so strict that transgressors are declared legally 'dead' and are prevented from having any contact with the 'living.' . . . Scott is a writer to watch."—*Publishers Weekly*. A Main Selection of the Science Fiction Book Club.

65351-2 • 384 pp. • $2.95

The "Silence Leigh" Trilogy

FIVE-TWELFTHS OF HEAVEN (Book I): "Melissa Scott postulates a universe where technology interferes with magic. . . . The whole plot is one of space ships, space wars, and alien planets—not a unicorn or a dragon to be seen anywhere. Scott's space drive and description of space piloting alone would mark her as an expert in the melding of the [SF and fantasy] genres; this is the stuff of which 'sense of wonder' is made."—*Locus*

55952-4 • 352 pp. • $2.95

SILENCE IN SOLITUDE (Book II): "[Scott is] a voice you should seek out and read at every opportunity."
—*OtherRealms*.   65699-7 • 324 pp. • $2.95

THE EMPRESS OF EARTH (Book III):
65364-4 • 352 pp. • $3.50

A CHOICE OF DESTINIES: "Melissa Scott [is] one of science fiction's most talented newcomers. . . . The greatest delight of all is finding out how she managed to write a historical novel that could legitimately have spaceships on the cover . . . a marvelous gift for any fan."—*Baltimore Sun*   65563-9 • 320 pp. • $2.95

THE GAME BEYOND: "An exciting interstellar empire novel with a great deal of political intrigue and colorful interplanetary travel."—*Locus*

55918-4 • 352 pp. • $2.95

Here is an excerpt from the new novel by Timothy Zahn, coming in October 1988 from Baen Books:

TIMOTHY ZAHN

DEADMAN SWITCH

I was playing singleton chess in a corner of the crew lounge when we reached the Cloud.

Without warning, oddly enough, though the effect sphere's edge was supposed to be both stationary and well established. But reach it without warning we did. From the rear of the *Bellwether* came the faint *thunggk* of massive circuit breakers firing as the Mjollnir drive spontaneously kicked out, followed an instant later by a round of curses from the others in the lounge as the ultra-high-frequency electric current in the deck lost its Mjollnir-space identity of a pseudograv generator and crewers and drinks went scattering every which way.

And then, abruptly, there was silence. A dark silence, as suddenly everyone seemed to remember what was abut to happen.

A rook was drifting in front of my eyes, spiraling slowly about its long axis. Carefully, I reached out and plucked it from the air, feeling a sudden chill in my heart. We were at the edge of the Cloud, ten light-years out from Solitaire . . . and in a few minutes, up on the bridge, someone was going to die.

For in honor of their gods they have done everything detestable that God hates; yes, in honor of their gods, they even burn their own sons and daughters as sacrifices—

A tone from the intercom broke into my thoughts. "Sorry about that," Captain Jose Bartholomy said. Behind his carefully cultivated Starlit accent his voice was trying to be as unruffled as usual . . . but I don't think anyone aboard the *Bellwether* was really fooled. "Space-normal, for anyone who hasn't figured it out already. Approximately fifteen minutes to Mjollnir again; stand ready." He paused, and I heard him take a deep breath. "Mr. Benedar, please report to the bridge."

I didn't have to look to know that all eyes in the lounge had turned to me. Carefully, I eased out of my seat, hanging onto the arm until I'd adjusted adequately to the weightlessness and then giving myself a push toward the door. My movement seemed to break the others out of their paralysis—two of the crewers headed to the lockers for handvacs, while the rest suddenly seemed to remember there were glasses and floating snacks that needed to be collected and got to it. In the brisk and uncomfortable flurry of activity, I reached the door and left.

Randon was waiting for me just outside the bridge. "Benedar," he nodded, both voice and face tighter than he probably wanted them to be.

"Why?" I asked quietly, knowing he would understand what I meant.

He did, but chose to ignore the question. "Come in here," he said instead, waving at the door release and grabbing the jamb handle as the panel slid open.

"I'd rather not," I said.

"Come in here," he repeated. His voice made it clear he meant it.

Swallowing hard, I gave myself a slight push and entered the bridge.

Captain Bartholomy and First Officer Gielincki were there, of course: Gielincki because it was technically her shift as bridge officer, Bartholomy because he wasn't the type of man to foist a duty like this off on his subordinates. Standing beside them on the gripcarpet were Aikman and DeMont, the former with a small recorder hanging loosely from his hand, the latter with a medical kit gripped tightly in his. Flanking the helm chair to their right were two of Randon's shields, Daiv and Duge Ifversn, just beginning to move back . . . and in the chair itself sat a man.

The *Bellwether*'s sacrifice.

I couldn't see anything of him but one hand, strapped to the left chair arm, and the back of his head, similarly bound to the headrest. I didn't want to see anything more, either—not of him, not of anything else that was about to happen up here. But Randon was looking back at me. . . .

The days of my life are few enough: turn your eyes away, leave me a little joy, before I go to the place of no return, to the land of darkness and shadow dark as death . . .

Taking a deep breath, I set my feet into the gripcarpet and moved forward.

Daiv Ifversn had been heading toward Aikman as we entered; now, instead, he turned toward us. "The prisoner is secured, sir, as per orders," he told Randon, his face and voice making it clear he didn't care for this duty at all. "Further orders?"

Randon shook his head. "You two may leave."

"Yes, sir." Daiv caught his brother's eye, and the two of them headed for the door.

And all was ready. Taking a step toward the man in the chair, Aikman set his recorder down on one of the panel's grips, positioning it where it could take in the entire room. "Robern Roxbury Trembley," he said, his voice as coldly official as the atmosphere surrounding us, "you have been charged, tried, and convicted of the crimes of murder and high treason, said crimes having been committed on the world of Miland under the jurisdiction of the laws of the Four Worlds of the Patri."

From my position next to Randon and Captain Bartholomy, I could now see the man in profile. His chest was fluttering rapidly with short, shallow breaths, his face drawn and pale with the scent of death heavy on it . . . but through it all came the distinct sense that he was indeed guilty of the crimes for which he was about to die.

It came as little comfort.

"You have therefore," Aikman continued impassively, "been sentenced to death, by a duly authorized judiciary of your peers, under the laws of the Four Worlds of the Patri and their colonies. Said execution is to be carried out by lethal injection aboard this ship, the *Bellwether*, registered from the Patri world of Portslava, under the direction of Dr. Kurt DeMont, authorized by the governor of Solitaire.

"Robern Roxbury Trembley, do you have any last words?"

Trembley started to shake his head, discovered the headband prevented that. "No," he whispered, voice cracking slightly with the strain.

Aikman half turned, nodded at DeMont. Lips pressed tightly together, the doctor stepped forward, moving around the back of the helm chair to Trembley's right arm. Opening his medical kit, he withdrew a small hypo, already prepared. Trembley closed his eyes, face taut with fear and the approach of death . . . and DeMont touched the hypo nozzle to his arm.

Trembley jerked, inhaling sharply. "Connye," he whispered, lower jaw trembling as he exhaled a long, ragged breath.

His eyes never opened again . . . and a minute later he was dead.

DeMont gazed at the readouts in his kit for another minute before he confirmed it officially. "Execution carried out as ordered," he said, his voice both tired and grim. "Time: fifteen hundred twenty-seven hours, ship's chrono, Anno Patri date 14 Octyab 422." He raised his eyes to Bartholomy. "He's ready, Captain."

Bartholomy nodded, visibly steeled himself, and moved forward. Unstrapping Trembley's arms, he reached gingerly past the body to a black keyboard that had been plugged into the main helm panel. It came alive with indicator lights and prompts at his touch, and he set it down onto the main panel's front grip, positioning it over the main helm controls and directly in front of the chair. "Do I need to do anything else?" he asked Aikman, his voice almost a whisper.

"No," Aikman shook his head. He threw a glance at me, and I could sense the malicious satisfaction there at my presence. The big pious Watcher, forced to watch a man being executed. "No, from here on in it's just sit back and enjoy the ride."

Bartholomy snorted, a flash of dislike flickering out toward Aikman as he moved away from the body.

And as if on cue, the body stirred.

I knew what to expect; but even so, the sight of it was shattering. Trembley was *dead*—everything about him, every cue my Watcher training could detect told me he was dead ... and to see his arms lift slowly away from the chair sent a horrible chill straight to the center of my being. And yet, at the same time, I couldn't force my eyes to turn away. There was an almost hypnotic fascination to the scene that held my intellect even while it repelled my emotions.

Trembley's arms were moving forward now, reaching out toward the black Deadman Switch panel. For a moment they hesitated, as if unsure of themselves. Then the hands stirred, the fingers curved over, and the arms lowered to the Mjollnir switch. One hand groped for position ... paused ... touched it—

And abruptly, gravity returned. We were on Mjollnir drive again, on our way through the Cloud.

With a dead man at the controls.

"Why?" I asked Randon again.

"Because you're the first Watcher to travel to Solitaire," he said. The words were directed to me; but his eyes remained on Trembley. The morbid fascination I'd felt still had Randon in its grip. "Hard to believe, isn't it?" he continued, his voice distant. "Seventy years after the discovery of the Deadman Switch and there still hasn't been a Watcher who's taken the trip in."

I shivered, my skin crawling. The Deadman Switch had hardly been "discovered"—the first ship to get to Solitaire had done so on pure idiot luck ... if *luck* was the proper word. A university's scientific expedition had been nosing around the edge of the Cloud for days, trying to figure out why a Mjollnir drive couldn't operate within that region of space, when the drive had suddenly and impossibly kicked in, sending them off on the ten-hour trip inward to the Solitaire system. Busy with their readings and instruments, no one on board realized until they reached the system that the man operating the helm was dead—had, in fact, died of a stroke just before they'd entered the Cloud.

By the time they came to the correct conclusion, they'd been trapped in the system for nearly two months. Friendships, under such conditions, often grow rapidly. I wondered what it had been like, drawing lots to see who would die so that the rest could get home . . .

I shivered, violently. "The Watchers consider the Deadman Switch to be a form of human sacrifice," I told him.

Randon threw me a patient glance . . . but beneath the slightly amused sophistication there, I could tell he wasn't entirely comfortable with the ethics of it either. "I didn't bring you here to argue public morals with me," he said tartly. "I brought you here because—" he pursed his lips briefly— "because I thought you might be able to settle the question of whether or not the Cloud is really alive."

It was as if all the buried fears of my childhood had suddenly risen again from their half-forgotten shadows. To deliberately try and detect the presence of an entity that had coldly taken control of a dead human body . . .